It's 1847, New York.

William Matthias Hallett is a fashionable dandy of the Manhattan social set. His life is laid out before him: a world of soirees, riches, and luxury. Yet all he wants to do is find an adventure so deliciously wicked that it will satiate his soul for an eternity.

Disguised in a lower-class manner, into the notorious *Five Points* he goes, seeking that spark of adventure. That is until it greets him in the form of his old schoolmates from Dartmouth College—a pair of Mohawk warriors who will up-end his world and all he knew it to be forever.

Beware Mohawks Bearing Gifts

The Cove Chronicles, Book One

SA Collins

A NineStar Press Publication

Published by NineStar Press
P.O. Box 91792,
Albuquerque, New Mexico, 87199 USA.
www.ninestarpress.com

Beware Mohawks Bearing Gifts

Printed in the USA
Second Edition
October, 2019

Print ISBN: 978-1-951057-66-4

Also available in eBook, ISBN: 978-1-951057-65-7

Warning: This book contains sexually explicit material that is only suitable for mature readers, scenes of graphic violence and gore, and references to child prostitution.

Author's Note

As there might be some issue with learning how to pronounce the Mohawk terms used in this work, I have included a pronunciation guide at the end of this story. My hope is that it will make your reading more enjoyable if you don't have to struggle with how to pronounce some of the terms.

Foreword

In creating *The Cove Chronicles*, I wanted to infuse the main characters with heroes rarely seen in an epic science fiction tale: Native Americans, namely in this instance, the *Haudenosaunee Confederacy* (or Iroquois) of upstate New York. You may know them individually as the five nations that originally made up the Confederacy: the Mohawk, Oneida, Onondaga, Cayuga, and Seneca. The Tuscarora were the first nation to join the Confederacy in 1722.

In this sci-fi melodrama I also wanted to explore the fringe scientific concepts my Native characters would be masters at manipulating. Thus, with apologies to Arthur C. Clarke, their advanced technology applications during a time shortly after the American Revolution would appear for all intents and purposes as *magic*.

To ensure I did no damage to the culture of the Haudenosaunee Confederacy—a culture I have deep respect for—I decided to off-world this whole saga by putting it into an alternate universe very like our own but with subtle differences that would allow me to tell the story as I saw it. This in no way diminishes the proud heritage of the Haudenosaunee peoples, just more of a *what if...*scenario I present to tell this fantastical tale with Natives at the core of the story—giving voice to the people and placing them beyond the stoicism shrouding them in many other works and historical recordings. They are real, fully dimensional people. They deserve a saga based on their own stories and legends.

The book you now hold is the first of a six-book series: three of them set during the 1800s with the following three set in current times. I have also borrowed from my husband's lineage as he is a direct descendant of the real Elizabeth and William Hallett of early American history. (Ever read *The Winthrop Woman* by Anya Seton? I highly recommend it.) The original Hallett's Cove is now Astoria, New York (shame on New York for changing the name).

As with many creation myths, this one also bears the mark of a battle of good versus evil and how the people will rise to meet that challenge—

in this case, the people of the Haudenosaunee Confederacy. For any Haudenosaunee reading this, I knowingly blended portions of the legends to suit my fictitious story. Please indulge me.

Another diversion from our collective timeline with regards to the great people of the Confederacy is there was a period during the Revolutionary War where the British promised to assist the Haudenosaunee (and potentially other nations) in establishing a truly sovereign nation on the same continent in exchange for their help against the rebellious Americans. The British reneged on their promise at the Treaty of Paris which ended the Revolution, and the established nation never happened here. In my alternate world, the promise was honored. So, the new Americans find themselves being contained along the eastern seaboard as the newly formed (and formidably enforced) border of the Akwe:kon nation is established. It is growing as more Indian nations join the Confederacy under *The Great Law of Peace,* seeking its protection from American expansion, thus creating even greater tensions for our heroes and their companions.

I hope you enjoy the journey of my ensemble cast and open your hearts to the rich cultural heritage of the great people of the Haudenosaunee Confederacy.

—SA Collins

To the four men who have shaped me into the man I've become thus far: William, my father; J L, my husband; Vance, my podcast co-host/producer; Jeffrey, my bestie of nearly forty years. This journey is, in part, an expression of my humble gratitude that you all had a profound effect on my life.

To my granddaughter, Keely, who was the sole inspiration for this epic tale.

"Any sufficiently advanced technology is indistinguishable from magic."

—Arthur C. Clarke

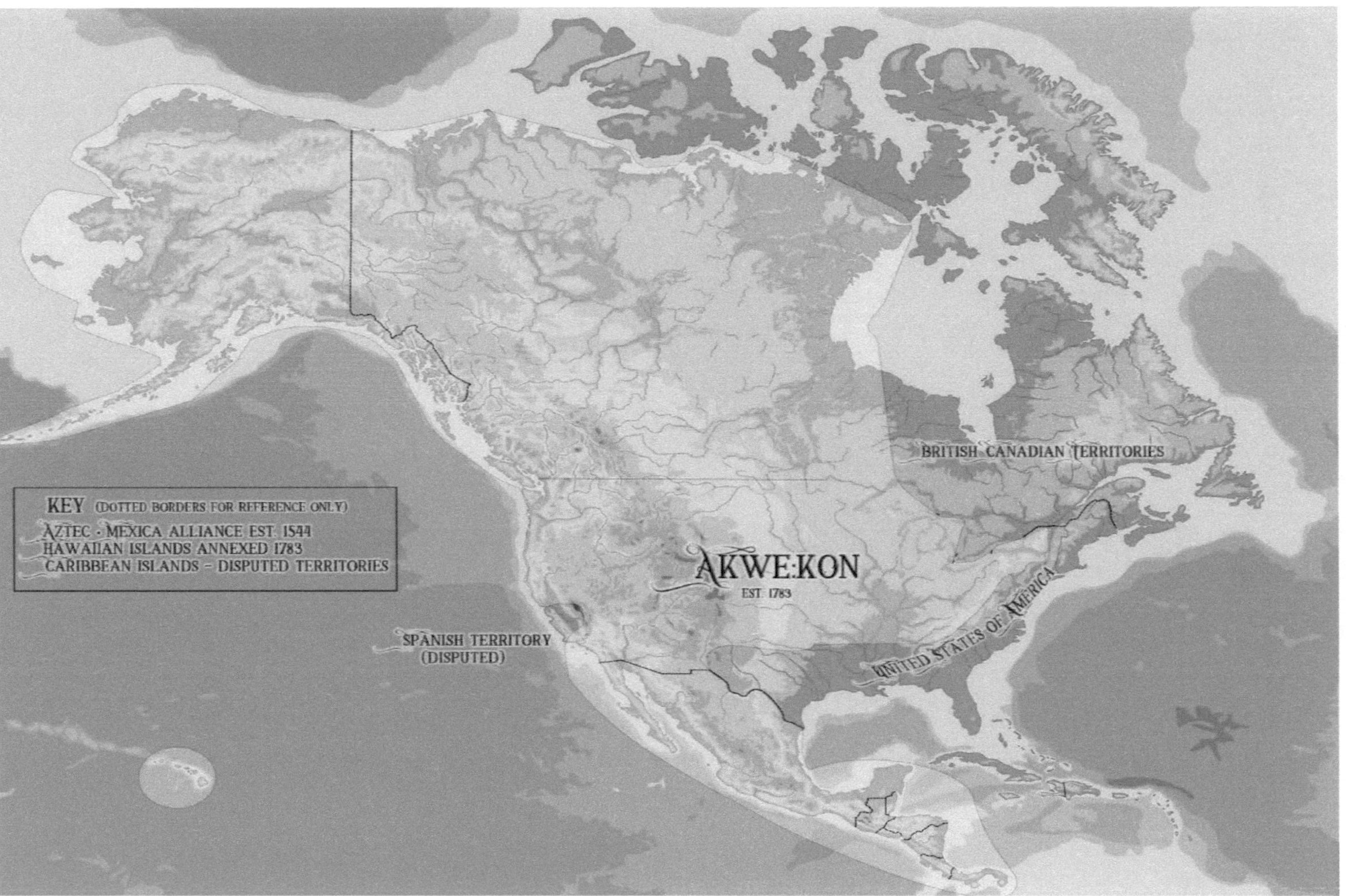

BRITISH CANADIAN TERRITORIES
AKWE:KON
EST. 1783
UNITED STATES OF AMERICA
SPANISH TERRITORY
(DISPUTED)
KEY (DOTTED BORDERS FOR REFERENCE ONLY)
AZTEC · MEXICA ALLIANCE EST. 1544
HAWAIIAN ISLANDS ANNEXED 1783
CARIBBEAN ISLANDS – DISPUTED TERRITORIES

Prologue

Wherein we learn of the legend of Skywoman and her twin boys, Spruce and Flint, and how that was just the beginning...

The Haudenosaunee Territories
As recounted by Tiyanoga to the people
October 21st, 1203
3:12 p.m.

"I speak to you now, the words and the voice of the people. Words that speak of our coming, our creation, and our enduring peace. These are the words of our fathers, our mothers, given to us since time immemorial. Hear now of the sacred warriors, the Tewakenonhnè, and learn what they tell us..."

We, The People, carry the story of *Skywoman* and of our creation with us. She resonates with us because she is the beginning.

From an early age we hear about her fall from the world of the *Skypeople*. Spying our world through a hole amongst the roots of the *Tree of Life*, she grew curious of our watery planet below. Ridiculed by the Skypeople for her curiosity, she was pushed from her world through the hole and fell in a fiery blaze to ours. Seeing her plummeting toward the Earth, geese flew high into the sky to ease her descent to our world. On their wings she watched in wonder as they glided over the vast oceans of the planet.

Knowing she needed a place to land, several aquatic animals scoured the water's depths to find some soil to put onto a great turtle's back. When they did, they created our home, Turtle Island. From the moment her feet touched upon the land, she began to seed the plants and create the beginnings of animal life that would populate this new world. They fell from the garments she wore as she walked around, and they took root and thrived in this strange new land.

Enraptured with her staggering creations, she gave birth to twins. The first, a virile strapping boy, she named *O'so:ra* (Spruce*)*, bringer of all good things in life. Yet, where Spruce possessed a robust body and a healthy glow, his twin, *Saweskira* (Flint), clawed his way from his mother's womb into this world sinewy and pallid in color and of ill purpose. One brother a bringer of light, love, empathy, and compassion. The other of darkness, malfeasance, calculated evil, and deception. Even in this, the balance of life must be maintained. The brothers, simply by being, kept that balance.

Would that their differences ended with their outworldly appearances. Our hearts are heavy knowing this is not so. But, as with all things in life, each responds and interacts with the world around them according to their own gifts.

Spruce moved about his world enthralled with every aspect of life his mother gifted them. His keen and sharp mind, coupled with his compassion and deeply profound respect for all the possibilities life afforded him, became the wellspring of his own creations. He demonstrated from childbirth his ability to imbue wondrous things on the island. Expanding upon the flora and fauna his mother started, he freely gave of himself to the world around him.

Flint, however, would toil his days away finding his brother's marvelous creations. Taking fiendish delight, he perverted them into beings of a darker purpose—bending Spruce's creation to his conniving will. Under Flint's maligned hand the common garden snake grew fangs saturated with poison to fill others with its toxic venom.

The boys moved about in a world immersed in brotherly affection laden with sibling competition. The latter trait, however, would come to shake the world to its core.

As their bodies grew in stature, so too did their conflicts. Smaller skirmishes between the twins eventually grew to outright warfare. Ultimately, Spruce found he could no longer bear to ignore the darkness that seemed to pour from his brother's very soul. Enraged and saddened by his brother's relentless assault on life, Spruce, bearing the heaviest of hearts, decided to put an end to it.

Thus, the brothers engaged, and an awesome battle ensued—a cataclysmic tussle that continued to rage with little regard for the passage of time. Whether one year or one million years, no one can say, for no one was there to mark its passing. What is known is the twins, in their epic sibling conflict, created the mountainscapes, deep canyons and gorges, as they flung their titanic bodies across Turtle Island, slamming each other into the fertile soil, hardening soft mounds of earth with brilliant fiery gazes that could melt the ground into sharp peaks, reaching heights this world had never known before.

When it seemed the world could no longer bear more of their anger, Spruce finally gained the upper hand and, in his victory, banished Flint to the shadows of life where darkness dwelled and bitterness and anger could make a home in him. There, in the oppressive darkness, Flint's heart grew black.

Though the battle ended, their sibling war was far from over.

Deep in those darkened places, in the blackest recesses of his banished realm, Flint raged, swearing he would not be gone forever. From those obscured caverns, sitting on an obsidian throne of his own making, he withdrew to lick his wounds and bide his time. For time, that uncontrollable but progressive companion, Flint knew would be ever in his favor. He counted on his brother's good nature leading Spruce to grow weary of watching for him. Flint felt all but assured he would work his way back to his rightful place to dominate the world his brother denied him. Patience and planning were all he required now.

Slowly, over the millennia, he crept back into everyday life, slithering through the cracks he created, testing his brother's resolve to keep him at bay. Whenever threatened by Spruce, Flint and his horde would retreat to their shadows, eager to fight another day.

But then Spruce did a thing his brother did not expect. For reasons no one can fathom, Spruce decided his works here were complete. Confident his brother was no longer a threat in this world, he became resolved to take his leave, to simply walk away. What Flint did not know, what he could not have guessed, was that his brother's gaze turned skyward—he sought life beyond their world. He wanted to return home, to the land of the Skypeople.

Spruce's final imprint on this land—he created the people of Turtle Island and imbued them with the knowledge to be the world's custodians, or balance-keepers. By them, the world would be cared for and treasured. They would become the check and balance against Flint and his minions should they rise.

For a time, it appeared to work. But patience was Flint's greatest weapon. He could wait several millennia if that is what it took to achieve his ultimate goal. So, Flint prodded the people. He poked at their defenses. Never so much as to do them great harm, but to test their strategic maneuvers and resolve.

Weary of smaller engagements, Flint reached into the world, revealing a shrewdness in his offensive tactics, eventually doing great damage to the people, weakening their defenses. Whispers from Flint in men's ears and in their hearts became commonplace. Meanwhile, Flint's work continued, maneuvering the people against one another to the brink of oblivion. In this, Flint's plan began to establish his evil intent: fear, mistrust, and deceit would he plant in men's hearts.

It worked.

As the infighting waged between the people, they realized they were losing too many of their kind to keep Flint in his place. The Onondaga Faithkeeper, in desperation, appealed to Spruce through prayers and offerings, begging for his assistance, explaining that the people were losing the battle, and all would be lost if he did not intercede on their behalf.

His heartfelt plea fell on deaf ears. For decade after decade, with further losses amongst the people, maddeningly Spruce remained silent—removed from their request. The people who remained, left to guard the planet, stood strong in their resolution to oppose Flint; they just did not possess the means necessary to defeat such a foe and in their weariness, their frustration festered between them, further playing into Flint's plan.

Under Flint's influence, the people argued amongst themselves about the correct way to defeat him. Flint saw this as an opportunity and played into this—pooling malcontentedness where he could, nurturing it, cultivating enmity toward their brothers and sisters.

On the eve of a particularly cold and bitter winter night, in the midst of a great battle, the people warring amongst themselves, tearing at one another to the brink of desolation, their prayer, long since forgotten, was finally answered.

He came.

Spruce returned one last time.

He returned to us not as we remembered, but as another great man: *Dekanawida*—known to us as the *Great Peacemaker*.

Dekanawida came to a man, a Mohawk man—*Aiionwatha*—who sat near a lake grieving over the butchering of his entire family during a recent battle. The Peacemaker consoled the man in his all-consuming desolation. Tears that seemed to have no end dried upon Aiionwatha's face as he spoke to the man, though not because of his words, but of the calming peace emanating from every part of him.

Resolved that the conflict had to end, the Peacemaker implored Aiionwatha to help him bring the people together. Using the analogy of a bundle of arrows, he explained how they needed to get the warring peoples to understand that a single arrow could easily be broken, but combined and of like purpose, they were nearly unbreakable.

The Peacemaker knew the words of peace should come from one of their own. Dekanawida stuttered to the point of shaking bodily just trying to convey a single thought—coaxing Aiionwatha to be that voice to the people. At first Aiionwatha was afraid no one would hear him. But Dekanawida assured him the calming and abiding peace that poured from his soul would warm their hearts and they would welcome Aiionwatha's words.

It was hard work to bring the people together, but under Aiionwatha's impassioned tongue, and the Peacemaker's influence, the people began to respond and see the way to the *Great Law of Peace*.

That was until Aiionwatha and Dekanawida came to the great Onondaga Nation. Here the great chief, *Atotarho,* was rumored to be the most removed from Aiionwatha's words. He had heard of Dekanawida and Aiionwatha's pilgrimage amongst the nations and wanted none of it for his people. As Aiionwatha continued to speak his words of unification and lasting peace, Dekanawida noticed that snakes moved within the hair of the great chief, whispering Flint's twisted words above anything Aiionwatha and Dekanawida could say or do.

Aiionwatha was resolved to give up when Dekanawida suggested he try one more time. While Aiionwatha spoke, imploring reason, Dekanawida stood behind the great chief, humming a soothing Onondaga tune that relaxed him, and began to comb the snakes from his hair, separating Flint's influence from Atotarho's ears. The snakes fell to the ground in cinders and ashes with each combining, leaving twisted singe marks on the ground around him—a testament to Flint's convoluted maniacal ways. The truth of Aiionwatha's words could finally be heard, and the unification was complete, uniting the original five nations—Mohawk, Oneida, Onondaga, Cayuga, and Seneca—to a common goal and purpose. The Great Law provided a method for other nations to join and the Tuscarora were the first to do so. Like that bundle of arrows, the Haudenosaunee Confederacy became strong.

But Spruce had a higher purpose in mind.

In their slumber, he visited each nation in the guise of Dekanawida. He moved amongst them as they slept, gifting the people with the ability to engage Flint and his twisted beasts. This gift, however, would come in the form of preternatural powers that would manifest themselves in unique and powerful ways. Not every man—or later, woman—would answer its call.

At first, Spruce chose warriors whom he observed showed the most promise; who were sound of heart and character and ultimately would not abuse the powerful sacred knowledge given to them by the Creator through the Peacemaker.

So, the *Tewakenonhnè* or Guardians, as they came to be known, trained under Spruce's tutelage in this way. As a warrior moved into his declining years, a new able-bodied young man of good mind and a great heart was called from the village into the Guardianship to learn its sacred knowledge.

Seeing the people had taken up the cause for themselves, Spruce decided to take his final leave from us. He gave us every tool we would need to succeed. The rest, he instructed, was up to us.

As he left, he approached the Faithkeeper of the Mohawk nation, and gave him a special wampum belt. Not of the white and indigo beads we crafted of our own, this belt, silver and shimmering like the ripples of a lake, is the most powerful and sacred of them all.

Gifted with this final tool to assist him in managing the Guardianship, he became the Guardian's first Central. I say to you now, as that Central, I bear the responsibility of the Guardian's care, welfare, and their training. I am not their master. I am their caretaker, their counselor, and their elder voice when need arises in the Grand Council for the Guardians to be heard.

"This is the way of the people; this is how the Tewakenonhnè came to be."

Chapter One

The Observational Prowess of William Matthias Hallett

The Cove Chronicle According to
William Matthias Hallett

Wherein we meet William Matthias Hallett, a man of independent means and stature, doing everything he can to put a swift end to it all.

All Hallows Eve—October 31, 1847
Satan's Circus, The Five Points, Manhattan, New York
8:53 p.m.

Satan's Circus. The name alone conjures up a visage of villainy.

My eyes took in the bright red effigy of Satan nailed to the doorway of the tavern, making no pretense as to what sort of clientele this establishment served, for gluttony and wickedness made a home here. It still did little to keep me from my current quest.

To be sure, as taverns went, she did not disappoint. The Circus was not where one went to hone one's craft of skullduggery and malicious behavior. If you had to perfect your craft, you had best do it elsewhere. Only the most proficient sharks, wildcats, and beasts could call the Circus their home. I could lay claim to none of that, though I did my best to blend in with the dregs who called her home in the chance that some thread of adventure would present itself.

Somehow, I had become somewhat of a regular. Clever enough to keep my nose clean and not falling in with any of the gangs who controlled the Points, I navigated these treacherous waters. Though, if pressed, there could be little in the way of my being able to entirely explain how all of this was accomplished. A pastiche of luck, concealment, and all the bottom of a braggadocio had allowed me to slip in and out of her timbered halls. There were moments where I almost thought, despite my wearing clothing of a lowly station amongst them, a cloak of invisibility had shielded me from them all. No one seemed to take notice unless I wanted to be noticed.

Which, for the most part, I did not.

From the moment anyone entered the Circus, their senses were accosted in such a manner that, if unprepared, would bring the strongest man to his knees. People who drank much and bathed even less peppered her halls and floors. The putridity of the smells was second only to the sounds piercing your ears: a raucous cacophony of braggarts and riffraff.

She is one of the busiest taverns in all of New York.

As I made my way to the barkeep to order a drink, I watched every conniving and devious cutthroat, and the harlots who hung onto them like leeches sucking the men dry, caught up in their usual routine of either getting drunk or getting someone else drunk so as to take advantage of their inebriation. Their game was always afoot.

Like maggots over carrion, the tavern was pressed to her walls with those who picked at the fetid remnants of life. Gold painted onto the fixtures of the hall had been tarnished by her clientele, soiling it to the dull hue they left behind. I could not help thinking that on her opening day she no doubt had been quite glorious. Looking at her now, it was clear she was but a tawdry remnant of her bejeweled past.

As I secured my seat with drink in hand, my eyes roved over the Circus. She boasted two levels, and the only places where a body could not occupy a spot were the large round columns running the gamut from floor to the second story above. Though many tried to cling to them from time to time if only to find some respite against the constant flow of hellions bent on consuming you and discarding your carcass in its wake.

Music played continuously from a couple of piano players who alternated at banging away at the keys with little ear to the line of the tune they played. For the most part the music went either enjoined in a drunken and off-tune chorus or ignored in its entirety. Unlike my normal life in Manhattan high society, I was all too aware that fisticuffs and knifings were standard entertainment fare here, and people took more notice if the evening progressed and bodies had not piled up. No one would spare a tear for lack of their presence; the Points did not permit you to care about anyone except yourself.

My eyes took note of this myriad of immigrants as they scratched at one another and at life; for they did everything to eke out an existence for themselves on these shores. In all of the commotion, it would have been difficult to spot an oddity within the torrent of drunkenness—save for one spot. A single well of calm stood out from the rest of the establishment: a darkened alcove and its inhabitants on the far side of the tavern to the left of the barkeep.

This alcove held my interest, the sole purpose of why I came back to the Points and the Circus time and again.

Having tried many of the other pubs and taverns within the Points, I turned to this very tavern in the hopes of observing something that deviated widely from the normal cutpurse fare—an adventure so decidedly wicked and filled with a sense of raw mystery as to satiate my soul for a lifetime. The gentlemen occupying the far alcove, no doubt the key to such an undertaking, held my attention captive.

For the past four nights the events surrounding these men varied little: they would sit in the alcove, each barely visible in the subdued light. The first thing I noted was how out of place they seemed.

Where everyone else bore the drab clothing of their lowly station, from what I could discern of these men's appearance, they seemed highly financed and respectable, as evident in the richness of their clothing—an island of wealth amidst the disenfranchised. Ensconced there, silent and immobile, casting about a wall of dark stoicism, they did little to dissuade me of my course. Indeed, their behavior did everything to secure my thoughts in the reverse. No service came to their table, and they made no attempt to gain the interest of a barmaid to change that.

They merely sat, waited, and watched.

The longer I observed them, the more intrigued I was by their presence and the great lengths everyone else went to *not* take any notice of them. These men, mysterious creatures confined in that darkened alcove, signaled to all around they alone occupied the top of the food chain—predators who preyed on other predators.

The alcove possessed only one source of light: a tiny candle jammed into a singular glass container. This poor excuse of a flame sputtered as if it had gleaned some prescient knowledge of the men's depravity as it struggled to cast some illumination against the three dark figures in close quarter. As far as I could tell, the only clear element in view, illuminated by their right hands lying on the table, displayed the same signet ring of a double-headed eagle, a symbol I had seen before but for the moment could not ascertain where. It gave me my only clue of their true identity.

From the outline the candle cast, they bore quite proudly their ostentatious attire, evident by the fullness of their black redingotes and framed in the soft ambient glow of lanterns hanging above the alcove. This allowed me to take note of their black furred hats.

These three men of mystery, large in stature for they nearly filled the alcove with their presence, always appeared around the same time each night. Yet, I could not recall the exact time of their arrival. Even the barkeep did his best not to look into the alcove they occupied. I believe I witnessed him visibly shudder last night as he had been watching the door and never spied their entrance, and yet, in that alcove, as sure as a tick of the clock, they sat.

Lighting, never in abundant amounts in any of the Five Points establishments, as dark endeavors require darkened quarters to operate, made it difficult to discern actions. This particular alcove exuded a darker purpose, one that kept even the more frightening miscreants of the Points at bay. For some reason I could not fathom, I found myself in exactly the opposite disposition—I was *riveted*.

For an hour or so, I sat and just watched them, forcing myself to drink the "cocktail" of ale that ran more in common to what I imagined pig's piss-water might have been.

From what I overheard, the barkeep spent the prior day buying up the dregs from other more well-established taverns' caskets of ale and tossed them together with little regard in the way of taste; for all I know he probably did add his own urine to the swill.

I heard one woman call it *Satan's Arse Cleaner*. She, being a frequent customer, and a lady of the evening, no doubt meant the double entendre when she would yell to the barkeep to "gimme the SAC." I did not think her commentary far off the mark on that account.

Yet I continued observing these three who held me spellbound. I do not know if they took notice of my stare. I talked to no one, just sat there, tolerated the SAC, and waited for my adventure to unfold, for I knew it would most certainly involve these men.

Around nine of the clock on each of the preceding nights, a young lad of no more than seven or eight strode into the tavern and walked right up to their table. No one stopped the lad; no one seemed to take notice of him at all, save for myself.

He would speak to them for but a few moments; then he would turn and leave the way he came. By the time I watched him go and turned back to watch what would happen next, the men would be gone. They seemed to vanish into thin air. The first time I witnessed it, I thought I imagined the whole routine. To be sure, I decided to gamble with my safety and changed my position to be closer to their alcove so I could observe their departure on the following night—again, to no avail. One moment there, and the next gone. The lack of lighting in the alcove did not help matters to be sure, but whether I observed from near or far, the result was the same: there one moment, gone the next.

Well, tonight I surmised would provide a new game. I knew I had the right of it. What put me onto it I could not say, but I felt it in the air. Tonight, the fifth night of this mystifying rendezvous, something was precariously at the tipping point. Disappointment would not be the order of the evening. I would soon discover the nature of their darker purpose.

As I sipped what I could from the devil's swill, I realized the men had waited much longer for the boy to arrive. They had no perceptible change in their posture to warrant that feeling, but the moment seemed pressed just a little harder. A tightening of the screw, so to speak. The edge to them was palpable. Whatever news the boy brought this evening bore the utmost urgency for these three men. As if on cue, the boy arrived as he had before. Despite seeing him the previous four nights, this time I bothered to take real notice of him.

A lowly immigrant boy, of that there was no doubt, he bore his station in his tattered clothes marked with the filth of the Points. But the boy's face, now there a marked change revealed itself to me. Most of the youth in this part of Manhattan were relegated to cutthroat tactics to survive their childhood, what little there was of it. That harsh existence etched a tough life upon them at an early age. To be sure, this young lad took his life in his hands, scratching out what little he could to keep his head above the torrents of the Points and make it to his teen years. He would sort out his adulthood once he made it that far.

Yet, in his countenance he possessed an almost angelic repose. A proper-looking lad who had the singular misfortune of being cast among the poorest of the poor, he no doubt stood out from the more average fare of the Point's child riffraff.

For a moment as my gaze followed him, I fancied seeing him cast in a different light altogether, one where he would have the finest clothing, food, and education. I guess what struck me most about him was that, save for our respective lots in life, he could be me at the same age.

Undeterred by others, he strode with purpose to the darkened alcove. A young man willingly engaging what the more aggressive and salient of the cutthroats dare not do. He spoke with them very quickly, and the men stirred. For the first time their faces came into the glow of the small candle's flame. It wavered, cowering a bit, as if their malevolence would snuff it from existence.

Each man, in that sputtering light, was revealed to be a foreigner. Their hats, now fully in view, were the tell-tale giveaway. Once they made themselves known to me, I identified them fully: *Russians.*

How odd to find them so far away from their home and in the Points. What possibly could they have to do in New York in this house of inequity? Though well groomed, each of them possessed a darkness to their eyes and did not bother to feign even the slightest element of any good-doing on their part. As the boy spoke, the men exchanged a silent but knowing look with one another, clearly taking whatever report he brought them to their liking. The man in the middle said something to his companions, gave instruction to the boy, and the most amazing thing happened: the three got up! Their quick movement caused me to jolt, and I dropped the cup of swill I had been tolerating. It clanked to the floor, though with the raucous sounds around me no one took note. Cursing at my obvious blunder, I scrambled to retrieve the cup. However, by the time I had set it right onto the tabletop next to me, they had taken their leave of the tavern.

I glanced at the door, only to catch a whisper of black redingote sweeping through it and out into the night.

At least this time, I have not lost them entirely...

I scrambled from the table to the door and out into the square that teemed with activity. I surveyed every option of escape. A key point to survival in the Points, you had to keep moving. A stationary man was a target for any number of assailants who would descend upon you and pick you apart. In some cases, that included the scattering of your bones, as well.

My sole quest at this juncture was to find the men quickly and keep moving along in this stream of sharks and piranhas. I eyed the small marshy patch that stood as the Points common. This tattered piece of bare earth, where meager strands of grass dared to show themselves, provided the only piece of undeveloped ground the Points had to offer as a public meeting place. A place where many a man had met their demise—publicly too. I did not wish my adventure to come to such a conclusion.

The Five Points existed where Cross and Orange streets intersected with Anthony, bordered on the east and west by Water and Mulberry streets. Hell's residence on earth, if there ever was one. And now I found myself swimming in the rip current of their existence.

And therein lay my current problem: I labored too long to find the men. A woman, who might have been quite striking save for how life had dealt her blow upon blow so now she bore a mere shadow of what God had intended at birth to qualify as beauty, made her way toward me. The purposefulness of her stride left little doubt that I had a target painted upon me, and I had only been on the sidewalk ten or so seconds.

However, I discovered an added benefit to my notice of her advance, for just behind her I spied the last of the gentlemen making their way down Cross toward Mulberry. I surmised their goal lay beyond the Points, but as to their exact destination, their plan escaped me.

The wharf, perhaps?

I did not know for certain. 'Twas the only thing I could think of lying in that direction. I tried in vain to circumvent the advancing barracuda harlot.

"Well now, a strappin' man like yerself. Where ya off to in such a hurry?"

She stood in front of me, attempting to ply her trade, as if I could not deduce her ulterior motive. I would have definitely been put off by the state of her teeth, which ran the gamut from putrid yellow to mildewing green and resolved themselves into decaying black. Her breath billowed about me, a mixture of the death that had already manifested itself within her and whatever ale she had consumed thus far to mask—poorly—the putridity of her pre-decomposition.

The harlot, for all intents and purposes, embodied a walking prostitute corpse. If I was clear on one thing, *Necromancy* did not fall under the classification of adventure in my book. I possessed little stomach for death. Little did I know how wrong I was to be on this singular, salient point.

"Eh, not interested," I replied with much haste and attempted to slip from the grasp of her left arm around my neck, entwined like a serpent hellbent upon consumption. Adam should have kept a better eye on Eve as the female sex had learned far too much from that reptilian encounter of biblical verse.

"Ah now, a virile buck of a man, howzabout a quick one in the alleyway?"

She ground her hip against my thigh, and the frailty of her form along with her breath nearly made me retch. However, I had not lost sight of her ulterior motive, which was to rob me of my money whilst she plied the dregs of her feminine wiles upon me. She did not think I noticed the sly movement of her right hand that ingeniously held a small knife where she was actively slicing the threads along my pocket and the few coins stashed there.

"I said, no, thank you." I slipped from her grasp, and she attempted to move on with my coins in her right hand. I promptly grabbed and applied the right pressure to her wrist and forced her hand to relinquish the coins back into my own. I smiled and moved on, the confident winner in our cutpurse mazurka. I pushed my finger through the hole of the jacket, silently cursing. At some point I would have to mend it but pressed on lest my adventure slip away from me. And I had little intention of allowing that to pass.

She stood there eyeing me with a knowing look, as if to memorize every last line of me so she could challenge me anon.

Good luck with that, m'dear.

As I moved down Cross Street in pursuit of the men, I spared a glance back at her and noticed that while she took stock of her loss, she unwittingly broke the rule of the Points as well, standing too long in one spot. For now, she was being accosted by some young boy who obviously intended to pickpocket her tattered purse.

"Barracudas, beware the little piranhas..." I murmured as I moved out of view.

I finally reached the corner of Mulberry, stopped, and scanned the other options on that corner until I spotted them to my right, heading down Mulberry toward the docks.

"Just as I thought." Though who I was speaking to was beyond me. I guess I took stock that I had survived another night in the Points and now had a lead on what might unfold before me.

With as much stealth as I possessed, I raced along Mulberry Street, and in my haste, I closed the distance to barely a half block behind the quartet. I could not see the boy, as the three imposing dark figures were surrounding him. Only when we moved several blocks toward the docks alongside the Battery did I notice the men had produced rather odd-looking walking sticks. Long and darkly metallic, as if made from a highly polished gun metal, gleaming in the meager reflective light. I had not noticed the sticks before, and this piece of male accoutrement would have sure caught my eye, for I possessed a rather large and tasteful collection of walking sticks.

The night air was becoming chilled along the river front. Yet, for some reason I could not discern, I became acutely aware that I may not be the only one doing the following. The hairs on the back of my neck stood on end as if, like a predator caught up in chasing his prey, I never bothered to take note that a larger predator was on my heels. I did my best to convince myself it was nothing more than the thrill of the oncoming adventure that had me so on edge and keyed up.

::This is not your game, William...::

I stopped suddenly as the voice played upon my ear, as if whispered to me and me alone. I looked around and found no one else, save for the quartet moving off further the longer I stayed and tried to figure out what had just happened. The only sounds were my quick, panicked breaths.

::You should go home, Will...this is not for you.::

I spun around, to find only breathing and most assuredly the rapid beating of my heart keeping me company.

Damn it all, that infernal voice!

At first, I might have mistaken it for my own inner voice warning me to be wary of what I was doing, but upon review, I realized the voice bore little resemblance to mine at all. Though, somehow, I knew I had heard it before.

Who in blazes could it be?

I had precious little time to think as my conundrum foursome made their way just beyond where I could make them out. I renewed my efforts to close the distance.

A few moments later, I found myself only ten or so feet behind them, worried now that whatever throng recently occupied this area had thinned out to a few people along the waterfront. I decided to duck into one of the building doorways to allow a tad more distance between me and my quarry, trying not to draw too much attention upon myself. The ruse worked, as I observed that one of the men to the rear happened to glance back just as I slipped from view into the darkened doorway.

Rather than suddenly appearing along the path at a later time, I decided to dart across the street and appear as if I had approached from dockside, merely paralleling their advance down the road. It was then I felt the "pursuer being pursued" again. Only now it seemed to overtake me and whip along the street as a gust of air that came from out of nowhere yet carried none of the chill night air. The breeze felt oddly warm and held a very familiar scent, though I could not recall, even with every part of my being working upon it, where I had smelled it before. So now I had a voice to pair with the olfactory sensation of a moment ago. I knew the two connected themselves somehow. I stalled momentarily as I contemplated this, before picking up the pace along the sidewalk nearest the docks, lest I lose my quarry altogether.

After a couple of blocks, I closed the distance between us to within a half block. We had traversed three full blocks at this point when they suddenly turned down a dark alleyway. This could not bode well for the boy. Even so, I still could not fathom why he would be in the company of such queer Russian figures in this part of town. Two of the men were sleek, with dark features and smartly clipped beards. They were encased in stylish black suits, and their waistcoats were of some of the finest damask-looking silver silk I had ever beheld.

My eyes roved to their more than fetching walking sticks. This feature allowed me to spot them. As I came to the entrance of the alley, I paused. This alley gave no quarter for relief from a survival standpoint for it was not open to the sky above, but a closed brick tunnel of a passage. Never a good idea to enter one unless you knew all access points to and from the enclosure. I did not relish putting myself through this, but I would not shirk my course now. I peered and squinted as best I could, to discern what little the light afforded me, which was not much.

Nothing. Naught but the dwindling echo of the men's footsteps at the far end.

Well, at least they have not dispatched the lad.

I walked closer to the opening and placed a palm against its surface. I turned my head a little to determine if my ears could pick up what my eyes could not. Steeling all the auditory prowess at my disposal, I concentrated on blocking the sounds from the remaining cacophonous ramblings of the dockside street and into the dark vacuum of the tunnel. When all hope had nearly escaped me, I heard something which made my heart race.

"So, are you sure that the requisite number of bodies have been procured?"

"Without a doubt, sir. Just as you required. I have them assembling as we speak to the right of the shanty, as you'll see, but remember I promised each of them a half-dollar as a token of your promise to provide them with better lives once they reach the west coast."

The boy carried himself well with these imposing figures surrounding him, but I could not believe my ears. For if they did *not* deceive me, and I had no reason to think they had, this lad established himself firmly in the trade of trafficking people to the west coast. I realized I came up short on a very important point in the boy's words. What west coast could he mean? The Pacific? Quite a feat, I admitted. Surely, he meant the west coast of Europe. But when I quickly explored that option, I found it did not make sense, either. Why would anyone agree to make the trek back to where they so recently fled? It had to be the western coast of this continent.

They cleared the tunnel. Their voices ceased to echo back in my direction. I had to press further along for a better vantage point.

"Well done, young Master Liam. Rest assured; they will have a better life. You cannot help but have a better one after the repugnant existence of this hellish squalor."

"Oy, that's me home you're ramblin' on about, there."

Silence.

Liam crossed a line. He may have the right of it, but as my father had been fond of saying when in such circumstances where you are clearly in a one-down position, you could be *dead right* as well. Which did you little good for the effort.

I began to creep slowly and as quietly as I could through the tunnel to the back courtyard where the quartet conversed.

A snicker all around met the boy's impertinence.

"Well said, young Liam. So noted. I meant you no harm. Just an observation that even you have to acknowledge. Your life, such as it is, is not the height of aristocracy, now is it?"

"No, but that's how I come to be under your employ, sir. I meant no disrespect by it. Just mindful of me ways and make no mistake about how low they are. But if I has anyfing to say 'bout it, there's gonna be a change in my life and for the bettah too."

Another laugh, this time echoed by the three gentlemen in chorus.

"Come now, Master Liam. Let us settle accounts then, shall we?"

"Ippolit, Ivanovich, do go and get these people processed through the warehouse. See to it that they are housed in the upper Hudson floor, and begin the sedative as soon as everyone is settled in. You know what to do with the children. Send Alexi to me so we can make final processing arrangements."

I had entered the courtyard and had the good fortune of finding some discarded crates and barrels near the mouth of the alley passage with which to hide myself. They afforded me some cover from which I could observe the men entering one of the doors leading into a small shanty structure raised above the ground. A young man of no more than twenty approached them. He too appeared immaculately dressed for such a nefarious operation.

Liam was correct. Next to the shanty was a collection of about seventy-five people of varying age and creed—all of lowly immigrant class. At this late hour, some of them had sleeping children, either upon their father's shoulders or in the crook of their mother's bosoms. They were obviously recently arrived immigrants; some still had the weary look of prolonged travel plainly upon their faces. To their left, a mass of luggage and belongings stood carefully arranged as if first- or second-class accommodations lay in the crowd's immediate future.

The two men, bringing Liam with them, moved up the short stairs to the porch, which creaked from rot and overuse. Its oddly slanted shingled roof of dark forest green that had seen a more colorful day seemed strangely out of place for this industrial structure. As if the house had always stood here and the surrounding behemoth of a building sprang up around it.

Grimy paned windows to either side of a Dutch door, coupled with rotting stairs and porch, gave the building the apparition of a man's face—all withered with age. The dilapidated roof, slanted slightly askew, completed the visage of the man wearing a funny sort of tilted hat. The stilts, upon which the porch stood, sagged from overuse and age. After the bottom half of the door closed, a gas lamp bloomed into brightness and illuminated what little was viewable through the years of city filth occluding the windows.

A burst of light crackled in the night sky but not so high that it rose above the courtyard warehouse. The people collectively took in an awestruck gasp of air, mesmerized by the glowing orb. I found I too was caught up by that glowing light, undulating whites and blues and little sparks trailing in the night sky. It seemed controlled from the tip of Ippolit's stick. When he moved forward, I felt myself pulled along with them.

My progress was stymied with a sudden unseen force thrusting me back into my hiding spot. That infernal voice filled my every sense, blackening the world around me, completely obscuring the hypnotic pull the glowing orb had upon me.

::Stay put, William, and do not *engage these men.::*

The black surrounding me faded, and the world came back to me. Despite the warning, I was in the thick of it now as I knew my adventure had finally begun.

I chanced a glance over the barrels to spy upon the collection of people again. The last of them was being skirted into the warehouse opposite the shanty and a large metallic door bolted behind them. Another two men leveled their sticks at the collection of belongings and slashed the air above them. The items floated into what appeared to be a giant tear in the middle of the air. The men took two steps toward the door and in the span of a single step completely slipped from view, as if vanishing into thin air. I was left quite alone.

From my secluded vantage point I watched the trio move further back into the main room of the shanty, still well within sight of the opened door. I needed a closer vantage point to get the fullest measure of what was going on here. I quietly darted from the safety of my cover to the porch steps. Keeping to the balls of my feet, I crept up the stairs. With catlike care, I took each step. As I gained a vantage point from the half-opened door, I peered cautiously over the closed lower half to witness this *settling of accounts* as the finely tailored, albeit sinister, leader of their crew indicated.

He settled himself into a large chair behind a rather plain-looking desk and laid his stick on the desktop as one of his companions went about lighting the oil lamps in the room. The room was as nondescript as the desk, the only other furniture a small bookcase behind the desk with a stack of what appeared to be accounting ledgers.

As Ivanovich moved about the room, I took note that he lit the lamps not with a match or torch, as I anticipated, but with the tip of his shiny stick. It crackled with a bluish spark the likes of which I had never seen. This manner of lighting the lamps only added to the sticks' mystique. I took great care to sink back below the doorway as he passed by to light the lamp nearest the entrance to the shack. Once he completed his task, he moved back to behind the young boy at the back of the house. Luckily, he did not completely obscure my view of the man behind the desk, nor young Master Liam.

"Let's see...we agreed on half a dollar per head, I believe you put it. You did demand a rather high price as I recall. And you procured...how many of them was it again?"

"Seventy-five, sir, counting the children n' all."

The sinister leader whistled loudly at the amount, though a certain spark in his dark eyes belied the largess of the sum. Evident upon their countenance, these men suffered little when it came to affairs of a financial nature.

"Now what would a young lad like you have to spend all that money on?" he asked, producing two coin bags onto the desk.

"Who's to say that I am going to spend it? I have plans, sir, I have."

"An enterprising young man, you are, Liam. You clearly wish to continue to work for us then, I take it? No?"

"Most definitely, sirs," he said as he removed his cap from his head and began to wring it in his hands, a sign he was growing more apprehensive the longer he toiled here with these men.

This piranha detected just how many teeth these sharks possessed. He, no doubt, did not intend to furnish them their next meal.

I understood his reason for concern. The longer I stayed on the porch, the more uneasy my stomach became. This young lad had more bottom to him than most of the men back at Satan's Circus who avoided these men like they had the plague. Yet, Liam stood his ground amongst these malevolent creatures. Impressive, to say the least.

My fear for the boy grew as I noticed the posture of the two companions shift ever so slightly. Almost imperceptibly so, though I caught it, nonetheless. I was unsure what would be the best course of action to save the boy—whether to call out or play the buccaneer and actually bound in unannounced.

Say nothing of the distinct possibility that if I did anything of the sort, what would likely happen is the boy would be killed immediately for bringing along an intruder. Or, worse yet, I might be captured and killed as well. Neither suited my purposes. But I knew I had to do something.

The larger, more muscular of the two companions had produced what looked like a stiletto from the sleeve of his overcoat. It glinted for a brief second in the lamp light. No time to waste...

"But other considerations need to be taken into account, young Master Brackett. Like the fact that you have allowed yourself to be followed. There is a brutish fellow hanging outside our door as we speak now."

Brutish? How dare he...

Before I could take note, one of the two men vanished, seemingly to slip into the darkness of the room to appear very quietly at my backside with the pointed instrument at my back.

Damn! Well this was it, for sure. My adventure had come and gone in the span of a few minutes and now to a miserable demise. And all I had to show for it? My feeble attempt to save the life of some miscreant who probably would be none too pleased to see me.

At my captor's prodding, I pushed inside the doorway.

Young Master Brackett looked positively murderous for my intended rescue. Well, damn him too.

Let them kill you as well. See if I care.

Only problem was, I was already trying to plan a way to save the little whelp. Sometimes I think I am seriously deranged and should sever all ties with humanity.

"Well now, who do we have here, Liam? A cohort of yours?"

"Never saw the likes of 'im before in me life." The anger in his face still plainly visible.

"He speaks the truth of it," I said. "I do not know who he is either. I...er..." I was trying to think fast but found myself coming up woefully short. The leader wearily sighed, not bothering to hide his boredom with my arrival.

"Seeking to displace his employment in favor of yourself, perhaps?" he offered.

An answer percolated upon my lips when the hounds of hell let loose upon the place. Though the next few moves came within mere seconds of one another, time seemed to run much slower so that every nuance of the ensuing fight lay forever etched upon my mind.

Without much in the way of a warning, the ceiling came crashing down in two places. I was blown off my feet onto my buttocks and down the short hallway, sliding to stop just in front of the door.

Two Mohawk warriors had crashed through the ceiling, landing atop of the desk with a loud crack. One of them sent some sort of powerful burst of light shattering the desk into pieces as they continued their descent through its remains to the floor.

The ringleader of the terrible trio retrieved his stick with the first sound of the roof cave-in. Instead of confronting them, he tugged his finger on a coat hook on the wall and a passageway opened and he slipped into the darkness of the small tunnel beyond. One of the two warriors gave chase, yelling for the other to remove the lad and myself.

Master Liam, however, in the middle of the blast, possessed the wherewithal to bound forward and grasp the coin purses from the desk prior to its untimely demise. He proceeded in my direction as I sat up and shook my head to clear the cobwebs from the blast.

Muffled sounds, as if heard underwater, very like cannons being fired in close quarters, played upon my ears. My body recoiled from the waves of sound and energy moving about in the small shanty. Light flashes and small percussive explosions rattled before me and my eyes, half-hidden by my hands to shield myself from the onslaught, bore witness to fantastical things. My ears, however, came up short on balance. I shook my head, banging the heel of my left hand against it to see if something inside had become dislodged. I knew, having taken anatomy at Dartmouth, this clearly could not be the case, but I did it anyway. It seemed to help somehow as Liam's voice sifted itself from the murky din.

"Oy, me white knight, get away from the door, you feckin' idiot! Or I am just gonna climb right over you to get out!"

I scrambled to my feet and turned to look down the hallway at what appeared to be the remaining two of the trio desperately trying to defend themselves from...

"Jacob?" I murmured to myself.

For indeed, one of the two Mohawk warriors was none other than my old college mate from my days at Dartmouth! I had not seen him in over two years since we parted company on our last day of school. He had been my confidant and best mate, but at no time during our near six years together did I ever see him as I did now.

Astonished, I started to walk not from the extraordinary fight as anyone with a clear head would, but rather toward the battle. As I came into view of the room, which by now bore little resemblance to only minutes prior, I stood slack-jawed.

Jacob stood where he had landed in the remnants of the shattered desk and proceeded to fight off the two blokes who, based on size alone, might have posed a serious threat to his continued health. However, evident in the dour expressions the Russians wore in the course of engaging my Mohawk friend, they did not have the upper hand in the fight. Indeed, they acted as if Jacob could dispatch with them with little more than a mere thought.

Blows billowed back and forth between the terrifying threesome but not with their fists or any weapons I could see. Instead, vibrations seemed barely visible as they rippled in the air between them, as if the finger of God were running along the fabric of reality in a constant volley. Jacob shrugged off the energy ripples sent his way by the other two with little effect upon his own aggression.

Taking no obvious notice of my entry into the room, Jacob took the offensive. His opponents tried desperately to fend off Jacob's assault by putting up some opposing force that attempted, quite in vain, to repel his impressive volley of power. Each brilliantly lit jolt, as if Jacob commanded Thor's hammer, only pressed them further to their respective corners of the battle zone. The larger, more brutish man, Ivanovich, called to his partner something in what appeared to be broken Iroquoian. Being a friend of Jacob's and having heard the language for the better part of my days at Dartmouth, I knew it, but could not decipher the exact phrase. It bore some sort of command, but the words were not in the right order.

One thing I did discern; the Russian men employed a coordinated effort to attack Jacob. I could not stand there and not do something, as he was my best mate from school. I searched the ground for anything with which to attack the brute directly in front of me. I spotted a long piece of wood on the floor of the hallway, probably from the demolished roof. It would do nicely enough for the task.

As I picked it up, I saw the men turning their shiny walking sticks so the ends pointed to each other without actually touching. An arch of power radiated from the tips. Like a bolt of lightning, it crackled to life. Jacob was about to counter their move when the other Mohawk warrior, who seemed familiar to me, though I could not envision where such a meeting would have taken place, appeared as if from out of nowhere by his side.

"Coward took off. Seems to have done a *ripper* on me. I got this. Take your friend and get him out of here."

"Battery Street meeting place?" Jacob replied, landing a bright bolt of light that collided with the men's arc of lightning. The result was a feedback along the lines to each man's stick, knocking them from their feet, one against the wall next to me. Ivanovich sailed through a rather dingy window I had not noticed on the side of the room.

"Right you are. As soon as I have had a go with..."

Jacob looked about.

"Lost one, have we?"

The odious man before me on the floor regained his composure and slowly stood up.

I spied his plan to change tactics. My chance revealed itself to me. I swung using all my might at his head. My strike collided with the unseen force that repelled Jacob's earlier assaults, shattering the wood. I bounced back against the wall of the hallway, my arms and shoulders throbbing with the contact reverberating throughout my body. The man took no notice of my advance. Dropping the last of the wood onto the floor, I slid down the wall in pain.

"Jacob, get Will out of here and find the boy!" The other warrior nudged Jacob with his shoulder to get moving.

Before I could respond, Jacob appeared at my side, and his hand gripped the collar of my shirt and waistcoat.

"Had enough of fun time, Will?" he asked with a slight grin, hauling me to my feet.

Oh surely, he cannot be so smug as to think I find all of this...this...whatever engagement we are in, to be fun.

Before I could say anything further on the subject, his hand moved to grip my wrist, and within the next instant we were out of the house and into the courtyard of the warehouse.

The abrupt change of the harsh light of the shanty to that of a subdued quarter-phased double-moonlit night was a bit of a struggle for my gaze to help me find my way. Jacob released me and turned his head slightly to catch me in the fullness of the moonlight's glow. He even had the temerity to smile at me!

The snarky bastard!

"Got an eyeful back there, did you?" he chided as he continued to stride out into the courtyard, scanning for what I could only assume was young Master Liam. I had every confidence the boy made his escape long ago.

As we continued to the far side of the courtyard, I could still hear percussive sounds from the building behind me.

I looked back to discover the little shack now completely dark save for the brilliant flashes of power Jacob's cohort leveled at his opponent. I turned back to Jacob. The younger warrior had miraculously joined us, coalescing instantaneously on the breeze. How he accomplished such a feat left me bewildered. This evening had become an exercise in the surreal and fantastical. Yet, despite what I had witnessed thus far, some small part of my mind tangled with this young man's name which still escaped me.

John, James? Like Jacob, I was fairly certain it began with a J.

We moved at a fast clip, determined to clear the courtyard. I did my best to stay close when my world rattled again. In truth, I have few words to describe the feeling. A sensation of a hook, painlessly but firmly lodged in my breastbone, gripped me and pulled the breath from out of my body, and I suddenly found myself air-bound, being hurled back in the direction of the house. My arms and legs flailing as if that was going to be of any help.

"Jacob!" My cry pierced the night.

Within the next moment, the younger warrior disappeared only to reappear by my side as I came to what I thought would be a body-crushing blow sure to claim my life. The irony that my desire for adventure had put me in harm's way not once, but twice in one evening could not have been more plainly felt than in this moment.

But no life-perishing breaking of the body for me. Instead, just as I should have crashed into the ground, my friend's mate somehow undid the force of the impact so that I landed upon a featherlight cushion from calamity. I came to a stop only inches from the ground. The sensation bore little difference from when I leaped into the comfort of my bedding at night. He held out a hand to me and, once clasped, pulled me onto my feet.

"Thank you...er, I am sorry I do not seem to recall your name."

Before he could respond, the shanty exploded. The young man held his hands out and seemed to contain the blast, so it rolled up an invisible bubble, keeping ourselves safe. In the next instant, the fire from the blast seemed to change into a volley of steam, to water, which collapsed onto the strewn debris. As soon as the fire was out, the bubble was gone, and the water came runneling about our feet. But the fight appeared far from over, it seemed. Four or five bolts of light shot past us. My young friend again put his hands out, and the volleys of light only seemed to dance upon the invisible wall he constructed between us and the attack.

"Flintlings on the roofline," Jacob shouted. "Two on the left, four more on the right."

"Take Will," he called to Jacob while they traded powerful blows with the dark figures bearing that odd-sounding name. "Get him out. What about the boy?"

One man on either side of us took a hit and fell from the roof, but their compatriots shot a brilliant blue-white light that appeared to tear at the air beneath the falling comrades. They simply slipped from sight before coming into contact with the earth.

Could this be what my young companion referred to as ripping?

"He seems to have found his own way out," Jacob added with little in the way of exertion on his part given the tremendous amount of energy flying about us. To them it seemed as if t'were nothing more than having a chat on a bright spring morning. "I could not find any sign of him."

"Made off with quite a sum, do you not think? Quick-thinking lad. I think I *like* him." Jacob smirked. His wicked smirk never failed to get a rise out of me. His devilish smiles alone brought about many adventurous nights during our days at Dartmouth. My reciprocating smile immediately took form in response to his.

Two more shots from Jacob seemed to burst from the palms of his hands.

The very air around his palms was alight with what looked like the dust glowing in a quickened swirl and compressed to a singular dark point in the middle. The power seemed to press in until it burst forth in a volley of pure energy. I was astounded by the enormity of it all.

I looked over at my savior who had not only employed the same tactic with his right palm but had erected a formidable invisible wall with the other that our assailants were having a most difficult time cutting through. As to our opposition, their power, while equally astonishing, seemed to come not from their hands at all, but their long glinting staffs. These appeared as the same highly polished reflective metal as the walking sticks, I observed earlier only now extended the length of a javelin. One of my younger warrior's shots was spectacularly brilliant but infinitesimally small, almost insignificant compared to the other exchanges that came before. Worry threaded across my brow for the first time this evening that they were running out of energy and our doom might come after all.

However, as soon as that insignificant sliver of light contacted its intended target, it not only shattered the glittering staff but burned the bearer to a cinder in a flurry of flame and smoke. The creature's shrieking cry of agony cut through the remnants of the blast.

"Nicely done!" Jacob commented as he pushed both palms together and condensed the power he amassed into a compact orb that grew in strength. "You will have to show me that sometime." Satisfied in the orb's compressed power, he released it so that the resounding explosion, once past our shielded wall, radiated across the roofline in a fiery ring of iridescent blues, pinks, and purples. The resounding shock knocked two of the figures from their stance, but they quickly rebounded and used that slicing motion to extract themselves from the scene. Their fellow warriors did the same, and the violence came to a speedy resolution.

This is not to say that Jacob remained motionless as the onslaught continued. He worked exceedingly well with his formidable teammate. Our best military could stand to learn a thing or two in coordinated warfare from my two Mohawk warriors. As the next wave tried to best us, he held his hands stretched to either side of him, calling up several cobblestones populating the courtyard and hurling them with considerable force. They glowed with such intensity the hair upon my arms singed as they flew by me. These fiery comets streaked across the night sky, lighting the air on fire in a maelstrom the likes that Lucifer would bring; collectively they pummeled the shield of the enemy, breaking down their defenses en masse. Sensing a turn in the fight, our opponents began to withdraw.

"That was fun!" the younger warrior commented with a bright smile that made his darkened eyes dance brilliantly in the moonlight.

"Not a bad way to spend an evening," Jacob replied, having come closer to us, also grinning from ear to ear.

This was their idea of a good time?

"Wait a moment!" I cried out, pointing to Jacob and rounding on his companion. "My arse nearly got handed to me not once, nay twice, but three times tonight and you both have the temerity to call it...*fun*?"

They exchanged a knowing, maddeningly silent look in a way the Natives did so well but offered me no reply.

"We better clear out in case they bring back reinforcements," the younger Mohawk added.

Jacob nodded. "Come with me, Will."

He placed a hand upon my shoulder and, gripping my collar, moved forward, pulling me with him. The moment he did, a pressure built behind my eyes, obscuring my sight. Before I could shake it out, from one step to the next, my vision cleared, and I found myself in the Battery, several blocks from the dockside courtyard we occupied a moment before.

Chapter Two

The Gating of Battery Park

Wherein William Hallett crosses paths with his past and unwittingly discovers the adventure he seeks.

Battery Park, Manhattan, New York
A few seconds later...

"Jacob, stop! Stop! Release me."

Jacob did as I asked. I stumbled for a second and then shook my head and the wariness cleared and I was able to stand up properly.

"But how?" I inquired as I gathered my wits about me with the sudden change of venue.

Jacob's companion arrived much in the same manner, simply appearing out of thin air. A ghostly and ghastly sight to behold. Having just gone through it, I could not say how it was accomplished, but the witchery of it did not escape me.

Neither of them took note of my frustrated query as they immediately became immersed in a very terse conversation in Mohawk.

Having spent the better part of my school days in our shared rooms with Jacob, I had become quite the Mohawk linguist. However, it was readily apparent, since we parted company two years ago upon our graduation, the dexterity of my Mohawk had become sorely lacking. I found I could only make out phrases like "new" or "unheard of" and something about a man named *Lord Flint* and another called a *Central*. It was all very confusing. I needed answers and, by God, I was going to have them.

"Look!" I chimed in the middle of their whispered heated debate. "Jacob, what in blazes *is* going on?"

I approached and placed my hands upon his upper arms and looked into those dark eyes. They seethed with a thousand different thoughts other than my petty questions, and he was of a mind that my inquiries could wait. I cared not for what he wanted; he had some explaining to do, and he best get to it, in earnest.

"Jacob, I know you. I have known you for years. We were best mates in school. And yet"—I moved away from him, swinging my arms around to show the enormity of what I had witnessed—"never in the entire time I knew you did I ever behold such...such—" I was suddenly struggling for the exact phrase. "—divinity to spring forth from your hands. Tell me, is it *magic*? I mean you read about these things, and true enough, though I know you and your people and their disdain for magic and witchery I cannot in all good conscience consider it anything but that. Yet, I know precious little of your private customs and teachings, so I am at a loss to reconcile what we have engaged upon this very night. Pray, tell me, so that I can make some sense of it."

I held him at arm's length. "On all that we had together as friends and the love I bear for you and your family and"—indicating the agitated young Mohawk who stood nearby with an odd sort of look about him, as if I had lost my mind, which I supposed I might have, but I continued nonetheless—"and *your* people. Pray give me *something* I can cling to, that will keep my mind from slipping into the abyss."

He stood there looking at me, though I could tell his anger or frustration had abated. His body became less rigid to my touch. His eyes softened gradually, and the Jacob I knew, whom I counted as more a brother to me than my own, actually bore the beginnings of a smile.

"You always were the dramatic one. And they are *your* people too, William, lest you forget. Your mother is *Kanien'kehá*, as is your grandmother."

And at that he pulled me roughly to him, embracing me fully, and we laughed for a moment. Upon parting, he turned to take in his companion.

That man, however, seemed even more wary of me. I took my first real look at him. He was a most *bewitching* man. Stunningly handsome and a strapping specimen of a man, of that there was little doubt. His age could be no more than a year or so off my own, yet in his manner, it was clear he possessed a singular wisdom about him. This was a young man not to be trifled with. He stood with such formidability, as if his young years bore a tremendous amount of worldly knowledge that would normally come from years of experience, as from a much older man. How he came to this sort of countenance, I could only guess, and from the looks of him in action, no doubt he had seen more than his share of battle.

This is not to say he appeared inept for the challenge, far be it. For here, before me, was a seasoned man of adventure. He physically appeared to possess the virility and proper muscular structure to hold his own in a fight. In truth, I smiled upon this fleeting thought. After what I witnessed coming from his own hands only a few moments prior, taking on several men equipped with weaponry that could level our best military, I doubted there could be any man upon this Earth who could engage *this* young man and have the hope to cause him bodily damage.

Yet, for all of his quiet bravado, he seemed to regard me in the most peculiar manner. As if he knew me or had known me at some point in my youth and, because of this, he already regarded me as an equal of some sort.

But in all good conscience, I could not ever recall having seen him before. As I thought upon this, to my great consternation, something moved about in the back of my mind that bespoke of a recollection, some wisp of a memory of him. It eluded me in spite of my efforts to wrestle it from its hazy repose.

If I had to guess, I suppose his eyes held the real truth of his character. For *if* eyes truly were mirrors to men's souls, as some lay claim, then this young man possessed a soul with an enormous depth and a keen sense of perception. An eagle-like perception that seemed to regard me with an intensity I could not begin to understand. A whisper of something slithered about me, not of my own accord. My body flushed with blood as if this young man could impress his emotions upon me. I did not know why I felt this, but I also knew it to be true. He, however, did little to acknowledge his effect upon me. True enough, there was honesty, clarity, and a trace of predator lurking about them. Yes, my initial estimation was spot-on: a most *bewitching* man.

"Will, I want to introduce you to Josiah Lightfoot," Jacob began. "No doubt he might appear somewhat familiar to you. We all attended Dartmouth at the same time, though he was a year behind our own."

He nodded. "Joss, please."

Dartmouth?

"Well, that is it, of course," I replied. Could I force a bigger lie through my teeth? For I still could not place him, no matter how I tried.

I shook his hand warmly even so. His body softened to my touch, and any apprehension of the moment seemed to take its leave of him. We were old friends now. Though pleasant the situation had become, I was still pressed to find answers to what I saw.

"But, Jacob, you still have not answered me," I replied. "Evasive as ever, I see. But, come now, enlighten me, my brother."

All I had was question upon question, and yet again, as in our days at Dartmouth, *he* had all the answers—only then it had been about his people, or as he reminded me, *our people*, and their plight.

He released a protracted breath, resigned to the fact that if it were any other person, save myself, he would not have bothered to discuss the matter at all. I sat down upon a bench nearby. School was obviously in session, and my good friend was about to teach me a lesson I knew was going to change my perception of the world, and all I knew it to be, forever.

Josiah rounded to the backside of the bench and allowed Jacob to have the floor, so to speak.

"It may seem that we have all the answers to your queries, Will, but I assure you we have many questions ourselves as to what just happened tonight."

"But surely, what I saw...what you both can do..." I began.

A curious change of expression, deep concern, colored his countenance. As if he was inwardly debating whether to acknowledge what we both knew to be plain.

"Oh, come now, Jacob, this was not a sleight of hand or mere trickery to charm the maidens of a tavern as you once did. Though now I am of a mind to wonder whether what I thought was sleight of hand was, in point of fact, something altogether greater."

I stood up and rounded on Joss.

"And *you*..." Joss's eyes widened with my advancement in his direction, clearly not ready for the conversation to steer his way. "What was—" I remarked as I mimicked his hand compression bit from a few moments ago, throwing my hands out in pantomime indicating the radiant blast. "—*that*? And then there is the disappearing and reappearing...and *who* were those men who attacked us?"

I wiggled my fingers and leaped from one place to another to draw attention to their disappearing act.

They seemed deeply amused at my folly, biting back a deep belly laugh that I thoroughly deserved, for to be honest, I had to admit I was making a right fool of myself. My theatrics warranted their less than serious response.

But there, at the very least, I had it out. It was not lost on them either that I was aware of my embarrassing display. I retook my seat along the bench to convey I sat at their mercy.

Jacob just stood there—placidly stoic as ever, with a slight grin blossoming across his face.

He had me, and he knew it. Joss, at least, had compassion enough not to fully smile, but his eyes were alight to such brilliance it would no doubt take him very little to spill over into a right state of laughter at my expense. I deserved it. Thankfully, Jacob took pity on me and my poor theatrics.

"Will, there is a war going on right under your nose, though you do not see it." His voice held no trace of mirth from my levity before with this dark proclamation.

"Except for instances like tonight," Joss chimed in.

I sat there staring and not knowing how best to encourage him to finish his story. I continued to blink with no reaction, so he decided to press on.

"Well, our people have been at war with a foe that has gone on for more than six hundred and fifty years."

"A war?" I queried, standing up fully at the sound of that word. "Jacob, I hate to break it to you, but the war with your people has long passed. Regardless of its outcome, it is what it is. I know the Confederacy had split and spread between America and Canada only to be reunited with help from the British to form a proper sovereign nation. And I am most pleased that other Indian nations have seen fit to embrace the Great Law of Peace and join the Confederacy. It is a most proper ending to that most calamitous set of events after the Revolution. So, I am at a loss by what war you mean."

Jacob continued. "This all happened well before your people came to our shores—that is to say, your grandfather's people, at any rate—we, Joss and I—are part of a warrior society within our own Confederacy."

"*The* warrior society?" I queried, recalling while at Dartmouth we had discussed our tribal affiliations and governance.

"Not exactly. Our affiliation is a *secretive* one. Even our own people do not know of its existence—well, at least not openly. After witnessing what you did tonight, can you say you blame us for not divulging our existence to the world?"

"It would not do the *Guardianship* any good if we did," Joss added as he came around to Jacob from the other side of the bench. I was still perplexed by this young man. It appeared as if he was always at Jacob's side. Yet, try as I might, I could not recall any instance where I witnessed this pairing. It was infuriating, though I did not outwardly express an ounce of my roiling consternation. And there were moments, especially when Joss spoke, that cleaved into me so deeply with their familiarity. There was a comfort in his voice instantly garnering my trust. *Why* was that so?

No need debating it...Jacob trusts him, so that should be well and enough for you.

Somehow, my bottom in the discussion manifested itself, and instead of retreating I moved directly toward Jacob rather purposefully.

"So precisely *what war* would this be? Last I checked, the Confederacy had more than its hands full in establishing their sovereignty these past twenty-some years much less engage in a war. And *you!*" I bellowed. Thinking on it, I did not know why I chose this particular point in time to turn on the one person who probably showed the greatest care for my wellbeing. Each time my life stood upon the precipice of death, Joss possessed the wherewithal and sheer strength to keep me from harm's way. But, I was in a right state and not in complete possession of myself.

"What was that you were doing anyway? Damned impressive but no one—not even the fastest of runners I have ever witnessed in my life, and I have seen quite a few in my day—can outrun the way you seem to slip from one place to another completely unobserved. You are truly an astounding man, Mister Lightfoot, saving my skin from the brink of death not once but three times this evening. So, what say you? Have you *anything* to shed light upon this dark mystery?"

"You are...*welcome,*" Joss murmured softly, tilting his head slightly in deference to me.

Grinning at his sudden cheek, I sighed.

"I suppose I deserved that."

A pause. We regarded each other.

"So, what now?"

"That is what we were discussing. What we witnessed tonight was the pinch of the game, and it has all changed from that moment."

"What? You mean to say this sort of thing was not, well, for lack of a better term, *normal*?"

"No," they answered, quite resolute, in unison.

"Though on the whole, not nearly the tight scratch we feared," Joss added with Jacob nodding in agreement.

"You witnessed our first encounter," Jacob offered. "Thus far, we have had the odd incursion from Lord Flint by way of maligned creatures hellbent upon attacking us. To be sure, cunning and evil in their own right, but nothing even remotely close to the men we encountered tonight."

Joss turned and whispered something to him that I could not quite pick up.

Jacob silenced him by raising his hand.

"Now this Lord Flint," I inquired. "He is your foe, I take it? From what nation's flag does he sail under? Russian? English? German? Danish?"

"Well, none of the aforementioned, actually," Jacob replied, studying my reaction. Which is exactly why I did my best not to outwardly respond. I was not going to make this any easier for him.

"You mean to say he is..." I ran out of options, hoping they would fill in the unknown.

"Will, I think you had better sit down." Jacob indicated the bench once more. "It appears we do have quite a lot to explain."

"Jacob..." Joss intoned under his breath, clearly not happy with this shift in the conversation.

I had little doubt he grew agitated with Jacob's admission. Clearly, though Joss was loyal to his fellow warrior, he was of a different mind than Jacob on the matter of my knowing about their little war.

"Joss thinks it is a mistake for you to know about who we are and what we do. I am not so sure. William, our war is a complicated tale. Oddly enough, you actually know how it all began."

Astonished, I could not recall knowing anything of the sort. The perplexing look I wore prompted him to remind me.

"Think back, Will. You remember all of the questions you had about our people when we first met? When you reminded me that your own grandmother and mother were Haudenosaunee and yet you had question upon question about our ways? I started to tell you the stories of our people. Stories you said you vaguely remembered from your youth when your grandmother used to tell them to you. Stories you thought she made up as a fancy tale to tell a restless little boy who did not want to go to bed. Do you remember?"

Now *that* I did recall. And I remembered my favorite among them.

"*Skywoman*? The creation story?"

"Exactly. Well, it is quite clear it was not so much an allegory of our explanation of how the Earth came to be as it was a near-literal translation of real occurrences on this planet."

He waited to see if I was buying the tall tale he peddled.

"Go on..." I was unsure of how this was all going to play out.

I recalled the tale about the Skypeople and how a tree of light became uprooted and one woman, who was known to us only as Skywoman, became fascinated with the small water-covered planet she saw below. Her husband became outraged that she was so taken with it, and one day he pushed her through the hole and she descended to the Earth. Geese guided her on their wings, and she came into contact with various animals, each of whom tried in vain to provide a place for her to land. Then one of them swam deep into the water and came up with some soil, and they piled it upon the back of a great turtle and, thus, the North American continent was born.

This was how it came to be known to the people as *Turtle Island*.

Skywoman was responsible for the seeding of the soil, so all plants and the beginnings of life came from her. She also bore twin boys: Spruce, virile and true, who created the fauna of the Earth, and his twin brother, Flint, who, out of jealousy, maligned some of his sibling's creations—which is why we had snakes, spiders, scorpions, and the like. Creatures of a darker purpose.

"It appears, Will, that the story of Skywoman has more truth to it than we knew. Skywoman *existed*."

I began to form a question, but Jacob stalled me with a raise of his hand.

"In time, Will, in time. As I said, she appears to have truly existed. A certain wampum belt, far older than any other we possess, tells the tale. Only our Central, the chief of our society, can read the belt and tell the story. But she did exist. And although there is often an intermediary daughter who usually is credited in the stories with having the twin boys, it appears Skywoman was their mother. Why there is that singular discrepancy is a mystery but, be that as it may, it was Skywoman who bore the twins. True enough, they were called Spruce and Flint. Now, here is the tough part for you to grapple with."

He studied me for a moment, appearing unsure how to proceed. Joss's agitation seemed to have waned after hearing of my maternal line being Haudenosaunee; clearly he did not know I possessed the blood of the people.

"Will, did you not ever wonder why I did so well in our astronomy classes at Dartmouth? That I appeared to latch upon some of the broader, more esoteric, concepts?"

"Jacob, you were always a good student. It was your keen mind and depth of heart that I valued greatly in our friendship. But yes, I do recall how of all the subjects that one appeared to come naturally to you."

"Well, there is an element about the universe we have come to accept as a member of our society that seems at odds with some of the concepts we learned in school. It was easy enough for me to separate and do well in class, but we, the Guardianship, have it within the story from the Central's wampum belt that the Skypeople did exist. And Skywoman, Spruce, and Flint are not of this world, but one of advanced means."

I was flummoxed.

Another world? One like our own? With life and technology beyond our comprehension? It was beyond me. New questions were already taking form with that admission, for I was struggling in earnest to grasp the greater concept.

It just did not seem possible.

"Another world?" I teased them. "Eh, go on with yourselves, then."

They did not respond.

They were *serious*.

I paused. I had to. After this much information, I could not do otherwise than to stare into the emptiness of the park.

I became completely still. Those words stopped my tirade cold in its steps, and the reality of the situation came cascading down upon me like the water from the burning shanty, cold and immediately shocking. We stood there and silently regarded one another.

Then I laughed, louder than I had ever in my life.

Overwhelmed by the sheer absurdity, I bellowed at what they proposed. Say nothing that one of my dearest friends and the man who saved me from a bone-crushing fall stood there, bewildered at my sudden nerve-laden laugh. I owed Joss my life, and here I was repaying it by guffawing with all the temperance of a crazy man. I was ashamed beyond all recognition, though, knowing Jacob, I was forgiven well before I began that march of madness.

Within a few seconds Jacob was laughing as well, and I could swear a smile was beginning to form across Joss's face.

We gathered ourselves, and Jacob approached me again. He placed a gentle hand upon my shoulder. I immediately brought him to me and hugged him warmly. It felt good to see him after those two long and often lonely years.

He had spoken the truth of it. If there was anyone whom I could never doubt would stand between myself and harm, it would be Jacob. A dance spent too many times within taverns between here and Ithaca and in far too many brawls where I was more than fortunate to have him fighting at my side. Usually because my inebriated mouth brought our troubles.

We parted from our embrace, and Jacob slapped me upside the head mockingly. "Carry on with me, eh? We have been through too much in such a short time for you to doubt me now."

"I know. Everything was just too much to take in. I mean, Jacob, why could you not tell me about all this back in our school days? Fearful I would expose you or something of that nature?"

"Something like that."

He was smirking at me again.

I did not know how to respond, but he continued before I could allow my pride to rise up again.

"Will, you have to understand. This is not about America and *my* people as you so incorrectly put it. Nor is it about any other threat of that nature. And you are quite right. The Haudenosaunee are not in a position to wage a war. But this war was upon us well before the recent events you speak of."

"But the things you both can do! With the powers you possess, how in blazes' sake did we ever dominate your people to gain a foothold on this continent?"

"Because as a warrior party we Guardians are engaged in this war that has been raging for well over six and a half centuries. This war takes precedence over anything else. Though our Confederacy was under attack from the British, the French, and then you Americans, we had our own battle to fight that was already underway. Secrecy is paramount. We were not allowed to expose our abilities in the open. Can you imagine the consequences if we did? Our people would be hunted to the point of extinction. Our calling is greater than that. We are fewer than we have been in a great long while, but we endure. We are working toward a resolution in the Grand Council to bring our numbers back up again. But all of our actions as Guardians are covert and *must remain so.* In fact, this little engagement happened only because we knew those particular buildings to be fairly abandoned."

"Or so we thought," Joss added.

Jacob held his hand out to me. I reciprocated, and he dropped my pocket watch gently into it.

"Thanks, old man." I slipped it back into my waistcoat pocket without bothering to note its condition. I would tend to its cleaning later. How I lost it was quite beyond me. But as ever, Jacob was there to tend to what I could not.

"Jacob, should we?" Joss asked, indicating that they should probably depart.

Jacob nodded in agreement, but I was not quite finished with them yet.

My world had ceased to stop spinning. This was precisely the type of adventure I sought, and I inwardly rejoiced that I had clear access to my goal because of my intimate association with these *Guardian* warriors. However, it was equally evident that I still had so much more to absorb about their cause.

I shook my head slightly.

"What about the boy?" I queried. "Is it a problem that he knows about your little war?"

"Yes, but since his actions have already brought him into our enemy's fold, it is clear he has had some knowledge of our conflict for some time. But we cannot allow this to continue. He has been elusive thus far. But we will get to him and remedy the matter."

It was a troubling statement, and very foreboding. Its implications upon the boy became quite plain for me to decipher. I must have worn my doubt on my face all too well.

"What is the matter, Will?"

"Hmmm? Oh, I am just trying to gain a handle on it. The sheer enormity of what you speak of is quite overwhelming. It shall take me a good long while to process it all."

The men looked at each other, and their demeanor changed slightly. Something had passed between them of which I was not privy.

"Actually, Will, no. It will not."

"Whatever do you mean?"

Jacob's mouth formed a hard line. I knew that look. He was about to say something he regretted already.

"You will not be remembering any of it," he added, taking a small step in my direction. "It is the way it has to be. No one can know of our existence."

"You think I will speak of this to anyone? Who would believe me? Surely you are not going to save me from them just to take me out yourselves?" I asserted, rather worried over this looming prospect I had not considered until this very moment.

Joss looked at the ground, not wanting to meet my troubled gaze.

"Will, I would never put you in harm's way. Unfortunately, knowing about us has done just that. So, we have to remedy this situation."

"But how?"

Joss disappeared, and I knew it had already begun. I spun around to run the opposite direction, knowing full well with their speed and agility it was of no use, but I had to try.

With a little luck...

But there was not going to be any—good or bad. I took only two steps and Joss was there, pressing a lighted palm to my forehead, and all my thoughts sank into a consuming darkness. To my satisfaction the contact seemed to rebound upon Joss. He let out a small yelp as if shocked by the experience.

As my consciousness slipped from me, I heard Joss query in the far-off distance, growing fainter.

"Do you know where he lives?"

Gasping for air as if I were held underwater too long, I awoke with a start. Shaken by the change in surroundings, I discovered I had obviously been asleep, sprawled out on my receiving room sofa. I sat up fully and spun around so my bare feet came into contact with the floor. The small blanket fell from my chest to gather at my waist, and the coolness of the floor against my soles made me realize that my shoes and stockings had been removed.

Or did I do that myself?

I was at a complete loss. The most excruciating headache blistered across my mind, consumed me. My sole companion. I rubbed my temples to soothe the throb that persisted for a few minutes before it began to subside with mystifying speed. As I continued to slowly rub my head, I opened my eyes to the darkness of my home.

Had I drunk too much and staggered back here only to collapse on the sofa instead of the comfort of my own bed upstairs?

It would explain the headache and the slightly bizarre dream. But then again, headaches of that nature do not rapidly depart. I turned my head slightly, anticipating that movement might bring about the pain again; I was surprised when it did nothing of the sort. I pressed my hands to the sides of my face and rested my chin upon them with my elbows supported by my knees. I pondered what I could last recall. The only thing I remembered was getting dressed to go down into the Points and having a pint or two near Satan's Circus and seeing what adventure would befall me.

Adventure? Did it come to pass? Surely no adventure would lead me back to my own home in such a state.

I thought on it some more and discovered no memory to cling to that would explain my current predicament. I did have the distinct impression that something of a revelatory nature had become known to me, though why I thought this eluded me. Yet, I felt something altogether spectacular and wondrous had happened. If I could only recall what it was.

Most infuriating...

I staggered from the sofa, taking the blanket. I wrapped it about my shoulders as the house was quite cool. I proceeded up the stairs and began to fully undress for bed. I found my pocket watch and clicked it open to discover that it was still wound and the time now read 2:45. With little in the way of light, I realized I must have been asleep for some time on my sofa. I rewound the watch and set it upon my nightstand. As I prepared for bed, I thought on what could have transpired over the course of the evening. Yet, try as I might, I possessed no memory of making my way back home, or worse yet, getting dressed for the evening and my trek to the Five Points. All of it seemed but a blur—bits and pieces with little in the way of continuity.

Within minutes of stripping myself and brushing my teeth, I was in bed without bothering to redress. It felt wondrously sinful to climb into my bedding with naught between me and the sheets. Within moments of my head hitting the pillow, sleep consumed me and I fell into its delightful well of oblivion.

Leaves fluttered in the wind of the early autumnal day.

This could be none other than the sophomore year of my studies at Dartmouth. The rustling foliage mixing with the laughter from our little gathering. I was sitting at a bench, regaling a small collection of my friends with my latest tavern encounter. I turned and found Jacob by my side, as usual, with a smug knowing smile upon his face.

"So there we were, Jacob, in one of my finest suits, looking quite the dandy and passable for an exotic foreigner. I made sure to spread it around amongst the barmaids he was of Turkish descent to ensure the gossip spread admirably. We were not disappointed in the slightest."

My friends nudged one another and chuckled, clearly following the ruse that had played out the previous night. It was then I spotted a young man of decidedly Mohawk lineage at the far end of the common, sitting on the grass with his back against one of the trees lining the grounds in front of Dartmouth Hall. He had a sketchbook out with all of his attention pouring into whatever it was he found so interesting. The passion he invested into that little book, as if he felt he needed to get it down before the moment escaped him thoroughly, stole my attention away from my mates.

The only problem with this scenario is I had not recalled noticing him on that particular day. It was as if the events from four years ago were relived and replayed. Allowing me to examine more closely that midday moment, giving me the opportunity to notice this other Mohawk man off in the distance.

"So do not hold us out further, William. What in God's name happened?" One of my friends, Robert Johnson, coaxed me further.

Only this time around I did not pay him or any of the others further attention. Instead, I stood up, and the other boys around me seemed to vanish in soft tendrils of memory that faded with the breeze. Only Jacob remained seated and watched me moving beyond the events as they had played out that fall day years ago. Jacob remained silent. His attention upon my next action. I started to walk from the bench toward this Mohawk man so absorbed in his sketching that he took no notice of my impending arrival. I stopped just in front of him and squatted so I could get a better look at his face.

I knew him...did I not?

A most bewitching man...

I could not recall where or when. I reached out to gain his attention and was about to speak when the scene changed to a different day altogether.

I was still in the same spot next to the same tree, only now I could see myself sitting back at the bench. This was a thoroughly jarring vantage point, watching yourself from afar, as if your body were not your own. However, this time I was back at the same bench Jacob and I usually occupied around luncheon. However, contrary to our usual rendezvous, I was alone. Obviously awaiting Jacob to make his routinely scheduled appearance. I sat and casually looked around for my best mate. My seated self had not noticed Jacob making his way to him, er, or my other self.

From my current dreamlike view I saw him approach and he was not alone. He was in a deep discussion with the same young man who had been sketching in his book earlier. This time, it was opened and they seemed to be debating, rather pointedly, something written in the book. When the young man pointed to whatever it was, it seemed to leap off the page and hovered in the air as if lifted by magic. Each time he pressed his finger to the book, something else would lift off and float for a moment. Symbols and words I could not decipher were dancing on the wind only to blow away before I could gain a grasp of their measure.

But there was one—one image I did understand most clearly. It was a sketch of a man. A man who appeared at first glance as any other save for his shoulder-length dark hair, impeccable clothing of the highest fashion, and a most notable stylish walking stick with a myriad of sigils etched upon it. However, before his visage faded upon the wind I noted that his eyes and texture of skin were remarkably different. The eyes were darkened to a singular point of light as if this were their natural state. The skin appeared to be mottled as if viewing it under sunlight through dense foliage.

I glanced from where my seated self was ensconced, contentedly awaiting Jacob's arrival, and stood there wide-eyed, thinking: Well, get up, you imbecile! See what is taking him so long!

When the seated me did not, I thought I should take the initiative. With tentative steps, I began to move forward toward them, picking up in purpose as I moved along the walkway. As I reached them, Jacob stopped arguing with the young man, and like Kerberos he suddenly seemed to have sprouted another head. A new face of his turned to look at me while the other was still carrying on the debate. This second eerie visage took me back a step as his stare bored into me, stopping all further progress. When it was clear I had stopped, wide-eyed, at my two-headed friend, the second face merged with the first. A clear warning to advance no further was plain. I was, however, permitted to observe.

The young man continued his debate, unaware of my approach, and was pressing his point in Mohawk, of which I knew some, ignoring the fact that Jacob divided his attention between us. Could I make out what his friend was saying?

Yes, I could!

Something about "standing guard" or "watching" and "part of their duty to note this peculiar talent." The words were similar, and the way he spoke them was not in the normal Mohawk vernacular I was used to hearing.

Jacob's "heads," to my great relief, remained one and he began to reply, but I noticed, through his flitting gaze in my direction, that he was still aware of my approach.

As soon as I took another step, an undetected hand to my right gripped my wrist. I was about to rebuff this harsh interference, but when I looked at who had assaulted me in such a manner, I was astonished to discover it was yet another Jacob, fully formed, who stood there and shook his head, not saying a word, but clearly implying that I should not be doing what I was doing—it was not for me.

He raised his free hand up, which seemed to glisten with a radiant glow. I had seen that before, though just where, I could not say with any great degree of truth. And he then pressed it to my forehead and a brilliant white light taxed my senses and I passed into a dreamless sleep.

Chapter Three

Morning's Sweet Deceptive Invitation

Wherein we find William Hallett starved for much more than his morning meal.

November 1, 1847
The home of William Hallett—New York, New York
7:16 a.m.

Another mind-crushing headache roused me to my senses. I had no idea what time it was. I felt about in the darkness of my room, feebly searching for my watch on my night table next to the bed until at last I found it. As I ran my hand around it to find the latch, I noticed some grit along the rim of the cover. I pushed myself up onto my elbow and squinted as best I could to investigate.

Most unusual—where did I pick that up?

There was little in the way of light coming from my adjoining bathroom window. A narrow shaft cut through the darkness, nearly blinding me for all of its harshness. That mind-shattering brilliance only succeeded in adding to the thumping in my head. I grabbed a nearby pillow and fell back onto the bed, smothering myself with it until the headache slowly subsided. All things considered, it did not take too long, and I noted this was not the first time one of my headaches had done so.

I had the great fortune of having one of the few buildings with the new running water systems. If I lit the fire downstairs, I could even have heated water for a small period of time. These modern marvels had just started to appear in Manhattan. Their arrival afforded me the opportunity to have my own en suite bathroom complete with running water. It was one of the few luxuries I allowed myself, as I was always cognizant of keeping up my appearances.

For all the agony of that shaft of light pressed upon me, my eyesight was still accustomed to the absolution of a darkened bedroom. Gathering my courage, I pulled the pillow aside and renewed my efforts to discern the time. I struggled to make it out, squinting so my long lashes could cut away at some of the glare, which in turn made it quite difficult to accomplish my task. I made every attempt to bridge the gap between delirium and coherence. Thus far, delirium held the better hand.

"Blast," I muttered as I scrambled out of the warmth afforded me by the thick bedding and into the coolness of the room.

The brisk sensation of the early morning air surrounding my naked form banished what little I had in the way of sleepiness. Ignoring all caution, I went to the large window of my bedroom and with a forced gusto threw back the curtains to welcome the morn and to finally gain a better view of my watch. Bright lights and throbbing headaches be damned.

I scratched my head—as well as a few other body parts of a southerly direction—and stretched broadly, exuberant in the blood flowing to my reawakened limbs. In the harsh early morning light, I noted it was just past seven and one-quarter hour.

"Splendid, I have not missed the morning market entirely," I spoke aloud to myself as if hearing it would heighten the experience. Sadly, it did not. At times, this house seemed enormously big with silly old me puttering about.

Enough with the mental ramblings, William. Best get to your morning or there shall be little to show of it on your breakfast plate.

Only then did something catch my gaze outside my window. There, across the roofline of a lower building adjacent to mine, I discovered Widow Van Tassel and her maid staring at my naked and virile form. Having nothing to be ashamed of, for no one could fault me for not possessing a strong and masculine body, and thinking it a lark, I smiled and waved at both of them. The widow seemed to have fainted. She was tended to immediately by her maid who blushed brightly and appeared only too glad to have something else to do in looking after her charge. As was customary of their gender, they feigned impropriety on my part, though I noticed the widow kept an eye to my manhood during her fainting spell so I had the right of her countenance on the matter.

Glad I could give the old girl a rise in the morning was my way of thinking on it.

I was sure our next encounter would be filled with all sordid things both implied and expressed.

A smile mellowed on my lips for my morning mischievousness, as I slipped away from the window. I grabbed my dark-green velvet dressing robe from the hook on the wall and struggled into it as I went downstairs to the cellar to stoke the fire to bring the bathing water to a warmer temperature for my morning ablutions.

Luckily, the charwoman I paid to clean the house and prepare it each morning had already come through and amongst her other duties had the water heating. I added some coal to the furnace and made my way back upstairs. I relished the idea of sinking into a warm tub to soothe my limbs and freshen up for the day.

Nearly an hour later, all scrubbed up and presentable, I dressed in a cream-colored fine silk shirt tied off with a stylish cravat. To this, I added my charcoal-gray pants, along with one of my finer frock coats of dark forest green, accented with a deep rust-colored waistcoat close enough in hue to match my dark-auburn hair and set off my green eyes to most brilliant effect. I descended to the foyer, eager to start my morning.

As I approached the door, I paused to pick up my dark-green tall hat and the rust-colored gloves, sealing that matched ensemble for all to see, collected my cherrywood walking stick, and moved out onto the street. I knew I cut a dashing morning figure for the market. If there was one thing I was most certain of in myself, it was that I knew how to impress others with my manner of dress and charismatic style. I held no qualms about being something of a dandy whilst mixing with the elite of Manhattan's social strata.

To be sure, I am not being self-centered in that appraisal. I have learned to be most attentive to what works or did not work in my appearance and demeanor by measuring the reactions of those around me. Over time I gleaned which physical attributes to emphasize and which to play down. There was a great deal to do with the former, and thankfully, given the blessed breeding between my British and Mohawk bloodlines, I had very little to worry about with the latter. It was thusly so for my twin sister who possessed even greater attributes to assail the senses.

This appraisal of my more salient characteristics came from my grandmother, Elizabeth. Though clearly biased, she had the reputation of being forthright and shrewd in her estimation of others. I did not think she cut me any slack based upon the blood running through my veins being so closely aligned with her own. She would cut me off at the knees if she thought I deserved it. I did everything in my power to *never* give her the opportunity.

From my days as a wee lad, she declared me to be a heartbreaker to all who would listen. I was most fortunate that she also instilled in me the need to be aware of my attributes but never to dwell upon them openly, for that would surely seal my fate as a pompous ass and would do little in progressing me further along in life. Conscious of the effect but never to the point of preening as the cock 'o the walk, as it were. I liked to think I had it down to a science by now.

Ever my rock, probably more so than my own parents come to think upon it, I knew I could rely upon her honest opinion of whatever endeavor I chose to partake in. This dispensation of praise as well as scorn in equal measures assured me beyond all doubt that her guidance guaranteed I would be a better man for my efforts. My dear sister was never too far behind and did her very best to keep me humble, if exceedingly loved. Rebecca loved to dote upon me. While I loved her tremendously for it, there were times when her form of love could border on overbearing and I had some push back. She usually got the message conveyed in those circumstances.

Grandmama, on the other hand, always told me I was her dearest grandchild. Exalted as that familial title may be, it was not easy to bear, as she expected a high level of excellence where I was concerned. Say nothing of how my dearest twin sister felt with that bestowed affection, whilst she did her best to slip from being under my shadow, as she put it. I loved my sister dearly, but like Grandmama, she knew exactly how best to needle and fester beneath my skin. And Rebecca was a master at navigating familial waters. I oft took my cue from her.

Moving to the street from my front door, I was lucky enough to hail a calash to cross the five long city blocks to the market on the eastern part of Manhattan with as much haste as I could. My arrival bordered on the utmost lateness of the morning, and I did not wish to miss all of the fresh buys.

As I rode along the street watching the city slip by, I had a smile upon my face as I continued to ponder the women of my family. Though with each progressive city block I passed, I found my thoughts drifting from them to my dreams of last night.

As if through a fog, my dreams sifted my way. Little memory-laden tendrils caressed my mind but did very little to fill in the gaps of the previous evening's events. My brow furrowed as I concentrated on the subject of those dreams—a man, just out of focus, who seemed to be the subject of those spectral images lingering in the farthest reaches of my mind. Though I could not say why, it seemed most important that I remember the fullness of the dream and, more importantly, the man. But alas, in my hazy, diminishing memory of my restless sleep, I would possibly never recall the exact events of that hypnagogic drama. The result of which vexed me terribly.

Then I recalled the condition of my watch from this morning.

I had plainly forgotten to tend to it and had absentmindedly put it into my waistcoat pocket as usual as I ventured out.

Using my teeth, I tugged out of my right-hand glove and pulled the watch from my waistcoat pocket. When I popped it open, I noticed the grit along its rim seemed to be not only dirt, but also what appeared to be ash or a burnt substance of some kind.

When was I near a fire that would tarnish my watch so?

I should think I would remember being so near a blaze to discolor it. Yet, no such fiery event came to mind. In fact, I found the only item I could be certain about lay in that I went out to seek adventure in the Points and came back much later in the evening with nothing to account for the intervening period. It was not like me to become so inebriated that I lost all recollection of the comings and goings of a given night's events. I vowed to myself to better curtail my imbibing of the SAC when traveling to the Points. It was not the sort of place you would want to lose yourself in.

The ride to the market complete, I stepped out of the calash, paid the driver, and marched into the brisk morning throng of shoppers. I passed the fishmonger's which had pretty much been picked clean of their best offerings. Not content with what was left, I moved onto the sausages and other daily meats. As I pored over the various items of produce, a familiar voice chimed on the wind in my direction.

"William, dearest. How wondrous to discover *you* here in the market this fine autumnal morning."

My ears would never deceive me with the caress of those dulcet tones—it was none other than Miss Sarah Covington.

Sarah was a new arrival from her home in Bath, England. Her manner was more proper than the socialites of her age here in Manhattan, the end result being social debutantes moved in a rush to take sides. They either detested her for being too highbrow for their company and thus toeing the line with the likes of my sister, or went out of their way to emulate her social etiquette—a role she coveted within the Manhattan social circles. She seemed to relish the controversy she stirred. In either event, it often made for very interesting social events where the younger fillies were at play in pursuit of a man to call their own.

Rebecca would never be the sort to be told what was appropriate or suitable. This is not to say she did not have an interest in any of the eligible males within our social strata. No, my sister's eye had roved much closer to home in the form of my best mate from Dartmouth, none other than Jacob Lysander Lyons. Their abrupt breakup was still legendary and highly gossip-worthy, a thorn Rebecca did her utmost to either soothe or at best ignore entirely.

Quite the contrarian, Sarah was the type of woman who thrived in the passing of gossip; properly placed gossip, mind you, that kept your name firmly entrenched in the social talk of the day. Her accomplishment in establishing such a foothold on the fabric of our social circles, since she had only arrived on our shores some six months prior, was a testament to her cunning ingenuity and deft hand at navigating the firmly entrenched social rules amongst the New York elite. She was clever enough to not go in for intentionally mean-spirited or crass gossip. But she did engage in using gossip as a means of information gathering and to put others into places of supplication when she felt it warranted.

Unfortunately, for myself, she was also unmarried and quite demanding of my attentions whenever we crossed paths at the same function. A commingling she did everything she could to cultivate and grow.

Indeed, many tongues were set afire from the first party we attended. We arrived in separate carriages but, having disembarked at the same time, I mistakenly offered her my arm to escort her to the door. As we entered the party, it appeared to all that we were attending the party together, something I was to learn later she did her best to encourage throughout the course of the evening with those to whom she spoke.

For quite some time thereafter, I had to make it clear we were but mere acquaintances and not embroiled in the romantic inclinations Miss Covington coaxed along in social conversations. So, my happening upon her in a public setting would run afoul to any protestations I might raise to the contrary of our perceived relationship status.

"Miss Covington," I exclaimed, bowing genially and tipping my hat to her. "Mere words cannot express the joy in finding you about this morning. Surely the sun will have to hide behind the clouds in shame for the most radiant star has deemed to bestow her beauty amongst us."

I knew I was laying it on a bit thick, but she was not alone and any rudeness on my part would have gotten back to my grandmother. For Adelaide Howard, a cousin of mine, was trailing behind in the next merchant cart, peering over some vegetables. I only noticed her accompanying Sarah in the instant before I opened my mouth. And my fortune could not have smiled brighter, as her first words to me only solidified my fears.

"William! Why, Sarah, I am pleased you had the fortune to find him here. Ah, sweet William." Adelaide kissed my cheeks in what I noted was the European fashion.

I suppressed the urge to dislocate my eyes to the back of my head at her obvious social aspirations in front of Miss Covington.

"I am going to see your grandmother and sister this afternoon for tea," my cousin added.

"Well, I am sure you will have a splendid time. If it is one thing Grandmama knows how to host, it is an afternoon tea."

"You are being coy, William. You well know your grandmother Elizabeth is a most formidable woman. I daresay *the woman*, but I am not the judge of such matters. I am all too aware of how very little she could not accomplish if she put her mind to it."

"Some would say the same of my sister..." I let it hang there, ever the one to thread my sister's dominance in the circles Sarah had of late been trying to usurp for her own purposes. We Halletts did not give ground willingly. I felt it my duty to ensure Rebecca's influence still reigned supreme.

Rather than have us stall in a quagmire of social etiquette, I pressed us along, gifting them both with a pleasant, if tight, smile as I presented an arm to each of them so we could continue to stroll along the path between the various merchant carts. Odors both pleasant and grotesque competed for our olfactory attention.

"You know, William, you must come to my birthday soirée I am hosting at my home in a week's time. I do believe I sent round an invitation, but you have not bothered to reply, you naughty, naughty boy."

Sarah tugged at my sleeve which I found irritating but did my best to ignore.

I gently patted the hand she had upon my arm and grinned as warmly as I dared without coaxing the vixen along too much. It was a very fine game to play. I prided myself on being the hunter in every situation, yet I could not, in all good conscience, consider Miss Covington as anything less than a hunter herself. She looked to be a woman who was quite accustomed to getting whatever her heart desired. I feared I was on the top of that list.

"Yes, well, I have been extremely busy as of late. So do forgive me for the oversight. I would be most honored to join you at your party this Friday hence."

I could not help but wish I would not have to deal with this conniving barracuda in such a social setting alone. Thankfully, whether by an alignment of the stars by sympathetic gods or some other source of divine inspiration, my sister's voice lilted over us all. I thought I had recognized the particular burgundy dress I had procured for her during my last visit to Paris naught but half a year ago. One cart over, she turned in the same dress that fit her so well. Like Adelaide, she too had been perusing the latest floral offerings though she somehow, through some preternatural feat I had yet to discern, had slipped in behind us unnoticed.

"Well, that should prove to be the highlight of the social season; of course, William should make an appearance, dear Sarah. *We* would not even consider missing such a monumental event."

My sister had a peculiar knack for rescuing me when I needed it most. How she managed it became a constant source of consternation. I could not explain the otherworldliness that seemed to guide her to these moments of sheer brilliance—to be exactly where I needed her to be without so much as putting voice to the request. Some sort of divine providence, indeed, a subscription neither Rebecca nor I ascribed to. And in truth, how could I hold her accountable for it when I was generally the sole reaper of its benefits? She was every bit the goddess, temptress, and leopardess I needed in my life. I could not begin to count how many blessings I should always find with her on my side.

To diffuse the moment, I smiled, doing my level best to dazzle Sarah with my brilliant grin. She demurely returned the warm affection, which made me inwardly cringe for I knew this sort of play could only lead to one conclusion where females of this sort were concerned: marriage. I was the morsel my sister, cousin, and Miss Covington would bandy about as if I were not present at all.

Though my more than formidable sister would do enough to stall, if not totally put off Miss Covington's latest desire to sink her claws into me. Rebecca and Sarah had a rather complicated relationship when it came to moving in our particular brand of social circles. While I knew she would not outright deny my sister's presence at her party, I also knew how much harder Sarah's pursuit of me would become with my sister's pointed observation over anything having to do with me.

Sarah, for her part, was clever enough to mellow that steely tone in her gaze when Rebecca mentioned attending the party with me. I had to play this carefully. Social engagements were a tricky thing to navigate especially where my sister endeavored to be involved—*best to let her take the lead*. The sudden inclusion of my sister into the mix did not bode well for Sarah's intended plans. I could still spy them mulling about, rearranging themselves, given the new twist Rebecca's presence brought to the conversation now.

Marriage, it was no secret to those who knew me intimately, was not something I cared to court at this juncture of my life. Though Miss Covington made that evasion infinitely more difficult. She was a woman with a one-track mind, and I was front and center in hers.

This very institution of marriage was so highly regarded by women in our stratosphere, yet I could not help equating it to a boat anchor rooting me to a life of familial servitude and negating any possibility of a rewarding adventure. From our shared childhood, Rebecca knew of my desire to see the world—a boyhood dream that never seemed to free itself from me. She found it as frustrating as it was *cute*.

Cute.

The pointed and sometimes crushing indictments of what one held most dear could border outright derision. The trouble was, she usually had the right of it.

The other staying factor in her biting assessments: she simply adored me. Some wagging tongues even had the audacity of pushing the absurd notion that there was something unseemly between my sister and me.

Being the ever-loving sibling I knew her to be, she was only too expedient in alleviating the effort necessary to play my cards to avoid, without any effect of impropriety or rudeness on my part, Miss Covington's navigation of these marital waters. With my sister present, Sarah's push to snare me lessened dramatically. I could not express more thanks in the loving glance Rebecca returned in that brief instance as she had time and again to confirm she was, as ever, my champion.

Sarah shot a curt if not slightly pained look at the turn of events my sister brought to the conversation that completely changed the dynamics of her little soirée.

Now, to be fair, I should be clear in that Sarah was not of a homely or unattractive state. She was, in all things considered, quite a lovely—almost statuesque—and charmingly agreeable woman save for her tremendous height. A singular beauty with but one fatal flaw: she was not nor ever will be the equivalent to my sister. For all of Rebecca's worldly charms, the one that professed itself in the most salient of attributes was her bewitching beauty.

I knew, being twins and nearly identical in so many ways, I also benefited from her physical attributes, but whenever she walked into a room every eye—man, woman, or child—took notice of my auburn-headed, statuesque sister. Her manner of dress was most impeccable—far exceeding my own peacock ways. The ladies of Manhattan set their manner of style and etiquette by my sister's clock. When she spoke, there were seldom any condescending opinions to be had, with the sole exception of mine. I never failed to cast a barb her way just to needle her lovingly.

Sarah, on the other hand, at nearly my height of six feet two inches, with ebony hair and a figure most becoming, would no doubt make someone a fine wife and mother. I was just going to do my very best to ensure that particular *someone* was *not* me. She was, in point of fact, no wilting flower of the social set. Not quite the bastion of society mores, but a formidable companion to my sister.

I smiled at Sarah, a mixture of relief and sorrow. Whilst Rebecca remained my champion, when it came to the topic of marriage, my sister maddeningly left it to me to navigate.

The little tartlet.

Adelaide's addlepated response was now ill-timed, given Rebecca's joining the conversation. But not having the sense to stay her thoughts for looking like a fool, she pressed forward, making an awkward situation even more so.

"How marvelous, Sarah," she exclaimed with all the charm of a viper cum co-conspirator. "William can be your date for the affair!" How sad that Adelaide could never keep up with how rapidly the dynamics of social conversations could diverge, leaving my poor cousin bringing up the rear. Not the brightest star in the heavens, but a darling girl, nonetheless.

"Well, Rebecca will arrive with him," Sarah commented, with a slight tone of derision, but carefully modulated into a more welcoming statement, though I doubt that was an easy effort on her part.

Whatever party you attended, if my sister and Sarah were in attendance, then you had little doubt that fireworks of a verbal nature would be had by the end of the night. My sister gave far more than she got.

By now, I had taken my sister's arm on my right and Sarah's on my left, leaving poor Adelaide to bring up the rear in our little shopping contingent.

I noted thus far that Rebecca, while acknowledging the importance of the party Miss Covington proposed, had not commented on whether or not she would attend.

Keeping things as neutral as possible, I flashed my brilliant smile upon them but, sensing the right of the situation, decided to contribute nothing further, choosing instead to purchase a paper cone of delightful *pommes frites* from a vendor who had started to make their presence known at the market.

Taking one into her mouth and giving it all the relish of how good it tasted, Rebecca made her move.

"Now, far be it from me to push in on a private affair, but I would so love to attend your birthday soirée. I am sure it will be the height of the seasonal calendar. Oh, if there's one thing you really know how to do, Sarah, it is entertain. I had just mentioned to the *Times* society reporter on what exquisite functions I have attended when they were held by your family. Always such joyous times."

Sarah smiled warmly at being so complimented out in the open. If Sarah thrived on one thing, it was public opinion. It did not go amiss how many society matrons were still milling about with their servants with an overly attentive ear to my sister's effusive commentary on what delights for Sarah's birthday celebration surely hung in the balance.

"Well, but of course you should come. Why, it would not be a true society affair if Rebecca Hallett did not make an appearance."

"Oh, I shall ensure it will be more than an appearance. It is not every day you get to attend a societal affair as you observe one of your own growing *older*."

And there was the dig, the way my sister operated when it came to managing the society fillies and debutantes of Manhattan. Sarah was painfully aware that in her twenty-sixth year she had yet to snag a husband. The thorn Rebecca placed firmly in her side did not go unnoticed by those same society matrons listening to her effusive comments earlier.

Sarah could only smile and add, "Yes, well, the prospects do seem to be looking ever in my favor. Do they not, Mister Hallett?"

I smiled and nodded to acknowledge the point but knew better than to contribute. Rebecca had this well enough in hand.

"Well, I would love it if you could be my attendant at the party, Mister Hallett. It would so make my day."

"Hmmm, that leaves me without a date," Rebecca replied, taking another fry from the cone. "Well, I am sure I can find someone to accompany me."

"Yes, I am sure, *even at your age* and with your commendable beauty, men would be lining up to accompany you to the event."

And there, the cycle of digging at each other had run its course. My female companions and I enjoyed the *pommes frites* as we continued our stroll. Within the hour we had arrived back at the beginning of the market. Having purchased a few items for my morning meal, and wanting them to remain fresh, I was eager to return home. Though I am afraid my desire to take leave of Sarah and my cousin took them quite by surprise.

"Thank you for a most lovely morning stroll, Miss Covington." I kissed her hand and bowed as courteously as I dared without any allusions to romanticism and bade my cousin farewell, having her promise to send my love along to my family. Before they could hook me into a prolonged end of our morning, I gripped Rebecca's hand and quickly departed, near to the point upon the market where I found them with her in tow.

"May I take you anywhere?" I offered as we climbed into the vehicle.

"Dockside, and, William—" She tore her gaze from our collective estimation of Miss Covington's pointed stare to catch the fullness of my attention. "We need to talk, and soon. There is much I have come upon that warrants our combined intellect."

I tapped the side of the calash, and the driver took to beginning our journey.

"Dockside, for Miss Hallett, if you please, driver. South Street Seaport area should be sufficient."

"Right you are, sir."

I turned my attentions back to Rebecca only to find her gaze troubled. Even more alarming was the slight quiver to her hands. Something had spooked my sister to her core.

"Of course, we can talk. I know you have the tea with Grandmama. How about you come by tomorrow evening? You can stay in the spare bedroom. That way we shall have all evening to talk; will that do?"

She sighed a tremendous relief and hugged me for good measure.

"Oh, William, I knew I could count upon you to help me sort through this."

I commented on Sarah's attentions toward me and then to her pointed focus in my direction as we departed. Her eyes riveted upon me in the most disconcerting manner. I spotted her watching me from afar. I knew it would be pointless not to acknowledge her, so I tilted my head slightly and gave her yet another smile and a small wave.

"Yes, and it appears my situation need not be the only topic on offer tomorrow eve," Rebecca added.

As we reseated ourselves in the calash, I dared to spare a sideways glance only to discover they had moved on. Not entirely sure about Miss Covington's expression, I pondered it. Suddenly it came upon me that it was not the simple gaze of a lovestruck young woman smitten with the prospect of an attractive eligible male. No, in her penetrating fixation upon my person, unnerving me to my core, she bore the look a predator manifests whilst stalking their prey. There was simply no mistaking it. Any witness to the event would not mistake it as an *I find you attractive and desire you as a mate*. Rather, it was an *I shall devour the very essence of your being with such a voracity that the universe will have little evidence of your prior existence after I am satiated* sort of look.

I bristled and did my utmost to shake the sensation away. Rebecca eyed a retreating Sarah and Adelaide and turned a questioning eye in my direction.

"Is there something I should know, Will? You look like you have seen a ghost."

"Not a ghost, Becks. A monster, perhaps."

Minutes later, dockside, I kissed my sister with promises of looking forward to our night together whilst guiding her to our cousin's ferry service half a block away. The bevy of looks from the dockhands as we passed only confirmed Rebecca still could hold a man's eye.

Twenty minutes later I entered my house and quickly dispatched with my outer clothing, hat, and gloves. I slipped the walking stick into its holder by the door, and made a note in my calendar on the writing desk for Miss Covington's birthday celebration on Friday, November 5. I took my morning purchases into the kitchen and settled into cooking a breakfast.

As I ate, I could not help but let my thoughts roam over this morning's events. More than anything it was the quiver in my sister's hand I fixated upon. Rebecca never was one to doubt herself. If she could not hide her anxiety over whatever plagued her, I began to ponder what effect it should bring upon me.

Not good. She is going to have questions. Questions I am not sure I want to have answered.

Steam clouded the windows of my kitchen, warming me against the coolness of the morning as assuredly as the meal I just consumed. I pulled out my watch again and ran my hands around the ring of the crystal. There were still remnants of grit and ash to be found along its edge. I scraped a little from the ring onto my thumbnail. I rubbed it between my forefinger and thumb. I tasted the grit which confirmed my suspicions. Indeed, little doubt remained that the ashen substance confirmed its recent presence near a fire. There also appeared to be a certain degree of wetness to the grit.

Water...

Fire...

A cannon blast? Light?

I continued to rub the grit between my fingers as if I could somehow decipher what secrets it held and unlock the concealed events of the night before. A divination reading of some sort.

"Do you know where he lives?"

That voice! Foreign from my own, yet intimately familiar all at the same time.

More percussive sounds, shouts, wood cracking...

My watch clunked to the tabletop, and my head began to throb as I sifted the details of last night from the muck collected there, keeping them buried deep within the recess of my memory. I mentally pawed at them. I moved from rubbing my temples to the heels of my hands resting against my eye sockets. My fingers combed through my hairline in the vain attempt to physically pry something loose from my mind.

A face...

Indian... A Mohawk*!*

Jacob!

Yet, as I thought longer upon it...decidedly a Mohawk man, but *not* Jacob. Though close. This was maddening; like something that hangs upon your tongue but cannot find the measure to make itself fully known. You struggle with it in your mouth, but your mind cannot seem to form the words to ensure its release. A damnable nuisance.

I had not laid eyes upon Jacob for well over two years since we parted on our last day of school at Dartmouth.

...or had I?

::It is not going to hold, Jacob...::

The voice, instantly both familiar and foreign, came to me as if whispered in my own mind! I stood up from my seat with such haste the chair crashed to the floor. I staggered around with my arms outstretched as if wary of someone entering my home unwelcome and unannounced.

This was intolerable.

"Who said that? If you have an *ounce* of respectability about you, you will show yourself immediately!"

::?!::

That last was not so much as a thought as a feeling pouring into my mind and washing over my body. Pure confusion added to the myriad of emotions playing within, as if *I* were now the intruder of my own being.

How can this be?

I strode from my kitchen through the dining room and into the main receiving room. I scanned the rooms as I made my way through them. Upon reaching my front door and surveying my home from this vantage point, I was relatively assured I was alone, which only added to my false sense of security. I turned the latch of my front door. It was still locked, the bolt secured in the usual position.

So, no one entered from the front, and I was in the kitchen by the back entry. A window perhaps?

I went about the lower floor again and found all of my windows securely latched.

Then a feeling of anxiety swept over me, though it was most assuredly not my own. I was apprehensive, to be sure, but not to the point I experienced now. This was someone else's feeling, separate from my own, yet it coursed vigorously through me, nearly overpowering every ounce of me in the process.

I gasped at the flood of emotion. Then a sudden snap of withdrawal as if a line had been severed prematurely. I sank to my knees with the sensation. I was numb to all feeling. I was sinking into an abyss of darkness that seemed to fog over my eyes. I was passing out yet fully cognizant. My body completed its descent to the floor.

I sensed this other "person" receding, growing fainter as if I were the one dying in the process. I rolled onto my back. I did not have control of my own body. I was trembling from head to toe. I did not know how much more I could take.

::It seems I cannot separate from him...::

The young man's voice moved within my own head, attempting to uncouple from my mind and body.

"Do...not...leave..." I whispered to the room.

How I had gained enough control to say these words befuddled me. In truth, I did not have much control of my own body.

:: Jacob, it is too painful...for us both. I am going to lose him. No, I do not know why this is happening! But we are linked. Do you not think I know how this looks? I cannot go any further. If I do, I know I will kill him, possibly even myself!::

I was trapped within my own body as if I were peering at the happenings of my home through a window, allowed to watch but restricted from any personal involvement. To make matters worse, only one part of the conversation made itself known to me. Jacob was obviously responding, but I was not able to hear his words.

I was about to lose all hope when the most powerful release coursed through me. I was coming back; and I was not alone.

I lay there panting like a dog caught up in the humidity of a summer's day in the sweltering city heat. My body was numbingly cold, but my head and chest were on fire. My breathing and temperature slowly returned to normal. I started to drift out of consciousness. I closed my eyes, content that I was whole again, or at least the part of me under duress returned whole again. I doubted that whoever moved about me was deeply concerned with my morning's revelation.

When I opened my eyes after some rather focused quiet breathing, I was surprised to find not just one Mohawk Indian within my receiving room, but two. One of them was the very same young man from my dream of last night. While my old school chum, Jacob, squatted beside me to get a better sense of my current state of mind. I attempted to rise when Jacob placed a hand upon my chest and whispered softly.

"Easy, Will. Do not push this."

He turned to the young warrior to his right who remained standing, and although he spoke in fluent Mohawk, I found, despite my being rusty with it, I understood far better than I thought possible.

"The Central needs to be advised of this. You know we cannot keep this to ourselves. These changes are coming far too rapidly. The game has changed, Joss. I know you have reservations about bringing anyone else into the conflict, but in case you have not taken notice, he already is involved in our conflict. Those, what did you call them, Flintlings?"

The young man nodded once to acknowledge the term's origin. I found it strange, the feeling of having a presence in his body as well as my own. The duality of it—most bewildering in the extreme.

Jacob continued, "These Flintlings are going to be watching him. He is known to them, now, as you well know. To think otherwise would be folly. I hoped clouding him would prevent him from pursuing it further. I think when we—well, to be more precise, you—clouded his mind last night, it might have caused this bonded link between you."

"The thought had not crossed my mind."

That was a lie. I knew he felt differently on the subject, although in my subdued state I was not in a position to press the point.

"He's aware of us now," the not-Jacob Indian uttered. An odd admission, given his previous deception.

"You mean he is not fully clouded?"

"I do not believe so. I can sense his listening in on our conversation. Even though we are talking in our language he is getting the translation through me. He is—" At this he looked at me and his gaze softened. Where I expected a hardened glare, I found none. "—a *resourceful* one."

"You say that with a rather admiring tone," I murmured.

A smile warmed over him; he was pleased with my last comment. *Most peculiar...*

"I believe I can remedy the situation, though."

I felt a change in his presence, almost as if he had taken me by the shoulders and forced me out of an unforeseen door and into the black abyss. Without him as a lifeline, I began to slip from consciousness.

No!

:: I am sorry, Will. Jacob can never know... He would not understand. I am not sure what else I can do.::

As I descended into the darkness yet again, cast out by this young man whose name still escaped me, I knew there was sacrifice in his tone. He was paying for something personally. It was this very *something* he kept closed off to everyone.

And that I was privy to his thoughts, he became most alarmed I might uncover that certain something he was guarding. I felt him let go entirely, and I passed from the land of the living and into the world of dreams...

I stood on a stretch of shore across from Manhattan, looking out over the East River. A radiant blue sky hung directly above me. The landscape, in all of its sumptuous glory, filled to the brim with a lazy afternoon haze.

Across the river I spied another man. By his manner of dress, a Mohawk Indian. Only his side of the river bore no resemblance to my own. The starkness of contrast between our two beaches left me with the impression he might have been in another world altogether.

For his side was not the city of Manhattan as I knew it, but instead a city torn asunder, as if consumed by some unseen behemoth with big swaths and furrows cut into the landscape. Buildings lay in ruins, some still smoldering—long spiraling tendrils of smoke snaking into the darkening sky, adding its gloom to its cataclysmic palette. No one, save my new Indian companion, occupied his side of the river. Manhattan in ruins—as desolate a place as I could scarce imagine.

Where a thriving wharf should have been stood a collection of shattered ships and mangled docks. The warehouses that stoically laid their claim as brick-and-mortar edifices now lay in a scorched rubble.

I looked up at the sky and spied where the brilliant blue of my own world darkened and became a morass of grays and blacks roiling with absolute desolation on his side. Cast in the midst of the rubble, he seemed infinitesimally small. I could scarcely make out any discerning features save for his costumed silhouette of our people. Though I could not say how, I knew him to be the very same whose body and mind I had just shared before finding myself here.

Joss? Josiah, was it not? For some reason the name flitted across my mind.

The landscape changed, and what represented two pieces of land cast apart by the vastness of the East River swayed with such force that the two opposing sides of land came close to each other. This young man and I were now but a few hundred feet or so apart. We lurched about with the shifting of the landscape but somehow managed to stand firm.

The wide East River had condensed into a rushing and (far more than usual) turbulent rivulet. How or why this was so, I could not reasonably attempt to explain. Yet, I could see him as plainly as he did me. It was the young man...standing there, his rifle in his right hand, the butt of it firmly planted on the ground. Almost as if on watch, guarding against something.

And I did know him.

It was Josiah.

It was Joss!

I had the right of it now. I called out to him and waved. He just stood there, watching me, though not with the stoicism I had witnessed before. Instead, he wore a mask of despair, of personal rejection. He seemed resigned to the fact there was no absolution from his solitary harsh predicament.

"Joss!" I called and waved my arms high above my head in a vain attempt to capture his interest.

Choosing to ignore my efforts in gaining his attention, he turned to go back from whence he came to his shoreline. Though I could not see any indication of a town or village that he could call home anywhere in the distance. I continued to call, but he was slowly disappearing into the haze of the wintry blizzard.

He was now but a pinprick upon an ash-white, slightly smoldering flurry. Whereas I stood in the comfort of warmth and stability.

Without any warning, the river became vast again, churning with such ferocity that for the first time since I came to find myself upon this spot I knew real fear.

To my great horror I spied the long back of an enormous eel or some other seafaring creature of gargantuan size as it cut through the torrential waters with relative ease. There was little doubt it would take a much mightier current to sway the beast.

I took a step back, unsure of where it was going, but most confident that when it broke the surface, I would not be so close to the shore.

As if hearing my thoughts a loud volley of water burst into the sky and the creature reared up out of the river. A large, worm-like beast with eyes to either side of a maw that could consume any number of the ships in the New York harbor with little effort on its part.

My eyes widened as it opened its mouth and let out such a deafening roar. Coupled with its breath—fetid and rotten with ages of sifting through the muck of the ocean floor—it knocked me to the ground. As I peered between the fingers of my hand I saw within its circular orifice sat row upon row of sharp fanged teeth, larger and more menacing to the fore and smaller toward the back of its throat.

Surrounding its head, long tentacles waved about, each ending in a glowing green bulbous tip. A pointed stinger protruded from the upper end of each bulb. But the horror of it did not end there, as each fluidic sack contained something to make my blood run cold.

Each one bore the head of a family member, various teachers, clergymen, braggarts from the Points, and even the tart who had tried to rob me in the Points the night before. All monstrously waving about in the threatening barb-laden mane of this monster of the deep.

They all had terrified looks upon their faces, as if their last moments of terror were forever trapped in that poisonous sack. Eyes no longer truly seeing, clouded and white, they were. Their mouths forever frozen in their dying screams before their lives met their abrupt demise.

Each barbed stinger dripped with what appeared to be sickly toxin, ready to pierce my skin and rob me of my life. They lashed about in exacting strikes to make it plain that the creature could make good upon its threats.

My father and mother did not escape being amongst those stricken faces. In the grasp of my abject fear, I noted only one tentacle did not have such a maligned and wicked visage to carry. Could its purpose be intended for me?

I scrambled to get up and run, but the creature lunged as if to scoop me up whole, when a brilliant cast of light slammed into its backside, causing it to lurch forward from the impact. It swung around to take in the assailant from the opposing shore.

I paused in my flight and looked around the leviathan's body to discern who had the temerity to launch such an attack and found that small speck of a man in the distance led the charge. I prayed Joss had changed course and proceeded to close the distance between us on the opposite shore.

Every few seconds another blast of light, emanating from this advancing dark speck, collided with the creature. Each collision left a blistering point upon its body, bubbling along the surface of the creature. Roaring with pain, it found itself hard-pressed to put up a defense against such a powerful onslaught, choosing instead to change tactics by diving under the water, leaving little need for deduction on my part that it chose to flee rather than engage.

The speck became larger and soon I was able to determine who it was, yet my eyes could not reconcile what I saw. For as Joss drew near, running toward the beast as it descended, he held his hands out, palms exposed. A point of light seemed to spark before him and directed at the beast when he released it.

The creature slipped beneath the surface but that did not stop the attack from Joss. Instead of backing off, as I had expected, he did the opposite and increased his speed and continued to attack with his balls of light. They slammed into the water's surface with such force that each strike brought wave upon wave of water shooting into the sky.

He did not stop at the water's edge. Before I could warn him of the creature's terrible visage, he leaped from the broken dock and launched himself into the air, very nearly taking flight as the creature burst from the water's surface to engage Joss in battle.

::Will, I cannot do this alone.::

His voice moved about me. Whispers I could discern with such clarity, even within the maelstrom of the heinous creature churning within the dark waters of the river.

::Will, do you trust me?::

::Will....::

::Trust?::

::Do you?::

::Trust.::

:: I would never let it harm you.::

::Trust me?::

::I need your help...only we can stop this.::

He was successful in reaching the head of the creature, grabbing one of the tentacles. The creature began to attack Joss in earnest, the barbs lancing this way and that, but failing to connect because of some unseen repellant force blocking their every move.

He was truly astounding to behold.

::Will!::

My head was spinning. The voices moved about in my mind. Some to the fore, while others were further back but still discernible—echoing Joss's words in a mesmerizing chorus.

"I do not know what to do..." I called out.

The hand that did not hold him in place, rooted to one of the tentacles, pointed parallel to the creature's skin. A brilliant stream of light emanated from his palm, cutting a gaping wound along the creature's side. The creature shook violently and keened a terrible high-pitched sound, nearly breaking my sense of hearing. This time it was successful in shaking Joss off.

He fell from the terrible height of the creature's head and plummeted quite fast into the waters of the turbulent river.

"Joss!" I screamed, shredding my voice in the process.

::No, Will. Think it. I will hear you. I am here with you.::

He was still alive and sounded quite unharmed.

The creature lunged back into the water, chasing Joss within its murky depths.

I stood there, grappling with these events. None of this made sense.

::Is this a dream?:: I thought at him, feeling utterly ridiculous in the belief I could even mimic his talents.

::Do you want it to be?::

By Jove, it worked!

::What does that mean?:: He ignored my last.

::It is going to attack again.::

He was right. As if listening in on our conversation it chose this particular moment to rise up out of the water in a massively colossal move. Only this time, there could be no mistaking its ferocity as nearly half of its body rose, towering well over fifty feet, casting a fresh surge of terror about me.

::Will, trust me!::

I did not think I had much of a choice.

::There is always a choice.::

In the next breath, time slowed; a peace seemed to descend over the chaos. Stilling it, freezing it into a horrific tableau. Even the raging waters became solid, unmoving.

Before I could react, it seemed he was right behind me. I felt the warmth of his presence, and somehow, I knew. I knew he, or rather we, would overcome this aquatic terror. His words punctuated the narrow stretch of skin just beneath my ear in caressing puffs. A part of me shivered with that whispered contact.

"That is it, Will, let go. Surrender to it. Surrender to me. Allow me to move through our connection. Together, we are strong, you and I."

Miraculously, I could spy him still on the other shore, dripping wet, his hands outstretched, a gentle but purposeful green-amber glow emanating from his palms. But his words rang into my left ear as surely as if he were standing behind me. Indeed, I felt his warmth as if his chest were to my back. I did not know how he accomplished it, but he seemed to occupy two places at the same time.

"Trust me, Will. I can see the right of it. Just let it flow. No matter what courses through you, remember I will not let any harm come to you from it. I am sure I know why the connection exists as I think your power will increase my own."

::Power? What power? I do not possess...::

A smile broke upon his face.

A smile? Such confidence when we should most assuredly meet our doom?

::Ever the dramatist...I suppose I shall have to learn to deal with it. You have a power I cannot even conceive of. Look above you.::

Abiding his words, I looked up. Above me was a sphere. A swirling silvery mass of light and immeasurable power. Its low hum casting wave after wave across my body. Arcs of electricity moved about the green-amber marbleized light rippling within.

"What is that?" I asked.

::I am not sure. I have my suspicions, but whatever this link is between us, it was strong enough to punch a hole in the fabric of the Guardianship. I do not know what that is, but I have a strong feeling it is meant for you. For us. It is our path to victory. I feel it.::

"But how?"

::Concentrate, Will, use the link. We need to cultivate speaking to each other this way. The more we use it, the stronger it will become. Save speech for public conversations. Our planning should always remain thusly. Agreed?::

::Agreed. But I still do not know how...::

::Will, you said it yourself. Not to me, but you confided in Jacob. You are Haudenosaunee. You get it through your grandmother and through your mother. It is passed matrilineally as with everything in our culture. But there will be time enough to explain all later. I cannot hold time much longer. We have to do this together. I think it is a test to ensure our connected state. Though by whom and why I cannot say.::

::What do I do?::

::For the time being, just let go. I can help guide you. But I think that orb above you will reveal its true intent as soon as I release the flow of time.::

I sighed. Resigned to the fact I had little to go on other than trust. This was all so overwhelming and new. First the attack of last night, then the connection between Joss and myself, and now this...

::It is new to us as well, Will. Last night, the war irrevocably changed for us. New beings, new weapons, and now you. We are not entirely sure we know the right of it all. Just know that if it gets too dangerous, I will get you out of there. That is why I am keeping my distance from the fight. I will provide the necessary cover. But it appears this fight is yours. When I let go, it will all happen pretty quickly, but just try to stay out of its way. You might do or say something that will be foreign to you. Just let it be. Are we clear?::

I swallowed hard and nodded. His countenance brightened at the prospect of our pairing. It coursed powerfully through me, flooding my veins—such an undeniable sense of confidence in what we could do together.

::On three...one...two...::

Three never came, just the rush of the moment crashing all around me. The creature's mouth opened, row upon row of teeth flexed into a bite position, a jagged forest of desolation.

A roar issued from its throat. I was unsure of how to react; my senses became overwhelmed with terror. The tentacles struck with lightning-like precision, but never met their goal. They were repelled by the very same unseen force protecting Joss, now enveloping me. Their venom oozed along that clear wall, the faces of my family and friends bashing against it time and again, their mouths held agape in final screams of terror before they became a prisoner of this hideous beast. It simply was too much to bear.

::Trust, Will....::

Trust. I remembered my pledge. I looked at the orb such as I could with the beast gnawing, gnashing, and striking upon my shield.

"Well, if you are going to do something, then let us get on with it!" I bellowed at that object floating above the melee.

At the sound of my words, whether interpreted as a command or not, I was unsure, its skin, more translucent than the swirling internal mass, doubled in size. Suddenly, I rose off the ground.

The creature reared up, not willing to allow me any means of escape.

As I came up to the creature's maw, it pulled back as if unsure. My body became flush as if with fever. My clothing started to burn from me. Charred remnants flew into the air, billowing about in fiery cinders.

::I have to fight this monstrosity naked?::

::Let go, Will. Now is not the time for modesty. You are resisting the orb's power as it moves through you. You are overheating. Look at your skin.::

My skin glowed a rustic amber, and I beheld tattoos that seemed to undulate, cascade, and move about my person. Sigils and glyphs whose meaning or purpose I had no way of understanding. A rather large and complexly drawn one caught my attention as it slithered across my chest. My right hand instinctively grasped it as if to tear it from my flesh. I fought the desire to resist as this whole event bordered on sheer madness, but I let whatever was going to happen take place as it should.

::That is right, Will. Let go. Trust it. Trust me...I am right here with you. Feel me. Let me move through you. We can do this.::

Well and good enough for him to say as he was down on the ground and away from the mouth of the beast.

I clutched at the moving sigil and pulled it off my chest in a form of pure energy. Its power within my hand both burned and tingled simultaneously. I marveled briefly at the sensation. Instinctively, something switched in me. I hurled it at the beast.

It passed through my shield and collided with the creature's head, scorching its skin, blistering the crown of its hideous face. It roared and began to lunge forward. I quickly took another sigil from my chest as it moved across and hurled it at one of the creature's eyes. The contact from the blast shattered its eye socket. The beast wasted no time in dispatching me. The orb sensed this and moved to my head with such speed I thought it would destroy me, but its translucent skin enveloped me in a protective sphere just as the mouth closed around me.

::Joss!::

::Trust it, Will. You will be fine. I know it.::

I was consumed in darkness, the teeth of the beast, those terrifying fangs moving to tear at my defensive sphere were but the last visage upon me...a sudden blaze of light, a cacophonous blast, and then utter darkness.

Once more, I fell into the abyss.

For the second time in the span of an evening, I awoke gasping for air, as if plunged deep into a watery tomb and finding myself nearly drowned as I finally broke the water's surface. My lungs screamed for oxygen. I discovered no watery grave for me for I thrashed about in my own bed. My clothing lay neatly on a chair in my bedroom. My body was soaked from what I could only assume was sweat. My breathing slowly returned to normal. I ran a hand through my damp hair.

"Well is *that* not odd?" I proclaimed into the coolness of the room. Though not expecting a reply, I could not say shock did not consume me when none came. "You are quite alone, William. So, stop talking to yourself, lest the world will think you mad."

I chuckled and paused when I thought I perceived another chuckled at me as well. Silence. No, quite alone.

Secretly, I wished someone would explain. Odd events had been happening to me since my last voyage into the Points.

Could I have taken the Mickey and therefore not be fully in control of my own faculties?

A plausible, if thoroughly unsettling, thought.

I flung the covers back and crawled out of bed. My bare feet hit upon the coolness of the floor. Seeing my dressing robe lying across the foot of my bed, I reached for it and slipped into it, relishing the warmth provided. I maneuvered out and onto the landing at the top of the stairs. From the balcony, I looked down upon the lower floor of the house. Nothing was disturbed. All appeared quiet, just as it should. The angle of the light, however, made it plain it was late afternoon, almost dusk.

How could my day have escaped me so? What would have kept me so long in bed?

I walked back into my room and went to the clothing. I looked it over, and it all seemed to be there. I checked it over to determine if I had worn it at all today. I knelt to gain a closer examination. I found the stirrup that rides under my shoes, keeping the lines of my pants tidy, was sufficiently muddied, which led me to believe I had worn these clothes this very day, as was evident by the slight dampness of the grime I found there. But somehow, I was stripped of them, carefully tucked into bed, yet never recalled going through that process.

Though, someone else had occupied the room...did they not?

I pondered that because, for some reason I could not fathom, I had the distinct impression there had been another "someone."

Or was it some...ones?

I rose and proceeded down to the lower level to search for any further evidence of my having been about in my lost day.

When I reached the downstairs receiving room at the foot of the stairs, I noted nothing really out of place. I am a man of tidy means, and upon first review, the room reflected that. Only as I proceeded further did I note a subtle change: the sofa was slightly askew. As if pressed back to make room for something on the floor. I looked around to get a better grasp as to what that *something* might be but found no evidence. Neither on the floor nor the sofa to give me a clue.

I moved the sofa back. I proceeded to my writing desk in the room. It appeared exactly as I usually leave it, save for a notation I had made, somewhat in haste from the looks of my scrawl, that I had a birthday engagement at Miss Covington's on Friday next.

When did this happen?

I could not recall with any clarity having been invited or making the notation as such, yet it plainly was in my own writing staring back at me from my engagement calendar.

How odd.

I drifted from the desk and through the dining area and into the kitchen. There I found evidence of my morning meal still laid about on the table as if I had been disturbed while eating and rose in alarming haste, evident by the chair thrown back onto the floor. The pans and various cooking utensils were strewn about the stove and kitchen counter. This was completely unlike me. I always made a point of returning everything back to its original clean and polished state whenever I prepared my meals. To leave it as such and take leave for a prolonged nap was highly unlike me, regardless of any sickness or injury on my part.

"Well, this will simply not do," I muttered as I righted the chair and began cleaning up the kitchen as it should have been. Within a half hour the kitchen looked as I liked.

As I moved back to the desk, I spotted my watch lying under the sofa. I had not noticed it before. But there, clearly outlined in the dimness of the waning afternoon light, I could make out its shape.

I scrambled to retrieve the watch from its hiding place. As soon as I touched it something within my mind clicked. I swear I could almost sense movement within my head. A barrage of imagery flooded my mind. The walk this morning with Miss Covington, the invitation to her birthday party, her odd look as I departed...followed by the strangest images yet: beheaded people in bulbous containers, a large eel-like beast, New York in ruins. What did it all mean?

I sat on the sofa and shook my head at the dizzying array of thoughts now clamoring for attention, when a certain image made itself known to me.

Jacob and...concentrating harder upon it...*Joss*! That was it! They had been here! I knew it, though I could not speak to the particulars just yet. I got up and began to pace the room. As I played it over in my head, I could now recall being laid out on the floor.

Which is how my watch came to be under the sofa. It must have been in my hand when I...what? Fell? Collapsed? Yes! Collapsed! That was it. I was sure of it now.

And then Joss and Jacob appeared; though not through the front door, did they? They had been discussing in Mohawk something I could not quite put my finger upon, try as I might to think harder upon it. All that resulted was the beginnings of a maddening headache.

"Blast!" I exclaimed as I made my way up the staircase, two or three steps at a time. I needed to redress myself and return to the warehousing district. As to why that particular part of Manhattan bore the focus of my thoughts, I could not say. But I knew for some reason my answers, if only in part, lay there.

The adventure began to unfold before me. Nothing would keep me from it now.

Chapter Four

Unexpected Alliances

Wherein William Hallett retakes his rightful place in the adventure of a lifetime. Guardian protestations be damned.

November 1, 1847
The Warehouse District, New York
6:45 p.m.

I bustled along in the calash I hired just outside of my home and set to thinking about recent events which still, even at this moment in time, slowly revealed themselves. What confused me so—they did not appear to me in any apparent order. I had bits and pieces that lent a clue as to the time of day or location, but little else.

From what I could make out, I pieced together events that seemed to start after my last full recollection of heading off to the Points two days prior. Conversations, both where I was an active participant and others where I merely observed the goings-on, began to unfold as if they billowed to the surface of my morning coffee. With some, I could even recall the nature of my attire—which helped immensely in determining a location and, more to the point, *who* I pretended to be. But the visages of Jacob and Josiah were the most troubling, for I could not recall how they had moved into my daily routine over these past two days, when it had been well over two years since I had beheld either of them last.

Jacob had not darkened my doorstep since our parting of the ways after school ended, though I prayed, silently, many days he would. I missed him terribly. I thought to write or to go back to Akwesasne to see him but decided I would only be a nuisance. A remnant of a schoolboy past. He surely had other things to tend to that no doubt would have a greater toll on his time than a lost chum from Dartmouth.

Only one thing appeared to link all of these pieces—a particular warehouse down in the South Street Seaport area. I could not speak to the exact location of the building, but I assumed it would reveal itself only if I investigated the area. I pulled my dark rust-brown redingote closer against the chill from the early evening air along the waterfront that had eked its way into my bones as we drew near South Street.

The coat, a behemoth hide from a bygone era, was the only fashion faux pas I allowed myself. It, along with several others in various hues, had belonged to my grandfather who had purchased them while visiting relatives in England during the winter of 1819. Its cut was in the old style, a tighter fit around the torso blending to a very full waist and back, which translated to an abundance of warmth. I relished its voluminous soft woolen fabric. It was an old family relic that my grandmother had bequeathed to me upon my grandfather's premature death at only forty-nine of consumption, from what I was told. Though I cannot say with any degree of surety what they claimed was the cause of his untimely demise bore any real truth. My sister shared the estimation that we did not have the fullness of the story yet.

Grandmama always thought these coats cut a romantic figure on a man—saying her husband could move her to swooning over him whenever he wore them. With the numerous portraits of him we possessed, I tended to agree. My grandfather was a stunningly handsome man.

Anytime I donned one of his coats I felt particularly close to my grandfather, so it meant a great deal to me—a man I had never known but knew intimately from family stories. Indeed, a portrait of him walking in a forest glade, where he wore this very coat, adorned a prominent place above the familial fireplace back in Hallett's Cove. I suppose the garment symbolically represented my ancestral roots, and as such I wore it proudly, despite its sentimental, out-of-fashion flair.

My grandmother would often berate me for its use when nearly everything else I had continued on constant rotation in favor of whatever was fashionable at the time. I would counter that only because of the redingote's signature silhouette could she discern me from any other gentleman in a crowd. This retort invariably would garner a giggle of appreciation.

Presently, I was unsure of my course now I had arrived, the revelations my investigation would make known to me; the resolution to this dilemma had me on edge. With little thought, I instinctively pulled the collar of the coat around my face, inhaling reassurance from the fabric against my nostrils, as I often had done as a lad wrapped up in it, sensing the spirit of my grandfather would somehow protect me from harm.

I swore I could smell the familiar fragrance my grandmother said he often wore, a whisper of a slightly heady spice mixture now lost to time because I failed to inquire about it as a lad. My grandmother claimed she could not recall its exact composition, but I fear it was more from the fact she was too close to him. Any element that would bring about a remembrance of him would lead to pangs of mourning. I am sure it was enough that I wore this coat as often as I did. She needed constant tending to after the horrific loss of her husband, son, and daughter-in-law in so short a span of time. It fell to me to be the man to whom she clung to keep the family pressing ever forward in life.

Emboldened with thoughts of my family, I reseated myself, having noted that in my unease I cowered within the confines of the calash. In all my years pursuing adventure, I never expressed myself in such a manner. Thus, reacting like this was a complete shock to me.

This is utter nonsense! You will either find what you are looking for and gain the answers you seek, or it will be a complete waste of time, effort, and money. In either case, you have faced far worse scenarios, William Matthias Hallett, so you would do best to find your bottom!

Having given myself a good mental thrashing, I realized my little diversion in thinking had allowed the calash to narrow the distance from my home near the northern center of Manhattan to the warehouse district along the wharf without my noticing the intervening city vista until we arrived. Most of the inhabitants and workers of the wharf had departed for their homes or taverns for their evening meal.

Which is something you should be doing as well, instead of chasing a veritable wild goose into the Warehouse District.

As we rounded on South Street near the tip of the island something seemed to snap into place. This spot was immediately familiar. I knocked on the side of the cab with my walking stick to alert the driver I wished to depart. He pulled over to the side of the road along the middle of a city block, and I paid him his fare, asking if he could return in a half-hour's time.

"I could, sir, but there are a number of men meeting at the Queen's Head only four blocks west from here. I will no doubt be on standby in that vicinity along with the other carriage services."

"Very well. I should require sustenance, in any event, as I have not had dinner. I will make my own way to the tavern, and after my meal I will be once again in need of your services."

"I may run a few trips uptown for the gents what comes out of the Queen, but rest assured I will return to ensure your safe passage home."

For this, I paid him double his fare, and we nodded our agreement on the bargain.

He cracked the whip, and the calash sped off in a loop back half a block the way we came before turning onto Water Street.

I watched him make the turn, marveling how only a few blocks beyond the Queen lay the Points, well-moneyed civility mere blocks from murderous cutthroats. How infinitesimally small this island could become at times. Everything so near, compressed upon itself so there was naught one could do but take notice of another. Yet, at the same time, the city seemed vast and increasingly sprawling just in the few years I had come to call her home, often employing building up, rather than out, to accomplish this largeness to her.

I turned and proceeded down the sidewalk alongside a particular warehouse building. Moving along the next block, I came to a darkened alleyway leading to an inner courtyard one hundred or so feet away. It carried about it the dank mustiness of the wharf along with the requisite lack of light and hearty welcome. At its opening, I placed the palm of my right hand against the side of the tunnel.

Nothing.

Ah, wait. Like my watch, it may be tactile.

I removed my glove and replaced my hand upon the stone archway. Nothing revealed itself. I was about to give up on the whole endeavor when a shiver threaded through me. I recalled a fight of some kind taking place at the end of this very tunnel. I had been witness to it all.

I hastily tucked my glove into the pocket of my redingote and tentatively proceeded down the darkened walkway. I came to the end of the tunnel and found the inner courtyard awash in activity. One whole group of men were working on removing charred debris from what could have only been a wooden shanty of some sort.

A number of men appeared to be guards, standing around the working men, as if there to ensure no one intruded upon their work or shirked their duties.

Luckily, I had the good fortune of avoiding detection and found a collection of barrels near the entrance, which provided a fair amount of cover, though I had to stoop to remain concealed. As the men worked, slowly the realization came to me. This was where the charred remnants had become embedded within my watch.

I had been here! Confident in the revelation, I was eager to discover more.

I started to stand straighter to peer over the barrels when a hand came out from the darkness and wrapped around my mouth, completely startling me. We were in such close proximity I could smell mint upon his breath from the exertion of pulling me to him. I spun around, only to find Joss, his finger pressed to his lips, signaling I should remain silent. I nodded my assent.

::Will, this is not the place for you to be right now.::

A voice in my head again. I recalled this happening before. *Joss and I can communicate this way. How truly astounding!*

::Well, you did not think I would spend all night lounging luxuriously in my bed, now did you?::

He smirked. Something flitting across his mind that he immediately quashed, shaking his head instead.

::No, what little I know of you, I would venture to guess it is the last thing you would do, I am sure of it.::

::Oh, well spotted, you! So, what seems to be happening here? And why are you here and where is Jacob?::

::Jacob is near the burned-out building listening in on their conversations and noting the nature of this whole operation. We are trying to gain a handle on what these Flintlings are on about.::

::But, why can I not see him?::

I started to peer over the barrels again, only to have Joss grab me from behind and bring my backside up against his chest in a quick move. A wave of coldness came over me, making my body tingle.

::Do not move or say anything just now, Will. While I have you in my grasp you are hidden from their view. This is how Jacob can be amongst them and they have no way to detect his presence. There is someone coming down the tunnel. Hold still...::

I did as instructed. I found my eyesight had shifted somewhat. Everything seemed to lose any trace of color, as if I could only make out shadows and light, in hues of black, white, gray with subtle traces of dark blue. Joss's chest rose and fell slowly against my back. I did my best to match his. I am not sure why, but for some odd reason, it seemed to make sense.

::Very good, Will. You are learning.::

I was about to comment when three men came out of the tunnel. Each dressed ostentatiously, complete with fur coats and fur-lined hats, and they were in a deep conversation. I was assaulted by many voices at once; the sensation was akin to a chorus of different men's voices talking at the same time. While my eyes took in only three men there could have been more than three hundred voices talking about different events and subjects.

Joss seemed to notice this.

::Will, you can filter this. Follow my lead.::

And with that, I found I could sense a slight pull along our shared link as if he had outstretched his hand and offered to guide me along. Within a few seconds the other voices fell away until I heard none but the three men who had passed. It was not so much their verbal conversation as their thoughts surrounding the topic.

::They seem to be connected to one another mentally, Will, much in the same way we are, but not so clean a manner. It seems to flow along like a massive river of communication. You have to focus upon the intended target. It does take some getting used to.::

With his help, I was able to sort out and listen. It appeared we had come upon the leader of their group.

"See that Alexi has the current number of bodies being shipped to this warehouse as we need to determine how many we can move through the portal once it becomes active. Ivan, contact your brother at our headquarters and inquire when we can expect the *Báthory* to arrive. I want to ensure nothing will cause Lord Flint to look unfavorably upon this operation. Ah, Irina, as punctual as ever. See to it that our latest arrivals have been processed after their meal and are secured in their quarters before we begin the conversion."

We both moved forward, though remaining in contact with Joss's hand upon my shoulder. A woman approached the men, spoke with them, and moved off toward a large bay door to the far side of the courtyard. Her long braided blonde hair and pallid skin stood in stark contrast to her dark clothing.

Joss was about to comment further when his attention was suddenly pulled toward the burned-out shanty. Now under Joss's cover, I spied Jacob plain as day moving about the workers. He was doing his best to listen into their conversations but keep a respectful distance. Jacob seemed to notice something out of place that garnered all of his attention.

I spotted it as well.

Three men and one woman disrobed from their current disguises to reveal themselves as Indian warriors. From the looks of them, they were not Mohawks, as my friends, but another nation of Haudenosaunee, the Seneca.

"Guardians," I whispered with a mixture of awe and recognition as the term came to me with their first assault.

They began to attack the Flintlings with large blasts of lighted energy. Two of them were taken unaware and were blasted from their feet and flew into the air only to level their javelin-type weapons in midair, tearing a hole in it, and slipped from view altogether. They suddenly reappeared on the other side of the courtyard, ready to engage in battle once more.

"Damnation! The Jemisons. Jacob is going to be quite beyond himself."

With that Joss released me and dashed into the fray, though sparing a look back to issue one final order.

::Stay where you are, Will. You will only get in the way. I will come for you as soon as it is sorted.::

Within the next second, he had moved with alarming speed, as if slipping the spanning distance in the blink of an eye. The coolness enveloping me was ripped away with his leaving, and decidedly warmer night air rushed about me. I began to perspire from the sudden change in temperature, as if I had just run a mile and come to a sudden halt.

I was pacing like a caged animal in the confines of my hiding space. Yet I knew Joss's last was no mere warning. These warriors were on a level I could scarcely comprehend, let alone take part in. Bodies on both sides were tossed about like rag dolls with lighted volleys of energy cast about. There was a great deal of shouting and commands bellowed from both sides.

However, words between Jacob and Joss played across my mind during the heat of battle. Joss had commented that I was *learning,* though to what he was referring came at a complete loss to me.

As if peeling back upon an onion, another memory presented itself: Jacob made a point of how Joss occluding my mind earlier might have brought on all of these new experiences. It vexed me so to think upon it and, despite such ponderings, have little to show for the effort.

Not being of their caliber, I peered out over the barrels to witness the battle fully engaged. Jacob had joined the four other warriors and was busy castigating them for their actions in what I could only assume was Seneca because the vernacular was slightly foreign to me, with the words sounding different or modified so much that I could not say with any certainty I understood the fullness of their meaning. Joss had drawn out three of the Flintlings, when more horrific creatures came from the warehouse proper.

Only then did I realize their intent to engage had nothing to do with my Guardian warriors, but instead they had turned their sights upon me! A collection of maniacal beings with maligned and grotesque features of ragged sharp teeth that jutted out in various directions and had but one purpose—to rend flesh from bone. In the immediacy of the moment I realized one thing: I was their intended target and it was going to be *my* flesh torn from *my* bones.

I did not know which way to go as several of them were moving along the roofline and nearly clearing the side of the building facing the waterfront which meant that soon I was going to have a contingent coming through the tunnel looking for me. Not knowing which way to turn, I decided the best course of action might be to move toward the only protectors I had at my disposal. I cleared the barrels only to discover the group that had poured out of the warehouse door had completely sailed by Joss and the four Flintling guards and were en route in my direction. Joss was besting these new arrivals in their skirmish.

"Joss!" I called out as he dispatched the third Flintling guard and took that very moment to discover me in my present predicament. He vanished on the spot, seeming to sink into the ground and ripple across the courtyard with all the alacrity at his disposal, flinging cobblestones burning white hot from the ground with him in a wave that completely curved to either side of me. The acrid meteoric swath swirled in a fiery maelstrom so intense I held my arms up to shield my face from the heat.

The hellish bombardment did its job as I spun around to see the stones pierce the flesh of these ghastly beasts, searing them to cinder on the spot. Joss appeared next to me a moment later. He grabbed the upper portion of my left arm and called out to Jacob, "Jacob, we need an out!"

"Do it, now!" Jacob called back as the Jemisons and he had finished off the remaining Flintlings they had been fighting.

A glance at the door said their troubles were not going to be over as more continued to pour out of the warehouse. One of the Jemisons began their assault again as soon as another garrison of the vile beings were spotted emerging from the doorway—the building just seemed to be birthing more of them the moment the previous assault was routed. Despite the best efforts of Jacob and Joss, the numbers of our foes were too great. We were being overwhelmed.

Joss turned to me as the new wave of foul fanged creatures, almost running on all fours, moved with alarming speed in our direction.

"Will, on the count of three, hit the ground."

"You and your counts of threes..." was all I could think of saying as it had not boded well for me the last time he put it to me, though on balance, that had been a dream.

"One." He began to compress his hands, and a tiny spark of light ignited between them. "Two." The light became brighter as his hands closed their distance in half though it appeared he was expending great effort to bring them together. I spied fragments of our surroundings losing cohesion, sucked into the vortex between Joss's palms, as if their matter were being drawn to Joss's plan of attack. I could not help but think some resisting force was at work. The air around us grew more silent as if Joss's action were siphoning all sound and matter from the immediate area. "Three!"

And with that he ceased to compress the matter and dragged me down with him as the small spark burst in a radiant arc. The deep-sounding concussive release vibrated, and it swept across the courtyard, shattering any facing window and leveling the rest of the Flintlings and their horde—save for Jacob who apparently had prior knowledge of Joss's actions and had shielded himself from the attack.

The Jemisons were not spared its force and found themselves flattened in the process as well. Jacob drew the four Jemisons together and then gripped two apiece in each hand. He slipped from view, taking the Jemisons with him.

I felt a hand upon my shoulder and knew before it happened that Joss and I were being lifted from the scene.

In the next instant the seven of us were back in Battery Park, which thankfully was again quite unattended. I was beginning to think the very absence of people in the evening hours was the cause for this being their current rendezvous point.

I stood up from my supine position and dusted myself off from the debris of both locations. Luckily, not much appeared to have collected upon me. Joss stood up as well and walked with all haste to Jacob. I had no other recourse but to join them.

"Jacob, what were they doing there? This was supposed to be our assignment."

"Yes, but lest you forget it is Thor Jemison's nephew who has gone missing from the village. I am sure he is most eager to gain his safe return."

"But to go in and to start a fight, this is not the way, and *he* knows that!" Joss said, pacing a bit in agitation. It was the most anger I witnessed in him thus far, confirming my estimation that I never wanted to be on the receiving end of Joss's ire.

"Easy, brother. Calm yourself," Jacob begged as he placed a hand upon Joss's chest. "Let us be thorough with this. You can suppress their gating, right?"

"Aye. But I thought we were agreed I was not to demonstrate that particular ability to the Guardianship."

"All things being considered I would agree, but you know the Jemisons are hot-headed and all-believing in their superiority. This would not be the first time they have gone in where we are sworn not to take sides. Coupled with the loss of one of their own, this has the potential to become a powder keg. You know Thor; he is all too willing to jump into the fray and make inquiries later."

::Thor?::

::You know of our tales in meeting and mixing with Vikings long before the English arrived. His name comes from the influential convergence of our two peoples.::

Unknowing of our small cerebral side conversation, Jacob continued, "Fact finding is not one of their more salient qualities. I only wish Samuel knew of their joining our investigation. No doubt he would have put the Jemisons on notice for any intrusion into our assignment."

"What do you mean, on notice?" I asked before I had the wherewithal to keep my mouth shut.

"Guardians can be removed from action for breaking our vow. It is quite rare but not unheard of. To do what they did," he added with some resignation on their behalf, as he kicked the foot of the largest man of the unconscious quartet, whom I took to be this Thor they were conversing about. "Well, I am not so sure I would be of a clear head if it were my sister lamenting over a lost child at the Flintlings' hand."

"But how did they know that Flintlings were involved at all? We have not spoken to Samuel yet of our findings. No one but Will, you, and I know the recent events of the past two days. It does not make sense."

"Sure, it does. Think upon it, Joss. What other way would they have gained the knowledge?"

Joss's face became a collage of anger, abhorrence, and confusion all at once.

"They were following us?"

"It would appear so. Though as to how and why they decided to follow us is a mystery, I must say."

"Maybe someone tipped them off?" I added, seeing how Jacob did not retort for my taking part in the debate.

"Hmm." Jacob pondered my last. "Highly unlikely. Assignments are between the Central—currently it is Samuel Brant—and the Guardian in question. In this particular case it was handed to me with the implicit instruction that I bring my apprentice, Joss, along with me for added protection. No one else is present when those assignments are handed out."

"And we do not speak openly of them, either. This anonymity might seem strange, but it is a way for Guardians not to reveal the goings-on of the organization since none of us know what the other is up to. There are ways of finding out, of course, but it takes some doing. Jacob and I have been extremely cautious to keep this whole set of events to ourselves as we do not even know what these Flintlings are up to. And now, well, let us just say they will be far more difficult to observe as they will no doubt put up ways to detect our intrusion. The stakes of this battle just became a little higher," Joss disclosed as he moved over to watch the Jemisons closely for any signs of their revival. "They should be coming around shortly, Jacob."

"If they are not listening in on our conversation to plan their next assault."

"You would be right in that assumption." A dark baritone voice came from the man they referred to as Thor.

The foursome all opened their eyes and rose at the same time, which was completely alarming. Thor was formidable, at nearly six foot three with a massively built frame. He was dressed as any other ruffian of the Points and would have blended in with their sort save for his reddened complexion and shaved head, with the patch of hair braided on the right side of his head and cascading down onto his chest. His sleeveless arms each bore a band of tattoos in what I could almost assume was a most interesting cultural motif upon his thick biceps. This was a man, much like my Guardian friends, not to be trifled with. Although whereas Jacob and Joss had a calm countenance dictating warriors who balance reason with action, Thor displayed none of the former and much of the latter.

The other two males were of similar appearance though I could not tell if their arms were tattooed as Thor's. I did see a broad tattoo across one of the men's chest as his shirt was unbuttoned halfway down his torso. I noted neither Joss nor Jacob had any such markings. Then I recalled Jacob informing me that of the Haudenosaunee nations the Seneca's traditions differed most from our Mohawk bloodlines.

"A family affair I see, Thor," Jacob remarked flatly, neither hinting one way or the other what his true feelings on the subject might be.

"When we had not heard from you—" Thor began, only to be interrupted by a terse Joss.

"Heard from us? How can you...?" Joss asserted, advancing a single step toward the quartet. In unison they took a counter step back, which to me revealed the most telling element between them because they were far more dangerous looking than Joss. However, their response did make me think when it came to their Guardian abilities, Joss was the one to whom they deferred, despite the pressing mood of the Jemisons.

"Joss, please," Jacob pleaded, putting out a hand to stop Joss from advancing.

"Jacob, this is absurd!"

"Yes, Jacob, *it is*." Thor cut Joss off again.

Things were heating up faster than a wildfire in the middle of July.

"Were it not for us, you would not have any recourse to find young Thomas."

::Thomas?:: I inquired.

::Thor's nephew. He went missing naught but a year or so ago. From the Seneca village just outside of Little Valley. We tracked his disappearance to the city, which is how we came to cross paths with you.::

I nodded briefly, at which the woman from the group seemed to suddenly take notice of me, though why she bothered to wear a mask of discovery, as if I had not been there all along, was quite beyond me.

"And what of him?" She stepped forward and pointed at me in accusatory fashion. "I do not recall his being within our ranks. Why put him in the middle of all of our troubles? Last thing we need is some white man thinking he can start telling us what can and cannot be done about finding *our* Thomas."

Before I could respond, Joss stepped in.

"Tess, do not presume you have the right of it. You actually owe your thanks to William, as it was he who led us all to this current situation."

"Some thanks. He is the one out hiding while the rest of us are risking our skins trying to find—" she replied.

Joss's hands flared with a spark of brilliant blue-white light, and he nearly growled his retort. His voice deepened as it gained power, echoing around us all. "You would do wise to keep your sister at bay, Thor, lest I give her a lesson she will not soon forget."

Tessa sprang forward, but Thor, for once, decided upon discretion and held out a hand, stilling her from progress in our direction. Though he spoke with a dark voice full of pressing intent, his eyes bore the real expression upon them: one of fear that Joss meant what he said. Knowing I was not of their caliber or class of warrior, it was safe to assume I was only too glad I had Joss to rise to my defense. I was willing to let him do all the talking.

"Tess, enough. Joss is quite right; it appears we do owe...*Mister Hallett* our gratitude," Thor gritted out quietly, with a slight nod in my direction. The unease I felt from his little deference to me cannot be fully stated enough. Like coddling a viper.

I was thoroughly surprised at the use of my name because I could not recall at any time since coming into contact with this quartet its having been mentioned.

I nodded curtly. Tess backed down, albeit unwillingly, and Joss relinquished his hold on the power within his hand. It slipped away from our world with a brilliant spark and was gone.

"I should add that William is no *white* man," Joss continued.

"From where I stand, he looks that way to me." She spat in my direction, recalling Joss's threat of retaliation. Wide-eyed she further offered, "No offense."

"None taken, I assure you," I quietly acknowledged.

These were to be the only words from my lips through this discourse. But Joss felt the need to press his point.

"He *is Kanien'kehá*, and you would *do well to remember* as such and treat him accordingly. Or need I school you of his lineage?"

He looked pointedly at the foursome, clearly not through with his intimidation routine. Though why it was of the utmost urgency to press the matter, I was at a complete loss. I had no further intent of crossing paths with these people if I could help it in the slightest.

"Joss..." Jacob held a hand up to his apprentice. Joss turned and walked away, closing the distance between us. His eyes were ravenous, as if he wanted nothing more to do with the Jemisons than I did.

I pursed my lips in his general direction, doing my best to convey that I appreciated his defense even if it was a bit over the top, which seemed to catch his eye. His anger abated almost immediately, and I could swear I made out the slightest blush coming to his face in light of the deepening night sky. He smirked, confirming my suspicions before he turned back to the group. His face, a mask of cool indifference.

Thor, doing his best not to outwardly show it, was rather leery of Joss's temperament when it came to defending me. Upon my word, the only thing that was completely clear to me was what I had assumed to be a cohesive unit band of warriors seemed to have some factions. Whatever their differences, it was abundantly apparent that where Joss and Jacob were undoubtedly capable of taking care of themselves in a fight, something I had witnessed, the Jemisons were of a very different mindset. And the two had little else in common other than both springing from the singular actions of this Spruce fellow who seemed the cause of it all. I resolved I had enough of the tension between these Guardians as I was about to take.

"Thor, see reason," Jacob pleaded. "This whole investigation must move along at a pace to ascertain what the Flintlings have been up to. From what I have gathered, it is something deeply troubling and on a much larger scale than we have ever dealt with before."

"Flintlings?" One of the two men behind Thor finally spoke up.

"Joss's term for the creatures under Flint's command." This got a collective nod from the quartet as the name seemed to make sense to them.

"I think we know what they have been up to." Thor asserted. "That much is surely clear."

"Yes, and I think your intrusion into our investigation quashed whatever gains we might have gleaned from their operation. They will definitely be alerted to our presence now. It was a bold and incredibly stupid way to insert yourselves into the situation, say little for what more harm it could bring upon poor Thomas. But that thought never did occur to you, did it?"

Two of the young men who until now had remained stoic, save for their fiery stares, grumbled with Jacob's decisive reprimand of their actions. But Jacob chose not to let that be the end of it. Instead, he pressed forward with his own assault on the Jemisons' shortcomings.

"No; what you decided to do was to blunder in on our carefully laid plans to gain a fuller understanding of their work so we could report it in complete detail to the Central and the Guardianship at large. Now, as it stands, we have very little to go on other than generalities and weak suppositions, and I am sure it will not be any easier to penetrate that warehouse thanks in no part to your bombastic approach. They will no doubt be figuring out a way to detect our presence even if we mask our physical bodies. As ever, Thor, the wake of your solution lacks a finer touch. A bull would do better peddling fine porcelain."

Thor crossed his arms at being called out. He was taking the tongue lashing, but it was clear he was not liking it. Joss took this moment to clue me in on the background of their disagreement.

::Thor may be a braggart within the Guardianship, but he knows all too well that Jacob and I are closer to Samuel, our Central, than his family is. The Jemisons have enjoyed a central role within the Guardianship for nearly two centuries. It is not a role they are willing to relinquish so easily. They may be a bit overzealous in their actions, but we are all still on the same side. Jacob will set it right. I am sure of it.::

::And I take it your glowing palm there is the confidence vote in Jacob's favor.::

With his back turned to me while he faced the others, he realized I alone could view the small blueish spark radiating in the middle of his right palm. He no doubt detected my sarcasm as I felt a similar sensation as he grinned a little, sending that feeling along to give me a clue as to his response.

::There is nothing wrong with being prepared. Unfortunately, with Jemisons you have to be prepared for anything. They are a volatile family within the Guardianship. Never engage them alone if you can help it, Will. Remember that.::

::I had no plans on having them over for tea, if that is what you are referring to.::

"Point taken," Thor offered. "However, you must appreciate the stress my family is under in finding my nephew. His safe return is paramount for us."

"That is all well and fine, but we must do this methodically. What happened tonight might have endangered the boy rather than helped his situation."

Tessa glowered at Jacob's accusation. But Thor's stance held her and the others in check.

"So, what do *you* propose we do now?"

"Well..." Jacob began.

Then everything became still and silent. Jacob's mouth seemed to be forming a word but now was frozen in formation of his response. The tiny spark still radiated on Joss's palm, only now I could see its undulations more clearly and they rippled in his hand. I looked around the park and noted that everything else had stopped as well. Anything that had been active and could make a sound in the vicinity seemed to have been silenced at once.

"That would be my doing," a man's crisp tenor voice sounded from behind me.

I spun around to find I was not alone in being able to move whilst the world seemed to have come to a grinding halt. A man equal to my height of six foot one stood before me. He was immaculately dressed in a frock suit of rich black, a waistcoat of finely brocaded purples and greens, and a beautifully tied cravat at his collar. He could be no more than ten years my senior. With his long blue-black hair cascading down his backside and his lightly ruddy but smooth complexion, he was decidedly of Indian origin. If I had to guess, I would assume he was Mohawk.

"Wolf Clan. Or at least, *I was*," he replied with a twinge of sadness. Which jostled me completely because I could not say with any certainty how he could glean where my thoughts wandered.

"What do you mean? You can hear what is going on inside my head?"

"Only when you are concentrating upon it. Everything else is quite a bit murkier. So, do not fret. It is not like I pry. I merely picked up what you were broadcasting so I could ascertain how this—" He paused and held his arms out at the chronologically frozen landscape around us. "— was going to be taken in by you. You are a wonderment to both sides, William Hallett, of that I am quite sure."

"Both sides...? You mean you are one of these...er, *Flintlings*?"

"*Flint-lings*, is it? Well, I cannot say I am fond of the term, but then we Haudenosaunee have not had the best of luck when it comes to others naming us, so I guess I cannot complain too much. *Iroquois* used to irk me as well, but to answer your question, yes. In point of fact, I am their leader, second only to Lord Flint himself."

"So why the theatrics? Surely you could have found a more opportune moment to make yourself known to me. I mean, if they discover you..."

"But they will not. *You* will see to it."

"That is a fairly impertinent statement to make of me when you know so little of me."

"True, but if your behavior this past week since coming into our little squabble is any indication, then I believe I have the right of the situation."

"A *squabble*, is it? My dear good man, this is more than a—"

I held up a hand in the general direction of my companions frozen in their tableau of terse discussion. Even with Jacob's face slightly contorted in the formation of words, I could see the right of it. Noble savages, indeed.

"More than a squabble, yes, yes. Allow me my small amount of humor. But when you have been around as long as I have in the fight, the back and forth between both sides gets to be tiresome. It has all devolved into a sibling squabble as far as I can see it, and believe me when I tell you, I like it not one bit, but there is nothing to be done about it but play our parts to the bitter resolution. I can see it coming. There will be no sweet reward for whichever side comes out on top. We were both duped into this arrangement by Flint and his brother, Spruce, but it is we poor pawns upon the field who will pay the greatest price."

My face must have had a quizzical gaze, because he smiled and indicated that we move to a bench just to the right of my glaciate companions. I tried to mentally reach out to Joss but found there was a strong resistance, as if I were swimming upstream with an equally powerful current pushing me ever further back the way I came, so I decided not to press the matter. Whatever this man had done to gain us some time with which to converse, it was clear I was in this alone.

"Yes, until I release us to normal time, then I am afraid you will find Joss a bit mute on the subject at hand. But not to worry," he added as we seated ourselves at the bench, "I am not here to harm anyone. In fact, I am here to warn them all through you."

"Through me?"

"Really, William, if you insist on repeating each comment I make, then we will be here a very long time indeed. Let us instead get to the point of the matter."

Holding up my hands to chest level in mock surrender, I nodded my understanding. All things considered, I did not see how I had much of a choice but to accept his terms. If this man could stay the flow of time in this manner, I did not think there was much in the way of recourse I could bring to the situation.

So, we sat side by side with our backs against the bench, gazing out onto the mouth of the Hudson River. Anyone who might have come along would have thought we were sitting in a gallery admiring a life-sized portrait of the harbor, a painting so detailed in appearance you could reach out and touch the ships dotting its landscape. Yet that is where the folly of this lapse of real time collided with my perceptions, for I knew it was not a painting, but the real world slowed down to an infinitesimal rate.

As my eyes took in the view, I noted a small bird coming into one of the trees close to the water's edge. It was caught in flight; along with its wings its feet were outstretched, little toes straining for the branch just out of reach. I knew exactly how the poor feathery creature felt, as if it could be cognizant of time halting his progress. This whole set of events: the Guardians, the Flintlings, bodies being trafficked, now a young lad gone missing. My mind labored to grasp the enormity of it all. Mentally, my toes were exactly in the same position as that poor winged fellow.

"Yes, it can get that way sometimes."

Running a hand along his pants to remove some unseen dust, my companion sighed wistfully at my thoughts, resigned in his own way to the battle, though I did detect in his manner a saddened weariness. Rather the hardened soldier pressing ever on, here this man sat, an embattled soul who no longer cared what the fight was about. He wanted nothing more to do with it. He longed for the day when he could lay down the sword, metaphorically speaking, and rest, with nary a thought about past glories or disastrous defeats. Just to allow the end to claim them all was the only requirement.

"You cannot know how I long for it. Though, given the current state of things I fear that once the battle *is* done, I too shall fade from existence, cast upon the wind, flesh from bone till there is precious little left, I am afraid."

Another wistful sigh broke from his lips.

"But that is not why I have come here to talk."

I raised an eyebrow, thinking his ruse was being revealed, and he smiled. I was glad to see being from the *enemy's camp* he could do that. He turned slightly so he could view me more fully. I turned to meet his gaze.

"You must not think of me as your enemy."

Now this had my fullest attention. I could not believe the audacity of his statement. Did he think me a fool?

"Calm yourself, William. I shall explain everything in as little time as I can."

"We appear to have all the time in the world, as you have halted it from its natural procession."

"Josiah is quite correct; you do have a flair for the dramatic, William."

"*I* do?" I countered with a thumb over my shoulder at the stilled city behind me. "That is rich coming from the likes of you."

He smiled again. Calm, cool, and collected. He would not always be so, but I run ahead of myself.

"The world has not stopped so much as you and I have sped up. I noted your eyes moving over Joss's palm. It is wondrous to behold at this speed. But even I cannot keep us suspended like this indefinitely. We *will* have to rejoin the others."

"You mean *this* is your doing? Will any of this cause bodily damage upon my person?"

I was alarmed that he could be so cavalier when his actions could undo the fabric of my being.

"Calm yourself. It is nothing like that. And by the by, it would take a far greater exertion of this ability to cause you any lasting effects. You will be right as rain as soon as we have finished our discussion."

"Well, that is a great comfort. So, then let us not waste any further time."

He pondered for a moment, no doubt where to start his tale, while I did my best to discern whether I could put my trust in someone I just met under these strange circumstances. Before I came to my conclusion, he arrived at his.

"I know you will not believe me when I tell you all of this, but I am hoping that in time you will see the right of it all. This war has been going on for well over six and a half centuries. I should know, because I have been around for a majority of those years."

I raised an eyebrow at his pronouncement. It was hard to fathom since the man before me looked no more than thirty-two or thirty-five years of age, and a rather well-put-together young man at that. He knew, of course, that his credibility had just stretched to the point of unbelievability, but pressed on, nonetheless.

"You mean to say…"

"I am over five hundred years old. Yes, quite. And I do not doubt you will not believe me when I tell you this. But it is true, and you cannot imagine how much I wish it were not. That I could have died as I should have back then, but did not, is a constant source of sorrow. Instead, I had this manner of existence befall me."

He shook his head slowly. I could tell his sorrow over his drawn-out life was heartfelt, yet I could not still reconcile that he was over five centuries in age. It did not add up to what my eyes beheld.

"All right. Say for the sake of expediting our conversation, I do believe you. You still have not answered, why *me*? Why *now*?"

"I will come to that soon enough. For now, just know I have witnessed this conflict from every possible angle, even those that have yet to play out, over the long course of half a millennia. You want to know the truth of what I see?"

I nodded in the affirmative, for someone this old, no matter his alliances, surely could impart some modicum of sage advice in this conflict.

He smiled as if he sensed my thoughts, but rather than comment, continued, "At best, the Guardians will ultimately prevail, though through no fault or talent of their own. I just do not believe our Lord Flint has the wherewithal to show up his brother's scientific prowess. Flint is good, better than good, actually, but compared to his brother? 'Tis like the difference between a fine silversmith artisan working with precious stones and a blacksmith doing the same sort of work. The smith might be able to pull it off, but it would not be nearly as nice or as valuable. Flint is a brute when it comes to the finer forms of scientific application. I am living…" He snorted disdainfully at the comparison and regrouped. "I am the sole existence of his ineptitude with his application of the concepts his brother lives and breathes."

"Wait, so what you are telling me is this whole scenario, the war, the Flintlings, the Guardians, the whole lot of it, is because two brothers are having a pissing contest as to who can calculate the larger numbers?"

"Well, not so much in that manner, but yes, metaphorically, you have the right of it. I mentioned that my existence is proof enough. You see, I am something of an anomaly. I exist by pure happenstance. My death, or what should have been so, was my rebirth into the semi-human form you see before you now. I cannot die, not easily that is. And the longer I live, the stronger I seem to become to either side doing any amount of damage to me. Though your companion over there"—he indicated with his left hand with a slight wave in Joss's direction—"he is *the* true treasure. He will be greater than any of them, or even all of them combined. I never would have come to the conclusions he has in his own mind about what it means to be a Guardian. He, and others who will likely follow him, chiefly the Central if he has any modicum of intelligence about him, will surely rise up and set our operations back tenfold just by adopting his manner of using the *Dark*. You are quite lucky to have found each other. But perhaps it was ordained to be so."

I was stunned at his last. *Found each other?* Could he be mad, or was my mind playing against me that he was alluding to something altogether obscene in the manner in which he made this bold innuendo?

He smiled, and I found his dark eyes looking on me with such concern it stilled whatever retort I had conjured up.

"You do not see the wholeness of my statement yet. But I know what you both are. You complete each other, William. In ways that will reach far beyond the physical, mental, or I dare say spiritual, if there is such a thing. After living as long as I have, I find it hard to hold on to that precept."

I found his sadness nearly crushing at this point. Men often think upon immortality and what they can achieve if only they had unlimited time. I fear that being face-to-face with just such an individual, I would say nay to such an offer. It was only when faced with him now, and the enormity of his existence, seemingly without end, it made me sad for him, as it was clearly more than any one man should have to bear.

"You must not fret for my sake, William. It is a harsh existence at times, but rewards are to be had as well. You see, it is because of my immortality and autonomy within the *Flintling*—upon my word, I will have to get used to that one—structure that I have been able to play both sides from time to time. The Flintlings"—he smiled at coming to grips with Joss's new term—"share one common thread. They are all tied, quite literally, to Flint. From his lofty and remote position, he can take out any member of my army on a whim for any impertinence on their part, real *or* imagined. I have no such tie to him. It is only because I have served his purposes willingly for these past centuries that I have gained his unwavering trust."

"But why become involved in his actions at all? Why not simply walk away from it?"

An obvious tactic to my mind, yet I could not fathom why he did not choose such a course of action.

"Well, therein lies the rub, as they say. You see, in all the time in my previous life, I had not taken a wife or had need for any sexual or lasting relationship. These are things that predominantly occupy men's minds in our youth until we are fulfilled with wife and offspring. When I was wholly human in my Guardianship, I foreswore any such relationships because I knew the rigors of Guardian life were not conducive to a stable family environment. Now, all things being what they are, no physical contact or romantic involvement can give me the sensations Flint has through the one hook he has instilled within me, keeping me invariably tied to him. I am almost ashamed to speak upon it, but I want you to know the fullness of the arrangement. It is important that you understand the nature of my part in all of this. Only in this can I hope to gain your trust as this whole torrential endeavor plays itself out. Times have definitely changed, William, and I fear only through you do I have a means to an end. I want this to be over; I am no longer in the thrust of the battle for the win."

He paused, and, brow furrowed, contemplated matters that were deeply troubling to him, but not ready to make known to me.

Of one thing I was certain: this man, for whatever reason, stood on the precipice in revealing something deeply personal but vitally important to my understanding of what was to come. I had to admit the revelation, painful as it must be, was the start of my trust in this man. As men, we are taught to trust our feelings and have them temper the logic that carries us forward. Yet, we are often ridiculed for any public display of any personal nature because as a society, men are not to have open displays of emotive responses.

To have this rather intimate moment with him was profoundly moving. I do not know if I could be as honest and open with myself as he was with me. The closest thing to which I could compare this situation was the quiet conversations I had shared with Jacob back in our college days. It was the one male friendship I knew would last throughout my life. The man's next words pulled my rambling thoughts back to our discussion.

"When I spoke earlier of my autonomy within the Flintling structure, I was not being wholly honest. Flint does have one tie to me, and it is a powerful one that keeps me irrevocably bound to his cause. You see, whenever he is pleased with what services I have provided for him, I am consumed, mentally, physically, and emotionally with such sensations they nearly drive me mad. They are all-encompassing and can last from several minutes to, quite recently, nearly an hour. I tell you now, William, if there ever comes a time when you feel there is no other way to deal with me, you must realize in these euphorically *pleasurable* moments I am at my most vulnerable. I am quite mentally and physically incapacitated to defend myself and lost to those sensations entirely. Though I should tell you I do get a premonition that I am about to be overcome with them and have learned to hide away from the world whilst I am lost to it. So, targeting me will not be an easy task, I can assure you. Unbelievable as it may seem, I find that even after all of this time, I still do possess a survival instinct."

He had turned away from me and stared straight upon the mouth of the Hudson as this admission was probably more painful to him than he initially thought. I watched him for a moment. A part of me could understand his addiction to that sort of euphoric reward.

How could anything ordinary mortals experienced even begin to compare with the level of which he spoke? It did not take me much time to deduce there was nothing physical or emotional, probably, that could compare to the wild sensations brought on by Flint. Here next to me was a man who had extraordinary abilities, a long and experience-enriched life, sage wisdom borne by the length of that life, and still, with everything at his disposal, he was as trapped as the moth to the flame. If one such as he could become ensnared, what chance did we all have in surviving such an ordeal?

"Indeed..." Reading my thoughts again, he smiled, though joylessly, bittersweet contemplation over this damnable existence.

"But we are not here to dwell upon me," he continued. "The game has changed for the Guardians, William. On this singular point, this entire conversation balances. Do you understand me in the fullest? Up to this point, they have only had to deal with Flint and his maligned creatures exacting their toll upon the people and within their ancestral lands—this is no longer the case. Up to now, the Confederacy has taken enormous hits to its population, which has historically been written off to warfare, disease, and destitution. However, know when I say this: Flint's malignant assault of the Haudenosaunee was engineered to appear as such to the outside world. Indeed, the manner in which we struck was so successful, to the degree even the people of the Confederacy believe it is disease brought by the European settlers which wiped out a good portion of our population. So too has the Guardianship been assaulted over time. During the last seventy years or so, our side has been systematically working to remove Guardians from the warrior society, *The Great Culling* as Flint termed it. And a horrendous culling it has been. It is vital you pay strict heed to my words at this juncture, William, for herein lies the foundation of our army."

I nodded.

"The Flintling army, as Joss so eloquently calls us, is comprised of the dying bodies of Guardians. We turn them at the moment of their expiration. Do you understand the fullness of what I am imparting to you?"

My eyes widened at the horror of it, which I supposed was signal enough that his message impressed upon me.

He extracted a flattened disc made of the same dark metal I witnessed in the walking sticks. He handed it to me for closer inspection.

On the whole, other than its unusual metallic properties, it was rather unremarkable—save for the sigils etched delicately upon its surface, visible if you turned it at a slight angle to catch them in the ambient light.

He continued as I examined the disc.

"Flint has engineered a device so cunning and devious in nature that it bends nature to its will. As the body begins to expire, this device becomes activated. Using it at the time of death, we quite literally break the breastbone by plunging a rather sharp point on its underside…"

He reached across to the disc and, by applying three fingers in a certain sequence upon those sigils, the device sprang to life, startling me. The device produced a sharp dagger-like underside. It pricked my finger before I could move it out of the way.

"Blast," I mumbled, moving the device to my other hand and licking my finger clean of blood.

"I do apologize for that; I should have said something. But do not become alarmed, William. As I have said, I intend no harm to you or your companions. I am only here to explain the manner of how things have changed."

He took the device from me and demonstrated how upon the underside the metal seemed to have liquefied and dripped down to a lethal-looking spike that could easily break the breastbone. Alongside the sharpened point were many undulating tentacle wisps. They appeared to have a sentiency, searching for what I could only assume was a body to infect. This young man ran his thumb along the base of the point, and the whole device retracted back to its inert state.

"It is programmed to work upon anyone with Haudenosaunee blood, and, more to the point, an active but expiring Guardian. While you fit the former, you are not active, so it would have little interest in you at this juncture. Which brings me to my next point."

He put the disc into the inner pocket of his frock coat. I secretly hoped it would be the last I would ever look upon the horrid thing. Indeed, as I thought upon it, some small part of me began to fester a desire to destroy them all before they could inflict any further damage upon the Guardianship.

If one of those ever comes near Joss…

He smiled for the first time with unrepentant joy. "You see, it's begun already. Your first thought is to defend him; this is a most excellent sign, William, ah yes, a most excellent sign! I implore you with everything that

I am *not to fight it.* The very success of the Guardianship will well depend upon your defense of him at all costs, and he, you. But again, we have fallen off the mark and time is, quite literally, running out."

The harbor lurched to life briefly; a general rumble echoed around us.

"My next point is equally pressing: our operations have expanded globally. Flint has taken the army he has stolen from the Guardianship and dispersed them to the four corners of the planet. They were instructed with but one goal in mind: cull the minds of men for their most nightmarish and terrifying thoughts. The thrust of his amassed army is to instill fear in mankind. Terror will be the manner with which we strike. For when humans are fearful, they are also unbalanced in thought and in action and behave irrationally. We are using this to our greatest advantage."

"So, our nightmares are our greatest weakness, then? This is how Flint thinks he will dominate the planet? Come, now. The whole thing is absurd."

"Is it, now? Tell me then, William. What frightens you most? What dark things lurk in the depths of your mind that would scare you beyond all reason? And do not waste my time with mere nuisances. I speak of evil so obscene as to take your very reason away. *That* is what we have been mining from society. To that end, Flint has created four specialized factions of the army at my disposal, sharing common elements across all societies. Chief amongst them is the ability to project imagery into others and to slip in and out of their reality with extreme stealth. We can make men see who and what we want them to see. The calamity to befall mankind will be of their own undoing once we insert the proper scenario into their minds."

He allowed that to sink in before he continued.

"The rest of it will spring from their own fearful devices on how to confront or run away from that which truly frightens them. Terror breeds the worst in men. You know this to be true; you have seen evidence yourself time and time again. In point of fact, it is the very modus operandi of the Five Points. Fear ultimately begets supplication. It is the natural way of things. Predators pursue their prey using this tactic. It is a fundamental tenet of nature. Oh, to be sure, one man may be able to control his irrational reaction, but a group of people under duress will find it a much harder influence to break. So, to answer your retort, yes, this very premise will open the door for Flint to dominate the planet. And the operation begins this Friday hence when our ship is due to arrive in New York harbor."

After he explained the enormity of it all, I wished I had not spoken out of turn. I became somewhat embarrassed at my schoolboy outburst. He chuckled and patted my knee nearest him. I took it to mean he was aware of my embarrassment but chose not to speak further. It was damned infuriating that he could peer so easily into my mind, but I was not able to do the reverse.

"All in good time, William. In a related matter, the Jemisons are quite right in that their nephew is within our grasp. Quite a lucky find, as he came to us almost willingly."

When I displayed an arched eyebrow mocking his statement, he chuckled and held his hands up as if to surrender.

"Well, the manner of his arrival is not so important as I should say he is unharmed and well taken care of. I have seen to that. But they have reason to be alarmed for he *is active and rogue*. Thus far, I have been able to keep his Guardian abilities subdued, but he will be obvious within the next few days or so. You will need to extract him within that time. I will only be able to contain him for a short while longer. Do you understand?"

I nodded my understanding and made a mental notation to relay the message to Jacob once time restored.

"Lastly, I leave you with this as it pertains directly to you: there is something coming your way. I wish I could explain further, but to do so might encourage you to make rather poor choices and might compromise the success of it reaching you. I only speak upon it because it is quite overwhelming in nature, and I do want to press upon you that you of all people need not be frightened of it. I do wish I could be more forthcoming, but trust me when I say when it does come to pass, you should not turn from its approach. For only you will be able to manipulate it, and I daresay it will be the one possession of yours that will enable you to protect Joss as much as he will come to defend you."

Another slippage of time rippled around us. The ship across from us appeared to creak and stutter forward in the water for another moment. We had moved to where he had found me.

"I must return us to our time, as I cannot hold on to this speed much longer." I found this statement most unusual because there appeared little if any stress borne across his countenance. For all intents and purposes, he seemed as calm as the moment I had first met him.

"We shall meet again when time and the manner of my approach is agreeable. Once we return to our time, you will not remember all I have spoken upon. The information is there but will reveal itself when you are confronted with an applicable situation. I take my leave of you, William. It will have been but a second since you departed from their company; they will have little knowledge of your disappearance. I *will* find you again soon enough."

And with that he was gone and the whole world lurched forward. Jacob resumed the point he was making. It took me a few moments to recall where that was, but already I experienced the dizzying effects of coming back into the world in full. A ripple of gooseflesh moved across my body and my head began to throb. I rubbed the temples to ease the pressure, and when I opened my eyes, I saw the group standing there as before save for the sole exception of Tessa who was looking at me, appalled.

Seizing upon her wild gaze, I found I could not remember my previous thought, as if her startled look wiped my last memory from my mind.

"Well, I would suggest that we proceed..." Jacob noticed Tessa's odd glare in my direction. The others caught sight of it as well and followed its imaginary line to where I stood.

"Is there something you want to add, Tessa?" Jacob asked, not sure why she looked at me in such a manner when nothing seemed to warrant it.

"He...he was there, and then I could swear he moved over to that bench and was sitting with someone else, a man I did not recognize, and then in the following moment, he was where he stands now."

Joss turned around and looked at me with nothing but concern in his eye.

::Then I did not imagine you trying to talk to me just now?::

"When? Just now?" It was out of my mouth before I had the sense to speak to his mind directly.

"You see, he knows he did it! Who was the other?" she commanded as she brushed Thor's hand aside and approached me, a growing vehemence in her eyes.

If Thor's arm did little to dissuade her from advancing, a shield, courtesy of Joss, repelled her back a few steps when her body collided with it. It appeared to do the trick. The collision caused light to ripple about the Jemisons' group. Thor's eyes narrowed upon Joss as if this was a personal insult of some sort. Again, I found myself the center of their discussion and feared this one was not going to fare better than the last.

"Jacob, tell your boy to mind himself before I take care of it for him."

"I would like to see you try," Joss stated icily. He cocked his head slightly as if he were looking at a rather odd laboratory experiment. "It would be quite hard to make demands when there is not any air for you to breathe."

The Jemisons fell to their knees clutching at their throats. Apparently, Joss was quite capable and more than willing to make good upon his word. The ground rumbled with the power he was exerting.

I felt a strong pull at my insides as if part of what he did came from within myself. It was not painful in the slightest but left me very depleted and uneasy.

"Joss!" Jacob called out to his pupil. "Release them! This is not the way we deal with our own!"

An audible popping percussed upon the air, and the group's oxygen returned to them in a rush. They were on all fours, gasping. Thor rose, a look of utter vengeance in his eyes. The rest of his family mirrored his contempt for Joss's actions as they too gained their upright positions.

Joss moved in swiftly to Thor and the Jemisons, clearly not intimidated by their bravado. Though Thor seemed to talk a good game, he was clearly taken aback by Joss's swift action. The fear of Joss's last move was still burnished upon Thor's eyes.

"Let me be clear on this singular point. William is off limits. Anyone from your family or the Guardianship sympathetic to your position, so much as *twitches* in his direction, I will know about it and my actions will be swift and decisive. *The Guardian code be damned.*" The last he saved for Jacob's benefit.

"Joss..." Jacob tried to placate his apprentice, but it was apparent Joss had just graduated his training to a master level even Jacob could not quite reach.

"Save it, Jacob. I have had quite enough from all of you. William and I are in a completely new Guardian territory."

He looked around the group with a fervor that up until now I had not known he could possess. I could not quite tell from where it sprung, but I was all too glad it rose in my defense rather than being directed toward me.

He resolutely continued, "I am all too aware what talents I bring to the Guardianship, and it is presently, for reasons I cannot fathom at this point in time, inexplicably bound to William. I am also keenly aware that what I do, I do for the service of the Guardianship and the defense of the people. So, anyone who threatens this new shared ability has taken a stance against our cause, be they Flintling or…" He looked pointedly at the Jemisons. "Well, the rest of my point is no doubt obvious. I am sure by now the Central is aware of our shared ability, so in the interest of clarity, I will reiterate my point once more."

He rounded on them all. "Not so much as a twitch in his direction or I will quash, with all of the vehemence we have against our common foe, any harm that comes his, nay, *our* way. We have too much to work out between us, and any advancements that might grow from this shared link are paramount. So, in effect, defending William is defending the advancement of our cause. *Everyone* should be ready, willing, and able to come to that defense."

He moved amongst them, staring at each in turn until they could no longer look him squarely in the eye, coming to the last to meet Tessa's cold glare.

"Spare me the witch hunt tactics, Tessa. Even *if* what you say is true, William's abilities are only starting to manifest themselves, and they might make themselves known in all sorts of chaotic manner. We each remember how our abilities came upon us. Though he is not active yet, I feel a strong presence within him."

He turned and faced me fully for the first time this evening, his eyes full of awe. I was not sure I was fully comfortable being on the receiving end.

The next he spoke almost in a whisper to me directly as he approached. "Yet, it is stirring. I do not know how any of this is possible, but I do know it is for a purpose. And *we need* to explore that purpose."

::All right, enough, you are embarrassing me. Next you will be talking of marriage and setting up our household. Let us just get on with whatever the group needs to do next.::

I knew I was blushing at my jest, though he showed no outward acknowledgement of my jocularity. He simply nodded and gave a look at Jacob to indicate he could proceed as before and walked over to where I stood. He took a stance just to the right of me, with his arms folded in front of him in a protective manner. With all of this male squaring off going on, all I could do was roll my eyes slightly at the watchdog attitude.

To be sure, I was quite pleased he came to value our shared ability, but I thought the protection was bordering upon being beyond excessive. I glanced at the Jemisons. Their resolve that I was the devil incarnate seemed to have abated, albeit slightly. Now they only looked upon me as an annoyance, and not with the all-consuming disgust of earlier.

"Yes, well, as I was saying earlier. Let us continue with the observations of the Flintlings within the warehouse compound. I believe your nephew is still alive and within those walls. Before you revealed yourselves and the mayhem descended, I was listening to two of the Flintling guards discussing a boy within their ranks. Their description of him seemed to match that of Thomas."

The Jemisons appeared quite animated at Jacob's revelation. Jacob was quick to cut them off before their next move.

"However, thanks in no part to our small incursion, I would be willing to bet they have closed up operations for the evening, if they have not relocated them altogether at this point."

The thought regarding their operations popped to the fore in my mind. How it formulated or became revelatory was beyond me, as if a small voice whispered in my ear.

"He is active and rogue," I blurted out.

Everyone stopped what they were doing and turned in my direction. Even Joss turned to look at me.

"And exactly how did you come upon this information?" Thor asked. Stern, quizzical gazes leveled themselves at me. To my surprise, Joss and Jacob seemed to have joined them.

I stuttered. In all honesty, I could not recall how I knew this, but I was certain I did know exactly his current condition.

"I...er, I do not know exactly. I just do. I cannot explain it fully but, Joss, I know it to be true. Look inside, you can see the certainty of it."

Joss faced me directly. His eyes searched my green depths, and I stared right back into his darkened brown. I felt him root around in my mind, and I tried with every ounce of my being to stay out of his way.

Then we both physically stumbled forward a step as he ran into something in my own head neither of us had ever encountered before.

"Aw!" I called out, sank to one knee, and gripped the sides of my head, succumbing to the pain as he slammed up against it.

"What is it, Joss?" Jacob asked as he moved closer to us. Thor and the rest of the Jemisons had chosen to close the gap between us.

"I have no way of knowing, but there appears to be a barrier in his mind I am unable to penetrate."

"Well, stop trying because you are giving me a massive headache in the process!" I roared, far louder than I had intended. But having someone beating against your mind with reckless abandon hurt far more than I could bear at the moment.

"My apologies, Will. I was only attempting to figure it out. I did not realize doing so was causing you such pain."

Without any purposeful thinking on my part, I reacted in what I could only guess was from a more emotive part of me, a focused thought. Joss immediately put the fingers of his right hand to his own temple.

"Well, now, it seems you *do* know how it feels."

I was not too pleased. His banging around inside my mind had gotten to me. It was the last time I would toss aside any reason for reticence on my part. From now on, I would be a much more willing and active participant. To my way of thinking, if I had not stood aside and left my mind as a series of opened doors, I might have discovered this barrier far sooner than Joss had.

Thor smirked at our little bickering.

"It seems that the *teniteron* have had their first spat."

Though Thor chose to use the Mohawk phrase, rather than their own Seneca for an espoused couple, the other Jemisons chuckled at his jest of Joss and me having a lovers' quarrel. I sarcastically grimaced at them whilst I continued to rub my temple. The pain had finally started to dull to a small but manageable throb.

"I guess he *is* Haudenosaunee, for he gets my meaning." Thor grinned, and they all laughed. Even Jacob seemed to think the jest was good-natured enough and only shook his head and smiled.

I spared a glance at Joss, and he alone seemed to make no response to their derisive comments or to my inflicting the same amount of pain at his clumsy search of my mind. What was there in his eyes, though, held mine for a moment before he looked away. That singular pained look would nag at me for the rest of the evening.

When the laughter finally subsided, Joss spoke up on the matter.

"He speaks the truth of it. I too can see he knows the boy is both alive and active. He needs to be taken to Akwesasne so he can complete the ritual and begin his training."

The mood grew more solemn as the Jemisons contemplated this new revelation fully.

"I can add that we have not much time," I interjected. "A week at best. I do not know how I know all of this, but I am most certain that the time to strike is sooner rather than a lot of planning later. I can offer you all my home with which to formulate our plans to rescue the boy if it would be of any assistance."

The others looked at one another, leaving Thor and Jacob nodding. Both sides agreed to my offer of a base from which to operate. Finally, I felt like I could contribute to the whole endeavor.

"Brilliant. So, how are we all to get...?"

I never got to finish my query as the others seemed to have figured this out quite quickly. They all made some sort of physical contact with one another. Joss grabbed my hand in his, and we all gated to the inside of my home. It was an effective, if somewhat clumsy, method as the two large silent Jemison boys slammed into a side table and my sofa. They straightened out as soon as they gained their bearings.

"Yes, right. Well, I have some food in the pantry. Joss, if you would help me get that settled, I believe we can get..."

Then the whole room slowed down again. I was subject to the same effect I had witnessed a few moments ago in the Battery.

"Christ on the mount; not again."

My head throbbed, and I clutched the temples of my face in pain. A brilliant shimmering light engulfed me from behind. I turned around, squinting into it, and found a young Indian boy standing in front of me. The light dissipated, and the darkness of the room crept back to us. In the next instant the whole room sputtered to life again.

"Thomas!" Tessa called out, and the Jemisons immediately surrounded the boy.

"How?"

"I am not sure...but I am not alone," he replied, looking over his shoulder. Holding on to his uncle Thor's waist like a waif clinging to a rock in the middle of a raging current that threatened to sweep him away again, Thomas seemed genuinely happy to be reunited with his family.

Thor returned the tight grip; a sense of resolute peace seemed to overtake them all.

Joss moved to me quickly as he noticed I was in pain.

"Are you ill, William?"

"Please, Joss, call me Will, and yes, but the pain is subsiding," I answered as I shook my head to clear the vestiges of its throbbing sensations.

But when I had stopped shaking my head, I found I was losing my balance. It had nothing to do with any dizzying effects. Rather, the room began to physically shake, and a ripple of light started to emanate from the same spot the boy had appeared. This time, tendrils of light cast through the torn crevice. They hung in midair, as if an illuminated squid were breaching the hole, attempting to score its next meal. These smaller tentacles were followed up by longer and larger variants. One of these translucent strands moved through me, causing a slight tingling sensation, only to recoil as it encountered something within me that it did not care for so much. Others shot further into the room, through furniture, objects on tables, and the other Guardians. The boy whimpered as if he knew the nature of the creature and it had been the cause of some deeply seeded alarm.

As a tentacle arm swept near him, Thomas whimpered louder and sank to his knees while keeping a terrified hold of Thor's right leg. Thor responded by picking Thomas up off the floor and holding him close, turning slightly to put his own body in the line of fire.

Tessa put up a repelling field just as the next arm lashed out in the boy's direction. It collided with the field and seemed to change tactics, as if it detected the protective barrier concealed its intended target. All of the arms seemed to focus on this one spot, battering it relentlessly. The percussive sounds clashed with Tessa's shield, increasing with each attack. To Tessa's credit, the Jemisons were well protected.

"We are leaving...Tessa, Marc, John," he called to the others who nodded their agreement and closed ranks. Thor regarded Jacob directly. "Apologies, Jacob, but we have Thomas to consider." And with that, they gated out of my home, presumably back to their village.

The shimmer began to collapse, the shaking of the items in the room subsided, and normalcy restored itself. We heard an audible pop as the tentacled creature removed itself. Whomever or whatever had put him within our grasp and the subsequent reach to remove him again provided us with a mystery to solve.

"Well, now, what do you possibly make of all that?" I asked my fellow warriors. They looked at one another with the same bewildered expression I feared I was wearing. It was clear no one present had a definitive answer to the conundrum.

"Clearly, though, we can at least be comforted that the Jemisons will no longer be a thorn in our side whilst we investigate this Flintling incursion further," Jacob offered.

Joss and I could only concur as neither of us desired an extensive planning session with that omnipresent quartet. Their departure, though unexpected, was unanimously well-received.

"Although, I have to admit I believe we have not seen the last of them," Joss added as they followed me into the kitchen.

While not wholly sure about either of my guests' hunger, I was famished since my dinner plans at the Queen's Head had not come to fruition. Luckily, with my mental link to Joss, he knew of my hunger coming upon me or my intent to satisfy it as he followed into the root cellar at the rear of the house. We returned to the kitchen table with some cheese, bread, and a collection of cured meats I had purchased the day before. We proceeded to make a meal, and I brewed some coffee for them while I enjoyed tea.

Over the course of the meal, we examined how much we had gleaned successfully before Thor and his crew had derailed our investigation.

"What concerns me most is they seemed to be operating with little regard for how they are perceived by the people of New York. Almost flagrantly operating right under their noses." Jacob shook his head at their audacity.

"And why not?" I added as I finished my last bite of dinner and washed it down with a decidedly tepid cup of tea. "Did you not sense the ominous feeling just going through that tunnel to the courtyard? I am quite sure any person other than a Guardian would have serious doubts about proceeding further along that trail. They do well enough with protecting their operations. But I do get your meaning. They demonstrated little in the way of covertness when it came to their arrival and departure within the Circus."

"But the question remains: do we intend to proceed along the same lines, or should we bring this to Samuel's attention now?" Joss queried. "And if we do, just how large is this operation? Do we really have the measure on that point?"

I looked at Jacob for a response and, for reasons I could not begin to guess, blurted out, "It is a global organization now, well beyond the borders of our homelands."

They looked stymied at my sudden proclamation. I was aware my own eyes mirrored theirs with this sudden admission.

Where did it come from?

"Joss..." Jacob breathed slowly. "How?"

"I can only surmise this knowledge lies in part of what is hiding behind this impenetrable wall in William's mind. One can only guess what other treasures of knowledge are concealed there."

I concentrated on it for a moment. As best as I could feel within the confines of my own mind, the information seemed to appear from out of nowhere. Though I could say, with some degree of certainty, that we should heed the information with great reverence and due respect, even if I could provide no reason why this feeling persisted in the first place.

"He is speaking the truth," Joss commented as he poked around in my head more tentatively. "I can sense the information is sound even if we have no way of knowing who put it there."

::Careful now, this is how we got into trouble the last time...::

::I am watching what I am doing, Will. The last thing I want is to cause you any harm.::

::I am aware of that, but since we do not know what we are truly dealing with...::

"Would you both like to join the realm of the talking? I am feeling left out here," Jacob sighed.

"Well, I do not think we are going to solve any great mystery tonight. Why not make yourselves comfortable here and we can pick it back up in the morning?"

I could sense immediately that Jacob was for it. Obviously, days of wandering around in the wilderness, and giving up the comforts of home, had taken their toll. He rather looked forward to some stable warmth and food.

"It is not as bad as all that," Joss offered. "We do have some hidden posts along the outer perimeters of the state lines. They are warded against intruders making themselves at home. So, we do have ways of maintaining a home life away from home. Think of it as a self-supported Mohawk housing," he revealed with a small twinkle in his eye, devilish in nature. He knew by saying as much he had admitted to listening in on my thoughts.

"Yes, well, why settle for that when you both are more than welcome to share my home while we investigate this further?"

Jacob agreed with a grin, and we both regarded Joss who seemed to be struggling with his reply.

"Oh, Joss, just say yes. Your heart could not be clearer on the matter."

Two could play that game of mind reading our foremost thoughts. His eyes widened for a moment before he allowed the smallest of smiles to mellow across his handsome face, knowing he could do little in the way of complaining at my peeking back.

I got Jacob settled in the den of my home on the chaise lounge I had recently purchased. His eyes lit up as he scanned the walls of my study and the numerous volumes lining them. "I shall be most comfortable here, Will. Thanks."

After stoking a fire in the room and providing him with ample bedding, I left him to his reading.

Joss followed me up to the spare room I had adjoining my own. Though small, I had set about furnishing it with the bare necessities of a bed, a small writing desk, and some books from the library below. I indicated that he had access to my bathroom through a shared door near the rear of his room. After I inquired if he needed anything further, he said, "I shall sleep peacefully here."

Though I knew he wanted to say more, he decided against it, so I bade him good night and proceeded to settle in myself.

Only after my head hit the pillow, the soft moonlight from our nearly half double-moons cascading upon a corner of the bed linens, did I find sleep could not pull me into her embrace.

I tossed and turned, re-fluffed the pillow, tried different positions to gain some comfort to drift off, when I felt Joss tentatively search me out from the adjoining room.

::Cannot sleep either, eh?::

::Blast! No. I find my mind is full of partial answers to questions that have not been asked. It is as if I am racing around trying to put the pieces of a puzzle together yet I have not a clue of what I am assembling. Do you get the fullness of my meaning?::

::Well enough. I have been silently watching your, for lack of a better term, mental dance. Will, when stressed, I have found it is best to calm your mind to these random thoughts. You are pressing for

answers when maybe the thing to do is merely observe. Do not give in to the impulse to react to everything you are presented with. Sometimes observation is all that is required. I would have thought your grandmother would have instilled that in you by now.::

This link between us was as intriguing as it was infuriating. I could sense he turned on his side of the bed, physically facing my direction as if talking across the expanse between two beds in the same room. I did not hide how his last rankled me, and I sensed he knew it as well. I also discerned he had not meant any harm by it. As I belonged to a matrilineal people, my social and cultural instruction would have come from Grandmama; he knew I should know that. His comment no more than an *observation* of my upbringing, perhaps. Of course, in sharing a consciousness, he knew my immediate thoughts on the matter.

::Yes, there is some of that. But I also know there are elements she did impart to you that you appear to have forgotten. A great many things I will have to remind you about how we are as a people. I know this whole situation is odd. It has me shaken as well. Why is there a connection? What purpose could it possibly serve? I struggle as well with the idea of having you move around in my mind is for good or ill. Yet, I know you have never taken advantage of our shared link, and I am ashamed I have used it rashly without much in the way of considering your feelings upon the matter. This is all new to me, William. I have only ever had to contend with my own fears, thoughts, and assumptions. To have yours added to them is extremely bewildering. I fear to ask you this, but do you trust me?::

His last reverberated within me, calling up the dream where he had posed the same question—a moment when the world of dreams converged with the world at large. I knew I should respond. It was a simple enough question, though I had the dickens of a time coming up with an answer. I found for the first time in a long while, all of my thoughts seemed to quell at once as if someone of great importance has entered a party and the guests immediately stop their smaller conversations to take note of the impressive arrival. Whilst my head was still sorting it out, I knew another part of me had already come to its decision some time ago. And then there was a flushing in my heart when he asked me. I hoped he did not misinterpret that sensation.

::I am afraid that was far too personal. Forget I inquired.::

I could feel him retreat from my thoughts and found myself mentally scrambling after him.

::No, Joss, no. 'Tis not the cause at all. Not in the slightest. Of course, I do. I only faltered because it was the first time anyone has ever asked such a profoundly personal question of me. With Jacob, it never was a point of discussion. As mates, we relied upon each other throughout our schooling. We were, or rather are, the best of friends. More like brothers actually, as I know more about him than I could possibly about my own brother. My fondness for him knows no bounds. Our trust is born out of that relationship. It was until you asked me in the manner you just did that threw all thought from my mind.::

I found myself smiling at this last thought.

::I will say this, Joss, you do know how to gain my attention.::

Nothing. He was still withdrawn. Oh, to be sure, I could sense he was still there, though it felt as if he had turned his back upon me, shutting out further conversation. I lay there fuming, trying to resolve my emotions where my feelings for Joss lay and how this new shared consciousness was going to play out between us.

"Hrmph," I muttered as I slung myself to the other side of the bed.

I felt him smile at this.

::Oh, this surely caps the climax, Josiah! You present me with nothing short of an icy reception, when I am attempting to engage you, yet let me have a moment of frustration and suddenly you find my predicament humorous. You are truly a wonderment.::

I did not need to feel his humor across our link for he laughed openly in the next room.

The next instant, he was upon me in the bed jabbing me in the ribs as I caught up in the bedding, struggling to free myself in the darkened moonlit room. My foot collided with his head, giving me quick respite from his tickling, as I struggled in vain to pull myself free.

His laughter mingled with my own until we crashed topsy-turvy onto the floor, a mix of bodies and bedding. In a swift move that surprised even myself, I was able to leverage my body, to drive him onto his back with me straddling his chest. Triumphantly, I pinned his wrists to the floor, my face inches above his own. We stared at each other breathing heavily but both wearing smiles of satisfaction, any ice between us fully thawed. I looked into his dark, near-black eyes and he into my emerald green. This was someone I knew would always be there. Protection, trust, and devotion to our common cause.

::Like the boughs of a pine...:: His eyes still searching my own.

::?!::

In the middle of our panting from the quick overexertion of our bodies, we heard it and it stilled us into silence. A scratching and scraping of wood in the darkest recesses of my room. Something had joined us in the middle of our horseplay. I immediately released Joss's wrists, and we maneuvered amongst the twisted bedding so he could sit up beside me as we struggled to discern what moved about in the dark.

All was silent again; even our breathing had quelled to where you could almost hear the movement of dust in the room.

::Should I light a candle?::

::You need not bother. I have my own means of illumination.::

Joss held out his right hand, and a spark of brilliant blue-white light glittered above his outstretched palm, casting light into the darkness. There, at the crook of the doorjamb with the opened door partially obscuring him, was Thomas Jemison.

Joss and I stared gape-mouthed at Thomas. He was dressed as before in my living room, suggesting he had not been back home for any great length of time. How long he had been hiding in my room neither of us could say.

"William?" the boy asked tentatively. "Is that you there?"

I crept forward on all fours to the end of the bed with Joss close upon my heels. I could not help but feel immensely relieved Joss was here with me. Normally, I would feel assured of my capacity to deal with nearly every situation that should befall me, but in this current dilemma, I knew I was well beyond any hope of bearing this ordeal alone.

As soon as I reached the foot of the bed, the boy scurried out from behind the door and in a flash had me in a tight embrace, sobbing as he rambled on.

"I went back with Uncle Thor and the rest and then...and then...the fighting started, the cre—crea...creature." He chewed the last phrase, gnashing it in his teeth as if he wanted nothing more than to rend it from his mind.

Indeed, it must have been terribly horrific for him to realize the creature's first attempt at procuring him from my own living room had failed, only to discover it had been successful in pursuing him to his own familial home.

He blubbered on. "The creature that came here"—more sniffles punctuating the darkened air—"well, it followed us back to our village."

I pulled from his tight embrace. His arms shook as he wanted nothing but to have someone or something to cling to that would remain stable. Yet the question remained: *why me?* I knew the boy less than Josiah or Jacob did. Yet, here I was giving as much comfort within my arms as he needed, stranger to me though he be.

"Tek:orens..." Joss called Jacob by his Mohawk name, a name I knew should only be used either amongst family members—myself included— or in times of importance. In a flash Jacob gated into my bedroom doorway, the fullness of his figure nearly eclipsing the expanse.

"What is the...?" He saw Thomas sobbing in my arms.

"Look, um, why do we not pick this up downstairs?" I murmured as I rubbed the back of the lad still struggling to compose himself. "I think we should get Thomas something to calm himself."

A few minutes later, with Thomas doing little to extricate himself from my person, I had to rely upon Joss to prepare a batch of hot tea that would hopefully soothe Thomas's distraught emotions.

As Joss put the kettle onto the fire, stoked the stove, I gently extracted poor Thomas from my lap and sat him down at the table where he placed his head down upon the surface, silent sobs still wracking his body, evidenced by the small motion of his shoulders. Joss sat on the chair I had left for him.

::For some reason, he wants to relay his experience to you. I am not sure why this is so, but please, Will, be patient with him. If something truly has happened, we need to learn of it.::

::Exactly my thinking, Joss. Do not fret on that account.::

"Well now, take a deep breath, Thomas, and try to explain to me what happened. Now you said you arrived with your family at your home. Then the creature that tried to apprehend you here seemed to follow you there. Is this correct?"

Thomas raised his head, and in the fullness of the kitchen lamp I saw a boy haunted by whatever tragedy had transpired this evening.

After a long breath to calm himself, he looked to each of us in turn before settling upon my face to confide.

"When it appeared, we did not have much in the way of notice. I had only been reunited with my mother in front of our home and was thoroughly glad to be there after so long an absence. Then the air crackled and I knew, I knew what it was: it found me. I turned around and watched the tentacles reaching for me. My mother screamed and tried to hide me as best she could. As I peered around her, I saw my aunt Tessa engage it, only to be swept away along with my cousins Marc and John. They had little time to react as the creature struck with such swiftness, I could only watch completely afraid.

"Uncle Thor moved between my mother and myself as people all around began to run away screaming for their lives. Uncle Thor was able to get a few shots on it, which seemed to give it some pause. It recoiled back onto itself, and we all thought it was in retreat when it took advantage of my uncle letting down his guard and swept him into the air well past the tree line. And then...then..." He began to sob in earnest.

I patted his hand to let him know to calm himself.

The kettle whistled, making the boy jump, so Joss got up and poured some water into a mug and added the tea and brought it over to the table with some sugar and cream Joss had dispatched from the root cellar earlier.

After preparing the tea, I handed it to Thomas and only after he had taken a few sips did I broach the subject again, all too aware to tread as if upon thin ice. His frightened face expressed his very fragile state. His next words, I feared, would present the root cause of his trepidation.

"When you are ready, Thomas."

He put the cup down after his fourth sip and attempted a small smile for my consideration. Something threaded across his gaze, something I could not quite make out, yet clearly troubling, held my attention. I tried to take as casual a stance as possible. I did not want him to fear that we would judge him too harshly on whatever action or inaction might have been taken on his part.

"'Tis hard, that's all," he murmured.

"Take your time. An accurate portrayal of the events is paramount, not the time in which it is relayed."

He sighed again.

"After Uncle Thor was knocked into the forest, I screamed aloud my anger at its assailing of my family. I began to yell 'no' at it most vehemently. And to my surprise it recoiled as if I had struck it profoundly. And then I knew. I *knew* what I had done."

I spared a glance at Jacob and Joss, their concentration on Thomas and his story plain upon their faces.

::It is him, Ohnehta'kowa.::

::What do you mean, it is him? He caused it?::

::Most definitely, thus his trepidation over telling us.::

Thomas watched both of us. For a moment I wondered if he could listen in on our mental conversation, but then realized our facial expressions probably accomplished that for him well enough.

"Go on, Thomas," I encouraged as gently as I could.

He nodded, and the curious thread I had spied earlier slithered across his countenance, indicative of something unspoken but important just the same.

"It was me. I realized that when I was yelling at it. It appeared to heed my call. It was under my influence. Then I realized I had caused it all. When I finally assumed I could control it, I banished thinking about it from my mind and at once it fell to dust and blew away upon the wind."

For the third time, that thread of something not measuring up in his tale slipped across his gaze. For some reason, I felt the need to recoil from it. Alas, I knew I probably put too much upon him and I resolved that I must have imagined the whole thing.

The room fell silent. We regarded one another until the silence seemed deafening.

Finally, Joss's smooth baritone broke into the room. "Thomas, I know this is difficult for you, but I need you to clarify something for me. You said earlier that Tessa and your cousins were swept away. What happened to them? Where were they flung? Into the forest with your uncle? Did they survive?"

The boy moved his fingernail along a well-worn groove in the tabletop, contemplating his words carefully. Indeed, his very careful contemplation disturbed me greatly, completely underscoring how his narrative all seemed slightly askew, off-balance, and not wholly the truth. Be that as it may, I felt another sore point coming to the fore.

"This is the part I do not know how to answer. When it swept through them, Tessa tried to defend them as best she could, but the creature was too fast. They got sideswiped and fell away into the darkness behind the creature. I could only watch as they seemed to fade from view, as if their bodies were torn apart upon the wind. I have no way of knowing where they went. Only that they were nowhere to be found after I sent the creature back from whence it came."

"And where do you suppose that would be?" Jacob inquired.

"I have no idea, Uncle Jacob. I fear I've trapped them with the monster I sent away."

::Uncle?::

::We are all related one way or another, Will. It is the nature of our Confederacy, you ought to remember that. Jacob's younger brother married into Thomas's family.::

Jacob's face became a stern line of concentration.

"And what of Thor? You said he was flung into the forest. Did you ever locate him? How did he fare?"

"After I sent it away, the dark hole it used to tear into our world collapsed. When it did, it shattered several homes in the village and put everyone around me to sleep. They fell where they stood when the creature's hold upon our world collapsed. I first checked upon my mother and she was alive, but I could not rouse her, regardless of what I tried. I spent the following hour moving amongst the brush trying to locate Uncle Thor, but I could not find him. I fear he is lost as well. I dragged those I could back into the few houses or buildings nearby as it was growing colder. I didn't know what else to do, so I came back here."

"Thomas, I guess we had better explain something here," Joss offered. "You are not going crazy. All of these events are as terrifying as they are spectacular, yet they are very real. And there is a reason for it all, and why it reveals itself to you now." It seemed to calm Thomas a bit.

Joss then looked back to Jacob who spent the next few minutes explaining the existence of the Guardianship and their common cause and how he fit into this new world that had suddenly opened up to him. Thomas had little time to assimilate this information; Jacob pressed his next point as soon as his Guardian history lesson was over.

"However, if what Thomas has said is accurate, we had better get to the Allegheny posthaste. Only then will we have a fuller understanding of what has transpired."

As I was in my dressing robe and nightshirt, I had to ascend the stairs to gain a change of clothing. Joss had already taken the quicker route by gating back to his room and had nearly completed his transformation as we discovered him walking out into the foyer at the top of the stairs. Thomas followed me upstairs. It was clear I was not going to shake him off anytime soon.

"I will see you downstairs. Hurry, Will, as we might have quite a cleanup on our hands."

In the bedroom, with Thomas sitting contemplatively on the bed whilst I shucked myself out of the nightshirt and into my regular clothing from earlier this evening, I could not help but feel that this all was a step backward. Yet, part of the recounting by Thomas had me confused.

"So, tell me," I asked as I slipped my shirt over my body and tucked it within my pants. "Why me? Why not your uncle Jacob? Or Joss, for that matter?"

I came to sit next to him on the bed as I proceeded to put my right shoe onto my foot. The left was more difficult, as the bedding was still strewn about the room, which required my digging around to recover it.

"I think I am not mistaken in this, am I?"

He sat watching as I reseated upon the bed next to him and went about putting the other shoe on. He hopped off and assisted me.

"No, you're not. Though, I hesitate to say why it is you."

"Whatever do you mean? You come to me out of a perceived bond of trust, and yet with the same breath you claim to withhold information because you cannot discern whether to trust me or not? Come now, Thomas. You will have to do better than that, I am afraid."

He just sat there, squatted upon one knee, and eyed me with a rather conspiratorial air, displaying a maturity far beyond his young years.

"It's because of *him*, you see," he uttered in whispered tones as he looked about the room—as if he expected someone to be listening in. The mysterious air about him seemed to crystallize in that moment. Thomas was a boy of vast layers and complications.

"He's what told me to trust you. *He* said that of them, William Hallett was the one I was to trust most, as *he* trusts you as well."

"He? He *who*? Joss, you mean. Well, of course he—" I was duly interrupted for being so far off the mark.

"Not *him*"—he looked about the room as if from the darkened recesses of my bedroom someone could spring forth and catch us both unaware—"*Lord Tiyanoga*. I know you know of whom I speak."

I became quite dizzy at the mention of the name. For a moment, the room spun. I had to fight to remain upright. Something seemed to stir within me. I knew who he referred to but could not place meeting such an individual.

Thomas seemed to realize I was under some sort of duress only when he touched the side of my face. The bed shook violently. We were all eclipsed from my bedroom only to reappear, bed and all, crashing onto the kitchen table, making a disaster of the furniture in a calamity of noise and broken wood. The moment we hit, Thomas sprang from the bed as if prodded by a hot poker, to stand about five feet away from my prone body.

Joss and Jacob came running to the doorway from the front receiving room after hearing the commotion.

"Will, when I said to hurry, I meant you could leave the bed upstairs," Joss teased as his eyes twinkled at the remnants of my bedding and kitchen table.

I allowed my eyes to relocate themselves to the back of my head, it being the best I could come up with as a retort. Yet, it did beg me to recall a time when my life was so much simpler before my maternal family, adventure in hand, had decided to come calling. My furnishings probably wished I had left things well enough alone.

"We still need to hurry, Will," Jacob added as he moved into the front room followed by a very amused Joss.

"Yes, yes. I suppose the cleanup will have to wait," I insisted as I got up from the colossal mess and moved toward the receiving room.

Once assembled there, Joss placed a hand upon my shoulder and Thomas took his place in front of his uncle Jacob and we gated to the Seneca village along the Allegheny River.

Chapter Five

Allegheny and Akwesasne

Wherein William Hallett and his staunch warrior companions assess the damage to the Seneca village of Salamanca—Little Lake.

November 1, 1847
Salamanca Seneca Village
along the Allegheny River, Akwe:kon Nation
9:55 p.m.

The wind whipped around us as we looked upon the devastation throughout the village. Joss and Jacob cast a silvery-blue lighted orb each. They hovered above our heads, illuminating a wide swath around us. We moved down from the small ravine to within the village confines in a matter of minutes. The lack of movement within the village only added to the nightmarish quality of the scene.

As we neared the center of the village, the central longhouse of traditional construction of bark skins and wooden branches stood untouched by Thomas's onslaught earlier this evening. Seemingly unrepentant of his imposed calamity upon the village, Thomas took off to the far side of it in a rush.

"She's over here," Thomas called over the rush of wind. "Come on, hurry! I thought they would be awake by now."

"The night air is ghastly." I spoke loudly, nearly making myself hoarse in the process. "It cannot be healthy for the people to be exposed to the winds like this. Can we not do something about this?"

::Actually, yes we can.::

Joss took his hands and clasped them together and blew gently into them. His action caused an incredible rippling force to billow from his hands in a cascading array of colors, completely engulfing the village. Almost at once the winds died down; however, as they slammed against Joss's efforts, a dance of light undulated over it in hues of blues, greens, and yellows not unlike the Aurora Borealis.

For a moment I lost myself to its beauty. That is, until Joss mentally goaded me that we had more pressing matters with which to attend.

::I shall make pretty lights for you later, William. As many as you wish, if it be your pleasure.::

::Yes, yes. Poke fun at the awestruck schoolboy I am. You have found me out, have you?::

::Ohnehta'kowa, I would wish it no other way.::

I chose to let it go at that point. Joss seemed to agree that I should.

About fifty feet ahead of us, there on the ground, just in front of his home, lay Thomas's mother with a blanket covering her body. While the strong winds were not life-threatening, they would surely bring on some colds for those who had collapsed out in the open. Thomas was not strong enough to haul everyone inside for comfort. He tried his best to find cover for them.

"That *is* better." I smiled. "How is it done, actually?" I asked as we came to Thomas's home.

"Bit of a trick, really. It does not prevent the wind from blustering through, but only filters it a bit and thusly slows it down a pace. The lighted effect seems to emulate the Aurora, so I can only assume it has some sort of magnetic effect that creates this slowing process, but on a pinpointed localized level."

"She is over here! I did not know what else to do, so I just went around covering up those I could not move. She will be all right, will she not?"

Joss inspected her briefly and nodded to me.

"She will be fine. You did well, Thomas. Better than most, I dare say," Joss reassured the lad.

We spent the next fifteen minutes or so getting her, and the rest of the family, settled into the home. They all appeared to be strewn about it in various states of activity when they succumbed to Thomas's rogue abilities, thus rendering them unconscious.

"We are going to need some help to get everyone sorted," I commented as I helped Joss move Thomas's grandmother back into a seated position.

"Where did Uncle Jacob move off to?" Thomas asked Joss.

I had wondered that as well but figured it would sort itself soon enough. Though a part of me could not let go that Thomas's story seemed too trite, a little too planned out for it to be a random act of violence. I chose at this juncture to keep this opinion to myself as I didn't want to raise suspicion without evidence to support the claim.

"Probably went out into the forest to search for Thor" was all he offered as he continued to work.

I nodded my understanding, but inwardly I wondered how long the rest of the cleanup would take with just the two of us to accomplish the task.

"How are we going to deal with what people have seen tonight? I mean, we cannot expect them to just ignore the sighting of the beast nor the damage done to the first few buildings at the front of the village. How are we to deal with that when they come around?"

"They are not going to come around until Thomas decides to let them wake up," Joss said calmly as he put some of the grandmother's weaving tools back into her lap.

"What do you mean? This is *Thomas's* doing as well?" I whispered as Thomas had moved into the home, probably in search of others who needed tending.

"Most certainly. Will, you have to understand that when we are called into the Guardianship the abilities become active and, until such time as you receive proper instruction, emotions often dictate how they are expended. And since emotions dictate that, it is rather safe to assume their appearance will be peppered with wild abandon or emotionally chaotic. In this case, I believe we have another *me* on our hands."

That was a bold admission on Joss's part. I was not sure what to make of it, actually. So, I decided honesty was best. "What do you mean by that?"

"I know you do not recall my being at Dartmouth with you and Jacob, but I assure you, I was there, and it was a most difficult time for me. Some rather bizarre and truly spectacular situations were caused by me, although to my credit, I had no idea what was happening. Only when Jacob made me realize I was the root cause of it all, the wild rogue activity ended and my real training with him began in earnest."

I had to admit I could not recall with any real clarity, aside from the dreams I had where he was definitely present, Joss being there. However,

I did remember rather odd situations that seemed to crop up in my next-to-last school year and how Jacob always seemed to excuse himself as soon as we received word of their occurrence. I had no idea Joss was involved in them at all.

Joss appeared uncomfortable at this deeply personal admission. I could see as well as feel it.

"So now it is up to me to be the next thorn, eh?" I inquired as I nudged him good-naturedly.

He smiled. "One can only pause in wonderment at what devastation you will wreak, *Ohnehta'kowa*," he imparted with a noticeable twinkle in his eye.

"What's with the Mohawk moniker?" I had noticed his use of it earlier, but only now, while we were relatively alone in setting Thomas's family to rights, did I choose to inquire. He only smiled and continued to work, choosing not to acknowledge my query.

::You will have to figure that one out for yourself...:: he teasingly sent to me as he made his way to the front door and stepped outside.

I caught up with him in front of the council longhouse.

"This ought to be impressive," he said to me as he took a step away from me while holding out a hand in my direction to indicate I should stay where I was standing.

He held his hand in front of his mouth as if he were blowing something unseen from his fingertips as he whispered softly: "*Kyenawa's...*"

The soft breeze from his breath billowed glowingly from his lips and took flight with a quickened pace as soon as it cleared the top of the tree line. There it dispersed like a firework into the night sky for points unknown.

He turned back to me with a soft smile on his face, as if he knew the next few moments were going to startle me.

Suddenly, trails of light came cascading through the air, growing in luminance and size. They passed through the wind barrier to land softly upon the earth, revealing what I was sure were other Guardians. Several gated within the village, while others seemed to prefer the showier arrival. In all, close to thirty Guardians assembled.

"That was truly most spectacular!" I called out to Joss who beamed at my exuberance.

"Thanks, my brothers and sisters. It appears we have a rogue on our hands: Thomas Jemison. Please see to the people of the village and let us put a twister of some sort in their minds to account for the damage to the buildings and such, as I get Thomas to release them from their stupor."

They all broke off into smaller groups to complete the task. With so many at hand, the cleanup was going to happen far quicker than I had imagined.

I moved with Joss back toward the Jemison home when it occurred to me, I had no idea what he meant by *putting a twister* in their minds.

"What image will they communally put into their waking minds of what occurred here? I mean so much could go wrong in the telling. Will they not compare what they saw with one another?"

"And how many people have ever agreed on every small detail of a calamity, William? Each person carries their own version of the same tale, homing in upon that which most caught their attention. It will be no different here. The Guardians know that. This is not the first, nor will it be the last time, we have done this."

I had to see his point. As long as they all agreed on a twister touching down upon the town, the particulars would be debated for some time, but would soon fade into the consciousness of the town's collective memory, with smaller details becoming blurred with the passage of time.

"So now what?"

"Now is the harder part: convincing Thomas of his continuing part in all of this."

I did not envy Joss in this. I could only hope whatever small trust he placed upon me would give him some comfort that he was not in this alone. I would be here to help him through it as best I could. Despite my abrasive introduction to his family, I had to appreciate their predicament and could admit that, given the same set of circumstances, I too would probably be equally as pressing to gain my nephew's safe return.

As we made our way to the front of the home, we saw to our left Jacob had returned carrying Thor, which was quite a feat. Thor easily bested Jacob by one or two inches in height, and by several pounds. We adjusted our course momentarily. I guessed Thomas's little set-to would have to wait a while longer.

"How bad is he, Jacob?" Joss asked as he ran to assist his former teacher.

"Bad enough that he is not healing as cleanly as I would like."

They carried him to the doorway as I held the door open. Once inside, we moved him to the simple rope bed along the side of the wall. Thomas came, and his eyes widened when he saw how pale and withdrawn his uncle Thor had become. To see Thor, a large and towering figure of a man, in such a sorry state was very disconcerting to the lad who clearly admired him.

"Is he dead? How bad is it?" Thomas began to ask, the tension in his voice rising with each word he spoke.

"Calm yourself, Thomas," Jacob said. "I will admit he looks rather bad now, but he will recover. Our Guardian abilities assist us in healing very quickly. You too will be able to do this once you are fully trained."

Joss called for the lad.

"Thomas, I need to talk to you for a moment. It is rather important that you pay attention to what I am saying, as it concerns you and the people you see around you."

At this, Thomas diverted his whole attention to Joss. His eyes remained wide with anticipation; evidently, he correctly thought he had caused more damage than he had initially ascertained. We pulled Thomas to the fireplace as Joss started to build the kindling and wood for a new fire, as the house had become quite cool.

"Thomas, did you not think it odd that after so long an absence no one, including your mother and your family, has come around?"

Thomas contemplated this and looked about. He took note of his mother and grandmother before casting his eyes further back into the home to the extended family he had grown up with, the enormity of everyone he knew and loved still unconscious in their home and how it all could be related to him. A realization crept upon his countenance.

"You mean *I* am the one keeping them asleep?"

"That is exactly what I am coming to, Thomas. You need to release them from the sleep you have them under. We have other Guardians modifying their memories to cloud them from the creature you unleashed upon the town. They will think it nothing more than a freakish accident concerning a twister that developed from out of nowhere. So, your monster will not have existed as far as they are concerned. But to complete the process, you need to let them wake up. It has to be by you. Until you release them, they will remain exactly as you see them now."

"But what if their memories come back to them? What if some of them do remember it was me?"

I decided to sit next to the hearth and console Thomas.

"Thomas, to them they have no way to connect what they truly saw with you. Only *you* know about that connection."

Jacob finally joined us.

"Thor will be fine after a few days' rest. His wounds are healing now at the normal rate. He suffered a punctured lung and some bruises that will surely hurt for a few hours or so after he awakes."

Thomas looked relieved. He moved over to his uncle who was still as if in peaceful slumber, save for the bloodied hole in his clothing that appeared to lash his right side along his ribs. Thomas sat on the side of the bed and then leaned into his uncle's uninjured side, placing his head against his shoulder for several minutes—a debate going on inside him. Then he sat up, a resolute expression upon his face.

"What do I need to do?"

The wood was set alight by Joss blowing upon it. It was clear he was extremely talented with his preternatural gifts, but I could also see signs of his showing off.

::Was that for my benefit?::

He smiled only briefly before bringing his expression to focus upon Thomas.

"It is rather simple actually. Your abilities right now are being guided by your emotional state regardless of how you might be trying to control them with your mind. We are emotional creatures, Thomas; there is no shame in that. But you have to take responsibility for it. Your brotherhood within the Guardianship is handling the smaller particulars with the village now. But the rest is up to you. To allow them to wake up you need to just let go of your fears of reprisal. But you need to wait for a moment as we need to populate the others in your family here to allow them to think they all witnessed a twister instead of your imaginary creature."

He nodded, and Joss and Jacob moved about the family and whispered into their ears. Their eyes fluttered and rolled around as if in a deep guided dream. A few of them mumbled something back to Joss when he spoke to Thomas's elder brothers.

"Pay that no mind. Sometimes, it does elicit a nonsensical response. Very like talking in your sleep."

After they had returned to the front room, Joss nodded to Thomas that he could proceed.

"But what of Uncle Thor?"

"It will not work on a fellow Guardian, but then there is little to hide from him now, is there?"

"Thomas, I will take William and the other Guardians to the outlying areas of the village into the forest before we all return back from whence we came. However, Jacob will remain here for a few moments to work out your going to Akwesasne in the next few days for your formal acceptance into the Guardianship and your assignment to a mentor. Do you understand?"

Thomas nodded that he was fine with the arrangement. Joss moved toward him and placed a hand upon his shoulder with such kindness in his manner I was warmed by the sight of it.

"Your days ahead will be both wondrous and terrifying. Take each lesson carefully and apply yourself. Heed what your mentor tells you and I know you will do well. Your fellow Guardians await your joining us."

He looked from Joss to Jacob, and then lastly his gaze settled upon me.

"But what of Tessa, Marc, and Jonathan?"

Joss took a deep breath and looked into Thomas's eyes before answering, "I will find them. I swear it to you, Thomas. It may take me a short while, but I will be successful."

How he could make such a claim, I was uncertain. I had to trust that if he thought he could do it, then he must be sure of his abilities to do so.

We moved out of the home, leaving Jacob to handle the Jemisons when they came to. He informed us he would gate back to my house in Manhattan as soon as he completed his efforts here. I told him to make himself at home when he arrived. We would clear up the kitchen in the morning.

Joss whistled loudly into the night air, and those who had completed their work already were standing in front of the longhouse waiting for further instruction. Joss's call brought the few others who had not made their way out into the village from their respective assignments.

"Everything proceed without incident?" he asked the collected Guardians.

"What happened here?" asked one of the Guardians, an Oneida by the looks of him, though in the cover of night it was hard to tell.

"Thomas Jemison is active now. Jacob will take care of it with the Central. Go back to your previous assignments. Thank you for the assistance. It would have gone much longer without your help."

They all began to gate to other destinations, some of them departing almost immediately while others followed Joss and me as we made our way out of the village. As we reached the forest, Joss turned slightly to me and held his hand out. I took it with little in the way of thought, and within the next step we landed upon the upper floor of my home.

I shook my head as he released my hand and chuckled to himself over my still being amazed at the gating process.

"Does it ever get boring? You know, the gating to and from place to place," I inquired as a knock happened upon my door.

I stopped to take in Joss, slightly alarmed at an intrusion so late in the hour. I made my way to the door with Joss close on my heels and peered into the peephole that had become all the rage of late. I was thoroughly glad for its installation now. A weathered man stood there, of fifty or sixty years in age. I did not think an intruder would identify himself first if the ransacking of my home had been his call, so I turned to Joss and shook my head to indicate he need not worry and opened the door.

"Message for you, sir." He handed the message over, and I gave him a copper or two.

"Who is it from?" Joss asked. I cracked the family seal, knowing it was probably from Rebecca, given the lateness of the hour and how only she would not take into consideration my sleeping schedule if the message was urgent enough.

"It is from Rebecca. She wants to bring someone with her when she arrives here tomorrow night. Blast! I completely let slip from my mind the meeting I set with her until now." I turned to Joss. "No doubt due to the fact you seem to keep scrambling my brains about."

"I did no such thing. I merely—" I held a hand up to him to stall a protest that required no protestation. I knew the reasons Joss did what he did, with the end result being I was unsure how many more of these little surprises, Miss Covington's soirée chief amongst them, would reveal themselves now my memories were returning.

"Well, in either event, it appears I will have more than Rebecca to contend with tomorrow eve."

"She is coming here?"

I nodded at Joss's inquiry. We *both* knew what that meant.

"I better warn Jacob."

I got the most devilish smirk to snake upon my lips. "No, you will not. I think it high time those two mend their ways. You know and I know there were never two more matched hellcats. They are both just too stubborn over their breakup to deal with it." I turned fully to see Joss stall a smile at my plan.

"It would be brilliant to be there when they meet up again after—how long has it been?"

"Two years, one month, and—" I glanced at my calendar on the desk and quickly completed the math. "—fourteen days. But who would count such a number?"

We both paused, gleeful wicked boys that we were.

"Come now, let us see what damage has been wrought since we have to put it to rights before they all arrive tomorrow."

We took the stairs when Joss, who read the missive from my sister, asked, "Do you have any idea who this other person is? Could it be a suitor?"

I turned on the spot and sat upon the stair in the middle of the staircase.

"Would that not take it all?" I beamed.

He touched upon my nose, and such a brilliant warmth radiated there I longed for it to continue.

"You are enjoying this far too much. She has always relied upon you to have her back and she you."

"I know. That is what makes this whole suitor thing so delicious. I cannot wait to see how poor Jacob will fare."

He nudged me up from where I had taken a seat, and we proceeded into the thrashed remnants of my bedroom.

I moved into my now barren room. He stopped in the doorway as I moved into the room to collect my nightshirt and dressing robe from a nearby chair.

"But to your earlier question regarding the sensation of gating"—which I had completely forgotten I had inquired about—"the simplest answer is: eventually. I assume it loses something over time. As for myself, I am still amazed by it all."

"Really? You do not seem to be as captivated by it as I am."

"That is only because you are comparing it to your own emotions. You know where else to look."

I did. Though I just could not find myself to move as easily along the link between us as Joss could.

He leaned against the doorway with a slight smile upon his face and placed the message from my sister onto the desk nearest the door.

"So, are you planning to sleep upon the floor, or will you nest down in the kitchen?"

"Just be glad the bed I have in your room is large enough for us both. You will just have a bed mate until we can rectify the situation downstairs."

"I could always sleep on your sofa in the receiving room, Will."

"Certainly not. If I am anything, I am a superb host. I will not have you attempting to recline on a sofa that is barely sufficient to sit upon, let alone gain some much-needed rest."

"Fancy little Indian, are you not?" He indicated the quality of my nightshirt and dressing robe.

"I walk in two worlds now; allow me my fashionable proclivities," I replied as I began to change out of my clothing and into the nightshirt. For a few moments he stood there shaking his head and smirking at my nightly routine, though I did detect a blush moving across his face as I got down to my undergarments. As I pulled my shirt over my head, I noted he had slipped into the spare bedroom.

I carried the nightshirt and robe over to the spare room to join him as he began to slip off his leggings and mocs. After he shucked his shirt, I paused to appreciate the simple utility of the Haudenosaunee male wardrobe. Moments later, Joss changed from the comfort of his daily outfit into a simple loincloth suitable for sleeping, and here I struggled with overgarments, shirts, pants, undergarments, and various pieces that served only as ornamentation. I began to question for the first time the intelligence of my way of dress.

::But you wear your clothing so well. I do not judge your choice of them. This is simply what I know and have grown comfortable using. Why are you curious as to our way of dress?::

::Well, I suppose I should gain a better understanding of our people's ways. I feel I know so little about my Mohawk life. I assume I can lean on you for that. Unless you find me a lost cause.::

::Will, have no doubt. You are Mohawk; your lineage is clear. You just have not had much in the way of guidance in our way of life. You can always turn to me for that.::

"Thank you. I cannot tell you how much that means to me. Since I came into this whole new world of the Guardians and Flintlings, I have felt little more than a leaf upon the raging river, with little hope of purchase with which to grant me some sense of security. You have provided the security I desperately need."

"Wait here..." He gated out of the room, though to where, simply wearing his loincloth for protection against the elements, was beyond me. I did not have to wait long as he returned within a few moments with a beaded side bag in his hand. He threw it upon the bed and began to rummage through it. He extracted a beaded belt and a tightly rolled piece of blood-red cloth.

"Get out of that precious royal swaddling you have encased yourself in," he chided me as he unrolled the cloth, revealing it to be about the length of the loincloth he was wearing. I realized he had retrieved his spare clothing, though from where I was uncertain.

Reading my musings, he replied, "I have spare clothing set aside in various places. I can retrieve them when needs arise. These shall be yours now." He indicated the bag on the bed as much as the belt and loincloth he held.

"Oh, Joss..." I gasped, filled with awe at his offering, knowing that to refuse would deeply mar our new relationship. Not something I was willing to risk, given our being inextricably bound to each other.

Forgetting my near nakedness, I knelt upon the bed, running gentle fingers over them, and watched as he completed the folding around the back of the belt. A small smile broke over his face, bringing his eyes to light. Clearly, he was most happy in his offering. I only wished I had something to offer in exchange. As if hearing my thoughts, he had a reply.

"Just your wearing it will be more than enough," he murmured as he handed me the garment. "Come, let us have you try it on."

"I am afraid you will have to help me out a bit."

Shortly thereafter, I found myself wearing my first Mohawk loincloth. My slightly burnished alabaster skin, with a dusting of freckles along my muscular shoulders that mellow as they wend their way over my bare torso, standing in stark contrast to the rich colored fabric of the loincloth.

He placed two gentle hands on my shoulders as we regarded my reflection in the mirror. I felt him course along our link with such gratitude and care that I was undone by his gesture.

Joss beamed, watching me take root in my heritage, pleased he could do this for me. After sheathing myself in some of the finest material and clothing the world could offer, I was amazed at how much comfort, both in movement and luxury, this simple natural garment afforded me.

He pulled out the leggings, a pair of mocs, and a shirt. After another few moments, I was fully clothed in my maternal heritage clothing. A sense of pride seemed to swell within me that I had not anticipated. I nearly wept from the sensation. I know Joss did not miss my eyes misting up from the transformation at his hands.

"Joss, I never knew just how comfortable these really are."

"You wear them well; as if you were born to them," he added with a bright grin, no doubt pleased with himself.

I paused, turning this way and that, before bringing Joss into a tight embrace, so thankful for his offering. He moved his head from my shoulder to place my forehead against his, his hands on either side of my face, gently holding me there.

::Like this, Ohnehta'kowa. When it matters most, this is how we share that moment.::

I nodded, thankful for his teaching and his generosity. I knew, being so linked with him, our intimacy would be something I needed to embrace and let flow. It was a part of who we are. If I were truly honest, I longed for it to go on into the night; spending this singular touching moment with him and to share it thusly shattered what I knew about myself and the world around me. Joss sensed this and gradually broke contact between us. I felt bewildered and in a slight stupor for the loss of him. I needed to regroup.

"Yes, well, now to bed, eh?"

After a few minutes, with Joss lending a hand, helping me remove the leggings, the only part I would have to learn how to master on my own someday, I was soon down to a matching loincloth, feeling in a far better mood to seek some rest.

"It is amazing to me how close we are in size that we can wear each other's clothes, even down to our shoe size. Do you not think?"

"Almost as if it were deigned to be so," he commented again with a twinge of awe in his voice. Words concerning the relationship Joss and I began to share moved about me, though who said them and why I could not grasp, try as I might. But it seemed to take root in what Joss expressed and I did not know what to do about it. So, I tried something else.

"Joss, may I ask you something? Do tell me if it is too personal to speak upon, will you?"

He nodded and a trace of concern moved across his eyes.

"What does it feel like? The *conjuring*...I mean."

His eyes widened, then softened at the subject. Obviously, he was fearing something else altogether, though what that might be, I really could not say. He seemed to possess certain skills in keeping things from me.

"It is not *conjuring*, William, though I suppose, from your perspective, it might appear so. Conjuring, at least to my mind anyway, implies forcing something along unnaturally, bending something to your will. I do nothing of the sort. Do you understand the difference?"

I nodded, though to be quite frank, I really did not understand at all. I supposed he read this confluence of thoughts in the manner of my expression for he pressed forward as if I did not understand him.

"First off, when you come into your Guardian abilities, your vision changes. You can see connectivity everywhere. We talk about it as a people—it is part of our way of life. But to truly see it in all of its wonderment and radiant expression is breathtaking. Would you like me to show you a bit of it? I think I can across our link."

I nodded, unsure of what to expect. The night had brought about so many revelations. To be able to see the universe how Joss and Jacob saw it, nay, that is a gift I would not turn down whenever offered.

He motioned that we should take our places along the headboard. Me against it, with him facing me, sort of straddling my legs outside of the bedding. We were close enough I could feel the heat radiating off his bare torso in wave after wave, billowing about my chest, warming me thoroughly to the point where I did not think I needed bedding at all tonight.

He brought up his hands to the sides of my face so we could lean our foreheads together. Only this time, his instructions to me were quite different.

"Keep your eyes open. Stare into mine. It is the only way I can think of passing this sort of vision to you."

I nodded, ready for just about anything to happen. I steeled myself to his gaze, those dark-brown pools that begged me to swim in.

::Concentrate, Ohnehta'kowa. Do not let your mind wander. I feel when this happens it will be abrupt and completely disorienting for you.::

I was on the point of replying when his eyes flashed brilliant amber and my green eyes caught light as if an energy bolt had passed from his gaze to mine. I weaved about a bit. His hands moved from my face to my shoulders.

"Take it easy, Will. Try to remain calm and composed. It is very overwhelming the first time you feel it. Close your eyes for a moment and gather your breathing. Wait until you can breathe normally before you open them again. No cheating the moment, either."

I did as he bade me, taking time to steady myself and my breathing.

"All right, I think I have it now."

::Slowly, Ohnehta'kowa, slow-ly.::

I gradually opened my eyes and could not believe what I beheld. Everything seemed to light up; colors expressed themselves across the rainbow in every facet of my room, the walls, the bedding, Joss.

I audibly gasped, marveling at the air being drawn into me in a light of bluish mist, though did my very best to remain calm in the face of such majesty. This was science; this was what I had struggled to conceptualize in the midst of all those textbooks and lectures.

"You are seeing everything, the connectivity of life. Bacteria, cell division, everything that makes up life and even in the inanimate objects in our world. Everything we ever studied in school, every lecture points to this—what you are seeing now."

If I squinted harder, I found I could press my vision further and actually see into objects. Joss's blood flowing, little lights flickering across his head—under his scalp—as if his thoughts caused little storms here and there. The electricity of it all. Watching the vitality of life all around me in its myriad of colors and movements left me in wondrous awe, as a child beholding the magic in it all, the adult knowing this was the foundation of science at work. It was one of the greatest gifts Joss had ever or would ever give me—even if I only borrowed it for a while.

He let me slip from the bed but stayed close as I wandered the halls and rooms. The root cellar was a cornucopia of life and scientific expression that would remain with me every time I used it to store food and other items requiring its cold damp quarters for their care. Thirty or so minutes later we returned to the spare bed, and Joss reversed the process, leaving me feeling like a blind man who saw for a brief while, only to have it taken away again. I sensed Joss's anguish at feeling the need to take it from me.

"We still do not know if it will be your path yet or not. A great many things are still a mystery about you, William. What I have shared with you may be infinitesimal in scope to what lies ahead for you and your own journey. We simply do not know where Spruce is heading with all of this."

"You think he is the root of what is transpiring between us?" I had to ask because up until now, the only person I could link this to was Tiyanoga, and I was not too sure if it was a good place to start putting my eggs in that questionable basket.

We settled back into bed, side by side sitting up against the headboard, and he continued to pursue my original question regarding conjuring.

"Now you have seen the connectedness in life, when you inquire about what we do as conjuring, I hope you can see why, as a people, we do not conjure. It would go against that connectivity we see around us. So, we have to find another way. Think of it as more of a concept you have to visualize in your mind. You recall how we studied scientific concepts in school? Well, it is much more along those lines. You must see it in its entirety for it to manifest itself. A to Zed, so to speak. It is quite a bit to grapple with the first time you make the attempt. So much can go wrong."

My brow furrowed for I had not thought of my science classes manifesting themselves in this sort of application.

"To have something happen from the *Dark* you have to visualize what you want from the smallest level outward. Since it comes from your own mind and you do not have to write it down or say anything in particular to vocalize your intent, unless it helps you solidify what you are after, it all happens rather quickly, to be honest. But you *do* have to maintain concentration throughout its formation."

He held up his finger in front of us as if there were a piece of slate with which to elaborate upon.

"It goes like this. To write"—he began to move his finger along the air, writing the word *create* upon it, and the word materialized out of thin air in a blaze of fiery orange lines—"you simply have to think about the tip of your finger causing friction upon the air. Once the air catches light, you have to think about the formation of those movements. Not forcefully, but gently prod them along to keep them active. In the case of this word, *create*, I envisage each letter in my mind and the letters remain floating in the air because I have ignited the molecules of air along the lines traced with my finger. To remove it all I need do is banish the thought."

The word faded upon the air and was gone.

"But I have seen you perform some extraordinary effects like when you shield us from attack."

"Ah, that one is much harder but is part of our basic training and really no different in principle than the one I just demonstrated. Actually, shielding is one of the first complex abilities we Guardians learn to master as our continued safety heavily depends upon it. Essentially, you have to conceptualize on tightening everything in front of you."

I gifted him with a slightly exasperated look regarding his simple, if slightly inane, explanation.

He laughed at my consternation.

"Will, you are not thinking anything different from when I first had to learn these abilities. But when you use them as a Guardian, you begin to sense them all around you. It actually supports our position that everything is connected. If you are manipulating the Dark in some way, you are only borrowing that energy and transmuting it into something for your purposes."

"How is that different from conjuring, or bending it to your will? Sounds pretty much the same, if you ask me."

"Hmmm, I see your point. But there *is* a difference, if only slightly so. Conjure is forced, as if there is no choice in the matter. When you conjure, you are ripping into the essence of what is there and taking what you will with little regard for what state you leave it in or to what end it was used. Whereas, what we Guardians do is to change properties momentarily but release it back to its proper form. We manipulate the Dark only to what extent is necessary."

"But the word you just created"—I flitted my finger mockingly in the air—"would that not be considered a waste?"

"You would think so, but not really. When I lit the air with the word *create,* I was charging the air in a particular manner. The energy did not go anywhere...merely changed form. When I was done, I released it to its original state. Nothing was lost in the process. There is quite a bit more to it all, but essentially that is *how* we do *what* we do. What I have explained to you is how I have sorted it out over a great many lonely days and nights honing my abilities and logging down the results and my thoughts regarding them in my journal. Though there are two thoughts on the matter. The Jemisons are of another mind on the subject altogether. For them, it is divinely given by Spruce and therefore relegated to the supernatural. For me, I see it more as an extension of science. I just get to apply some rather complex concepts I dream up in my mind and make them play out in the physical world. For the two years I wandered the countryside of our nation, I spent a great deal of time perfecting my craft, but more importantly, I journalized all of the actions and reactions to what I put out there. A series of experiments all meticulously categorized and diagramed so we can gain a better understanding of what Spruce truly gifted us with as a means to stop Flint and his Flintlings from running amok."

"Is that not tantamount to playing God?"

"That presumes I am attempting to control and dominate what I can manipulate. I do not. I change its properties; that is all. Harmony at all costs. It is harder than it sounds."

I wanted to comment further upon it, but a yawn caught my throat at that precise moment.

"Bed...?"

As I had little energy left, all I could do was to nod in agreement. Within minutes of my head hitting the pillow, I slipped to the darkness of sleep—beyond the vale of dreams—or so I thought.

My grandmother turned the page of the small novel. She did not appear as if the story held her attention much as her eyes barely scanned the words on the page. Something else this night was pulling focus away from the trials and tribulations of Miss Elizabeth Bennet and her adversarial romance with Mr. Fitzwilliam Darcy.

A flash of lightning cascaded about the room from the tall two-story windows of the library of our family home. Within a few seconds the roll of thunder rattled those very same windows. Grandmama did not appear to be fazed by the storm.

A sudden loud creak emanated from the roof. It drew her eyes and ears to it, alert for anything further. However, with the storm it was hard to glean the subtle differences between the thunder and any other ominous intrusions.

Nervous energy seemed to propel her from her seat. She moved away from the Chesterfield to one of the seven windows interceded by a tall bank of books that lined the library walls. As she approached a window midway the length of the room, the sounds appeared to be divided—one to the roofline and any other odd creaks and unusual noises in the house, the other was...well, elsewhere.

"Oh, James...were that you were here, my love. You would know what to do," she murmured to herself.

She sighed as her thoughts came back to the present. A worrisome smile crept across her lips, for in that brief moment she allowed her mind to wander aimlessly through the milestones of her life. Then she snapped out of her reverie, her eyes focused outward across the East River. Beyond she could scarcely make out the silhouette of Blackwell's Island.

She moved along the room, stopping at each window and peering out into the darkness, ever searching for something amiss. She rotated the wedding ring suspended on the chain around her neck—a nervous habit. Her unease was evident.

A knock on the library door nearly made her jump as the maid entered. She was a slightly pudgy woman, with a round plump face but as kind a heart as you would find on anyone.

"Madam, the children are safely tucked away in their beds as instructed. Will there be anything else before I turn in?"

"No, thank you, Renee. You may turn in. I will see to it that this room is secured before I go to bed. Just want to finish my novel before I retire." She waved a hand in the book's general direction but did not bother to spend the effort of glancing at it.

Renee's eyes glanced to the unopened, abandoned book on the small side table. Her mouth crooked slightly, and she raised an eyebrow but seemed to know better than to say anything.

"Very well, good night then, madam."

"Yes, yes," she added, waving her off and out of the room without so much as a glance in her direction. Her eyes were riveted to the thicket of woods behind the house. With the last flash of lightning she seemed to think she spied someone standing at the property's boundary.

As the door of the library closed, Elizabeth moved slowly down the length of the room to the far window facing the back of the home. Another flash and roll of thunder pounded upon the manor. She moved purposefully to her goal. Her reflection briefly shone in each rippled pane of glass as she moved to the other end of the room. Reaching the far window, she focused her gaze with eagle-like precision. She scanned the tree line as if she had some ability to see into the shrouded grove of trees, revealing their darkened secrets with a preternatural stare.

Another brilliant cast of blue-white light pulsed into the room with the thunder pounding upon the roof of the house moments later as if God himself were knocking and requesting entrance. Still, even that did not alter her gaze. Her eyes widened ever so slightly for in that brief light she saw him. There amongst the trees, tucked just far enough from the light. But the silhouette was unmistakable.

"Samuel! Thank the creator..." she whispered to herself. She lifted her hand as if to motion to him to enter when she seemed to hear something that no one else could.

Whatever or whoever caught her attention, whatever they did or said stopped her cold, as if whatever she heard equated to a hand upon hers, stilling her actions. Every part of her began to tense as if ready to spring for a fight. She nodded once slowly, almost imperceptibly, that the meaning of whatever was relayed to her was well received.

A subtle change came over her. Instead of a slight tremor of fear threading through her, she seemed to take a breath to collect herself, and the serenity and confident peace, hallmarks of her character, came over her.

She quietly changed tactics, no doubt hoping to throw the others watching off guard and went about sealing the room. She closed the drapes and moved down the length of the room, going through the routine motions of closing the house for the night. She hoped whoever lay out there with Samuel would think she was unaware of their presence.

It took every fiber of her being to move about slowly and deliberately as if no danger lay pressing upon her. After the last drapery closed off the room to the outside, she moved a bit quicker. She made her way over to the book on the small side table and picked it up, all the while her attention returned to listening for noises both internal and external to the home. With the calamity of the raging storm, it was a bit difficult.

She clasped the wedding ring on the necklace around her neck and concentrated intently, trying to reach out to Samuel watching over the house. Her gaze scanned the room in that way when someone is very near to and whispering something dangerous into your ear, and you want to check the room for any who might overhear. Something akin to a queer shared secret.

A moment later and seven warriors appeared in the confines of the room, each dripping with the wetness of the storm. Steam spiraled off their broad torsos from the sudden change in temperature; the soft lamp light played off defined muscles. From the looks of them, a trio appeared. Mohawk men she seemed to recognize, followed by two Seneca, evident by their complex tattooed torsos, and two Oneida. If she knew any of the others, she did not outwardly show it.

A moment later an older Mohawk man appeared. He was fully clothed in the fashion of the day. His deep rust-colored Garrick redingote cut a sweeping romantic figure in the room.

She ran to him, the rustle of her full dark skirt breaking the silence of the room. She embraced him wholeheartedly, not caring at all for the wetness of his clothing or the other Guardians in the room.

"Not now, dearest," he whispered in her ear. "The children first. They are in danger. Who knew my grandmother's wampum belt would be so accurate?" He turned his attention to the others in the room. "Marcus? Geoff? Second floor, the nursery is the middle door on the right. Stand guard there; we will join you shortly. Go silently, draw no attention to yourselves."

The two nodded briefly before they vanished from sight, leaving only a wisp of their former selves that faded within a few seconds of their departure.

Five strikingly impressive young warriors stood stoically, but she could sense the power at their command. These were no mere Guardian warriors; they were the adept of that warrior sect. Their presence filled the vast room.

"Any idea who?" Elizabeth asked the older warrior as she surveyed the remaining Guardian contingency on hand.

"The she-witch Tituba, who else? Henry, take Ati'ron and Atená:ti with you and make your stand on the third floor as we discussed. Go quietly."

The three of them slipped away, leaving two who simply nodded and departed for the back of the home near the kitchen.

"We knew it might come to this. Are you going to be all right?" Samuel asked once he and Elizabeth were alone. A drop of rain fell from the brim of his hat onto his nose, and they both smiled for a moment.

"It is what I trained for, is it not?" she remarked, not looking into his eyes. It was too hard facing the precariousness of the moment. Instead she busied herself with brushing a few droplets of rain from his redingote. He drew her focus to his eye by lifting her chin with his right finger. Her eyes were misty in the candlelight.

"But it has been many years since you have had to put that training to the test. It is one thing to prepare and quite another to put it into practice."

"They are my grandchildren, from my only son. This old lioness will give them such a fight, the likes they have never seen."

"That is the Elizabeth I love."

A bittersweet smile broke across his face. How long he had regretted letting Elizabeth slip from his life. But he had his Guardian duties to attend to; after their parting she had built a life here in the home of a prominent family whose very name was a point on the map of New York. Only now, after she became a widow and a respectable period of mourning, had they rekindled their romance—albeit slowly, quietly.

"Samuel, why now? What spurned it on so?"

"Who knows why she does what she does? Maybe she is being ordered to do so? In either event, sending her along it is clear Flint's horde is bent upon taking the children. But at what cost?"

"Let them come and try." A fire burned in the back of her eyes. Samuel brushed a wisp of hair from her face that had escaped her delicate coif. How her defiance only made her more radiantly beautiful. It cut him more deeply and profoundly at this moment. It was not lost upon him that this was going to be a fight, and though equal in numbers he had to admit Elizabeth had not near as much training in dealing with one of Flint's greatest warriors. The outcome could spell death for any of them, not the least of whom were the children themselves. He knew the stakes were that high.

His greatest fear was if Tituba and her retinue could not extract the children, then they might be on order to kill them. Neither of which would be a simple thing to subvert.

A tug as if someone had pulled at his coat sleeve caught his attention.

"It seems we have run out of time. The gloves have come off. They have entered the home. Come now." He kissed her forehead briefly before they parted.

He slipped from the room with lightning speed, pleased she had remembered how to slip-run and had followed. Within a matter of a few seconds they appeared in the center of the nursery. The room was silent and undisturbed. Elizabeth scanned the room. Where were Marcus and Geoff? Samuel seemed to sense Elizabeth's apprehension upon entering the abandoned nursery.

::They are here. It is a new tactic we have developed. It is how we keep watch over the home but do not draw attention to ourselves. Not too unlike the light trick Flint's warriors use.::

For a moment they stood in the nursery. All seemed as it should be. Then a small wooden toy on wheels began to move as if pushed along by an unseen finger. At first it was so slow one might have missed it. But then it picked up speed and flung itself across the room where it suddenly caught fire and spun into a brilliant cast of flame and sparks about the room. All at once chaos seemed to rain down upon them. Like some venomous spider moving in for the kill, Tituba descended from the roof line and landed with a thunderous clap. Not a haggard piece of female flesh as Elizabeth might expect from one so old, she was radiantly beautiful, wrapped in a shroud of undulating black clouds. Her luminescent skin cast a cold blue hue to the room. She spared little time moving toward the children.

At precisely the same moment of her arrival, the two warriors slipped as if out of thin air to guard over the nursery beds. A wall of amber luminance engulfed the alcove and the beds, sealing the children and the two warriors who stood ready to take her on directly. Marcus and Geoff simultaneously took a stance poised to pounce into the fray if warranted. Samuel wasted no time in pulling punches. From his position near the doorway, he lashed out at her with a blast of power he seemed to call from the very air itself and hit her fully in the back. She lunged forward before spinning on the spot, and with a shimmer of silver metallic flash she countered with a volley of energy directed at the two of them.

Elizabeth slipped from the doorway in time to miss the blast, but Samuel was not so lucky. It hit him square in the chest and threw him across the hallway through the facing door and into that room before he landed squarely upon the floor in a heap of wood and the volume of his coat. Elizabeth took the moment of calamity to put herself between Tituba and the two Guardians. She realized the best thing she could do to help Samuel was to draw the witch's attention.

"Come for my grandchildren, have you? Well, witch, do your best."

"Little one, you are no match for my kind. I was tormenting Guardians well before you were born. The Salem trials were but a dalliance on my part. Even your Guardian abilities cannot make up for the centuries I have had to develop mine. Stand aside and I shall spare your life.”

“My life is full. I have nothing to lose but the children. And make no mistake, I will not go quietly. So, do your best.”

Tituba stopped and tilted her head for a moment as if to gauge her words more fully.

“My best, eh?” And with that she slipped from sight completely, leaving another in her wake.

Elizabeth’s heart nearly stopped cold. For standing there, in the very same clothes she had worn when last she laid eyes upon her, was her daughter-in-law. What could she have to do with this witch’s attack upon her own children?

“Rose, nay, it cannot be you.”

“Can’t it now, Mother? Did you really think I wouldn’t come back for them?”

Elizabeth’s mind raced. How was this at all possible? Before she could ask, a crackle of debris told her Sam had survived the blast.

A cacophonous crash came winding its way up into the nursery from downstairs. The others were becoming engaged in battle. She could hear various items being cast about the house along with the other Guardians defending the home as best they could. A scream came from downstairs. Obviously, the melee had woken Renee, her maid.

“But you are...?”

“Dead, gone, which would it be, Mother? Which would be more expedient for you to assume control over my children’s lives?” Rose spat her words as she paced slowly back and forth as if circling the defenses the three of them had put up between her and her goal.

“Their lives...? Rose, this is not you. You know I have only cared for them as a grandmother should. John has not been the same since you disappeared. None of this makes any sense. What kind of mother could abandon her children for six months?”

“Six?”

That last seemed to throw her. She obviously had not realized it had been so long since she had seen them last.

“Yes, Rose. Six months. They never stopped asking for you. You cannot imagine the amount of grief John has endured in your absence.”

She thought she was getting somewhere with Rose. Her words seemed to have stopped her progress to take the kids.

In the distance Elizabeth could sense Samuel recovering from the attack and returning to the fight.

::Do not be deceived, dearest, she is not who she appears to be. Look closer. You will find she is not the daughter-in-law you knew. Be prepared to do what I taught you.::

Samuel was right. She focused her eyes closer upon her daughter-in-law and noticed there were differences in her appearance that could not be explained away. Her skin was mottled and gray in hue. As if her corpse had been revived and brought forth to cause confusion. She also noted that the visage of her daughter-in-law was carrying the same small silver stiletto about six inches in length that was of a dark but highly polished metal. Sigils appeared to luminesce about the length of the shaft. Rose stopped her pacing and noted what had captured her mother-in-law's gaze so intently. Her voice rasped with a soft and maniacal laugh, as if something darkly secret was about to be revealed.

"Noted that, have you? Well, old hag, it's my ticket to my children."

She lashed out at Elizabeth with a stream of icy blue light that should have taken her out. Instead the other Guardians had pushed their defenses to envelop her. The blast hit the shield and radiated about the room, singeing the walls and various items of furniture and toys. The room shook with the blast, but the shield held.

"Do not worry, Elizabeth, they cannot get in. Marcus and I have been perfecting this manner of defense all summer. It seems to be tied to our bodies; so as long as we live and breathe the shield will repel whatever they throw at us. We are fairly invincible," Geoff added aloud over the din of the attack, choosing this moment to launch an attack of his own.

"No, Geoff!" Samuel yelled from the other side as he attacked Rose and engaged her directly, drawing her line of fire to defend herself.

Geoff already succeeded in knocking her about the room. She was becoming unbalanced from the physicality of the fight. She obviously was not as well trained. Her talents with Flint's silver device was not as thorough as she let on. She attempted several attacks of her own, but he was able to deflect them easily enough as though he were merely swatting flies while continuing to assault her.

Geoff turned his attention to Samuel, not fully realizing what line he had crossed that should alarm the Central so. He had not long to wait before he realized the damage his deeds caused. Within the next instant Tituba had made her reappearance, only this time she appeared within the confines of the shielded area, shocking all three of them. She appeared to be neither here nor there. Her whole visage vibrated and flickered as if she had one foot planted in this world and the other in another realm unseen.

Tituba moved with all haste in attacking Marcus, the closest of the three Guardians. Her form fluttered in and out of existence. It was hard to tell what she was up to. Only when Marcus screamed in absolute agony and Tituba's form seemed to become more solid did they observe her right arm was firmly embedded in Marcus's chest. Blood spurted from his mouth, and the shield began to collapse under the direct assault of his body.

Geoff spared no time reaching Tituba and brought both hands up to the sides of her face. A searing white light issued from both palms and began to press in upon Tituba's head. She writhed in pain herself and her form seemed to flicker. She appeared to be losing cohesion. Elizabeth wished she knew what to do to assist, but this was well beyond anything Sam had shown her. If she survived this onslaught, she made herself a promise; she was going to increase her training tenfold. As it was, she felt much like a spectator at a gladiatorial match but with a seat not inside the arena, but upon the stage itself.

In his agony Marcus reached up and pressed a palm to the front of Tituba's face, and with all he could muster he applied the same brilliant pressure. She left off her attack and vanished to the other side of the bed.

"Geoff, the shield!" Samuel called to him. Elizabeth looked in his direction and noted that in the course of their fight Samuel had successfully captured Rose. She was unconscious in a heap on the floor. Samuel had her small device in his hand.

Geoff removed the shield, and Samuel plunged forth to engage Tituba. In her confusion he flung her to the other side of the room far away from the children. At that moment three of Flint's army moved into the nursery. They were quickly becoming outnumbered. Marcus's chest had healed from Tituba's attack and he seemed to be back to full battle mode, so he and Geoff engaged the new arrivals. They easily beat them back into the hallway where the two Guardians from below joined the battle and dispatched two Flintlings. Within seconds the numbers game had reversed itself, and it was the Guardians who held the advantage.

Elizabeth took up a position between the two beds. The children somehow had slept through the entire onslaught. Only then did she notice though the shield that walled them off before had been removed, Geoff and Marcus had somehow encased the beds so nothing, no sound, vibration, or disturbance, would shake and disturb their precious cargo. No one, least of all Elizabeth, seemed to notice a pair of little boy eyes that had opened to the fight.

When Elizabeth looked up, Geoff approached her and held out the small silver javelin belonging to Rose.

"Sam said to figure out how to use this quickly. It may be our only hope in getting rid of her." He looked over his shoulder. The fight between his Central and the she-witch was about evenly matched. Marcus, in the hopes of seeking his revenge, had started to assist Samuel in subduing Tituba. Geoff winked at Elizabeth before he too returned to the fray.

Elizabeth's attention turned to the doorway of the nursery as Renee appeared and the vision of the battle overwhelmed her. She screamed in absolute terror at the sight. Samuel cursed, and with a small flick of his wrist Renee crumpled to the floor.

::She is fine. Just asleep. It was the best I could do.::

Elizabeth nodded and went back to looking in the dimness of the room, trying to make sense of the sigils upon the device's surface. She was wishing for more illumination when a brilliant point of light appeared over her head. She looked up to see a young Oneida Guardian smiling at her. How they could honestly be entrenched in battle yet smile as if it were nothing but a lark was beyond her. She was trying to keep her wits about her, and here they were like boys in a wrestling match. It was all good fun despite the life and death dangers involved.

"Here, I think this one might help." She looked up to see the four Guardians simultaneously attacking Tituba, yet she was still able to hold her own. Sam was right in that she had to be one of Flint's best if she could handle four attacks at once and still be standing.

The room began to reverberate as if the air was being siphoned off at an alarming rate. Wave upon wave seemed to tug at their very bodies. For a moment the smile faded from the young Oneida warrior. A look of concern moved across his face. Elizabeth saw the nature of his concern for it appeared Tituba had stopped trying to fend herself from the assault and instead had begun to turn the tide in her favor by collecting their combined assault into a fine point of concentrated energy. Elizabeth realized as did the others that Tituba meant to unleash it and take them all out simultaneously.

Elizabeth ran her fingers along the surface of the device until her index finger covered the sigil of three concentric circles with a jagged line running through it. She concentrated with every ounce of her being on pulling everything around her inward and pressed down upon the sigil. The small javelin vibrated, and her whole body began to tingle as if ants had poured out from its core and were racing all over her. In the next instant she found it hard to breathe—not because there was a lack of oxygen but because there was far too much. It was as if she had entered a wind tunnel. She could hear the others struggling to maintain their balance in the tug of energy between herself, the Guardians, and Tituba. The windows imploded inward from the struggle. Elizabeth forced her eyes open and, in the maelstrom, she saw that not only had she diffused Tituba's tactic; she had completely leeched the energy from everyone around her. The Guardians had all collapsed upon the floor but were still conscious, simply unable to help her.

"You think to best me? You brash vulgarian, how dare you think to take me!"

"Really? Is that the best you can serve? Your words are cantankerous upon the ear but what little good they may do you. In all of your years it is clear you have not fought someone who has so little left to lose. Come at me and my own, will you? I will cast you back into the pits of hell from whence you came!"

Tituba was beyond any modicum of self-control. She charged at Elizabeth. Without so much as another thought, as if the device itself instructed her next move, Elizabeth dropped to her knees and with all of her might jammed the small javelin into the hard-wooden floor. In that instant everything stopped. It was as if time itself had bent to her will. Tituba was just a few feet from her, her arms outstretched. She was pulsating with raw power, causing her to flicker slowly from this world into another. The flurry of dust and debris caught in the air also seemed to hang suspended by the magic of her action. Then the floor rippled and the walls began to undulate. Time snapped back into motion. A swirling mist sprang forth from the tip of the javelin still protruding from the floor. The dense material swirled around the room. From within the thick mist doorways began to open, and a great pull began on the members of Flint's army. They were being drawn into the openings that lined the room.

Try as she might, whatever Elizabeth had succeeded in doing was enough to thwart Tituba further. She was caught irrevocably in the pull of the open doors surrounding the room. Her black clouded shroud with undulating tendrils—not too unlike a dangerous octopus—seemed to try to brace her from the enormous pull of the doorways. The tendrils reached out to the structure of the room and ceiling beams to hold her in place. She looked like an enormous black spider in a very large web. But it was not going to hold her long. The boards were beginning to creak under the strain. The Guardians around the room slowly began to pull themselves up. They seemed to be unaffected by Elizabeth's tactical maneuver.

Elizabeth stared directly into Tituba's face. "Back to the pits of hell from whence you came..."

"This is not over. I shall come for your grandchildren, and you shall be made to watch as I torture them."

"And I shall be ready for you. This," she said, indicating the room as the others of Tituba's party lost their last grip upon this world and slipped into their malevolently glowing crevices, "is but a taste of the reception you shall receive if you ever make the mistake of crossing my family again."

A small murmur came from the doorway as Renee began to regain consciousness.

"Just to show I have no qualms about dispatching any of you." A tendril of Tituba's shroud had reached out and gripped Renee about the waist. In a quick move Tituba hauled her into the void; Renee screamed in terror as she left this world. Tituba's grip on their world lost its battle, and she too was extracted from the room into the ether. Elizabeth dashed after her maid only to be stopped by Samuel who held her back.

"Marcus, Geoff, Ati'ron, go after them," Samuel instructed. Within seconds the three Guardians had slipped into the same openings as they closed behind them.

The room fell into swift darkened silence.

The jarring nature of that all too real dream and the cold light of dawn brought me from my slumber. Only part of me was rather cold as Joss, in his deep sleep, had rolled so that half of him was lying on top of half of me with his arm draped across my chest and his hand upon my shoulder, his waist-length hair fanned out across both of us. I did not mind it so much as it did provide a level of warmth against the coolness of the morning. The soft puffs of air from him billowed softly against my neck as he slept. Not wanting to rouse him, I gently tugged upon the bedding to cover the rest of myself and pondered what wonders I had witnessed over the past several days.

The dream seemed to be so very real. Had I heard it in hushed tones not meant for my ears as a lad? I could not with any certainty recall it one way or the other. I made a mental note to ask Rebecca about it.

One thing was certain: I had found my adventure.

A gleefulness to that revelation brought a smile upon my lips.

"You are gloating, William."

He stirred, gently extracting his arm from my chest. A part of me found myself missing his touch the moment it was gone. Words, as if from a far-off dream, came to me though from where I could not recall. I just was certain as I was lying here next to him that the subject of them was my association with Josiah.

Though your companion over there, he is the true treasure. He will be greater than any of them, or even all of them combined... You are quite lucky to have found each other.

Again, the phrase held me spellbound as it had before—*found each other.* Yet, it continued to play in my mind, if not my heart.

You complete each other, William. In ways that will reach far beyond the physical, mental, or I dare say spiritual...

I could recall for some reason that Joss had been threatened in some form, and when I rose to intervene, this strange voice demonstrated nothing but pure delight.

You see, it has begun already. Your first thought is to defend him. This is a most excellent sign, William, ah yes, a most excellent sign.

Why I thought this just now was perplexing to me.

"I apologize for my manner of sleep. It is unlike me to be so forward."

I frowned the tiniest bit, as I was missing his touch, if anything, for the warmth it provided.

"'Tis nothing to concern yourself with. I took no offense, Joss. In fact, I rather liked the warmth it provided me. Are you not feverish with that much warmth radiating about you?"

"I do not feel any different actually, but yes, at first it does feel feverish to some extent until your body gets used to it. They say it is because of the way we do what we do. The energy moving through us causes this as a side effect. Again, I did not mean any impropriety by it."

"Joss, why on earth would you suggest? I would never..."

He looked everywhere about the room save for looking at me when I desired it most, a bit ashamed for what he thought was an imposition on me. I chose to fight his misplaced embarrassment with a little humor.

"Besides, think of all the money you will save me in burning wood when I can have you warming my bed?" I smirked, and for a moment his eyes widened and something insanely warm flushed through my body and I knew it was from him.

Only these thoughts...felt different. Though I could not grasp them fully, as he pulled them back with a slight shake of his head that I should not make further inquiries of them.

I had pleased him tremendously with my comment. I did not quite know what to make of it. I knew we were linked, and Joss would now be an irrevocable part of my life, but I could not, with any real focus upon the topic, think of a more suitable man to share this sort of aberration than Josiah.

Another flush confirmed he was listening in on my thoughts.

A slanted smile eked across my face.

"Come on, we have a house to set right after we pick up some breakfast. I think Jacob is probably up by now."

"He is. He is reading." Joss tapped the side of his head.

"How can it be that only you can hear me, then?"

"I do not know, really. What you and I share is very different with how I can communicate with the rest of the Guardians. With them it is what they release to me and I to them. Much as in the manner we are talking now. With you..." He shrugged, unsure of how to go on.

So, I tried to let my feelings of how much I was pleased by our special connection flow back to him. I did not know if I was doing it right because I felt like a feeble child with it all. But his smile faded quickly as it made his eyes go wide. He immediately sprang from the bed, and with a word about having to use the facilities he was in the bathroom, leaving me to wonder what I had done.

::It is, uh, nothing, Will. I, uh, just suddenly had to relieve myself...that is all.::

Somehow, I did not think he was being fully frank with me on it.

Early in the morning, after we stuffed ourselves with breakfast, Jacob called us into the library. We expected he had discovered something warranting our attention regarding our recent developments. Unfortunately, this was altogether a different matter but no less troublesome.

"This is what I wanted you to see. It has nothing to do with our current investigation, but I think I need to bring this to Samuel's attention nonetheless." Jacob indicated the press clipping he had snipped from today's paper.

Joss and I turned our heads slightly to read the short article. Though few in words we instantly knew why it raised an alarm in Jacob. The title alone was enough to cause concern: *Astounding Weapons Testing in Virginia.*

Reading through the piece, I noted it might have not been enough to raise a brow with my lot in Manhattan—rising tensions between the United States and Akwe:kon was commonly acknowledged. Though the descriptions of these weapons brought a rush of blood to my face—their pointed analysis bore no good will to my Indian brethren.

"No ordinary cannons, these," Joss read aloud. "No cannon balls, no powder, indeed no propellant or projectile of any kind. It is as if *the lightning of God* is being channeled from the Almighty himself scorching the land, blasting rocks as if they were cheesecloth. Indeed, these new advancements in weaponry might just signal our government is gaining an even footing in our continual confrontations with our neighbor to the west."

A protracted breath shared by us all billowed from our lips. Jacob began to look through older papers I had not bothered to toss to see if there were other mentions of these hair-raising advancements. We left him to his task.

The rest of the morning Joss and I spent setting the house back to rights. Over the course of the next few hours Jacob, Joss, and I worked out times when we would move back to the warehouse district to see what we could do to spy upon our Flintling enemies.

At this point, Jacob and Joss had fully moved in, and my home had finally become a base of operations for our investigation. We converted the library into a makeshift office from where we could meet and compare our observations. I had procured some time ago a medium-sized piece of slate that I had mounted onto a rolling frame so we could make notes upon it we could share. At the time I had been unsure why I had made such an extravagant purchase as there did not seem to be a need. Now its use was immeasurable.

As Jacob's room had been converted into one from which we could strategize, our sleeping arrangements required adjusting. Jacob had taken up the spare room as I had purchased a new bed frame which took up a decidedly larger portion of the room but allowed for Joss and me to share it quite comfortably.

The hours ticked by. Joss and I kept glancing at each other with a fiendish glee that seemed to grow the closer we anticipated my sister's arrival, when the hellcat romance reunion could begin. Truly, a small part of me winced that I knew what was in store for them both, but Joss quickly reminded me this is what precisely had to happen to bring them together again. They were meant for each other. Two flames never burned as brightly as they did.

::Jacob was never the same once they parted on that ill-fated day.::

::What I wanted to know is why they felt the need to break up in the first place? Rebecca was never happier than in the arms of Jacob, and he with her. It never made sense to me.::

::It was Jacob's pride that got in their way from what I could make of its aftermath. He did not think the life of a Guardian would do well as a proper means to support a Manhattan socialite.::

I openly winced at that. Rebecca had never said. It was the one subject she closed down the moment I even hinted using it as a topic of conversation. Quite literally we four became emotionally arrested from that horrendous day.

::Well, I can understand why she will not talk about it. To have her upbringing become the brunt of Jacob's abolishment of their relationship was a stupid move on his part. Rebecca has more money than she knows what to do with. Our family prospers without even trying. Oh, now I see why Rebecca became so incensed at their breakup.::

::Incensed? She leveled a tree! Even I knew not to mess with her after that.::

::'Twas but a sapling and you know it.:: I smirked for his cheeky estimation of my sister's physical prowess. He openly chuckled, bringing Jacob up from reading something in the local paper.

"What are you both planning that I do not know about?"

"What? Us? Plan?" I replied, backing my way out of the room with Joss joining me near the door.

"Uh, we need to see to the food for tonight's session. I may have to procure something from the local meat market to augment our dinner plans."

"Augment? Why? It will just be the three of us as before." Jacob rose from the settee and put his spectacles into his shirt pocket. In truth, he did not need them, but he thought they made him look studious in school. If the fillies near Dartmouth only knew of Jacob's proclivity for playing the field and ever being the master of deception and ploys to bed a girl. Then I realized he had stopped all of that six months before we graduated. That was the time Rebecca had begun to assert herself at my school, prepping me to move back to Manhattan and family life. I had not realized until this very moment that all of Jacob's wanderings had stopped from the day she had arrived on campus.

::Hellcats, indeed.::

"Um, well, you never know when the odd guest might make an appearance," Joss offered. I nodded profusely. We were bungling this badly. We needed to take our leave of him, and be quick about it.

"I shall accompany Joss to acquire some additional food just in case."

"In case of what? You both are acting most strange. What is going on here that I am not privy to?" He stood at his full height and crossed his arms, pointedly staring at both of us.

One would think two men intellectually linked could manage this situation with a far steadier hand. We failed miserably.

We both ducked out of the room but not before I popped my head back in to add, "Oh, one never knows. Best to be prepared and all that rot, no? We shall endeavor to return shortly."

Joss's hand gripped my collar, and we gated out of the house back to the alley next to the day's market. Never had I been more thankful for Joss than I was then.

A few hours later, at Joss's prodding and laden with such an abundance of purchases we did not think we would ever eat it all before it spoiled, we gated back to the kitchen of our home and proceeded to stow our goods in the root cellar for keeping.

Jacob had left us a note that he would be back in time for supper but needed to seek the Central out for some advice. So, at least we had the afternoon to get our collective arses together and present a united front for this evening's entertainment.

"Well, I hope her intended suitor eats like a starving dog; we bought so much food. Why did you not stop me? It will surely go to waste."

"William, you are sharing your home with two active Guardians. Believe me, the food will be consumed. We may appear to eat lean whilst on assignment, but we can hold our own in an eating contest. Of that, I can assure you."

Jacob returned, and whatever business he had with the Central so plagued upon him he seemed to forget all of our obtuse conversation regarding tonight's unexpected, though thoroughly prepared for should they arrive, guest.

Jacob brought us up to date with the latest developments. Thomas had been taken to the Guardian Central who saw fit to assign him under the tutelage of his uncle Thor. Though Jacob had reservations about this assignment, there was little he could do about it. Joss figured it was a battle best saved for another day.

Chapter Six

When Next We Meet

Wherein Joss and Will are on pins and needles waiting for Rebecca to arrive, bringing a new element into their investigation and the potential of a lovers' quarrel that has been two years in the making.

November 2, 1847
William Hallett's Home
Manhattan, New York
6:55 p.m.

As the seventh hour of the night drew near, we still had not heard from my sister. Jacob returned to gathering notes and jotting strategies and plot points on the slate board. He also added news clippings regarding the change of ownership of the warehouse the Flintling operations had been using to another company that dealt in textile manufacturing.

It appeared from everything we could ascertain on the transaction the Flintlings had definitely pulled up stakes. To tie the final knot on our dossier of the property, Joss returned to the site and confirmed that no Flintling activity seemed to be hidden amongst the new owner's import and production of textile goods. The operation there was legitimate. The thread we had been following to them unraveled at this point. We would have to begin anew. Not a welcome prospect by any means, but it was what we were left with.

Still Joss and I could not stop thinking about tonight's events and busied ourselves where we could around the house. I think we traded off rearranging a floral decoration I had on the small table behind the sofa in the living room by my count at least six times—three apiece.

Joss checked the food options in the cellar and saw to the meal he had been preparing for us. He was careful to include Rebecca's guest, should he decide to stay, which was no given considering Jacob's heated jealousy over any man who looked my sister's way.

Mostly, Joss and I whistled a lot. More than we probably should have. I think it gave us away.

"Are you both going to keep whistling that nameless tune?" Jacob barked from the confines of the library down the hall to where we milled about avoiding him. "What has got you both so incredibly wound up? Is dinner soon? I am famished," he asked as we entered the room, glancing up over his spectacles from the news of the day. His handsome face bore not a care in the world.

::*Little does he know....::* I sent Joss's way.

Joss suppressed a smile that made me want to break out giggling like a schoolgirl who just ran into her fancy of a boy.

At this we discovered, quite to our amazement, that Joss and I could not keep a secret of this magnitude. Well, not one as big as my sister's impending arrival, it seemed, without turning into those very same addlepated lovesick girls in the school yard. We hastily retreated to the safety of my kitchen.

::*We are not that bad, William, and you know it.::*

I chuckled, bringing a small snort from him.

::*See? We cannot even keep this small point to ourselves. Joss, we are terrible at this!::*

"What are you two going on about?" Jacob popped his head in the door as Joss added a few spices to the meal as it continued to simmer, and I marveled at his prowess in the kitchen. His arrival startled us both. He continued, unfettered by our response. "The reason I know this is because you both smile, chuckle, and, Will, I have heard you giggle twice just now. And that flower arrangement has been changed five times by my count." He thumbed toward the flowers in the living room that despite our mucking about with them looked pretty much the same as the morning I had brought it in.

"Six times," Joss offered, not helping in the least. I turned my head to glare at him and he shrugged.

Jacob crossed his arms and stared, waiting for an answer.

I let a warm smile break over my face in a feeble attempt to disarm him with my charm and went to him. "'Tis nothing, Jacob, I can assure you. I think we are all just hungry and waiting for Joss to give the signal it is ready. Why do you not go back to your reading and collecting data? I am sure Josiah will be calling us to dinner soon."

"It is almost ready. Just waiting for one important ingredient to arrive, er, uh, simmer."

::Even that we do not get right...waiting for an ingredient to arrive? Is it coming from Madagascar, Joss? Hmmm?::

::It was but one little slip of the tongue. I am sure he did not notice. Will, I think you let your mind run away from you. It is fine. You shall see.::

Without letting this escalate any further I pushed Jacob back toward the library. As soon as he crossed the threshold and entered the room, the knocker on my front door shook my senses. I glanced at my pocket watch and saw it had barely turned seven of the clock.

I hastily made my way down the hallway away from the library to the front door. My sister was not known for her patience to enter my home if I did not answer in what she deemed to be an adequate amount of time. In truth, I did not think even gating would suffice to complete the distance in the time she thought required.

Joss called from the kitchen, "I have taken the food directly off the flame. It will keep for a few, but we really should eat soon."

I nodded and waved generally in his direction without stopping as the door began to open. I reached for the handle and flung it back, surprising my sister.

"William! My, you startled me. I did not know if you were upstairs and did not hear me knocking, so I let myself in."

"Fine, fine." I gave her a most welcoming hug, relishing the dark silvery-gray silk dress she wore, accented with a black velvet collar and a masculine-looking white cravat about her neck. My sister loved to play with gender when it came to her form of style. She always loved to press the boundaries of what was acceptable to wear for a woman of her stature and breeding.

My eyes roved over her shoulder to a most beguiling young man of no more than seventeen. In his stance I observed a well-built figure in that farm boy way, though his clothing did not appear soiled or torn. Given my sister's association with the missionary orphanage—the Crossroads—they clearly had been provided to him from the shelter where Rebecca must have met this strapping fellow.

"Oh, William, this is Christian Stuyvesant. I met him through the Crossroads. Well, he came to us late one night about half a week ago."

Not forgetting my manners, I guided them both into the receiving room of the house and closed the door. I went to shake hands with the young lad only to discover he was carrying a medium-sized chest in his hands.

"Just leave that by the door there. We will tend to it later."

He did as I bade and then returned to us as Joss came out of the kitchen.

"My, my, whatever are you cooking? William, you seem to have outdone yourself." Her eye landed upon Joss making his way to us, and my sister's response was rather surprising.

"Oh! Joss! Can it truly be?"

She rushed over and gave him a warm hug which pleased Joss enormously. It was probably the last time good feelings would be expressed tonight, so I allowed Joss to enjoy himself in my sister's embrace. We all meandered closer to the kitchen, finding a way to slip a hugging Joss and Rebecca into the kitchen so we could all marvel over his concoction for the evening.

I opened a few pots he had left in the oven to keep warm and noted the cooked meats he had put into a skillet along with some herb-seasoned roasting vegetables and potatoes in another pot.

As I stood, I glanced Christian's way only to discover that since Joss and my sister had now parted from their embrace, he watched Joss with a most peculiar gaze. I did not know quite what to make of this lad. If I had to venture a guess, he may have come to the Crossroads seeking assistance, but his involvement with my sister went beyond that of a wayward boy who sought help. His affections seemed to stem from the attentions my sister paid to him, unrequited, unacknowledged, and painfully growing in spite of the warmth she had for him and his care. A most revealing look and one I did not take lightly.

::Joss, the lad is in love with Rebecca though she does not know or return those affections.::

::It may just be a schoolboy crush. But we shall take special care with him when he and Jacob cross paths tonight. I sense something is different about him. Something I cannot quite place. Something that bears remembering and taking note upon, but what it can be I cannot sort just now.::

I marveled at my sister's fondness for Joss. She held him at arm's length, eyeing every facet of him, before turning her sights on me.

::I have a small confession to make regarding your sister, Will. When Jacob broke her heart on the day of your graduation, I took it upon myself to see her from time to time over the following year—more to ensure she was coping with the loss than anything else. There was nothing amorous about our meetings, you must believe me. I just hated seeing her in such a state as when you both departed that rueful day. I had words with Jacob over it, and it very nearly ended our apprenticeship because of it. Do forgive me for not telling you about it until now.::

In truth, I did not know what to make of it. Joss and my sister had had this relationship for well over a year, and she had not even mentioned it to me once. Still I could not hold him accountable for it. I had only brought him and Jacob back into my life recently. Given the nature of everything going on, I am sure we just did not have the time or place where he could impart such an understanding between my sister and him.

::Do not fret about it, my friend. I am only too happy she could turn to someone to confide in. If it were not me, than I am glad it was you.::

I tried my damnedest to not let him sense the pang of hurt I felt over his replacing me in her grief over the loss of Jacob in her life. But as I told him, and I firmly believed it, I am glad she found solace in someone with which to cope. Rebecca turned to me with her arm around Joss's waist.

"I could never quite understand how you let this one get away from you." She playfully gripped the lower part of his face, smooching it a bit as a mother would do to tease her son in front of a prospective girlfriend. He endured it with the sentiment that she offered in her caress.

I nodded, sending such thanks to him so he would know how much his presence in my life meant to me and how thankful I was for his willingness to endure my family's idiosyncrasies.

"What can I say? I am but a fool."

As ever the tactful one of any given situation, Joss was prepared with words of eloquence I knew would rescue me from Rebecca's barbed sisterly teasing.

"You shall suffer the fool no longer, not while I am around."

Rebecca beamed, standing so beautifully there in the lamplight of the room.

It was clear she meant something deeper than the connection Joss and I shared, or at the very least her hinting at a real romantic level to our relationship should have been a fait accompli by now. All I could recall from that horrid day was that she had come to me, her heart breaking from the horrible things my friend had said to her before taking off to points unknown.

Jacob had only advised me that the Guardianship had given him an assignment, and he had left after seeing Rebecca. He would not cross paths with me again until our recent Flintling incursion. Yet, on that day, wiping tears from her face, she had commented on her own stupidity for putting her heart in Jacob's calloused hands—which I would not believe for one minute as I had lived with the man for four years and sat there stupefied over these horrific events. I could also not reconcile the way he had ended things with her. We both felt a supreme loss, and I was hurt by the breakup because it was my sister who bore the brunt of it, say nothing of the love I bore him. Betrayal did not begin to cover the well of emotions Rebecca and I had shared on the long journey home.

The ride home had been unbearable, but somehow, we managed to remain close after my return to Manhattan.

"Well, I always knew you two would make a home for yourselves." We made our way from the kitchen toward the library.

"William is kind enough to allow us to remain here while we investigate a Guardian matter."

"We?" she called over her shoulder as I opened the door to the library for her.

We stepped in, and Jacob turned from making notes on the slate board. It was then everything stopped, Rebecca partway into the room, a mere eight feet or so from where Jacob stood at the slate making a series of notations. Christian stood to my right, along the wall of books lining the shelves on that side of the library, his eyes roving over them all, but coming back to the threat he definitely perceived Jacob to be from the stern look he cast his way. Joss stood next to me by the door, which he brilliantly kept open as a means of escape, in case one was required.

:: Ohnehta'kowa, short of her blowing up the house, rest assured I will work very hard to put things back together in your beautiful home should the worst come to pass.::

I glanced his way for a moment, thinking he was making a joke of the situation, only to find he was not. I looked about the room briefly and began to fear for my home and our lives. This was underscored by observing the steely stance my sister took and Jacob's visible displeasure at being surprised in this manner. It told me the welfare of my house, though it clearly hung in the balance, was probably the least of my concerns.

"I had hoped you were not stupid enough to show yourself in my brother's home." She rounded on me, completely startling me to where I gasped like a matron who suddenly discovered she had descended into her soirée with friends dressed only in her undergarments. It was not the manliest of gasps, I can assure you.

::There is hardly anything matronly about you...::

::Joss, please, this is not the time...::

"*You!* You are the fiend who has broken my love's heart. You scoundrel! I shall have you, meet me..." Christian never got to finish his lover boy's pledge and calling for a duel thanks to Joss.

When Christian pushed against Joss and made his way rather quickly to defend my sister's honor, Rebecca turned with the tightest smile I could see and held him back.

"Joss! Please!" she called to him like she knew about his Guardian abilities.

Joss sprang into action and put a glowing white hand on the boy and uttered, "*Sátien tánon.*" Christian collapsed upon the nearest chair in a stupor it did not likely seem he would recover from too soon.

Rebecca had other ideas. "I would watch him. He seems to sort out commands like that and becomes all the angrier for it." It startled the three of us that a kid of his stature could be subdued by Joss but could somehow shake himself free from it of his own accord. I, for one, having been the brunt of those hand memory wipes, just wanted to see the lad do it.

We turned instead to Jacob and Rebecca's icy reintroduction, which had not melted in the slightest. Their stares at each other said to me two things: firstly, her arrival put them right back to that moment he had walked out of her life two years ago as it was plain from the pain expressed on both their faces, and secondly, despite their cold stares at each other, they were still most ardently in love.

::Get ready, Will. Jacob is about to say something stupid that will set Rebecca off. It will not be good. For this house, or for us.::

I could not help myself but began to delicately reach for the breakable whimsy items, some of which were irreplaceable, from the nearby tabletops. Rebecca eyed my removing them as a sign of weakness on our part. I froze with a teardrop-looking water paperweight and a small but ornate piece a Russian friend had procured for me, saying they were all the rage with the ruling family in Russia. I quickly set them on a small table behind me that suddenly seemed quite cluttered.

::Sorry, my own doing given Jacob's perceived anger with us.::

It was true: he now knew that we knew all along this would transpire tonight. We had no defense in the matter. From the way he stood at this moment, I would be eating crow for the better part of the year over this fiasco. Finally, I had enough of his false bravado.

"Oh! Stop looking at me like that, you big oaf! You would do well to patch things up with my sister. You both have been miserable beyond reproach. And do not deny it, sir."

"Do you not think I know this?" he all but barked at me, throwing the book down upon the desk. "William, I expected far more from you on this. But to sneak in your sister—"

"A sister who is *still* in the room, by the way. You can address me directly, you know, instead of hiding behind William's precious books and press articles." At that a few books flew off the shelves with a fling of Rebecca's hands. Joss and I began to cast our eyes about, then back to my sister whose anger possessed a strong palpability to it. A low hum began to permeate the room. The ceiling started to creak and groan in ways it never had before. Joss and I could not hide that we disliked this sort of thing as it usually came with surprises, and not the kind you expect at Christmas, either.

Up to this point we had been consumed with how my sister had responded to running into Jacob unexpectedly. Now our sights turned to an incredibly angry Jacob.

"Jacob, brother, listen..."

"To what? You already knew this was going to happen! Indeed when I asked this afternoon you both acted like lovesick girls straightening the house and rearranging floral arrangements in the room just to keep tabs on my well-being while you placated me with words about dinner and such. At first I thought it was a most welcome way to start a hazy Sunday morning, Now I see, after my prolonged absence this afternoon with the Central, there has been a great deal of planning probably to put your sister off our meeting as much as myself and this, this is the culmination of your efforts. To bring us together when—"

"When what?" Rebecca chimed in, her anger rivaling Jacob's, and I daresay the wild look in her eyes did not give me much hope that Jacob would be able to maintain his end of the angry lovelorn person in this situation. One thing was certain above all else: it never boded well when Rebecca's gaze became wide-eyed and crazed. This was a disaster in the making and one I wished had not happened in my home.

"Rebecca, control yourself. I cannot have you thrashing my home to settle what should have—" I held up a hand to let her know I was in full agreement with her and that my allegiances had not changed one jot even with the rekindling of being with my old school mate. I was fully aligned with her position in this matter. "Well, what he should have settled two years ago."

"Well, that surely caps the max, William. You told me you understood my reasons for breaking things off with your sister. You agreed they were sound and absolutely the best course of action."

At this point Christian rose, having broken free from Joss's formidable subjugation of him, and made for Jacob directly. Joss held him physically back.

"So, *this* is my replacement now, is it? A little young in the tooth, do you not think?"

"I shall have you, sir! You have insulted my good self which I am more than man enough to take, while you have also taken to insult this lovely creature who is kind and generous, and who I love and care for most ardently in the humblest manner. Miss Hallett is the very essence of refinement and gentility."

"Then you should see her with her knickers off. She's not quite so refined when she slashes a man's clothing to shreds in order to satiate herself with him, leaving him bereft of his former existence. She is hardly the delicate flower you seemed to have confused with the *lady* who stands before us."

"*Wá:s sentá:wha!*"

Joss's voice echoed loudly in the room as he sent a powerful ripple of energy against the lad, sinking Christian to the floor where he stood, a pile of muscle and bone. Joss spared a glance my way to convey that Christian would be quite heavy to lift by normal means.

::Joss, take him to my bed and keep him there. Tie him down if needs be. I shall do my best keeping these two hellcats from destroying my home.::

He nodded and gated with Christian to my room whilst I tried my best to insert myself within the melee of flying books and shattered delicate pieces that had once decorated the library. I hoped Joss could make good on his word and repair most of it since a great deal had sentimental value that trumped any real market value.

The hellcat couple stood but a mere two feet or so apart from each other. Their outward gaze was of utter contempt for each other, yet in their eyes, buried so deep, was a raging inferno of the love they still felt, neither one wanting to make the first move. I was about to give negotiation another try when Jacob's next words removed all hope of it succeeding.

"*Becks*, did you really think I had any other choice than what I had to do?"

Astonishingly, she did not lash out at him with claws bared. Instead, she put her hand to her mouth and giggled. In her anger that twisted-sounding giggle took on an infectious, if maligned, glee. It made me begin to smile, and indeed Jacob, woefully in the wrong as he was about to find out, snorted as if we all shared a tremendous joke. We did, neither of us menfolk realizing how a woman laughing did not mean all was well with the world. Indeed, we learned it could bring a terror with it neither of us was prepared to deal with. His last only made matters worse, thinking he gained the upper-hand.

The room began to tremble a bit, though by whose hand I could not say with any definitive measure. Books began to fall off their shelves; smaller items seemed to float in the air. Wind from an unknown source, since I noted that all my windows were shut, moved about the room as if we stood on the precipice of a gathering gale. Ignoring this, Jacob, still smiling warmly, stepped a tad closer to my sister—a colossal mistake in the making, but it was too late. Too late to turn this around. And the way she continued to laugh was as if every ounce of hurt and anger she had stowed for the past two years chose laughter as the way to make itself known to both of us in that room.

"Becks, Becks, you were, nay, *are* the love of my life. I never—"

He never got to finish as the low hum escalated to where it finally caught, and all of the senseless activity ceased to happen in the room. The suspended books fell to the ground; the wind coming from out of nowhere stopped. All that was left was my sister still caught up in her fit of giggles, though Jacob's words had them fading a bit as if she was really listening to what he had to say. Jacob glanced my way as I sat on the floor, trying to keep the pieces of a broken lamp together in the hope Joss could do what he said. Jacob took one more step, and I realized what was about to happen.

I opened my mouth to warn Jacob to back away. Her anger had only just started with him when the hand she had over her mouth to suppress the laughter lashed out and backhanded him so hard across the face it sent him flying into the air. He spun horizontally until he collided with the large slate board, cracking it in half, before he slid the length of what remained of the board's frame to the ground in a heap. That one smack had left him semiconscious and winded. He struggled to regain himself.

Gone were the giggles and laughter. She had *raised hell and put a prop under it* as Grandmama was fond of saying. This was a salient trait of the headstrong Hallett women, and the Hallett men knew better than to stoke that particular fire. She approached him, turned him over so he could see the fullness of her wrath, and straddled his chest. This brought a dry cough from him for her efforts.

"You do not *ever* get to call me that little love term again. *Ever*! Try it one more time and by the Creator above, I swear you shall end up in the infirmary with more injuries than one doctor should have to address in a lifetime." She turned to me, and I could not help but scoot back a bit. Her heated gaze softened considerably once she observed my reaction to her.

"William, my argument has never been with you. I know you see it all my way. But I need to see to Christian. He is not what he seems, and I fear Joss may underestimate him. This is why I came to you this night. To see what can be done about him."

"He is in my room. I believe Joss has tied him up in his stupefied state." I feebly pointed to the second story of my home, wondering if any of her antics had caused damage up there.

"Good thinking. We had him sedated most of the time at the mission, though he does behave much more rationally when I am around. Perhaps he *is* smitten with me. Would not be the first time we have used *that* to gain the upper hand when necessary." She turned a cold eye back to Jacob. "As for him..."

"You need not worry. He shall recover soon enough. Their healing properties are most remarkable. I will stay with him while you go check on Christian and Joss."

"There is a good brother." She leaned down and kissed my forehead and ran a loving hand down my cheek before she climbed over me and the debris of the room, of which there lay plenty, and made her way upstairs.

::War over down here. She is headed your way.::

::I thank you for the advanced notice, but she likes me, remember?::

::Yeah, you must explain to me how that all worked itself out. The consoling you spoke of earlier. I definitely missed something along the way of our schooling youth, say nothing of the year thereafter.::

I sensed his smile. He was most pleased with the outcome.

::How is the room?::

::Oh, sure you inquire as to the status of my library rather than your own former mentor. Come now, can you not spare a thought for poor Jacob as he lies here a broken man?::

::She really got one in on him?:: he inquired a second or two later.

::More than one I think. It went so bloody fast, but I am sure he will not be making the mistake of using his lover nickname for her.::

I eyed him trying to regain his breathing. In truth, I could not spare much in the way of pity for him. He more than made his own bed with the way he handled his parting from us both two years ago. I was half waiting for someone to deliver him the wallop he deserved. I probably loved him too much to have said it as plainly as my sister did. In that, she is the stronger of us two.

::I am sure he will mend soon enough, though as to matters of the heart, there I am not so convinced.:: I added a moment later.

::I give it to the end of the night before he can say it again.::

::You really think they will have it patched up by then? I thought I should hire a pugilist ring to let them really have at it. We could open it to betting and make quite the killing.::

He sniggered at that vision alone.

::I cannot speak definitively for your sister, but Jacob misses her far more than he lets on. Did you not see how wide his eyes went the moment his gaze fell upon her? I mean before the angry façade took its place. His first instinct was to bring her in his arms and ravish her from head to toe. She would be a fool not to have seen it.::

::And as you say, we Halletts miss nothing.::

::Well, I would not go that far...::

He cut off the link between us as I am sure that was when Rebecca entered the room and took his attentions from me. I slowly began to rise, as did Jacob. He rubbed the side of his face where her hand had connected with it. No doubt it still hurt quite a bit. He moved his jaw about to see if anything had become...*dislodged* by her attack.

I reached him and held out a hand.

"I daresay my sister takes round one."

He snorted and took my hand to raise himself to standing.

"She did all of...*this*?" he inquired.

"Well, I cannot say for certain, but with you caught up seeing her, Joss departed with that Christian boy who wanted to challenge you within an inch of your life, and I know *I* did not do it, so by process of elimination that would leave just her."

"Rebecca. A *Guardian*? No. There is simply no way she..."

"I do not presume to know all the ins and outs of a calling to the Guardianship, but I think she qualitatively carries enough Mohawk blood, as do I for that matter, to become Guardians should the calling come. Am I right?"

He picked up a broken statuette of Romeo wooing Juliet that I loved—thankfully, it did not appear too damaged. "Eh, no, I did not mean it in that sense. I meant I was with Samuel today. He would have warned me about it since he knows of my connection to you, that's all."

He turned around and saw the complete demolishment of the slate board and what remained of its frame.

"I think I can put it to rights again. It is a clean enough break. I thought I imagined it all once she smacked me across...she *did* do that, right? I had not imagined that part, had I?"

"No, she walloped you one but good. Far more force than I expected her to have too. And throughout our early sibling years we had a time or two to tussle about a bit. I do not ever remember it being an issue when I was younger."

His expression turned grim as he rubbed that part of his face her hand had connected with.

"Now that I think upon it, there was quite a bit going on before we came to blows, no?"

"I think she hit you harder than you realize. Do you need to lie down for a bit? Jacob, she had items floating in the room, books flying off the shelves, and then she knocked you across the room and split a rather thick piece of slate with your backside. That's a bit more than a slight misjudgment on your part. Save for the fact I am privy to your abilities and their ties to science, I would run screaming from the room that my sister had become a witch."

He snorted as he stopped rubbing his face for a moment. "Well, my face would not argue with you should you take that stance."

We both allowed ourselves a small chuckle over his summation of their reunion.

Jacob set about restoring the library back to its former glory whilst I ascended the stairway to my bedroom. There I found Rebecca trying to talk down an extremely agitated Christian. Joss had both of them under a shield of light that he assured me would hold should Christian find a way to break the bonds holding him strapped to the bed.

"Christian, Chris, please. This is for your own good. You know I mean you no harm, right?"

He stopped in his valiant struggles against the bindings Joss had him in. He seemed mesmerized by the tone of her voice. It was then Joss and I noted she slowly extracted a dark silver-like stiletto not dissimilar to those we had observed the Flintlings using. How it came to her, how she seemed so calm in bearing it, using it apparently against Christian to further subdue him, left both of us aghast.

Rather than interrupt we mutually signaled that we would wait for her to complete whatever she was going to do. She pressed a couple of sigils along the surface and put one end of the object to Christian's arm, and he calmed down to the point of being almost pleasant. A dreamlike state of consciousness seemed to overcome him.

"Here, observe his skin." She opened his shirt to expose his muscular chest, and there we saw the influence the wand held over the lad. His skin rippled with a silvery glow that seemed to emanate from within.

"Do not be alarmed. It only occurs with him."

"And you know this because?" I inquired rather pointedly, my brotherly ire notwithstanding.

"Calm yourself, because I tested it on myself and on one of the other children in the orphanage. While I could attain the same level of quietude of the child I tested, their skin did not have this glowing, luminescent effect that seems to move through Christian. Somehow, he has been altered. And here is the interesting part of it all."

"You mean there is more than one?" I ventured, much to her annoyance.

"Really, Will, I am not some simpleton who does not have an idea on how to run a decent experiment. And yes, before you go there, when I tried it on myself it did not work at all. Evidently the device is aware of the bearer and will not actively do anything to harm them, which I had hoped was the case. And yes, before you interrupt with yet another brotherly tirade of questions, I realize it was a rather stupid option to take without someone there to watch and intercede. Again, this is why I have brought this to you. Well, you and Joss." She leaned across the bed and took Joss's hand. "I am so glad you are here. I feel confident knowing your scientific prowess will give me a much better understanding of what we are dealing with here."

Jacob entered, and we all paused for a moment to gauge how things would proceed with his being present. Rebecca decided to continue despite her dander being raised with Jacob's arrival.

"The most interesting aspect is I discovered this."

She moved from the bed with a quick glance Christian's way to ensure he was still subdued. We all cleared the area at the foot of the bed to give her some room to work should she require it.

"It appears this device, from what Christian informed me, is called—"

"A *Mordant*." I finished her sentence without realizing I had the information within my head. Apparently, one more piece of surprise knowledge Tiyanoga had gifted me. "We have seen them before, only in full extended mode. At the Flintling compound. When you both fought them."

Joss and Jacob nodded but added nothing further.

"Precisely," Rebecca added as she took the center of the open space between the door and the foot of the bed. "Well, it appears this Mordant can replay the previous situations in which it has been used—sort of an audit of who employs it and why, I suppose. That is the only reason I can discern at the moment."

"But how did you...?" I started, but she held up a hand to stall me along that line of questioning.

"I think what I am about to show you will answer that. Do not become alarmed. All of what I am about to show you will feel very real, but we are watching the past. Your bedroom will appear as if it is has been transported when you see this. But it appears to be naught but a memory. Do you all understand?"

We all nodded our agreement so she could proceed.

She pressed some sigils on the device and set it on the ground only to join my side as we watched my room transform. Save for the bed furnishings, Christian and all, the walls seemed to melt away and turn into some small bedroom, though where I could not say.

"While you may see some images that could not have come from the device we now possess, I have come to believe all of these devices are somehow linked—they might even share a common narrative. Somehow, I have been able to watch several such narratives. The likes of which are quite alarming," Rebecca offered. "I have not pursued too many of them for fear that while I looked out, someone could be looking back in."

It was a noteworthy point, but we all signaled to one another the risk was worth it at this juncture if it gave us a clue to Christian's origins.

A shaking bloody hand rises over the headboard of the small bed along the wall of a very small bedroom. Fingers stretch and curl upon themselves as the bearer gasps for air, struggling to catch his breath— the pain evident in the rattled sound emanating from him. A head slowly appears, the hair twisted and mangled into a bloody mess, above the line of the headboard. The side of his head is drenched with blood, though whether his own or someone else's is hard to determine.

The nude body is that of a young muscular lad—Christian by the looks of him. He pulls himself slowly up into a seated position, his back to the headboard, his knees bent with his arms wrapping around them. He rests his forehead against his knees as he rocks back and forth, trying to absorb the carnage around him.

Blood-saturated walls and bedding dominate the room. Pieces of bone and flesh, a muscled arm here, part of a hirsute torso there, entrails strewn over the floor, litter the room as if a man of sizable stature had been literally blown apart. In the ceiling above, a portion of the man's skull hangs from the plastered ceiling, dripping blood and brain material onto the floor below.

Above the boy's head, stabbed into the wall, is the Mordant, sigils glimmering against the crimson-stained walls. Tiny bleeps and blips are the only sound save for the weary, overused springs in Christian's bed as he consoles himself with his rocking motion. His eyes, wild and frenzied, dart left and right trying to determine what he will do next.

The door suddenly rattles as someone pounds upon it. The knob is twisted and turned to no avail as it appears to be locked.

"Christian, are you all right?" A young boy's voice, barely heard above the rising commotion beyond the door. "Uncle Eddy heard the noise; the Hook is on his way. Are you all right?"

Christian, for all of his bodily strength, does not seem able to respond. He just sits there with a slightly bewildered expression to his face, as if he cannot make sense of the warning the young boy has expressed.

"He's coming...I can't stay."

The soft patter of footsteps echoes off away from the door.

A second later and another sound of footsteps, far heavier than the last, pounding their way to the door. It bursts open, nearly sheering it off its hinges, revealing a large beefy, leathered-looking man, his bald head and body profusely sweating—his clothing saturated with it. He possesses a grotesque scar that trails down the right side of his face, further distorting an already ugly individual. He is brandishing a nasty barbed-looking riding crop that he wields as if it is always at the ready to use at a moment's notice.

"This apparently is the Hook the boy spoke of. The older man is the brothel keeper, Edwin Wright. They all call him Uncle Eddy," Rebecca added.

A moment later, just behind the large man, is an older gentleman doing his best to present himself as an upper-class sort, though his manner of clothing only gives the barest appearance of such; upon closer inspection he would not pass the sneer of the truer upper-class set. This is Uncle Eddy. He places a gloved hand onto the stocky man, peering over his shoulder at the morass of Christian's room. He pushes his way past the large sweaty man and into the room, his eyes and mouth wide with the morbid devastation before him.

Younger boys, some dressed up with makeup and clothing to resemble little girls, stand cautiously behind the large man in the doorway—some peering around him while others look between the man's legs into the room. All of their eyes and mouths agape—clearly not trusting what they are seeing before them.

"What have you done, you whelp?" Eddy bellows at Christian, enraged but thoroughly disgusted all the same. He towers over Christian but does his level best to avoid touching anything. A piece of the dead man's brains chooses this time to slip from the shattered cranium above and land on the man's shoulder. He shrieks like a surprised elderly woman and quickly uses his handkerchief to push the brain matter from his shoulder onto the floor. He presses the same handkerchief to his mouth in a vain attempt to prevent himself from vomiting all over the room, only to realize there is some loose brain matter on the handkerchief nearest his lips. This almost succeeds in emptying his stomach onto the floor.

Christian shudders but does not answer.

As he does his best to shake out the handkerchief, Eddy takes note of the Mordant glistening on the wall above Christian's head. He starts to move for it when Christian springs up, surprising everyone with his swift move, and retrieves the Mordant from the wall, brandishing it like a pointed weapon to use against them, further infuriating Uncle Eddy.

"Don't just stand there, you imbecile! What am I paying you for?" Eddy rages at the large odious man who then moves into the room with as much speed as his pudgy frame will allow. But Christian is too fast for them and levels the device which has now started to bleep and make sounds, momentarily stalling the man's advance.

"Stop! Or...or I shall make sure it is the last move you will ever make!" Christian warns them both, waving the device between them. More boys have collected in the hallway to witness the strange scene before them.

"What's that there? You think you can best the Hook with...that? Take him, you arse!" Eddy scoffs.

The Hook moves again, and Christian's fingers slide upon the device. A strand of bluish light emits from the tip directly at the Hook and hits him squarely in the chest, stopping him. The bluish light seems to gather within him, overwhelming his bodily systems; he pisses in his pants. Not a good sign. The light seems to incinerate him from within.

His eyes melt in their sockets; his skin overheats and begins to slide off. His strangled cries echo as his large body withers to cinders and ash, bringing screams from the boys in the hall who scurry away in a patter of women's slippers and shoes.

Christian turns the device to the old gentleman.

"It seems, Uncle Eddy, we are at an impasse," Christian informs the man who now quakes as he backs up toward the lone window, shrinking from the bloodied curtains dangling there. "I think this more than ends our employment arrangement."

Christian moves from the bed and begins to gather his things, slipping into breeches and shoes and pulling a small rucksack from under the bed containing his few possessions and some clothing. He grabs a shirt from the sack, never relinquishing the Mordant he aims at Uncle Eddy.

"You'll never get away with this. This man was our wealthiest client. Someone will come looking for him."

"Well, then I leave it to your good judgment to deal with them. In either event, I will no longer remain here."

"They'll find you! They always do. And when they do I shall press charges."

"Say what you will. They will have to catch me first." Christian brandishes the Mordant as if he now has the means to truly disappear.

"No one will believe you! A boy-whore. They all know what you are, where you work. You can't go anywhere in this town without someone recognizing you!"

Christian pauses. He looks down at the floor. His lips form a firm line of concentration. "Then I shall have to go somewhere no one knows anything about me. Goodbye, Uncle Eddy. It was profitable, for a time."

He presses his way down the hall. Boys scurry from him as he makes his way down the stairs, his bloodied hand trying to hold himself upright, scraping along the tattered remains of once delicate printed wallpaper. He escapes to the main floor and out of the back of the building into an alleyway. The visual from the Mordant is quite jarring as Christian makes his descent.

"We'll all miss you...the boys and me. In case ya wondered or anything," a young boy says the moment Christian breaks through the back door, sounding very much like the lad from the bedroom door earlier. Christian turns to see the small waifish lad, clad in a white corset, leggings, a russet-colored wig, and tawdry makeup.

Christian stops and turns, bringing a hand up to the boy's face. He recoils the tiniest bit, noting Christian's exposed flesh is mottled, silvery in patches with long sanguinary streaks from the event in his room. The lad's expression softens as he seemingly remembers himself and the apparent relationship they shared. Christian runs a soft hand along his face—a caress as if from an older, dear brother.

"I promise, Tim. If I can find a way to get you all out of here, I will. Have heart. You've not seen the last of me. I'll remember you all. I'll save you if I can. Give the lads hope from me..."

They hug briefly and Christian moves off—Mordant in hand.

The scene dissolved, only to change like ripples in a lake as the walls of my room were once again transformed, this time becoming a forest clearing I struggled to recognize.

It is night. Tender spirals and wisps of fog linger along the forest ground, giving it an eerie appearance. A great ripping sound is heard, and light presses in from what appears to be a giant tear in the forest, as if the fabric of reality were torn by some cosmic being.

Christian slips through and plummets onto the ground before him, Mordant in hand. He slowly stands and gathers his wits about him, taking stock of his surroundings. Notably, he is without his rucksack but has found some place to wash away the signs of his earlier catastrophe. His skin shimmers with a mottled silvery hue under the double-moonlight.

He takes the Mordant and presses upon its surface. The device elongates into the size of a javelin. Christian drags the tip of the Mordant along the moist earth, creating a large oval in the dirt about four feet wide at its greatest width, three at its narrowest. This is followed by etching some sigils in the center of unknown origin.

He then stands back to survey his work, retracting the Mordant to a smaller stiletto.

Christian's fingers move along the device. A bright light emits from its tip, and he uses it to cut into his palm. He squeezes his injured hand over the oval, allowing the blood to flow onto the earth below. He kneels before the etched bloodstained earth and stabs the tip of the device into the oval, causing it to ripple as if liquefied upon contact. Christian takes a deep breath and submerges his upper body into the watery earth, leaving his kneeling half along the rim. The movement of his torso within the rippling earth suggest he is searching madly for something beneath.

"He informed me later that he was searching for his rucksack which he had hidden in a bush in Battery Park. He never did locate it. Came to me at the Crossroads with just the clothes on his back and the Mordant in hand," Rebecca commented, crossing her arms as she took in our subdued Christian there in my bed. It was an odd visual to see our reality so entangled with the one from the Mordant.

"But how are we seeing this if the Mordant is submerged like it is?" I inquired.

"You shall soon see. It is like I said; I believe they are all linked in some manner. It shall reveal itself shortly," Rebecca added.

"How did he come to know how to use it in this way?" I asked.

"From my own hand using it, I can only say when you use it, it makes a connection of some sort to your thoughts, almost anticipating your needs before you have them fully formed. From there, once it knows what you want, it will guide you to achieve it. It is quite...disconcerting how easy it is to get the hang of it." She nodded in the direction of the scene as new individuals had revealed themselves.

As Christian continues to search in vain for his sack, three people enter the clearing. One is a brutish hirsute man, thick with muscle and only wearing pants that are frayed midcalf. He is barefoot and carries a wild look about him. The other is a sleek man, clad in dark clothes of fine construction, with a silvery waistcoat, his long hair plaited down his back. He circles the oval, watching with great intent Christian's bottom half move about the edge of the liquefied earth. A tallish man of scarcely above my height of six feet, he appears of Mediterranean descent...Greek, Italian, or possibly Spanish.

The third to enter the clearing is a woman of decided beauty. Her skin glows a blue-white tone as if she too knows the means of casting about the same ethereal hues of the moons above. Her eyes and lips are the darkest red to rival fresh spilt blood. She, however, does not wear any clothing that makes itself readily apparent. Instead, she seems shrouded in a dark undulating cloud with sleek tendrils of darkness moving about much in the way an octopus would over coral. A beguiling and ghastly visage. Rather than join her companions nearest the unsuspecting Christian, she lingers in the branches of a barren oak tree, overseeing the events from that lofty position.

Wind stirs within the clearing, the beginnings of an impending storm as clouds can be seen in the distance growing ever near, pulsing with light, bringing a wrath of rain in its wake.

"What's he doin'?" The brutish man leans over Christian's backside, peering into the liquefied soil as if he can glean something from its murky depths.

"Does it truly matter? Get his attention; haul him from the damned thing if you have to." The sleek catlike man's voice has almost a lyrical quality to it—mesmerizing in tone and reach.

"Whatever you say, Alarico…it's your call," the brute murmurs as he takes out his Mordant. With a press of some symbols the device separates into a two-pronged fork. The man, with all haste, stabs Christian halfway up his back, the blood saturating the shirt in two large pools within seconds, thankfully missing his spine.

Christian pulls himself out as the brute retracts his Mordant. He licks the blood from it and savors the taste. This is a man who has a real taste for men's blood, evident by the manner of the ecstasy he expresses in sampling Christian's.

Christian coughs and more blood spews from his mouth, yet it is apparent he is already healing from the assault as he stands up with little pain expressed upon his face. Wiping his mouth, he turns on the man who violated him, the Mordant in his hand at the ready. The two square off, dancing slowly around each other, looking for a weakness with which to strike.

"You are a clever one, sorting out our Mordant's abilities so quickly," Alarico practically coos to Christian. Christian shakes his head slightly as if the mesmerizing effects of Alarico's speech begin to plague upon him.

"The way I see it, either I tried to sort it or I would be the one in a pauper's grave come the morning," Christian replies, noting the three of them fully now after the woman's movements caught his attention.

"Who are you?"

"The more prudent question should be: what are we, do you not think?" the woman in the tree replies as she lowers herself slowly from bare branch to branch—a most disconcerting movement, undulating as *she does in the veil of darkness shrouding nearly all of her save for her face, a leg here or there as she moves, and the ample bosom from the plunging neckline of her smoky garment. All of it possesses a bluish luminescent glow that Christian finds hard to look away from. She is a temptress, of that there is little doubt—an ender of men. Sirens could learn a thing or two from this creature.*

At last she reaches the forest floor, shifting in and out of view, as if caught between this world and the next, distorted at times to bewitch the mind and eye. Christian's stance becomes even more wary as the three of them surround him.

He moves into the center where the soil had once been liquefied, only now with the Mordant's extraction it has returned to being normal dirt and decayed flora once more. He turns this way and that, keeping each of his predators within his view lest they think they could best him.

Christian huffs in frustration at his predicament.

"Very well, I shall make the introductions. You deserve that much before we do, what we are going to..."

Alarico speeds to Christian with such alacrity the action is a blur. He clasps the back of Christian's neck and pulls him close enough that his mouth is but mere inches from his right ear.

"Do to you."

By some magic of the Mordant, we could make out every word Alarico uttered as if whispered into our own ear. My eyes could not quite remove themselves from looking upon the woman amongst them. She appeared to be the very same I had witnessed in my dream. Could it not have been a dream at all, but some sort of vision instead? A thread of dread began to swell within me.

Alarico's mouth opens, baring a barbarous collection of sharp teeth meant to rend flesh from bone. His tongue licks and suckles upon Christian's ear. Alarico slips back to his original position before Christian can react.

Christian furiously wipes at the side of his face with a murderous contempt for Alarico's minor assault.

"Vampyre?" Christian's accusation is not missed in his inquiry. Alarico bows, accepting the moniker with little offense. He rises and indicates the voluptuous woman to his right.

"The female you've no doubt cast your gaze upon is Tituba. A most beguiling creature, is she not?" Alarico continues, his tones playing heavily upon Christian's ear.

"Most alarming..." I murmured. *It seems their preternatural powers extended across the visual we witnessed.* Sensing my distress over Alarico's prowess, Joss nodded that he agreed, but bolstered my resolve to stand firm. The scene continued.

Tituba's visage flickers, slipping out of focus or altogether, as she glides her way across the earthen ground closer to Christian. He holds his Mordant with deliberateness as she approaches. A slow, creeping smile slithers across her face.

"Christian, is it now?" she murmurs. As with Alarico, this is a creature meant to lure men to their untimely demise. A true witch rather than the misguided failings during the trials of Salem.

"How have you come to know me? Pray not add lying to your witchy ways," Christian demands, though the tremor in his voice is plainly evident. He does his best to shore up his courage though it is plain upon his face this is but a losing battle.

A bubbly laugh devoid of any mirth, for she is a predator through and through, trickles upon her lips. She throws her head back slightly though her eyes glow as dark crimson orbs that know of the ninth level of hell. Satan's paramour on Earth.

"My dear boy, do you think it was by pure happenstance that poor Mister Michael Connolly, your most highly prized...paying companion...came upon you?"

She reaches Christian and her hand goes out to his face; he recoils, unsure of her touch. Her fingers curl in slightly as she resists, for the moment, granting Christian any such caress as he feared. A lascivious smile blossoms across her face, a predator casting a roving eye upon her precious prey.

She chuckles, sending shivers down Christian's back from the way he shakes it off. She leans in without touching but losing none of the voracity she desires to consume in the look she bears for him.

"You were targeted purposely. We knew of your lineage and that you might display rogue abilities of a Tewakenonhnè."

"I know not of what you speak."

She pulls back slightly, casting an eye to the hirsute man and Alarico, an arch to her brow suggesting this is a complete surprise to them all given the depth of information they seem to have on poor Christian. Alarico appears to have solved that little puzzle.

"He was born of a Mohawk woman who was assaulted and left the wee lad on the doorstep of a farmer further north in New York, only to escape at the age of eight and find himself without a home, food, or roof over his head. That is how you came to be under Uncle Edwin's employ, is it not?"

Christian seems most alarmed at the profound accuracy from the look on his face, that of sheer wonderment over Alarico's proclamation of his history.

"You seem to know an awful lot about me, sir. By what manner have you dredged my past to dangle it before me with the vehemence you so readily express?"

"My dear boy, have you not listened to a word we have put forth? We knew you would eventually show signs of being one of Spruce's lot and therefore an enemy to ours. It was our endeavor, through the now apparently deceased Mister Connolly—"

The hirsute man growls most dangerously at this statement, but Alarico shoots him a warning look not lost upon the others to stay his hand for the time being.

"To purchase your services with the sole intent of using that device in your hand to bring you to our side before your talents manifested themselves. You are, in a manner of speaking, our experiment."

He chuckles darkly, seemingly amused by Christian's folly.

"I dare say we had no expectation of your besting Michael as you apparently have. Quite remarkable. We...Tituba; Michael's twin brother, Malcom; and I are here to assess whether or not you are still salvageable for our purposes and if so, take you from this place to one of our own where you will complete your...transformation." He bows as if in deference to some greater cause.

"Our Lord Flint is most interested in you."

The quiver in Christian's voice plainly expresses the deepening dread that seems to take root in him as the details of his current situation reveal themselves to him.

"What if I cannot be of service to your cause?" Christian inquires, his hand with the Mordant shaking nearly equal to his voice. No doubt

he can see with the way he is surrounded his demise could come at any of his rival's hands.

Malcom is the one who provides the reply at this juncture. "Then we're given leave to dispatch with you any way we see fit. Given the abhorrent manner of my brother's demise, I daresay it shan't go easy for you. I, for one, plan on making it most painful and so great in length that you shall beg for mercy, of which you will find none."

During his pressing of their point Malcom has moved in closer to Christian, causing him to turn in his direction. His gaze widens as Malcom seems to slowly shift in shape, his fingers extended slightly with long claws, like that of a bear or wolf, ears that begin to grow into points, and even more hair pushed forth in such a manner it is truly astounding to behold. Malcom stops just a few steps shy of reaching Christian.

Tituba flickers for an instant, then reappears at the edge of their little circle around Christian, keeping him penned in but clearly wanting a distant view to assess the manner of executing their directive from Flint.

"Malcom, desist. We have not gathered the information our Lord requires."

Malcom glares at Alarico's warning and retreats a few steps but gives up none of his threatening change.

"A vampyre, a witch, and a lycan," Joss whispered under his breath to Jacob. I had a collection of the new gothic horror books within my personal library, among them Polidori's *The Vampyre*, *Hugues, the Wer-Wolf* by Menzies, and the infamous *Malleus Maleficarum*. I knew Jacob had read every one of them with such a fervor from our shared boarding room as I brought them along as passing literary fancies and his joy in consuming the writings of that nature tickled me to no end. Only now, pondering upon the visage before us, I began to understand that perhaps he was consuming them for an altogether different purpose.

::Jacob lent me the books when he did not think you knew. This is most disconcerting, William. Jacob sensed a shift in Flint's tactics was at hand. We argued about it constantly. It appears Jacob had the right of it, after all. Flint has seen fit to plunder the minds of men of their worst fears and has found a way to make them a reality. What more devilry can we expect from him now?::

Now the visual from my own dreams recalling those heated debates I witnessed made sense. Joss had been there all along, but somehow, I had been precluded from any such meeting of the two while at school. The idea did plague upon me as I watched Christian struggle with the enormity of how much Flint had accomplished in reaching into what truly would drive men to madness.

"Lemme make him talk, Rico. I may not have your particular talents, but I know how to make men talk about the things they'd rather not reveal," Malcom pleads with the posh vampyre. "And I need to know how the little whelp brought about the demise of me brotha..."

At this, Christian turns fully to face Malcom. "If Michael Connolly was indeed your brother, sir, then I can inform you I do not know how or why he expired in the manner he did. I did not even have the eyes with which to see it. I was facing the wall when it happened. This!" He turns the Mordant slightly in his hand so it is plain to Malcom and the rest. "This is the device of my torturous trysts with my client and your brother. He—" Christian pants and then swallows hard before continuing, no doubt the horrific end of Michael Connolly still playing out in his own mind as he struggles to put word to deed of that night. "—used it on me, bringing such pain for his efforts—always with my back to him so I could not see what he did but felt it so deeply that I could only liken it to servitude of Satan himself."

At that Malcom practically flies to Christian and grips him by the throat, the claws of his right hand pressing firmly against Christian's neck. It will take but one dramatic swipe with that hand and Christian will be in serious trouble. He well knows it too, given the heightened fear now expressed upon his countenance. Malcom growls most darkly, a certain degree of lust, though not of a sexual kind, more as if he wishes to consume the lad body and soul and would if Alarico and Tituba would allow it.

Despite Alarico's words regarding their orders from Flint, both he and Tituba seem to withdraw, leaving Christian to Malcom's mercy—of which he knows there will be none.

Malcom huffs twice before he makes his intent plain.

"Me brotha was all I had in this world, and you took him away from me!" His grip upon Christian's neck tightens, and he lifts Christian off his feet and flings him across the clearing into a large maple tree. But

rather than colliding with the tree, Christian turns at the last moment to face it and slips into it. The Mordant falls to the ground as Christian disappears. The bark buckles as a ripple moves up the length of the trunk to an apex where several large branches have separated from the main part of the tree. He emerges, unhurt and rather angry for Malcom's efforts.

A dark laugh echoes in the distance. Clearly, Alarico and Tituba are not visible but observing, nonetheless.

Malcom is somewhat alarmed at the ease with which Christian turned what could have been calamitous for his health only to convert it to his advantage by taking higher ground against his adversary.

"Your brother," Christian huffs with some effort, though it is quite plain that it is more out of frustration over his current predicament, "was a despicable man. And I can lay such claims at his feet because of the contemptuous manner with which he assaulted me, not just in person but in deed. If he was truly your brother, then I grieve for you. Not for his loss, but because you had the despicable fortune to be associated with him at all!"

::Well, if that did not seal the deal on his fate, I do not know what will.:: I thought in Joss's direction. He stroked across my mind to soothe my growing angst.

In a flash Christian descends from the tree and catches the wolf-infused visage of Malcom by surprise. He does not merely reach for Malcom but slams into him, disappearing altogether. Malcom shakes violently with Christian's assault, his skin buckled and split. Blood runs in gushing rivulets only to close again and reappear somewhere else. Eventually Christian emerges on the other side of Malcom, heaving gusts of breath from his lips. He holds his head in a cocked manner, angling it stiffly as if there were some effort in the movement now he has passed through Malcom.

Malcom spins around to see Christian assume modifications to his own body that mirror Malcom's, as if in passing through him he picked up the talents Malcom takes for granted. Christian appears to soak up whatever made Malcom and can now display his dexterity in newly shocking profound ways.

Christian swiftly moves in a blur to the other side of the clearing and retrieves his Mordant from the base of the maple tree. This time he does not level it in Malcom's direction. Instead he stares at it as if it means little to him now. His clawed fingers move over the device before he turns slightly to take in Malcom who glares with murderous contempt for Christian. For his part, Christian does not seem to see Malcom as much of a threat, as if he has all he needs to best the man now.

Alarico seizes the moment with Christian so focused upon Malcom and suddenly appears, gripping Christian around his neck from behind, his elongated slender fingers ending in what appear to be razor-sharp talons befitting a raptor. He hisses openly into Christian's right ear, baring needlelike teeth slick with vampiric saliva that drips like venom.

Malcom chooses this moment to rush Christian, thinking him subdued, only to watch in terror as Christian holds up the Mordant and his palm lights up white-hot. Both emit a cast of light so bright it briefly overwhelms the senses. When the light fades Malcom is embedded in a boulder several feet away, the rock slowly blending with Malcom's body, suffocating him. His strangled cries go unheeded by Christian who has turned in Alarico's grip and hisses back in defiance at the vampyre, matching him gaze for carnal gaze.

Alarico seems shocked at this turn of events but decides not to let it deter him. He leans back and with a sharp intake of breath seems to pull blood from Christian's body in a crimson shower. It glistens like tiny rubies in the air.

Christian repeats the same gesture before Alarico can inhale the sanguine-saturated air for himself, and returns his own blood to his body, further surprising the vampyre. It is apparent to them all that whatever Michael Connolly applied to Christian is working but in a manner rising to a level none of them anticipated. He is not only matching them move for move, but instantly knows how to turn the tables on his opponent.

I tucked this bit of information into my head as I glanced at Christian lying motionless on my own bed, thankful, at least for the time being, Joss was far more formidable than Christian's talents allowed.

Tituba twitches her way into the scene and, using hands that vibrate so fast you cannot witness their movement, begins to extract poor Malcom from the boulder. She seems to be making progress.

Christian smiles at Alarico before blasting him across the clearing. Alarico's free hand digs into the moist soil in a crouched stance, his eyes seething with rage, his Mordant evident in his left hand held above his back, poised to strike should Christian advance.

"Come at me if you dare..." Christian's voice slithers around the clearing much in the same manner as Alarico's did earlier. His ability to adapt and maneuver with these newly acquired talents clearly bests what the trio thought they would encounter.

Alarico smiles as if Christian's change to match him had been the one thing he hoped he would see. He slices through the air with his Mordant and disappears altogether though the tear in space, leaving Tituba and Malcom.

Christian rounds on the two of them as Malcom slips from the gouged rock and falls to the ground, his preternatural healing abilities slowly changing the blended rock from his own skin. It appears to be a slow and painful process. There is no getting up for him, it seems, too preoccupied with recuperation at this point.

Tituba turns her attentions to Christian.

"Well, little one, we seem to have misjudged you."

"Apparently so."

She flickers, changing her position to slowly advance in Christian's general direction though not in a straightforward manner, hoping to catch him off guard. He keeps his stance at the ready, Mordant in hand.

"I have had over one hundred and fifty years to hone my craft. Think you can best me as the others?" she murmurs, her voice making Christian shiver a bit as it caresses his ears. Having witnessed his earlier appropriations of their talents, it appears anything they share became a part of him—a point they have been slow to pick up.

"Give me your best, witch, and we shall soon see..." He matches her wiles tone for tone, enraging her. She comes at him with claws bared, her fingers vibrating and pushing their way into him. He writhes in agony for but a moment, bringing a rolling laugh from her lips for her self-perceived conquering moment. Then he lowers his gaze in a very controlled manner and looks her squarely in the eye.

"My turn..." And with that he seems to run some sort of charge from his own body. It courses through her immersed hands, causing them to flake off as if he were rattling her apart. She tries to slip from him, but his arms come about her, solidifying her from twitching out of this world as a means of escape.

"Let us hope Alarico can deliver your message to your Lord. I do not think you will be there to back him up."

At this he moves his hands so they clasp upon her throat, and he begins to squeeze. She writhes and tries desperately to jerk free of him, but his palms, burning brightly, keep her in place, the light from them radiating about her. She cries out in utter agony from his reversed assault, and for the third time, he bests them at their own game.

She continues to try to overwhelm him, but it is a lost cause. Anyone witnessing it could see the challenge is being met and reversed upon her. She finally is able to extract her hands from Christian's sides, though whether of her own accord or with Christian's exile of her from his body is unclear. Her hands go to his, trying in vain to gain her release from his death grip. He roars and she wails in a deafening crescendo until she bursts into tiny fragments that dissipate into the wind.

Christian stands, heaving large breaths to regain his composure once more. He walks slowly, stretching his sides one at a time to check for any lasting damage, until he reaches Malcom. He glares down upon the man before squatting over him, leering his last to him.

"I say to you, be warned not to engage me further. For you have witnessed how deadly a man I am. Your brother was a most despicable man. Intolerable, vile, and wretched do not begin to cover the thoughts I have for him and his memory. You've had your chance at retribution. Do not think it will go so easy for you should we cross paths again. Tell your leader, tell him from me, that I am not for him. I am for the first time in my sordid life my own man."

He spits in Malcom's face and rises, slashing the air with the Mordant and slipping into the darkened abyss beyond.

The scene faded from view, leaving the normalcy of my room to remain. Rebecca turned to us. We all stared at Christian lying quiet in my bed before turning to face Rebecca.

"Thoughts, gentlemen?"

We regrouped downstairs at the dinner table and settled in to what was left of Joss's amazing meal. The meat was a bit overdone, but it could not be helped as the viewing was paramount to our cause. We supped silently as we pondered what the vision brought us. Finally, Jacob broke the ice, startling all of us.

"It's one thing to think of him as a Guardian, but I have never experienced what he can do." Jacob eyed Christian who looked up from his plate but did not add anything to the conversation.

"A Flintling-Guardian crossbreed?" Joss inquired.

"Plausible...but how?" Jacob responded.

"The kind of sex we had, that's how" was all Christian offered before returning to his supper. The boy was ravenous. Joss supplied him with some additional meat and vegetables. He appeared thankful for the second plating.

"It is a good thing I made plenty," Joss commented and smiled at Christian to let him know he did not hold his hunger against him.

"What do you mean, the kind of sex? Without going into too much in the particulars, after all, we have a lady present," I added, knowing full well Rebecca's response when men made the mistake of protecting the gentility of women.

"You think I cannot imagine what two men would do together? Come now, I am no wilting flower of a sister as you well know, dearest brother. Spare no revelation on my account."

The last she said to Christian, but her voice softened considerably from the sisterly tone she took with me.

"It is not so much the sex as what he did to me while he violated me with his manhood every way come Sunday." He eyed the lot of us and added, "Beggin' your pardon."

"None needed," I offered.

"What *did* he do?" Jacob ventured where none of us seemed to want to inquire openly.

"He used that bloody Mordant on me. Caused me great pain and suffering. He was into pain during sex. It was a power thing with him. Wrestling me into submission, taking his way with me. Pardon my colorful language, Miss Hallett."

She waved a hand at him but nodded to give him encouragement to continue.

"He marked me, with the Mordant, I mean. It...did...*things* to me during the sex. I felt changes overcome me. Even after he left and I'd be lyin' up in my room recuperating—Uncle Eddy always let me have the rest of the night off if I was entertaining Mister Connolly. He was one of our biggest and highest-paying clients, you see. I was kept on well after most boys are let go for growing too old, manhood and all. The clients are into boys who can pass for little girls when they are all dolled up, you see."

We watched him intently, and when we added nothing he continued.

"Anyway, I was kept on for the clients who wanted things a bit on the rougher side. I'd been working for Uncle Eddy since I was a boy of eight. Made my way up." He smiled proudly at that, though his pride diminished when it was clear we could not sort how to be happy for a boy in his state moving up within the brothel. "I mean, I took on other duties. Saw to the boys like an older brother. Kept them in line, saw to their needs as best I could—feedings and such. I was good to the lads; they all looked up to me."

He suddenly became quite sad which alarmed us.

"I just don't know what will happen to the poor lads now I've gone. Eddy will be ruthless with them, I am sure of it. Though I took out the worst of his henchmen—that Henry the Hook. Right piece o' work he was. But I got the bastard!" He slammed his fist on the table, startling us all.

He looked at each of us.

"You don't understand. What with your life and the people you move about in. Those boys need me. But I can't go back there and work for Eddy." He shook his head, almost violently so. "I won't!"

Rebecca placed a placating hand upon his balled-up fist, and he seemed to calm down immensely from his frustration and anger over the fate of the brothel boys.

"We need to do something to help those lads. It is not right," I added, my own dander on the rise from Christian's tale.

"And we shall, *Ohnehta'kowa*. Jacob and I will see to it."

"I shall help you in that," Rebecca offered, but Jacob had other ideas.

"No. Let Joss and me take care of it. We know what to do. You are better prepared to go to the mission and explain what we have encountered and make the necessary preparations to receive the boys once the brothel has been taken down. How many are we talking, Christian?"

He counted them up in his head before replying, "Sixteen. No more than that I suspect. Perhaps less if some of them escaped when I left."

Jacob nodded to Joss and then turned to Christian.

"Let us make haste to the brothel. William, can you alert the authorities on a disturbance—where is it exactly?"

"Mulberry...just outside the Points. Capricious Hall. A right den of iniquity if there ever was one," Christian replied.

"Tell them to arrive in about an hour, then return here for safety. Rebecca and Christian will go and alert the missionary orphanage about the status of the boys and why they are coming to them tonight."

"Not to worry. They will take the lads in. If anything, to take them away from the sordid work they have been subjugated to throughout their childhood. That will be my selling point." Rebecca rose and moved to the sink to clean her plate.

Christian quickly finished his meal and took his plate to her. The look in his eyes for my sister spoke volumes of the infatuation he carried for her. Jacob took notice of the lad and had no doubt surmised the same sort of boyhood crush he witnessed in Christian's gaze over his former girlfriend. He seemed to let it go given the tenuous truce standing between him and my sister. Not a bad idea in the long run.

We all finished our meal and cleaned up while Jacob and Joss prepared their assault on Capricious Hall. I knew of the place, having spent enough time trolling the Points. Sadly, I even knew some of my kind, well-placed men within the social elite of Manhattan, if not the world, who frequented the establishment. It had quite the reputation even beyond the Points.

"Woe be to them if they are there tonight," I murmured to myself.

"What was that?" Joss inquired as he drew near.

I shook my head. "It was nothing, just absorbing Christian's sordid tale. I am glad we are putting an end to that place. Just one more level of evil this world needs to be rid of."

He agreed with me but added, "There is no greater evil than to steal the childhood from a child. There is no coming back from that. Not really. All we can do is to help heal what has happened and ensure it does not happen again."

The look in Joss's eyes told me Jacob and he agreed. This Uncle Eddy's days were numbered and could be counted with one finger. Tonight would not only see the demise of his establishment, but perhaps the demise of Uncle Eddy himself.

"Joss, are you going to...?"

He put a hand to my shoulder.

::It is best not to think about it. It would not be the first time I have had to make this choice, nor will it be my last. It is never easy to take this path, but take it I must. Jacob will be there, so it will happen quite quickly. But I will close our link for the duration of this attack. I do not want you to try to breach it. Do we have an understanding?::

I nodded and felt the need to pull him into an embrace. This caught my sister's attention, and she nodded once with a smile that could be interpreted a number of ways. I would corner her about it later.

Within the next five minutes we all departed, each to our separate destinations. I hailed a calash to the precinct nearest the Points in my attempt to get them to the hall within the hour. No small feat considering the disarray in which the police tended to operate. I also had the fact they were overworked and probably carried payments from Eddy to ensure they did not come calling upon the brothel to consider as well. I hoped my family prestige and status within high Manhattan society could carry some weight in the matter.

The precinct was awash in the dregs of the Points being hauled in for one crime or another. I checked my pocket watch and discovered I had naught but forty minutes to convince someone of the events about to occur at Capricious Hall. I made my way to the main desk to make inquiries about reporting what I knew would come to pass when it appears my cohorts had begun a full half hour earlier than expected.

Just as I approached the desk a lower-ranking officer came barreling in, raising a warning of explosions and fighting going on at the very same hall. Within seconds of his announcement I witnessed more cops in one location than I ever imagined possible. It was as if the building itself birthed them, fully formed and in uniform. They poured from every hall, every room, down the stairs. It was a sea of blue as they made their way out of the building into waiting paddy wagons. The whole main floor became awash with activity. Not wanting to add my name to any suspect list if I could avoid it, I let the stout Irish cop do my bidding for me and backed slowly out of the melee of the police station and tried my best for the next fifteen minutes to hail a way home.

Once within the confines of my home, I paced back and forth like a caged wild animal. Joss still had himself shielded from me. I could not sense or feel him.

Surely, he must be free of that morass by now. Gods above I pray he is safe and will return to me. I also had a terrible thought that perhaps I could not reach him because something bad had happened to him. Would I know if he died?

That only added to my anxiety over the events of tonight.

Again, Tiyanoga's words simmered across my mind. I still inwardly debated whether I should heed his desire not to fight my instinct to protect Joss at all costs or to do my best to remain distant. I could not reconcile that he was the leader of the enemy, and yet somehow when he spoke to me, I did not detect one modicum of withholding on his part. So, in essence, I supposed I believed him and the manner of his tale. To what end should I run with it? That was a different question altogether. One I was not too sure I had an answer to or one I wanted to answer just yet.

One thing I was more than sure of? Joss was central to where my life would go now. To what extent I could provide support and companionship worthy of him I could not begin to sort. I only hoped I could rise to the occasion as needs called for.

"Blast! Why have I not heard from them?"

I could stand it no longer. I pressed along my link to Joss with an urgency I hoped would gain his attention.

::?!::

Finally. Some response. I would take his confusion at my plea over continued silence.

::Are you all right? Did it go according to plan?::

::We are fine, Will, and shall return in a few minutes. We are ensuring the boys rescued do not end up in the hands of the police but at Crossroads as intended. Some were arrested. Jacob and I have been trading gating into the wagons and releasing them from their bonds and gating them near the missionary so Rebecca and Christian can care for them.::

::Will not gating open our world to them?::

::It appears too late for that. Evidently, they witnessed enough from Christian's departure and the stolen Mordant to know there are more mystical elements at work. We are only too glad to provide a cover story for them. Who would believe Mohawk warriors disappearing and reappearing across town? They have no proof, and it appears they are only too happy to be free of their Uncle Eddy to question our methods of escape.::

A moment later and they both appeared in my living room to find me a muddled mess fraught with worry. I hugged them both, much to their amusement. I cared not one jot whether I appeared silly or not; I could not bear the thought of something removing my dearest friends, indeed brothers, from me now they were so firmly entrenched in my day-to-day life.

Joss joined me upstairs, he to the spare room to retrieve his belongings and me to mine to prepare the bed. Jacob begged off that he had to return to Akwesasne to report what had transpired tonight but would return in the morning for us to continue to assimilate what we had gleaned from our exchange with the mysterious Christian Stuyvesant.

::Joss?::

::Yes, Ohnehta'kowa, what is troubling you now?::

I huffed a bit because while we could easily converse in this manner, I was a man stuck in my old-fashioned ways. I liked face-to-face conversations. Sensing this, Joss queried me gently with his next offering.

::Would you prefer my sharing your bed so we can discuss what is troubling you so? I can feel you are raging about something but will not permit me to see the fullness of it.::

A smile, warm and full as the midday sun, coursed along my lips. I did not know why I reacted to Joss so warmly. After all, he had accosted me twice trying to remove him from my mind only to prove he could not—though I was not too sure how I had managed such a feat given Joss's very persuasive methods to cloud something he did not want others to know.

::You will have to give me a moment as I am not wholly presentable for company in your room.::

I sighed. What could he possibly mean by that?

::Josiah Lightfoot, get into my room and in my bed as you are now. We have nothing to hide between us. I can sense your thoughts and emotions, and you have proven on more than one occasion that mine has a welcome mat you traipse over on a pure whim. So let us not stand on propriety now, shall we?::

::Will...::

::Now, Josiah!::

Suddenly a rush of emotions made me giggle as if someone had shared with me an off-colored joke or bon mot. Laughter bubbled along my lips only to be silenced the moment he gated into my bed on my left side. Thankfully, once I realized why he had tried to warn me I was in deep awe of his being so precise with his gating abilities because I knew without a doubt he was completely naked.

"My apologies for any perceived impropriety, Will. But I did try to warn you of my current state of undress."

"I know what you mean. And it is of little concern. We are both men; we both have the same parts and physicality to us. Unless you have sprouted something I have not witnessed that would shock me beyond belief?"

"I assure you, I am simply a man lying within your bedding. I just sleep far more comfortable this way. If you wish I will retreat to my room and dress more accordingly."

"Stop just there. To show you I bear no ill will…" I climbed out of the bed and slithered the nightshirt from my body and slipped back within the down bedding, so we were of like mind *and* body.

He seemed rather pleased with my action. A warm and soothing feeling emanated from him, immediately calming what might have been an awkward moment into something I grew to understand would become quite commonplace with us.

I turned on the bed, resting my head against my hand with my arm crooked into my pillow for support. He did the same. For a moment, I faltered. Everything seemed to stop. His eyes were wide, with a gaze so soft I found it completely mesmerizing to the point I nearly forgot myself and why I wanted to talk with him at all.

"You were saying something about what troubled you about tonight's events."

So, like a poor man with a diarrheic excuse of a mouth, it all poured out. A steady stream of my fears over Christian's life, what he and Jacob must have witnessed with those poor boys, and the profane lives they led at such a tender age. Being the only one of the team who felt completely sidelined because I could not do anything on their level to help. The absolute frustration of not being able to do anything about it.

As I raged I sat up for a few moments, knees bent with my arms around them. I noticed during this time that Joss, while still attentive to every word I ranted over him and my ineptitude to keep up with the rest of them, continually watched the fullness of my bare back. At one point he sat up and began to massage me, making me quite relaxed to the point my angered words became slurred.

"William, you know you cannot take on the world and all of its ills. Even Jacob and I know, with our talents, that there are limits on what we can do. Yes, they lie well beyond how mortal men can affect their surroundings or problem-solve a situation. But, what I can tell you is that…lie forward onto your stomach, your muscles are a mess. This whole evening has gotten to you and your body is literally tightened up. You are alarming me with how much of it you internalize and let get to you."

I huffed, not even thinking about our shared nudity, and flung myself forward onto the bed toe to head. He continued to work my muscles as he explained how much my being there for him now gave him far more courage to take on things than he ever had before. While the Guardianship was linked in a loose sort of way, what we shared was far more powerful and how deeply thankful he felt that I embraced it rather than tried to push it away.

I had an answer for that but found I could not put a voice to it because I could not speak the man's name who put it there. That too was infuriating—Joss, for all of his talents, could not access those thoughts, plans, and schemes from the other side. They would remain hidden until we needed them most.

The soothing of my body with his more than capable hands and the softness of his tone allowed me to fully relax for the first time in more days than I cared to remember. Ever the gentleman, when he realized I was falling into slumber, he slowly helped me turn back around in bed and tucked me in for the night. He turned the lamps out in the room, and I heard him pad his way toward the bathroom so he could return to his room through the shared door.

"Joss?"

"Yes, my William."

"Do not leave me. Return to our bed. I would feel so much more at ease with everything that has happened in so short a time if you were here with me should something find its way into my room while I sleep. I hope you do not mind the request I am making. I mean no impropriety by it, I assure you."

He slipped back into his side of the bed and pulled the covers over himself.

"Whatever you say, my William. Whatever you say…"

I gave into sleep's glorious embrace, knowing the greatest friendship I shall ever have did not mind keeping watch over me while I slept. As I fell, a silent prayer slithered its way across my mind: *Do not ever leave my side, Joss. I have come to count upon it, far more than you know.*

For a fleeting moment, as I lost control over my waking body, I swore I heard him sniffle back a tear.

Chapter Seven

Beyond the Pale

Wherein William and Joss learn of Jacob's trip to the Central bringing the Guardianship up to date on current events, only to find themselves in a quandary that can wait no longer.

November 3, 1847
William Hallett's Home
Manhattan, New York
9:35 a.m.

Jacob returned the following morning as planned. Rebecca advised us via messenger that the boys were being settled and Christian was in great spirits having them so close to him without the worry of Uncle Eddy or the brothel.

Jacob had more pressing matters to bring to our attention: Samuel was contemplating making a change of assignment with regard to Thomas's continued training. It appeared while Thor and Thomas were getting along, under observation of their sessions, it became quite clear Thor's continued ire for Joss's perceived sway over Sam would be a bad influence to put on Thomas at so important a stage in his training. To put it plainly, Thor, or the Jemisons, would not be happy.

For my part, I was not sure why this assignment was problematic. I thought there was no better way for him to learn his craft than under a respected family member. I only had to think of Tessa's vehement appraisal of Joss to realize they had the right of it despite my belief that family was always best.

::But you forget that Jacob is family, Will.:: He relayed his last to me from the bathroom as we prepared for bed.

::We are all related in one way or another. That is the purpose of seeking the approval of the Clan Mothers when proposing a marriage. We intend to cross bloodlines to ensure our infighting and warring ways will not return. If we are all family of one sort or another, then it will often stay our hand in a disagreement.::

While I understood their position, I took solace in the fact that at least he was getting proper instruction as to his newfound abilities. Training, for good or ill, was better than no training at all.

As to the whereabouts of Tessa, Marc, and John, Joss and I compared notes on what we thought had been their outcome from the engagement with Thomas's creation. The final result was either they perished completely, as evidenced by Thomas's own retelling of the events, or more along the lines of what Joss had assumed: they were trapped somewhere.

That somewhere, however, was not immediately accessible as Joss was sure it might be the thin veil where the Guardians gated from one place to another. Having gone through the gating process more than once, I could see the point Joss was making for as you moved from one place to another, in the infinitesimal moment between those two points you had a feeling of being in neither. It was not a wholly unpleasant sensation, but at the same time I could not fathom how I would feel being trapped in a place that seemed to be neither here nor there.

Joss took me out to the border lands surrounding Akwesasne, and we began to experiment gating from one point to another with me as a side-along passenger. Joss's thought was I could be the impartial observer since he was preoccupied with the actual gating process. I quickly became somewhat frustrated because while I could sense that separation, I had no way of figuring out how to peer into it. Joss tried it a few times himself to no avail. Maddening though it was, Joss was determined to figure it out. I posed that if they were in there now for what had amounted to several days, how would they have survived with neither food nor water? His explanation vexed me to no end.

"Think of it in this way then," he explained. "If we move but from one place to another in the blink of an eye, would it not be possible that the space in between could be running at a different pace? I mean what passes for us as a full day might be but mere seconds to them? Thus, several days be no more than a few hours at most?"

I had to admit I had not thought of it in that way. It certainly was plausible.

As it turned out we need not have waited long for an answer; though when it came it was not news to warm the heart. It appeared that when young Master Thomas had attempted to recall the creature during one of his training sessions, with the assistance of his uncle Thor to control the beast, Tessa had made her way back but spoke of a horrific time spent between the worlds. She said she and her companions could sense one another though they did not appear to have flesh and blood bodies with which to comport themselves. As a group or individually they could sense other Guardians, as well as what they assumed were Flintlings, moving between the worlds by gating. Several attempts were made to latch onto their movements when they occurred; however, all the attempts were to no avail.

Jacob spoke of Tessa breaking down a bit and crying over her cousins' fate as they appeared to have been among the first of the trio to try the crossing. She lost both boys in those attempts. She spent a great deal of time lamenting their loss, leaving her alone in the darkness. When Jacob pressed her for what she meant by "loss," she would not give a direct answer. He was left to assume they had perished in the ordeal, though Tessa banished all talk of her cousins' premature demise. So, a mystery would remain regarding her cousins.

Thankful that Tessa had been spared a "nonexistent" life in the abyss, Joss and I were quick to ask Jacob if the time they spent in the void seemed to pass quickly or over a great length. Sadly, he could neither confirm nor deny our suspicions—I say *our* when I fully acknowledge it was Joss who came up with the theory, but as we shared one mind, there was no other way to see it.

The reason for this was in no small part attributed to Jacob's lack of query upon the much-debated subject. We would have to wait for resolution upon the matter when next we saw Tessa.

In either event, Joss relayed, prior to our departure, what we discovered to Samuel, such as it was. He thanked us for the information and advised us he would put other Guardians onto searching for the missing Jemison brothers.

With that mystery stalled in its tracks, we decided wholeheartedly to press on with the one we had been pursuing before the whole Jemison quest had spun out of control and consumed our investigation.

It was a brisk Tuesday morning when I came downstairs to find Joss cooking eggs and bacon, and my tea already steeping along nicely in the small teapot. Jacob sat at the table with a plate scraped clean and only a smattering of biscuit crumbs dotting the unadorned white porcelain plate. He was looking over what I assumed were some of our notes regarding the recent events we had spied within the confines of that warehouse and what our next course of action would be as I arrived.

"Bit of a morning fry-up, is it?" I asked as I slid into my chair, already pouring myself the aromatic Earl Grey concoction I loved so well.

"Hmmm, one egg or two?" Joss asked as he proceeded to make three, knowing full well breakfast was always my largest meal.

I merely caught his eye and smiled, pulling a biscuit from the towel-covered bowl, still warm enough in my hand that I immediately slathered it with some butter and began to consume it ravenously.

"So, what is on deck for this morning?" I asked between chews as Jacob raised an eyebrow over my speaking with a mouthful.

Who knew Indians could be so touchy about table manners?

I smirked because it had always been so with Jacob. One of the first things I had to learn about him was he was a stickler for table etiquette, though in my own home where I was master, I realized he would just needle me about it to call up our shared past.

"It appears we are running low on food supplies," Jacob replied as he finished writing down the last of his notes. "Christian consumed more than we realized."

Only then did I realize it was not our investigation he was poring over but a shopping list. We needed to buy more supplies to support the three of us sharing my home. I had to admit when it was just myself, I spent more time out in the public houses than cooking for myself. Not that I minded cooking; in point of fact, I relished it. However, in a matter of a few days we had pretty much cleared the house of any victuals.

"Survival is first on our list," Jacob added.

"Well, no time like the present, I say. I have a stash of money in my bedroom I can collect that should more than pay for your little list there. What say we finish the meal and get this taken care of so we can concentrate upon the investigation this evening?"

"My thoughts exactly."

"Who is Sarah Covington?" Joss asked as he slipped the plate before me loaded with fried eggs, skillet-fried potatoes, and what appeared to be a half pound of sliced bacon, of which he swiped three rashers as he sat between Jacob and me.

"Just a lady I met once at a party some time ago. Why do you ask?"

"You have a date in your calendar this Friday evening. Is it a party?"

"Blast!" In all the events over the last few days, I had completely forgotten about it.

"I take it you are not looking forward to going?"

"No, it is not that. She is...well, for lack of a better term, *assertive*. And not in a way that makes single gentlemen like myself comfortable. She is likened to a muskie. A few moments with her and any man, no matter his steely resolve, would shrink after her ministrations. Yet for all my maneuvering, I did accept her invitation to her birthday party this Friday."

Joss and Jacob exchanged a glance. It was so brief I was sure they did not think I saw it, so I decided for the sake of secrecy I would play along with this little game to see how it played out.

"Would you both care to join me?"

They shared another look, clearly meant for my viewing, as Jacob raised an eyebrow suggesting the absurdity of my offer. We regarded one another for a moment. "Oh, all right. Forget I asked."

My mood turned sour. Jacob proceeded to gather himself but stopped short.

"You cannot expect savages such as ourselves to be well received at such an auspicious Manhattan social event? Come now, Will. You know the way these things must play out."

"But in school..."

"That was *in school*. We were but boys there playing the field," Jacob murmured, placing a hand upon mine. I was being placated and I knew it. So did Jacob, though I had to admit he had the right of it. I withdrew mine from his and spared him a small smirk. I appreciated his efforts.

"It is just...well, my old life holds little interest for me now. Truth be it known, I was floundering ever since we parted company that rueful last day of school. Family pressures to marry and set up household. To settle into some sort of business as befits my station."

My temper swelled as all those emotions I worked so hard to repress and endeavor to circumvent were surrounding me to the point of my being suffocated.

Jacob rose and looked at Joss who only nodded. Something had passed between them.

Did they talk about me when I was not around?

"I will wait for you in the library. Take your time; it is still relatively early, so we will not miss much of the morning market."

And with that, he took his leave. Joss watched me with a quietude that sapped what stormy anger had begun to take root.

"I will go with you to the party if that is your wish."

It was my turn to placate.

"Nay, Joss. I would not subject you to that coven of ignominy. They reek with it. I cannot believe I used to count myself willingly amongst their number. Gods in heaven, what was I thinking? When my path had been right before me throughout my youth. I belong here, with you and Jacob and our quest to stop these vile creatures before they overrun the planet. Not trading silly conversational quips to satiate a wanton filly whose social status is incumbent upon the quality of the stud she beds."

"And what a catch you would make, no? I can certainly see why she makes such a play."

My eyes snapped to his, searching for intent within those words. Surprisingly, his did not stray from my stare. This was new territory for Joss. In the short time I had known him, and the intimacy we share when our minds linked, he would be the one to bury his meaning within his words.

But before I could comment upon it or seek its fullest, he closed himself off to me. Completely. This was new.

"I only mean that given your family status and financial position, any woman with a modicum of social evolution would find you a most suitable jewel. Personal effects aside, it is purely a business arrangement where women are concerned. This is the very nature of why your world is established upon shaky ground. Your lot do not value your women and what place they should hold within it. They are to be bartered away like cattle. The only hope of acceptability is through marriage. You can hardly blame them for their actions. Were I in their position, I know I would do whatever I could to secure a man who would grant me that sense of security in life, say nothing of love and passion, though one would have hope they would enter the mix at some point. And if not, then at least there is a roof overhead and food in the belly. What more needs could there be to survive?"

"Ah, but therein lies the rub for me. I require nothing but love and loyalty and a strong sense of adventure. Life is meant to be lived, Joss. Surely, you above all people know that."

"All too well. Though my lonely existence can scarcely be likened to an adventure." He held up his hand to quash my protestations and continued. "There are wondrous and amazing battles and visages to behold, to be sure, but that does little to quell those nights when you are out in the middle of a forest with little in the way of companionship, let alone an amorous one. Adventurers rarely speak upon it, for their dalliances are few and far between. The adventure alone becomes their paramour."

He clasped my hand in his. The moment his hands locked upon mine, a shiver ran between us, causing the small hairs on the back of my neck to stand up. I had come to believe any touch between Joss and me was charged due to our connection and his status as a Guardian. Now, I was not so sure.

"William...*Ohnehta'kowa,* do not rush to abandon a life of wife, family, and fortune for the sake of adventure. You may soon find yourself at the end of a pistol with a life woefully cut short, and little to show of its passing."

Then he released it: a wave of raw emotion filled with countless days and nights of loneliness and sorrow at the hands of his *adventurous* life. It so overwhelmed me. It caught the very breath from my lips. My eyes swelled from the tears his words called from me. His next reverberated through every inch of my being.

"I only show you so you can make an informed decision. I do not want you to become a man filled with regrets of the path not taken."

He rose to leave and slowly withdrew his hands from mine, taking the wave of emotion with him. I was utterly spent from the ordeal.

As he passed the doorway, he called back softly. "Finish your meal; you need the sustenance. No reason to let it go to waste."

And then, he too was gone.

An hour later, the three of us moved along the street, choosing the stroll to the market over the use of a hired calash. We could have gated to an unobserved location near the market, but given the number of people and the brightness of the morning, we opted against risking that we might be seen.

In addition to tan pants and riding boots, I was dressed in a morning coat of dark purple with a waistcoat in embroidered hues of deep orange and green, a soft tied collar topping off a pale cream-colored shirt. I knew I cut quite a figure, yet I could not shake how out of place all this finery felt—confining after spending time suited in the life I had come to call my own. My birthright, my brave new...dare I think it: *adventure*. Now I only longed to get out of these entrapments and back into the more traditional clothing Joss had introduced to me.

::But, Ohnehta'kowa, you cut a dashing figure. No one can wear a morning frock coat quite like you. Though they do try. 'Tis a lost cause.::

I warmed to his compliment but found it interesting how he could think such things and yet have no outward appearance registering such a response. It left me feeling as if I were going slightly mad and inventing these responses all on my own.

Joss did nothing to allay those fears.

At times I succumbed, rather unwillingly, to the temptation to reach out to him only to find him completely sensitive to my probing, which in turn drove me into complete retreat. If he sensed my reticence, he showed no outward signs. Though occasionally, I swore I could feel him seeking me out in the same manner.

"Will, I suggest we gain the root cellar staples last as they should have the shortest time from market to the home as possible," Jacob said, taking no note of the unspoken exchange between Joss and me.

I nodded my agreement, and the three of us turned into the throng of the market.

The sights, sounds, and smells never ceased to amaze me, no matter the time of year. For the time being, my melancholy thoughts were washed away by the rush of the crowd, and I became enthused with the prospect of shopping, even if only for the staples of food and drink.

Moving about the vendors and shoppers, we collected several items to take back to our house. Jacob suggested he and Joss slip away and deposit the goods so they could return and complete any further purchases. I thought it an admirable idea, and we decided upon a narrow alleyway about a third down the street from the start of the market. It was a dank and musty passage that could bear little more than an average man's shoulder width.

With Jacob and Joss's collective imposing figures, not counting my own, we just barely fit. Having worked their way about a quarter into the alley, and after double-checking to ensure they were not being observed, they gated out of sight.

I waited by the mouth of the alley, simply observing patrons as they passed by. I tilted my hat to a couple of ladies who happened to be out shopping with their mother. The latter gifted me with a terse smile before whisking away her daughters further down the marketplace. I only smiled after them and shook my head.

::If they only knew...::

::Knew what?::

I had not realized that in my amusement I had left myself open for Joss to listen in.

::'Tis nothing, Joss. Just a mother thinking I am a cad for seducing her daughters when it could not be further from the truth.::

::More is the pity for her, then. Her daughters should only be so lucky.::

::Exactly my line of...::

I trailed off because at that moment, about four vendor carts down the street, Miss Sarah Covington came into view. She was discussing something rather tersely with another woman I did not recognize. However, with her was a young boy who looked most familiar. I only had a side profile of him as he seemed disconnected to the intense discussion between the two women.

::Will...?::

I know I should have replied to Joss, but the boy finally turned, his face passing fully before me, and I realized where I had seen him before. He was the young lad whom I had observed at Satan's Circus within the Points. The very same boy who was working with the Flintlings!

I do not know if my rising alarm caused some sort of jolt between Joss and myself, but in the next instant a gust of wind whirled up next to me, making everyone, myself amongst their numbers, cover their eyes at the amount of dust being blown about. When I could regain myself, I discovered Joss and Jacob were by my side, seemingly having gated right out into the open market, observable to everyone.

"What in blazes did you do that for? You both could have been seen!"

"You covered your eyes during that sudden gust, did you not?" Jacob asked, a small smile upon his face. It was then I realized the bluster of air was no mere accident; it was properly planned by these two.

"It is not something we do very often, Will, but if needs arise in an emergency, we have been known to cause a distraction using air, water, or some other naturally occurring element with which we can disguise our arrival."

"It is most effective, if a little overdramatic," Jacob offered when I looked slightly incredulous. "Joss figured out how to do it with little risk to the Guardian who called upon it."

"Well, there is the reason for my growing concern," I remarked as I quietly indicated the boy some one hundred and fifty feet down the street.

At this point, the woman and Sarah appeared to complete their discussion because the woman seized the boy's hand and was moving off into the crowd. I was curious to know how these two knew each other and in what capacity the young boy figured into the whole scheme. What had deceived me was that he was a bit more cleaned up than in the Points. If I had to venture a guess, I would lay odds the woman was the boy's mother or some other relative, due to the way he allowed her to scoop him away from the terse encounter with Miss Covington.

"That boy is the very same from the night at the Flintling warehouse," Joss added.

"The very same, and now he moves off without us. We should give chase; however, I see no way for me to pass the ever-observant eyes of Miss Covington. No doubt she would detect my presence. This is damned infuriating."

"Leave it to us, Will. We can manage."

::We will meet you back home once we gain further information from the woman and the boy.::

They moved off and another flurry of dust and air stirred about them. They simply drifted off into the ether, becoming fainter to the eye with each step, until I could detect them no more.

Now I had a choice to make. Either return home and wait for their arrival to learn who the woman and the boy were and how they were officially connected to our investigation or to put myself into the fray by engaging the ever-prescient eye of Miss Covington.

I gritted my teeth and pressed forward, determined to find out what I could about the altercation between the two women. As I closed within a few steps of her, she turned to face me, and for a moment I could have sworn she had a contemptuous look in her eye that softened to a slightly rapacious one as I came into view.

"Sweet William, how lovely to see you about in the marketplace. Why, we shall have to be far more careful lest the people of our fair city begin to think we are using the market as a ruse for our clandestine meetings."

Outwardly, I smiled warmly, though inwardly I was shuddering at the thought of being captured by this predatory creature.

"It is always a pleasure to run into you, Miss Covington. The day always seems to be a bit brighter after our encounters. I am nothing short of overjoyed that today will be such a day now our paths have crossed yet again."

"But I see no goods within your grasp. Could it be you *are* using this as a ruse?"

"Oh, I have a couple of recently acquired assistants who have already taken my purchases back to our, er, *my* home."

Her eyes widened at the slight miscalculation in my speech. She did not miss a turn, this one.

"Live-in assistants? My, we have moved up in life, have we?"

"Not so much, I assure you. Certainly, nowhere near the opulence of staff at Beekman Place."

I took her offered hand. She slipped it into the crook of my elbow like a constrictor clings to the branch of a tree. I was in her vise-like grip as she smiled and took in those who made our acquaintance while we strode further into the market. She clearly enjoyed the wide eyes and wagging tongues that both preceded and fell in our wake.

That I had the reputation of being cordial and gentlemanly to a fault, I think, only added to the gape-mouthed stares by the more matronly society members. Surely this would make its way back to Grandmama who would only be too glad some woman had started to make inroads to the coveted altar of marital bliss with me in tow.

My thoughts were obviously not my own as I could detect Joss sniggering at my revulsion in placating Miss Covington. I sent a retaliatory feeling of contempt at his amusement which only succeeded in magnifying it.

Only when we had sufficiently moved along did I dare broach the subject which led me to the current dance with the viper vixen.

"Pardon my intrusion, but who was that woman you were speaking with rather tersely? I only ask because it seemed you were engaged in a heated debate and I do not ever recall seeing her in your company before."

"And well you have not, William. She is a detestable creature who all but accosted me here in the marketplace, rambling on about how I influenced her employer and how her post was now threatened by my actions. She was doing her best to threaten me that I should hold my tongue. Yet I could not, in all honesty, ever recall having said influence over someone else's employment other than house staff at Beekman. That she would bring her poor child into the debate was but a mark upon her lowly character. I told her in no uncertain terms she was grossly mistaken, and I wanted nothing to do with her or her post with her employer. My denial must have upset her because she spoke with the most profane language and then took her leave of me. It was most disconcerting, and I wish to speak upon it no longer, for fear it will sour my day."

I nodded, for I could not think of a way to further the conversation along. We strolled quietly for a few moments when she embarked upon the subject of her birthday party just a few days hence.

"Now, William, you will be a dear and not arrive late to the party? I would not want anyone to think I was unattended at my own birthday party, now would I?"

"No, uh, we would not want that at all. Consider it confirmed that we will endeavor to arrive fifteen minutes prior to the appointed time."

She smiled, having secured me as her escort for the evening. No doubt it was quite the victory, seeing she accomplished it without my sister to intervene. Her smile held all the malice of predator to prey. In that moment, I knew what the forest mouse felt when he was beheld in the eyes of the owl. Unfortunately, I did not know of any way to avoid the situation, as our recent observation warranted a close examination of the mysterious Miss Covington. Thankfully, Rebecca would afford me some degree of security in dealing with the viper.

As I contemplated her story, however, I was not quite so accepting of her proclaimed effrontery at being accosted by a stranger. Their exchange had a distinct element of familiarity about it. I could not point to a specific part of their conversation though, if I had to guess, it may be the way Sarah had lowered herself to the woman's level by becoming just as animated and vicious, rather than the cool, collected, and austere woman I had come to know. That Sarah would have never deigned to associate with any familiarity those beneath her station.

So, as she clung to my elbow, nodded to the gossip-hungry matrons at our public association, and played every element of a girl basking in the glow of my attention, *I* knew the difference, and it sent rivulets of hyperborean chills to replace my blood supply. This overall wave of dread must have connected with Joss because I saw him quickly approach in a flurry of dust, from down the street.

"Now, where has my manservant gone off to?" I muttered, knowing full well, of course, that Joss was heading my direction. "Ah, here he comes."

A sideward glance to Sarah confirmed my suspicions about any ulterior motives she may have had in my direction; her face manifested a look of sheer terror at the sight of Joss, now a half block from our present course.

"Ah, William, you must forgive me. I have forgotten that I need to meet up with a woman who has graciously worked out the culinary arrangements for the Friday affair. Silly of me, really." She had already disconnected from the crook of my arm and was moving in the direction from which we had progressed. "Though it only occurred to me at this moment. Do forgive me, and I will wait with all anticipation your arrival Friday hence."

Joss moved with increasing swiftness to me, a pointed determination in his eye that I found both comforting and disconcerting at the same time.

"You just missed her," I commented to him as he came to take her place.

"We will deal with your Miss Covington soon enough. Will, I need you to come with me. Jacob and I followed the woman and the boy to a place we believe may be key to their operations." He took my right elbow in his hand and began to guide me back to the alleyway where they departed with the groceries.

As we stepped into the narrow passage, I began to feel slightly uneasy.

"Joss, can we get on with it? I really detest small tight spaces."

"Will, you do trust me. Do you not?"

"With my life, Joss. But why all the concern?"

"You shall see soon enough."

A sudden prickling came over me as if ants had crawled out of some crevice in the alley and consumed me whole.

::Steady, Ohnehta'kowa. This is something new for you. It will feel most uncomfortable but I assure you it is worth it.::

::Very well, just get it over with. This sensation is most distracting.::

We gated but not in any manner I had become accustomed. In normal situations—though I use the term advisedly as gating is anything but—the gating is a simple change of scenery as you seem to move from one step to another. There is a sensation along the lines of passing through icy-cold water, without the feeling of getting wet, and suddenly you find yourself on the other side.

This gating was nothing like that.

The prickly sensation intensified as we moved forward. Followed by a pressure behind my eyes, somewhere in my head, as if I had been rendered unconscious and was only now coming around. It clouded my vision. When it began to clear I saw we were in some sort of office building along the waterfront.

The room itself was tidy though a bit ostentatious for belonging to a seafaring line. A counter about two-thirds into the room separated the office from reception. Behind the counter were two impressively massive wooden desks facing each other but about five feet apart. Between them against the back wall was a large armoire, also of dark hue. A singular large mirror occupied its door, reflecting the occupants of the room. A richly overstuffed sofa stood along one wall with an equally ornate low table before it. The counter separating the office area from the reception was a darkly stained but beautifully carved piece of furniture craftsmanship depicting the same image that hung, just visible, from the window outside the front door.

The carved company logo was a woman of exquisite beauty crowned in a jewel-encrusted diadem complete with seaweed, starfish, and coral, her ebony hair flowing in the breeze. She was standing in the water to her hips, and her white dress seemed to bleed into the water turning it red as it swirled upon the surface. She had one hand outstretched, as if pointing to her goal on the unseen horizon, the other carrying a scythe. It was a breathtaking sign for intermingling of beauty and startling bloody imagery. Only, the carving had her hand really reaching into the open space of the room.

There before me was the boy, looking slightly apprehensive as the woman conducted an intense conversation with the rather austere and gaunt man. The man's skin was as white as porcelain, so feathery each wrinkle seemed like a crack that would wither at the slightest touch. His eyes were steely blue, which only intensified his cold unfeeling air. He was tall, dressed in a black frock suit befitting an undertaker. His shoulder-length white hair was slicked back as if he had just stepped out from a bath. He moved around birdlike, intricately put together but decidedly lethal should you cross him.

::How the devil is this all managed?::

::We are between places. It occurred to me how to do it when I considered all that Tessa had explained to Jacob. I reasoned out where I was going wrong when we tried it. They cannot see or hear us, and we cannot affect their world. We are but ghosts occupying the same space.::

I felt another presence beside me. Jacob, who looked not the worst for wear, if slightly transparent.

"I am glad you returned just now," he said. "It appears this woman is the ringleader for the immigrants she has collected for this Flintling operation. The young boy appears to be her son. He too is quite involved, though I fear it is by his mother's hand that he came to be so."

"Not very likely," I added. "You should have seen the boy negotiate his portion of the wages for procuring the people for this collection of scalawags. I take it they cannot hear us either?"

He looked at Joss who only shrugged as if he had not thought about it before. I rolled my eyes at their lack of forethought, allowing us to prattle on.

"If they did hear us, we would have known by now. As we are neither here nor there, I think it was safe to assume we would not be detected."

"I cannot, with all confidence, hear what they are saying. Can we not move in a little closer?"

They nodded so we glided over, catching the woman midsentence.

"As you well know, Mister Stephens, the cargo we have provided more than meets the quota your superiors have set for us. We cannot be held responsible for the incursions by the Natives. We were hired to perform a singular function, which we have done admirably, in my estimation. We have never inquired why you need so many people, nor what you do with them. All we expect is to be paid for services rendered.

As of last night, we are thirty heads over the total sum requested. I have come to collect for those services."

"I take it our agent has approved the transaction?"

"Yes, I secured it only last night. However, there was some discrepancy over our continued employment. It seems Miss Covington has decided to intercede in our continued negotiations. I have, however, put a stop to that and only just now came from speaking with her."

"I think perhaps, Mrs. Brackett, we should refer this to Mister Romanov. He has the authority to complete your transaction and you can feel free to discuss any further engagement with him, as he is Grigori's personal assistant. Follow me, please."

The Bracketts followed the frighteningly oppressive Mr. Stephens around the counter up to the armoire. Stephens paused and waved the Bracketts toward the large mirror.

If the Bracketts thought this an odd gesture, they showed no outward signs of it. Mrs. Brackett took the boy with one hand whilst she gathered her dress skirt with the other and walked with purpose straight to the mirror. She then stepped miraculously through the mirror, the boy glancing over his shoulder in our general direction. I was sure it was more of an afterthought of the more comforting world beyond the office's front door than any knowledge of our translucent presence.

Stephens completed the trio's departure through the mirror, which left the three of us pondering our next move. I say three of us, though more to the point, it was only I who had any doubts about it. Joss and Jacob had already started to drift toward the same cabinet, though we did not have to take the physical route of skirting the counter—we just drifted through it with all haste to the mirrored door. There, Joss and Jacob hesitated. The moment would go on far longer than I realized. The tingling sensation that constantly moved over my body in a flurry of cascading waves had slowed considerably; I could almost feel the progression of every little crawling sensation.

It was then *his* voice came back to me—and the full realization of who it was seemed to slip over the edifice constructed in my mind.

"William, I am only going to allow you passage into this part of our operation. Joss and Jacob will not be permitted to make the same journey. I am sure you understand my reasoning, as they could present numerous problems should their Guardian warrior blood come to boil and press them into action. I cannot have that. As you move through the

mirror, I need you to concentrate upon the word home—*are we clear? It is for their own good, as well as your own."*

"I understand," I murmured. Joss regarded my outburst with some alarm, for he knew neither he nor Jacob had made any inquiries of me.

"Excellent. I see our mutual trust is intact. This is a wise move on your part. I am going to release you from our timeframe, and you will move through the mirrored door. Remember to think upon home..."

I nodded and then we made contact with the mirror, or at least I did. As soon as my translucent body pressed forward, which I would liken to being pushed through an icy-cold waterfall, I felt a tremendous pull against me. As my body pushed through, I thought of *home.* Or rather the word *home* as my own never came into focus within my mind. A second later, and I was through and inside a cavernous warehouse. I could only assume it was some sort of conduit to the warehousing building I knew to be some four or five blocks from here, as the small waterfront office was nothing more than a small box.

"Do not be alarmed by the sensation. I am just casting Jacob and Joss back to their home. I do thank you for assisting me with that. I could not have pulled it off quite as easily without your help. Joss is clever. One day he will sort this all out and he will be quite my adversary. And undoubtedly you will be there by his side, helping him as you are helping me now. But that is as it should be. You belong with him. It is inevitable."

He spoke to me as a father to a wanton and reckless juvenile. I could not really attest to any fatherly affection in his voice, but there was an unmistakable confidence in the *inevitable* outcome, as he put it. I knew I should be concerned with Jacob and Joss's expulsion from the warehouse, but for some reason it did not concern me at all. Instead, I concentrated on what lay before me now I was beyond the veil of the mirror.

As I moved into the cavernous warehouse, where the darkness was disrupted by the light cutting in square shafts onto the barren floor, I marveled the expanse of it all. While I had no corporal body and therefore no sense of smell, I could only imagine, given my current visage, the dank mustiness of the warehouse would be quite overwhelming. I could just make out the backs of the trio some twenty feet ahead of me. I continued to drift forward, not really walking but sort of gliding upon the air. How I continued to manage this—as well as being translucent—while not being with Joss was rather unclear to me. I took solace that it remained so.

I soon caught up to the group as we turned a corner, and there before us was a collection of what I assumed were some precious cargo. It was secured in darkly stained pine boxes fitted with ornate and secure copper corner bracket. Each one, lying upon its backside, was fitted with some type of gauge that had a small tube moving from it into what was undoubtedly the top of the box. Affixed to the front, which in this prone position faced the ceiling, was a small circular glass pane allowing viewing of the contents.

Stephens perfunctorily made the introductions before stepping back into the black background. "Mister Ippolit Romanov."

A moment later he was gone; the shadows of the room consumed him. No one present seemed to have noticed his dismissal.

"Mrs. Brackett and young Master Liam. Whatever brings you to our establishment on so fine a morning?"

Ippolit Romanov, it appeared, was a rather slippery fellow. He was impeccably dressed as the more elegant undertakers would be inclined to present themselves to the public. He was tall, somewhat athletically built, judging by his frame, and extremely handsome.

His evident charm only added to the overall sensation that when dealing with him, you would do well to remember his beguiling manner was that of a cobra. His brilliant white hair was pulled tight to his head and braided down his back, with the tip of the braid coming close to his waistline. His sharply clipped goatee matched his hair color and the overall pallor of his skin tone. His eyes were steely blue. He was a sea of brilliant white ice crowning the monolithic mass of ebony clothing. The look was altogether mesmerizing as it was off-putting. It certainly held the boy's attention. He could not take his eyes off Ippolit.

Mrs. Brackett reiterated her tirade over her continued employment, which afforded me the opportunity to examine one of the cargo boxes in closer detail. The small window glowed in a muted but beckoning violet light that undulated in intensity. As I drifted closer, the glow became more radiant. I risked looking into the pane of glass. I saw a woman encased therein. Her delicate features not making the slightest movement, as if in peaceful slumber...and yet, I heard her. In the far-off distance, as if she could suddenly sense my presence and was trying desperately to gain my attention.

I peered wide-eyed, or at least that is what I felt like I was doing—without having a real body it was difficult to discern. The woman was of no more than twenty-five or thirty. She may have been all of sixteen for an immigrant life was unusually harsh upon the womenfolk, and their beauty soon wilted to a leathered memory of what was, at one-time, radiant. Her eyes were closed, and she seemed at peace save for the small wail that continued to echo forth in my direction, yet I was damned if I could make out what she was saying to me.

"'Tis not important, William. She is undergoing a transformation. They all are."

The familiar voice, as I now had finally put a name to it, completely shattered the last vestiges of her call from my mind. I moved away from the smooth dark wooden surface and glanced into the distance. I could scarce make out perhaps ten or fifteen other boxes such as the one I inspected, when the darkness blossomed into brilliance for a brief moment. Ippolit and the Bracketts seemed to take no notice, so I gathered Tiyanoga was permitting this viewing just for me. As the light became brighter, I could see the cavernous warehouse was immense. The number of caskets was well into the hundreds, if not thousands.

"There are a great deal more of these from various parts of the globe. You must see to it Jacob and Joss believe you on this point, William. It is paramount that we gain their acceptance of our mutual goal. We need to get the Central to acknowledge he is fighting a global incursion. The game is on a much larger scale than he can imagine."

::I still do not understand why you are showing all of this to me. Why would the enemy, nay, the leader of the enemy camp, choose to show his hand at this juncture? Surely, this is but a trap of some sort and you wish me to be the dupe in this no doubt maligned scheme.::

"Calm yourself, William. There is a great deal at risk here. If you recall, I have my own agenda in this little war that has been going on. I have waited well over five hundred years to find someone like you who I could count on to assist me in putting an end to all of this."

At that, I did recall the entirety of our earlier conversation. The weariness of his battle fatigue. The reason for my trust in his cause to put an end to this whole catastrophe of a war.

::It would go a great deal further if I did not have to keep remembering the cause we have both agreed upon in this endeavor.::

"I realize it is inconvenient, William. But with the connection between you and Joss, I cannot take the risk he will gain too much information all at one time. I have planted far more in your mind than even you are aware of just yet. They will reveal themselves over time when the right situation presents itself. I am, in a manner of speaking, protecting both my goal and your safety in this. I have not wavered from that position. I still stand by it."

::*So, the operation is global and the people in these boxes are going through a transformation of some sort. Do I have the right of it?*::

"Yes, but do be careful in your choice of words. I doubt if you relate it in such a manner, neither Jacob nor Joss will give it the serious thought it warrants."

::*Very well, I can see your point. But answer me this: what have the Bracketts and Miss Covington to do with this whole scheme?*::

"All I am willing to impart at this point is the Bracketts work for us procuring immigrants pursuing a better life. They are lured here and then processed for the journey to the west coast of the Americas."

::*And Miss Covington? Why should she be mixed up with this? I have had my suspicions of her as of late but have nothing but intuition with which to pin those assumptions. Is she involved? Is she a Flintling?*::

"That word still rankles me." I could almost sense his distaste in his voice. *"I cannot give you more information in the case of Miss Covington. Her part has yet to play out, but I will say this: your suspicion is warranted. Do be careful when dealing with her. She is most cunning and will not hesitate to do you harm if it precludes her from her goal."*

::*Which is?*::

"I am well over six hundred years old. Do you think it that easy to pry from me what I have said I will not speak upon? I know you are a far better adversary than that, William."

::*You cannot blame me for trying....*::

"Well, I am afraid it is time you returned to Joss. He is stirring, and I can sense his first thoughts are about you. Yes, he is attempting to gate back here now. Most clever fellow. Do pardon me the hasty way in which I give you back to him, but he is behaving like a caged animal. I fear he would find a way rather quickly if I do not return you with all haste."

::Yes, I suppose you had. Will this hurt?::

"It will not be comfortable, but you should get through it fairly unscathed."

And with that last, I was extracted from the warehouse in a whirl of dark, dense fog assailing my senses to such an extent I nearly vomited from the experience. When I thought I could contain my morning meal no longer, I was hurled into a darkened room of unknown origin. I went flying and collided with a table and chair which cast to the other side of the room with little in the way of damage. I could not say if I came off the same. I heard feet scrambling to my crumpled form.

"Ohhhh..." It was all I could muster. The simple groan brought about more pain. My head throbbed.

"Will? Will! Is that you?" Joss skated the distance between us and rolled me over, bringing about a whole new wave of nausea and pain.

"Ohhhh, dear *God* do *not* do that again!" I called out.

"Will, I am sorry. I only... You were not here. Jacob and I did not know what had happened. I panicked."

I rubbed my temples with one hand whilst the other groped around in the darkness.

"What? Do you need assistance sitting up?"

"No, come closer..."

I sensed him leaning toward me, and I found, through one semi-opened eye, I could just make out his face. I put my fingers to his mouth as he began another tirade.

"You realize, for a stoic Indian, you talk too much."

Through the haze Joss looked at Jacob with my fingers on his lips, and Jacob lost all composure and began to laugh with such conviction I thought he would possibly wet his loincloth. Joss pulled away from me and sat back down and began to laugh as well. I shook with silent laughter for but a moment when it caused my head to throb even more and had to stop. I winced in pain.

"Are you hurt?"

"Just a headache and my pride more than anything else." I waved my hand again in front of him. "I believe I can sit up now."

Joss leaned forward and gripped my hand. The connection sent a small tremor between us, and I felt the pressure that had built up in my mind from Tiyanoga's expulsion from their facilities along the wharf to...?

"Where on God's green Earth are we exactly?"

"The council longhouse at Akwesasne. Jacob has sent for the Central. We were waiting for him when I became impatient about not knowing your whereabouts."

I scanned the large room which had a central fireplace where the four walls had three rows of what I guessed was about fifteen-degree raked seating all facing the fire. A standard council house setting but built in the more modern colonial manner.

"Yes, I thought you might begin to worry about that. I am sorry, but it could not be helped."

"Will, is it my imagination or was someone else communicating with you while we were back in the shipping line storefront?"

"Your perceptions would be spot on there. It was the very same point of contact from the Battery when Tessa made a point of bringing it up."

"And who would this person be? A Flintling, no doubt?" Jacob had chosen this moment to join our conversation, though he was busy looking out of a nearby window, obviously checking on the arrival of the Central.

"None other than the top of their command. A man by the name of..." A dull throb echoed across my head, and I found I could not form the word. I stuttered. Joss and Jacob both drew closer, thinking I was having some sort of convulsion.

"I assure you I am fine, but for some reason I cannot reveal the man's name. Each time I make the attempt, my head aches and my tongue ceases to form the word."

"Can you spell it out?"

I attempted to think upon how I would sound out the word, as it was obviously Mohawk, but again the pain grew as I forced myself to bring it out.

"Perhaps if he wrote it down...?" Jacob offered.

"Nay, I think the result would be the same. I am precluded from divulging who this man is. He did inform me that I have a great deal more buried in my mind about their operations, but it will reveal itself when the appropriate time comes. Until then, it is securely locked away within my own head. We well know what the result will be if Joss attempts to breach that barrier."

"What if you thought it to me? Maybe I could sense it that way."

I tried, but the thought was blurred. It had no way to form any coherence between us. I looked at him inquisitively, and he shook his head that he got nothing.

I rose to my full height and began to pace around. I was pondering how much I remembered and what, if anything, Tiyanoga would allow me to impart to my two colleagues.

"I can tell you this. Their operation is far larger than we anticipated. I have it on good authority, and by my own sighting of their operations behind the mystical mirror, that they are in the business of procuring bodies. To what end entirely, I am not sure. But I can say when I made the crossing successfully, I found myself in their cavernous warehouse. I can only assume it is the very same which we have visited twice now. I do not believe we will be able to do so again. They seem to have fortified it against your arrival. Why T...T..."—I stumbled upon his name again and decided after the two attempts I would just move on—"my *informant* was showing me the inside of their operations because he wanted me to be clear upon the largeness of their current endeavor. We cannot be mistaken here. On this point he was most adamant. This is no longer a war between our homelands and the surrounding areas. These Flintlings have proceeded upon a global reach."

"To what possible end?" Another man's voice rang into the semidarkness of the room.

A shaft of light streamed across the floor from the doorway where he stood. This could be no one other than...

"William Hallett, Samuel Brant, our Central of the Guardianship," Jacob introduced us.

As Samuel approached, I moved to meet him halfway and we shook hands.

"A pleasure, sir."

"Oh, dispense with the formalities, William. I have been close to your family for many years. I know your grandmother very well. I am nothing more than a warrior trying to make sense of this whole new mess they have gotten us into."

The four of us moved to one side of the council house where Jacob and Joss took the second row and Samuel and I seated ourselves in the first. When I was unsure of what was the best course to proceed, Jacob prodded me along.

"Go ahead, Will. We do not stand on ceremony when dealing with the Central. Just relay to him what you saw and what you believe it means."

I pursed my lips for a moment, collecting my thoughts.

"I should back up and explain how this whole situation came about from the first instance at Battery Park."

"You mean when the Jemisons interfered with your investigation at the warehouse?"

"Oh, you know of it?"

"More or less. Jacob filled me in on the fiasco Thor and his family brought upon your sensitive probing of their operation. But as to the interlude between this Flintling commander and yourself, Jacob said it was best to get it from you directly. So, you now have my every attention."

I walked him through the experience of our first encounter, and the three of them listened quite intently. I sensed Joss's apprehension at someone else having access to my mind while we shared a consciousness, and I did what I could silently by sending comforting thoughts to ease his worries. By the time I finished my initial tale, Samuel's demeanor took a more somber tone. I sensed he could already see the fullness of the way their engagement in this protracted war had drastically changed.

"So, you encountered this same man again this very day?"

"Yes. Joss had retrieved me from this morning's shopping in the marketplace because I had observed a rather terse conversation between a Miss Sarah Covington, of whom I am acquainted..."

This brought about a smirk on Joss's face which I did everything I could to ignore and continued.

"And another woman who I did not recognize. This woman had a small boy with her of no more than seven or eight years old, who was none other than the very same lad we encountered on our first foray into the Flintling warehouse. From the way he was associating with the unknown woman I could only assume she was his mother or some other relative, as he made no protestation when she completed her argument with Miss Covington and departed."

"Sarah Covington is the woman I spoke of who we have been watching for some time now in Manhattan," Joss added.

This was not an entirely new revelation to me as Joss had commented as such, but I had not known their observation had been for so long a period.

::Why do you not think I was so interested in your datebook appointment? I have had deep suspicions about her for some time now.::

::As do I. But I suppose we will have to wait to find out the root of those suspicions.::

Samuel was eyeing me cautiously, as I had suddenly stopped my normal conversation to discuss this point with Joss.

"They are speaking mentally to each other," Jacob offered as a point of clarification.

"Yes, you did tell me about that, Jacob. Most interesting. And you do not know how this linking between you came about?"

"Well, I have my suspicions on that subject as well," I replied.

Joss raised an eyebrow at my announcement.

"I cannot speak as to *how* it happened, but I do believe I know *when* it happened. After the first encounter with the Flintlings, Jacob and Joss thought it would be best if I could not remember any details of our encounter. So, when Joss pressed his hand upon my forehead, I did pass out, but the object of his contact did not have the desired effect. Rather, as I recovered, I believe it is what led me to become connected with Joss."

"I see. Most interesting, and we shall come back to this later. But as you were saying, they had parted company and Jacob and Joss pursued the woman and boy, I presume?"

"Precisely. Which left me the task of picking up on the other half of that exchange by engaging Miss Covington directly upon the subject."

"Were you successful in finding out the nature of their exchange?"

"To a small degree. She did not seem to want to speak upon it fully, so I gave up the chase. I hoped Joss and Jacob were faring better by following the woman and boy."

"We followed them to a new shipping line storefront along the warehousing district. The Red Sea Line. Fairly new office, quite ornate and decidedly Russian in nature."

"Russian? Here on the east coast? Most extraordinary."

"We get ahead of ourselves," I reminded them all. "After my exchange with Miss Covington that came to no avail, Joss returned to the marketplace and was proceeding to me when Miss Covington became quite agitated and made a hasty excuse. It was not lost upon me that she only did so after seeing Joss moving with all speed to our location. Though I did nothing to let her know I had observed this singular point."

"I informed Will of our observation of Miss Covington but made a point of our quick departure back to the storefront. Jacob and I believed we were going to find out a great deal about their operations," Joss replied.

"You mean to say you are able to take Will through a *gate*?"

"Not just gating. We can share a great many other talents between us. He appears to be a conduit or an augmentation of my abilities, now we are linked."

"Jacob thinks it has to do with the fact that somehow there is a unique bond between Joss and me."

"Elizabeth, such a dear woman," Samuel offered and lost himself in remembering my grandmother fondly. I could not help but have a pang of jealousy over not knowing much about this part of her life. We were immensely close, but she rarely spoke of her life at Akwesasne before her marriage to my grandfather.

"Undoubtedly, your blood is a factor in this newly manifested ability. But do go on with what you found out at the storefront."

I thought for a moment, still unsure of how much I was going to be allowed to reveal. I knew I could not speak Tiyanoga's name, which was infuriating. I could think it but not share what I believed was vital information. So, I pressed on with what I was instructed to impart.

"When the Bracketts—we learned their name from their conversation within the storefront as they conversed with the clerk in attendance, you see. When they were referred to Mister Romanov—is that not the royal family name in Russia?" I just realized this small fact, and I found it most startling that a member of the royal family would be present at a warehouse in lower Manhattan.

"Well, that aside, the clerk, a Mister Stephens, a darkly frightening man who could give callous undertakers a run for their money, directed them to an armoire at the back of the establishment. The trio moved to it directly and without any hesitation, which leads me to believe they have traveled this path before. They moved directly through the mirror and disappeared from view."

"It was then that Jacob and I decided to pursue them through the mirror," Joss cut in. "I noticed Will seemed to be preoccupied and conversing with what I thought were his thoughts aloud, but upon closer inspection I realized he was speaking *to* someone who we could neither see nor hear, which I found most troubling."

I explained the conversation between Tiyanoga and me, and what happened after I was successfully across the mirror conduit. I then told them what I saw: the dark wooden boxes containing the woman, her attempts to engage me mentally, and the explanation Tiyanoga provided to me that silenced her plea. I relayed how many boxes containing bodies I saw. I did not need to elaborate on the size of the warehouse and how many bodies could be held in that building. I added this was just the culmination of their New York operations, but they were processing the same number of people from other continents. I could sense the men growing concerned at the fullness of my report. There was little doubt in their minds as to the scope of what we now faced.

"Why so many?"

"I think it is quite plain as to the sheer numbers they are amassing...it is an army they are raising."

"But you said you viewed a woman. Surely, they would not be placing females into battle. And, Jacob, you commented that there were children present when the Jemisons interceded."

"Samuel, I cannot say to what end the women and children are being recruited, but I can say the numbers point to either slavery or some sort of military action. I did get one more piece of information from my contact. And of this I am most certain: their operations are based just to the north of what was once called Yerba Buena. We know it now as San Francisco. He said it was a derelict fortress of some sort. We will need to ascertain which fort that may be so we can plan a line of attack or, at the very least, a reconnaissance to scout out further developments of which we may not be aware."

Samuel got up from the bench and began to pace around. Then, without another word, he vanished for a moment, only to return with a medium-sized, rolled item I could only assume was a wampum belt. I had been fortunate to see a few in my short life. However, this belt was unlike any I had ever witnessed before.

He rolled out the belt. The first difference was it had no discernible symbols in white. It bore no resemblance to our wampum belts other than it seemed to be woven in the same manner. It measured nearly as wide as the length of my forearm, and when Samuel unfurled and laid it on his lap, the belt's length spanned the distance between my two arms if I held them out in front of myself.

The beads were far different than our standard wampum. Rather than the requisite indigo and white, these beads resembled maracite, not too unlike the Mordants I spied the Russian Flintlings using. It was strange to behold yet had a familiarity that escaped me at the moment. I noticed Jacob and Joss did not seem quite as awestruck as I was over this particular belt. I could only assume it was a normal part of the Guardianship.

Joss seemed to sense my wonderment over the belt, and decided to clarify.

::Not insomuch as we have seen it as we know of its existence. I can only recall one other time I saw it in Samuel's possession. Jacob, as the Central's right-hand man, has probably been near it far more than most. I assume he probably has the gist of how it is used by the Central.::

::What do you mean used? It is a wampum; the most you can do is read from it.::

::It does that, and quite a bit more. This is no ordinary belt, Will. As you shall soon see.::

Samuel moved to the small table that Jacob had returned to an upright position after I collided with it earlier. As soon as the belt was unfurled, he took his blade and made a small incision in the palm of his right hand. He then pressed the wound to the silvery beads. The belt seemed to come to life, as if it were but a dormant creature that only required the sacrifice of blood to wrench it from slumber.

"I have quite a bit to show you three. If you will all gather around as this will undoubtedly concern us all, I am afraid."

The three of us inched closer. The belt, the moment it was unfurled, rippled with palpable energy. The very air crackled with it. Each individual bead seemed to glow in a cascading ripple of color and luminance. The effect washed upon us as well as radiating onto the surrounding walls.

Samuel moved his finger over the belt, and a lighted ripple seemed to follow his fingertip.

"It responds to your touch?" I could not help myself asking, as the belt was quite remarkable to behold. Having spent time with Joss working on how to reach the Jemisons trapped within the void, I was sure this was not, as he claimed, some form of ancient magic, but some part of science as yet unexplained but functioning fully within our universe.

"To my touch, sometimes my thoughts. Generally, it appears to perceive what I want to learn most. This belt has been in the Central's possession since the inception of the Guardianship, some five hundred years prior, going back to the first Central. His untimely disappearance in his fourth year as Central still holds one of the greatest mysteries for the Guardianship."

A ripple of gooseflesh moved about my body. I shuddered; why the mention of the first Central should cause such a reaction was deeply mystifying.

"Should we start a fire, Samuel? It appears Will might be a bit cold."

"It is not the temperature of the room I am reacting against. Pay it no mind. I am fine. Please, Samuel, proceed with all haste."

Samuel regarded me for a moment, his hawk-like gaze moving over me. This was a man in complete control of his faculties, Guardian or otherwise, and I knew well enough not to resist his hard stare. It was not directed at me personally, but rather was borne out of his shrewd management of the Guardianship and those warriors under his care and tutelage. I knew he was appraising me and what unforeseen talents would unfold due to the bond between Joss and me.

That penetrating stare defined me as a risk in his eyes, and he did little to hide the fact. Yet, I could also tell in his gaze if Joss was fiercely protective of our shared gift, then that was enough to hold sway with Samuel.

I knew Joss was his most valued asset. Jacob had all but confirmed as much to me in private. So, by association, I had to assume I too was now under that auspicious label. I was sure my being a completely unknowable factor had to rankle the Central. His whole job, as any commander in the midst of war, was predicated upon knowing to the fullest extent what was in his arsenal.

I represented a wild card he did not know how to play. It was by the grace of having both Joss and Jacob in my corner that probably secured my position thus far. But Samuel, while pleasant and capable, was not a man to allow an unknown to linger in his camp for long without some sort of action, which would label it for good or ill. It was on this point that my apprehension found a home.

Samuel moved his finger across the beads and wrote out a sigil of some sort. I was uncertain of its meaning; however, the belt seemed to know how to respond. Small iconic images began to emerge across its canvas. They slid from left to right across it in a fluid animated manner, like leaves upon the water.

"Each of these represents the Guardians in my care. They are the symbols each of you took when you were confirmed into our fold."

"Why do some seem distant and faded into the background?" Jacob asked.

It was then I noted what had escaped my cursory review of the images moving across the belt's surface. There were small symbols, roughly hewn. Some of animals like bear, eagle, or deer, whilst others were more iconographic in nature: a sun or some other simple shape such as a square or triangle. It was not until Jacob had made his inquiry that I noticed what he was commenting upon, for in the background, as if submerged in watery depths, were sigils that barely registered across the surface, almost as if they were lost to us. Some were so vague you could not, with any certainty, determine the shape at all.

"Those are the troubling aspects of what I have been observing," Samuel replied as he continued.

He pushed an index finger forcibly into the surface of the belt, and it disappeared beneath the surface, which was most alarming. I was not the only one who reacted with a degree of astonishment. But Samuel seemed to have done this several times as he simply hooked a finger as if to draw the obscured icon to the surface. Once revealed, it was a singular circle surrounding a small dot within its center. He tapped it twice. The image dissolved, and all of the other symbols drifted off the belt's surface. The selected sigil grew and began to change into a picture of what I could only assume, since I had never met the individual it represented, was the holder of that Guardian symbol.

"That is Grant Doxtater," Jacob said. "He is an Oneida confirmed two years prior to mine. I trained with him. I heard that he was covering the western door out into the plains territories. Samuel, what does this mean?"

"I wish I knew. Several times I have consulted this very part of the belt. I have counted well close to two hundred Guardians such as Grant's. They are all drifting, slightly obscured, as if lost to me. Here, let me set his aside for a moment and show you what should normally be appearing when I make an inquiry into the Guardianship as a whole." He flicked Grant's image in an upward stroke, and it seemed to condense into the small icon again only to float off the belt into the air where it glowed in a wispy radiant object lingering in the air. Samuel made the same sigil mark with his finger, and the flow of icons moved across the belt's surface.

"Here is yours, Jacob. This is how they *should* present themselves to me."

He tapped upon a head of a five-point stag. Rather apropos for Jacob, I thought.

The image expanded as before, but next to his image were several statistics about him: his birthdate, his Guardianship date, along with other pertinent details of his Guardianship endeavors, including two children he appeared to have sired. I raised an eyebrow at this and looked at him. He only smirked and shrugged at being revealed to have children he never spoke upon. It was the first sign that Jacob had kept something from me in a relationship defined upon our sharing just about everything. *Though obviously, not everything.*

Joss mentally reached out to me to reassure my questioning nature. I glanced at him, and he knew this was best left to another time when the three of us could discuss it.

"As you can see, I have just about everything at my disposal. The belt is linked to the Guardian. I can even track your current whereabouts to within a couple of miles. The belt is amazingly accurate in just about every detail possible. Including that you have children you have not yet acknowledged, Jacob."

There, it was out. Jacob shot a look in my direction. My pointed gaze met his.

"Perhaps because I was not aware of their births. This is the first I have heard of it. Does it relate who the mothers are?"

"Another time, Jacob," Samuel replied, looking between all of us. "Let us get to the more pressing matter." Clearly, it had not slipped his sharpened perception that Jacob's paternity was a point of contention.

He poked the errant icon in the air; it drifted down to the belt again so we could see the two images side by side. They were alike in many respects save for the fact Grant's was missing a tremendous amount of information that was clearly shown on Jacob's side.

"Were they all filled in as Jacob's?" Joss asked, turning his head slightly so as to gain a better vantage point.

"Yes. At least his was, until about a year ago. Then his icon slipped below the surface and became obscured to me. When I noticed its absence, I searched through the obscure icons and finally found his. It took me a while to realize I could probe beneath the actual surface of the belt and retrieve the more distant records. But the lack of information, the manner of which the icon finds itself alone are not what give me pause, although they are part of it, certainly."

He paused for a moment.

"No, what concerns me most is that the scales seem to have tipped to those who are obscured now, outweighing the number of Guardians whose symbols I can see with great clarity. When I was reaching well into the hundreds, I knew this was no mere occurrence, or happenstance, for that matter. This was an intentional or determined move on Flint's part to separate myself from those under the Guardianship. To what end this whole endeavor has undertaken, I am not sure, but the sheer numbers are alarming."

"Why do you think you have not taken notice of it until now?" Jacob asked quietly. His mood far more somber than I had ever witnessed in my rather good-natured companion.

"I think because our people were concerned with far greater problems than just the status of the Guardianship. This was during the time of the American Revolution and we were not only dealing with their war, but the effects of disease brought by the European settlers. Disease that nearly brought about the destruction of our way of life. I fear it was during this period of time when several of our Guardians were lost along the way and we had no real means to deal with their loss. The belt simply ceased to find them. I fear the worst for them. However, since their sigils still appear, I am hopeful they are still reachable and can be saved."

Jacob placed a reassuring hand upon Samuel's shoulder. "I wish you had shared this with me earlier, Samuel. This should not have been your burden alone to carry. At the very least, Joss and I—"

"Joss and you, what? Do you really think you could have changed the course of this loss? Really, Jacob, you alarm me in thinking along those lines. Whatever this is, it is a far greater challenge than the Guardianship has ever encountered. I fear it may well be our undoing. We are not in great numbers as we once were. Our calling has not come as steadily as before. And what we do have is factionalized."

He leveled a look amongst the three of us.

"Do not mistake me; I am well aware of the change in our course. I know Joss has the way of our future. But do not think for one moment that the rest will fall into line behind him. The Jemisons are strong and ever-present. Whether you choose to acknowledge their dominance over the Guardianship or not, it is a point I have to deal with politically every day. These things must be dealt with delicately. It is only because of your reports of a large Flintling army of men and women that our current course of action has been brought into play."

We regarded one another for a moment. The light from the belt played against our faces in the semidarkness.

"I cannot say with any degree of appreciation that I was happy to hear of Thor's intercession upon your investigation. But it was their nephew who had been abducted. There was little I could do to preclude them from retrieving him at all possible costs. I know what it has cost us with regard to your investigation. Believe me, I am all too aware of how foolishly Thor and his family played their part. I have spoken to him upon the matter. He feels it was warranted since they were successful in gaining the return of their nephew."

"Yes, but that was not due to any part they played." I spat out my opposition to Thor's accounts before I scarcely could believe the words had left my lips. "The boy came to me in my own home. He as much told me so when we were alone in my bedroom discussing his arrival."

Joss softly smiled at my cheek.

At least, I thought I saw him smirk at my outburst. Then a shiver of laughter rose between us. I pursed my lips and took in a deep breath to calm myself.

Samuel's eyes were alight as well, though his amusement did not move much beyond them.

"Granted. Young Thomas told me as much when he and I were alone to discuss his ordeal, which is why we must act now. And I think our course of action will be as shocking as it is difficult."

I did not need the connection between Joss and me to tell we were treading in unknown waters.

"Jacob, I think I need you to gain passage aboard a ship from the Red Sea Line if one exists. It is clear they mean to move the slumbering bodies of their army via a transport of some kind. You need to be there as our continued point of contact."

"Surely, I will be joining him," Joss said with all certainty.

In truth my heart sank a little at Joss's words. This was immediately quelled. Samuel had other plans.

"No, I think that would be most unwise at this juncture."

Joss snapped his head up from looking at the belt, clearly not expecting this denial. But before Joss could mount a defense, Samuel pressed on.

"Joss, do you not realize the risk the Guardianship would undertake, should you and Jacob both be present on the same transport and something were to happen? I cannot, in all good conscience, have my two most revered and talented warriors on the same ship sailing into unknown waters of the Pacific. No, Joss. *That* is final. You know my reasons are sound, no matter how much you rail against them. As you are so fond of saying, we *must be logical* about this. Therefore, Jacob, you will take young Master Thomas with you as your guide."

"But he is still a boy in training. Thor will have nothing to do with this, let alone the fact the Jemisons will probably rise up in opposition." Joss hid little of his disappointment in not being part of the action.

"Yes, they very well may. But Thor knows on this point he has little to argue. Thomas is the only one of the Guardianship who has been on the inside of the Flintling operations and lived to tell about it. He is the perfect candidate to lead Jacob into the unknown. He will be the best guide possible."

"But he has barely begun his training. Surely, you can see how it would be throwing him into the fray like raw meat to the wolves. He stands no chance of survival against their new arsenal."

"True, but that is where you come in, Jacob. You will continue his training whilst on board the ship, slipping away to the mainland when it is in sight so you can do so with relative safety of discovery. There will be plenty of time and opportunity. And it will cleave Thomas from the protection of Thor. I believe it is in the best interests of the boy if he is not trained by his own family."

"Then why did you agree to it in the first place?" Jacob asked with an arched eyebrow, indicating the irony of the moment had not escaped his notice.

"Because it silenced Thor in the middle of his tirade. Or do you not remember what an obnoxious arse he made of himself?"

Joss coughed to keep from laughing at Samuel's appraisal of what I could only assume was Thor's oft-childlike behavior.

"Yes, I do recall. Quite clearly." Jacob visibly blanched, recalling the moment.

"Very well, then. Let us not pretend we do not know what will be coming our way once I call Thomas forth and give him his new assignment. You can well expect contention from Thor on the subject. So, best be prepared for it. Do what you can to ameliorate whatever rubbish Thor has buried in there, within the short few days he has had in his training, will you?"

"As best and as quickly as I can, Samuel."

::*The divinity versus scientific approach, I take it?::*

::*The very same. I do not have to explain it to you how explosive this call by Samuel will be.::*

::*I can only imagine.::*

::*You might not have to. Rest assured, if we are left behind, the Jemisons may pressure us into what transpired at this meeting today.::*

::*They would not descend upon us en masse?::*

::*With arrows notched, if they go to the extreme I hear them capable of. There is a reason their influence has held sway over four centuries. The family has been problematic for warriors like me who tend to push against their view of things. I make them extremely uncomfortable. However, the only things that have kept them at bay are the talents I have formed on my own far exceeds theirs. I am, you see, the great unknown to them. Nothing is more threatening to them and their world of divine providence.::*

::*Then, by extension...::*

::*Yes, Will. That includes you. You can well remember how Tessa regarded you at Battery Park. Think of that magnified by the collective of the Jemisons' contingent within the Guardians.::*

::*Are there many of them?::*

::*They are singularly the largest family contingent within the society, numbering well into two hundred or so at last count. Now, with young Thomas their numbers have increased by one. Each increase only tips the scales at an exponential level because there are so few of us on the other side who heed my approach to what we do. It is a numbers game, and they have been on the winning side, either by genetics, or through coercion, on their part. They can be most convincing. Currently, there are only a handful of us within the Guardianship who have the wherewithal to push back. Jacob is another. 'Tis part of why I fight so vehemently for you. Until you came into my life, I was feeling rather alone. I mean, I can count upon Jacob for just about everything, but the gap of what was missing had not closed.::*

::Oh yes, and I am quite sure that your days were spent in a wonderful bliss of experimentation and solitude until my blundering thoughts came barreling in.::

::Actually, there was not much else to do. It was a lonely existence.::

That last cut me to the marrow. I knew Joss was accustomed to his solitude, as Jacob had expounded upon it at some length, so I knew it was not something my mind conjured up to put a label to his quietness. It was clear when I looked upon him that, aside from his very handsome and fetching dark features, his whole manner spoke volumes of the thoughtfulness and care he put into everything he did. Joss was an amazing individual. If I had to be mentally tethered to someone in such a manner, I could not have been blessed with a finer choice. There was comfort in the thought. A deep comfort.

He looked down from my gaze and proceeded to be occupied with the display before us, yet I knew where his thoughts were. I searched tentatively within him, only to confirm that they were...upon *me.*

"So, that is why it comes down to William and you." Samuel finished wrapping up this last detail point. Albeit a point I had missed entirely. I grumbled inwardly at my lack of focus on the matter at hand. How I was to cover that ground without demonstrating I was so easily led astray?

::At least one of us can pay attention to two things.::

A warm grin blossomed across Joss's lips, catching me up short in my lack of attention.

"Agreed, Samuel. We shall see to it that Jacob leaves with Thomas on the next outbound ship of the Red Sea Line."

Finally, hearing something I could grasp hold of, I joined in. "The ship leaves this Friday sometime in the afternoon."

"Can you tell me how you came to know that?" Samuel asked in bewilderment.

"I cannot tell you how I know...I...just...*do.*"

It was true. The thought simply popped into my head. Probably another nugget of information left by the persuasive, albeit elusive, leader of the Flintling army. I was growing quite weary of being a pawn in someone else's game, never mind that the game be with my Flintling friend, Jacob, Samuel, or Joss for that matter. Say nothing of Miss Covington's advances.

"Well, this does put us at a disadvantage. I really cannot see how we can work up the capital to pay for passage in such short order." Sam's lips formed a grim line.

"Well if it's just *money* impeding our progress, you need not worry on that account. I could procure passage for Jacob and Thomas. Today, in fact."

"Thank you, William. Your generosity is most welcome."

"Samuel, though I may not be a Guardian, shared connection with Joss puts me as close to its mission as I dare think anyone else has been. So, in effect, its goals have become my own. Please know I will do whatever you deem necessary to get the task accomplished. You have my word on that, sir."

Samuel regarded me for a moment. "You do your grandmother credit, William. I can see why she takes such pride in you."

His comment caught me off guard at the familiarity of mentioning my grandmother. I flushed with the compliment.

"Family, Will. Family. We are all family of one sort or another. The Clan Mothers see to it. Though we may argue with Thor and his crew, there is enough marrying between the nations and clans that his family is not too far removed from mine, Jacob's, or, I daresay, your own."

There was Joss again, responding to a thought I had formed but remained vocally absent upon. A subject I rather thought I was debating within myself. I stared at him, wide-eyed at his complete lack of discretion on the subject.

"You need not dwell upon the specifics of our ways, William. They will come along soon enough. You are home, brother. I am confident the link between you and Joss will give you the guidance you seek," Samuel continued as his fingers played upon the wampum belt, commenting on this Guardian or that one while Jacob took careful note. These were names I did not recognize, so I left them to their recollections.

He moved the display onto a different view altogether. Now the display was a map of some sort. Though from where I stood, I could scarce make out the specifics.

"I meant no disrespect, gentlemen. It is just hard with the link between Joss and myself to find him responding aloud to thoughts I was entertaining as my own."

I looked to Joss who appeared to be truly stung at my words. For that instant, I found I did not care. Then, the feeling mellowed, and I could see the right of Samuel's statement. I was welcome to comment upon Joss's thoughts as he was as open a book to me as I was to him. The reticence I had upon reaching out to Joss was my own. Indeed, every time I had explored that thread to him, I was never barred along the way—save for the mental poking we did on our first night in my home. But that was horseplay between two blokes. Joss and I finding our way as two men often do. The way Jacob and I had back at university. I struggled with looking at him now as I did not want to draw too much attention to it. He had to know what I was wrestling with, yet he gave no outward expression.

In point of fact, he was not barring me from seeing him wholly and unprotected. I could feel it now. I had unfettered access to everything within him. There was no guard between us. What held me back were my own preconceptions of propriety and privacy. Joss came to me, wholly and unbound. The only way this was going to work for us was for me to move as freely as he did along our shared link. Only then, we could ensure that whatever was building between us would have the greatest advantage in succeeding.

I looked over to him as he watched the belt's animations move before him, though I caught the smallest smile snake along his lips.

::Ohnehta'kowa, I was beginning to think you were never going to catch on.::

"...then, of course, that reaches all the way back to our first Central, Tiyanoga. And what happened to him is lost to history. It seems we shall never answer that mystery."

The room spun with those words. Those words, and the mention of *his name.*

There, it was out. The man whose name I could not speak. With it floating in the air, barely past Samuel's lips, I found I could not put together the words fast enough to explain to them that it was he who had been communicating with me. He, the very same man who held this mystic position in the Guardian collective consciousness, was now the leader of the opposition. Joss could tell I was agitated but could not reason as to the source.

::Everything all right, Will?::

::No! It is bloody not all right! I just cannot...::

The best way to describe what followed was just a stuttering vocalization that startled both Jacob and Samuel as it was completely unexpected in both scope and volume.

"Will, it is a mystery but one that has faded with time. No need to dwell upon it so," Jacob said as he and Samuel both looked at me as if I had become slightly mental.

How could I relate to them this man was the one whose name I could not utter? Frustrated, I walked away from the group for a moment.

"Will, was something mentioned that you cannot speak upon?" Joss asked, moving toward me.

I could tell he was closing in on the elusive piece of conversation I so desperately wanted to have but could not find the physical faculties to carry out. Closing my eyes in relief, I sighed. I nodded to indicate he was on the right path.

"Does this have something to do with Tiyanoga's disappearance?"

My eyes widened and I spoke sarcastically, far more than I had intended. "I am sorry, Joss. It is not you. I am just rather perturbed with myself. I know what I want to impart but feel like a newborn with no means to communicate my own thoughts on the subject. It is maddening in the extreme."

Now Samuel and Jacob had turned in our direction. Obviously, the use of Tiyanoga's name had piqued their interest.

"All frustration aside, is there some knowledge you have over our first Central's disappearance?"

"Not directly, no. I do not know what exactly happened but all..." It was happening again. I began to falter for words, and forcing their utterance only caused me to spittle all over myself.

"Calm yourself. If it is causing you this much distress, then allow us to do the talking."

I sat down along one of the raised steps of the room, where the council members would sit, to collect myself. Joss, as was becoming quite clear, sat ever at my side.

"Is Tiyanoga the man's name you cannot speak upon, but may have given you the information within your own head?"

I opened my mouth but was stymied. I could not get anything to function. It was as if mentally I was struck dumb. I only seemed to manage breathing and blinking with everything else a quick slide into the abyss of little-to-no functionality.

"Just nod if I am on the mark." He took my hand that had come to rest on my knee. It startled me at first, but he gripped it a bit tighter. "Let me see what I can. Do you trust me?" His eyes were pointed and precise, eagle-like in their precision.

I took in a controlling breath and let it out slowly. He nodded that I should take another and I did. I knew I needed to leave all of this to him. He joined me with those steady breaths. As we inhaled, I felt him slip up my arm and mentally course through me. This manner of his approach was extremely disarming in that he quelled any tension I had built.

But this was a slow burn within me. He was gently coaxing my body into relaxing. It was working. My limbs and then my torso slipped quietly into his mental embrace. He was so gentle and soothing as he made his way to my mind.

::That is the way of it, Will. Keep breathing slowly. In...out. Let me take care of this for you. Do not let even a thought move in your mind. Be still and let me try to do this another way.::

I slowly nodded as I continued to breathe.

I felt myself let go, and he was immediately there to guide me onto my back along the platform, easing me into a peaceful repose, hovering just above sleep. It was truly one of the most blissful things I had ever experienced.

The caress upon my mind was unlike anything I could have imagined. A rush of emotions and history of Joss's life poured through me, imprinting himself in every place within my mind. His memories now stood alongside my own, and not just the visualizations of them, but the emotions tied to them. Anger, pride, love—so much love there. I was but a feeble wanderer in that emotive land. He, the master. This was followed by loneliness and fear—of rejection and oblivion. At this, tears slipped from my eyes, but I did as he bade me. I let it flow. I did nothing to impede his progress.

As I took my next breath, he finally reached the part where I could mentally see Tiyanoga from our first meeting at the Battery. Only this time, Joss turned around from the little scene to take in the conversation. It was like those dreams I had earlier of our university days. Joss was where he was before when Tiyanoga and I sat on that bench and discussed the plans he had for me in ending this brutal war.

He was not still as the others were, trapped in their moment in time. He now was an active participant and walked around us as my memory of the meeting played before him. He studied Tiyanoga from every angle while Tiyanoga expounded upon his plan. Joss even squatted in front of him, cocking his head this way and that, as if memorizing the man for all he was worth. But it was an appraisal of one enemy to another. It was clear Joss was a very adept adversary.

When the memory had run its course, Joss quietly moved to me and placed a gentle hand upon my shoulder, and he returned to his place in it. With a nod at me he turned back around so he was where he ought to be in that moment.

At this, the memory faded, and Joss slipped slowly away.

"No..." I was anguished at the sensation of his pulling back, as if I would never know that sort of blissful repose ever again.

But pull away he did, and my body slowly returned to its waking state. When at last I opened my eyes, I was alone on that platform. I sat up and saw the men had moved outside the longhouse and were discussing something intensely. I made my way to the front door and wondered if I should make myself known first.

::Ohnehta'kowa, you can never hide from me now. The link between us is as strong as I can make it now. I have told them you are awake.::

At that I sighed, and almost chuckled at my predicament, for no one would believe me if I were to speak upon it. I wanted adventure. I just was not so clear as to the nature of what that would mean.

When at last I opened the door, Joss's eyes were immediately upon me, and I knew if given the choice between any other adventure and the one that had my brothers with me again, I would always choose the latter. They were family. They were home as I had never known it.

I had what I was looking for. Time to dive in and relish every moment.

As I stepped through the doorway, I was determined I was committed and going to be fearless about it. Propriety be damned. *Joss and I are together on this, and there would be nothing to tear that asunder.* I was never more certain of anything.

I felt him flush at my thought, and for once, I let it be and did not think too much upon it, just allowed Joss his pleasure. I took it in and welcomed it like a favorite blanket on a chilled winter morn.

"Ah, William. I am glad you are awake," Samuel began. "It appears we have precious little time to get Jacob and Thomas on that ship. Do you think you can handle a quick gating to the harbor? Are you well enough for that?"

"We have not much choice in the matter. But pay it no mind; I am as right as rain. Besides, if we need to get Jacob sorted, then let us proceed with all haste to the matter."

"Excellent."

With this, he turned to Jacob.

"I shall go and retrieve Thomas and advise them of the change. It will be met with some resistance, but I feel in the end they will see the way of things. I shall signal you that he is ready to be picked up, and you can retrieve him and return dockside for your departure. I apologize for the shortness of my handing you this, but we cannot miss this opportunity to observe them up close. Especially since we now know Tiyanoga is leading the charge on their side."

While Samuel was pleased at the six-hundred-year mystery of Tiyanoga's disappearance being solved, it was also plain that in solving this mystery, there was a fair amount of apprehension that the game had changed—and not for the better.

I was comforted that Joss had, in my brief nap, relayed the information about Tiyanoga. Plans could proceed with greater speed now Joss was able to access whatever Tiyanoga had put into place.

As if flitting across time, his words came back to me. As if meant for me, and me alone. Joss seemed to take no note of this playing back—or perhaps because he already viewed it, it had become old news? I did not know. Yet, Tiyanoga's words were clear upon my mind.

Though as I thought upon that, somehow, I was not so sure luck had any part. Indeed, as I looked upon him, I was struck by the divinity of it all. As if it were deigned to be so, and we had merely stepped into our allotted roles.

Joss arched an eyebrow over this thought but said nothing. I decided not to think upon it further and let that one slip into the abyss.

It seemed we finally found our equilibrium in the binding between us.

Chapter Eight

In the Gloaming of the Red Sea

Wherein William Hallett books passage for Jacob and Thomas on the Red Sea Line, setting a course that will prove to be a turning point in the adventure.

November 4, 1847
South Street Seaport, New York
10:14 a.m.

The gating to the South Street Seaport part of Manhattan brought us from a clear brisk morning into the thrust of a cloud-ridden sky threatening rain at any moment.

We stood on the sidewalk in front of an impressively built dockside edifice. We walked along when we happened upon the small archway leading into an inner courtyard, and I had the strangest feeling come over me to walk into it, as if something were drawing me in, yet I knew our sights were set upon a more pressing matter. I had not even noticed that my pace had slowed down as we came to the passageway.

"Will, is something the matter?" Jacob inquired.

I found the question to have much more buried within it than a simple query. It was not what he said as much as how. Those five words seemed to have more weight as if he were concerned for me in some manner other than any other friend or acquaintance would.

"No..." I replied in an almost dreamlike manner. This whole situation was most puzzling.

"Will?" He pressed his point, stepping closer to me.

"Hmmm?"

"The booking? *Remember?*"

I decided to leave it and accompany them further.

"Yes, quite. Sorry about that. I do not know what came over me."

"'It is all right, but our need to book passage is pressing, Will."

We moved on, but my thoughts kept creeping back to the small passageway and something I needed to convey to them but found I could not. I spared a glance in Joss's direction, and he regarded me with a little concern. I felt him move about me as we proceeded down the road, only to discover that whatever I had been mentally chewing upon bore no more concern than the change in weather.

"We will ensure that you do not get wet, Will. No need to worry over your precious clothing," Jacob chided me good-naturedly.

I caught them looking at me from time to time as we closed to the dockside offices. The office we were looking for was in the second set of buildings a block away, and noting the signage, it was the middle door of three. Overhead hung a freshly painted sign indicating the profanely beautiful woman of Red Sea Line.

"Rather foreboding image, do you not think?" I inquired, pointing it out to my companions.

Jacob smiled and shrugged. "I could almost mistake that for a public house."

I laughed and nudged him with my elbow, as his comment was to bring back our carousing evenings in various public houses around Dartmouth College. Joss smirked only slightly, but I chose to let it go and not press the jocularity any further.

We entered the office, and it appeared to be unmanned. The room was tidy if a bit ostentatious for being a seafaring line. Everything was where we spied it before. The mirror held a fascination for me as I knew what was on the other side. My companions noted my eyeing the armoire. Frustration moved across their faces. It was clear the mirror conveyed an altogether different sensation for them than it had for me.

Again, I noted the counter separating the office from the reception, its darkly stained but beautifully carved piece, the woman depicting the same image that hung outside the front door, her hand still reaching into the open space of the room. We took it in, marveling at the artistry. When we looked up, the same gaunt-looking man from the day before was standing there. We took no notice of his silent entry.

His arrival seemed to jar Jacob far more than me. Joss seemed unfazed. Having spent years in close proximity to Jacob at school, I sensed the tension in his body rise, though he was careful not to openly signal his wariness.

"May I be of some assistance to you?" The man spoke with a slight foreign accent. Slavic in nature, if I was not mistaken.

"Yes, my friend here was looking to book passage for himself and a young ward to the west coast, if possible. Do you have a ship scheduled to depart anytime soon for that destination?"

His eyes surveyed Jacob for a moment, and a look passed between them that I found hard to place. It was extremely subtle, but I caught it.

"First, second or *steerage*?" He pressed the last with slight derision, presuming it since my friend was obviously Indian. I found his manner most off-putting but decided not to make a scene of it.

"Sec—" Jacob began.

"First," I blurted out, interrupting him. Jacob started to protest, but I gave him *that look*. It said I was paying for the trip and would book nothing less. I wanted to ensure Jacob was well taken care of, so I was willing to part with the money to ease my conscience. Jacob knew better than to argue with me as it was a well-trodden road for us. I spared a glance at Joss who had moved about the waiting area and took note of a leaflet regarding their services.

"And will this be a cash transaction?"

"Will you accept a check?" I inquired as I removed my checkbook from the inner pocket of my coat.

He nodded and took out a receipt book and the boarding passes and began the necessary paperwork.

"The ship is scheduled to arrive later today and will be departing Friday hence at three in the afternoon."

"Splendid," I added. "They will be there."

Fifteen minutes later, we had concluded our transaction and were back outside the door to the office.

"Did not his manner seem a bit over the top?" I asked them.

"Yes, I knew it was getting a rise out of you. He *was* a haughty creature," Jacob concurred.

"As he was yesterday. Well, at least they can be counted upon for consistency."

We began our stroll back along the wharf. We were about to cross the street when we had the good fortune of a proper coach coming toward us. We waved it down and instructed the driver to return us to my home in midtown Manhattan.

We could have easily gated back to my home, I supposed, but I had already begun to surmise that the borrowing of the *Dark*, as Joss had put it, was to be used sparingly and only when absolutely necessary.

As with all borrowing in life, I assumed one did not want to impose too greatly upon the supplier—whomever or whatever that turned out to be.

A nod from Joss was all I needed to know I had been right in that assessment.

By the time Friday would descend upon us, Thomas would be reassigned to Jacob. This had necessitated a visit by Joss and Jacob to Akwesasne to sort out the details of the reassignment and the process going forward.

To say the Jemisons did not take it well would be an understatement of epic proportions. The only reason it did proceed at all was that ultimately, it was simply not their choice to make—that fell solely upon the Central.

So, reassigned, Thomas began tutelage under Jacob's care. In the process, Joss was recognized for being a fully-fledged Guardian and thusly no longer under the watchful eye of Jacob—not that he felt oppressive with Jacob before, or so he told me. One would have thought this would have been a welcomed thing.

Sadly, it was not.

Word had arrived from Rebecca that the boys were now placed with various farm homes and were happy for their new lives. Christian was in the best of moods and had been assisting her in learning how to use the Mordant to great effect. There was a mention about seeing Jacob, but it was not clear as to the means or reason for such a visit. Joss thought it meant Jacob had finally plucked up the courage to straighten things between them. I prayed it was so. But then I was sure Rebecca would remark as much in her note to me.

::Perhaps she wants to tell you in person when next you meet?:: he added.

He spent his time readying for bed in Akwesasne at his family's home whilst I settled down for bed in mine. His point was as good a guess as any. I chose to let it go and wait until the fullness of their meeting would reveal itself to us.

Joss arrived the day before Jacob and Thomas, so I had nearly a full day with him where we strategized over the next phase of how he and I would continue our investigation into the Red Sea Line. It was then his feelings upon his graduation to full Guardian status were revealed to be something altogether different.

"In all honesty," he commented as he put another set of maps into their tubes, "I am not too sure I am ready to undertake that role yet."

"Why would you say that? Jacob has said on more than one occasion I can recall that you were more than ready."

"In my abilities, perhaps. Though I do have my doubts about how I apply them. Never think I am so in control of my world that while I move decisively, I may do so for entirely the wrong reasons. I am a man like any other—my emotions do get the better of me on rare occasions."

"Noted. And yes, I do recall your last set-to with Thor and how you— how shall I put it delicately?"

He capped the tube and turned to me, his arms folded.

"Brought them to their knees? It was not a proud moment of mine, to be sure."

"Joss, I only..."

"Nay, William, you are quite correct in your assessment. I lost my composure when they came for you."

::And why is that?::

Silence. At first, I thought he was not going to answer.

Just as I was about to think he would go silent on me, heated emotions moved within me, to the extent I became flush with them. I audibly shuddered as it took hold.

He became alarmed and it quickly withdrew. He tried to busy himself with other maps in the hopes I would let it go.

I would not.

"Joss, what—"

He stopped what he was doing and closed his eyes. Embarrassment emanated from every part of him.

"Will, please. I beg of you. Do not ask me."

He left the maps and turned to me. Before I could begin again, he changed the subject.

"In any event, it is time for our evening meal. I shall get started on it."

With his next step, he gated away from me. I heard him moving about in the kitchen. I tentatively reached out to him only to find him wince at my approach. The message was clear: he needed some space away from me.

I sat down behind the writing desk and contemplated my relationship with Joss. He was truly a bewildering man. My original assessment of him had not changed one jot from the moment I encountered him. In point of fact, it had intensified many times the longer we stood in each other's presence.

Yet, he could also be exasperating and perplexing in the extreme. An enigma formed, core to who we were as men who shared the most intimate things. However, as our bond grew stronger, the more I felt us flung further apart. I wanted nothing more than to close that gap.

I sat there as he moved about the kitchen. For a moment, I let my mind take leave of the entire situation. It was then I heard him humming a song I had heard my grandmother sing to me as a boy. It was a traditional song; one I could only scarcely recall the words to. He was not singing the words, but his lovely warm tenor voice permeated the house. I did nothing to let him know I was actively listening, but assumed he would know if I were, at any rate. A casual feel his way and his song faltered slightly. I retreated. After a moment or two, he began his song again as he continued to prepare supper.

About a half hour later he announced that supper was ready. I started to make my way there when I stopped and tentatively reached out again and found he was more than agreeable.

Time and space had given him what he needed to regroup. I tucked that away about my new companion, hoping it would be a great guide on how to deal with his mood swings.

Most of all, I wanted us to work. I did not want to find myself constantly trying to sort out how to deal with our ongoing bond.

"It looks splendid, Joss. Truly."

"Thank you, William." He beamed as he poured me a tankard of ale.

I looked upon the spread. He had assembled quite a sumptuous feast. Two steaks of decent size, Onondaga potatoes and lima beans, a favorite of the Haudenosaunee, and a bowl of warm biscuits.

"Biscuits, how on earth did you manage...?"

He merely smiled as he poured himself some ale.

"You can *do* that?"

He sat down and put the napkin upon his lap, his eyes alight with how pleased I was in this small touch of his. He had surmised this quite correctly; I was a sucker for a good bowl of biscuits—the more buttery, the better.

"It is only a matter of pushing dough along at a faster rate than normally happens. 'Tis nothing, really. Just pushed it along to make them an option for tonight's dinner. Really, William. You think I would not take notice of how fond of them you are and not do something about it?"

I smiled as I collected two from the bowl, placing one on his plate. We bowed our heads and gave thanks for the meal before we dug in.

I discovered a great boon to our bond; it afforded us to eat and carry on a great and rousing conversation without speaking with our mouths full. That was truly one of the best things about it. To look upon us, it would have been nothing more than two men enjoying a silent meal together, save for the odd snort or giggle. The conversation moved along in a most engaging manner and, to my great delight, was filled with humor I had suspected bubbled under the surface of my companion. But up until this moment, I had no way to confirm if my suspicions lay in truth or not.

Joss provided a wealth of surprises and treasures I had only begun to understand and embrace.

The meal done, the dishes cleared, Joss and I were enjoying a cup of tea for him and another tankard of ale for myself, along with a pipe of Akwesasne tobacco to share. For a small while it was comforting to just be in the same space with him and not a word, thought, or emotion passing between us other than the delight of solid companionship. Not too soon thereafter, I segued to finishing the tea with him.

With my last sip, I set the cup down and knocked the last of the tobacco from the pipe. I took the cups and gave them a good wash and rinse while Joss dried them.

Without a singular word between us, I was flush with enough ale to leave me warmed thoroughly from within and without. The drink fulfilled the former, while Joss's company provided the rest.

After we secured the kitchen to its rightful state of cleanliness, we made our way to the staircase. Without a single word, he nodded his turning in for the night and made for the library.

"You are going to sleep in the library, then?"

He stopped a few steps away and turned slightly to face me.

"Do you not think I should?"

"Only if you desire it. I would not want to be an inconsiderate host of my guests."

"I only thought—"

"Yes, I know what you thought. Get into our room where you belong, Joss. Leave Jacob's chaise longing for his warmth. I have grown rather used to my sheets being as warm as you make them."

I knew it was a coy thing to say, but in truth, I truly liked that we shared the same close quarters. To my way of thinking, it only served to make our bonding stronger the more we spent time together.

If he were to take to the library, I knew he could reach me within a second or two, should something go wrong. But in this new world of Flintlings and Guardians the violence from their war could cause irreparable damage in those same few seconds. I simply felt more rested if he were in the same room. I did not want to admit to that just then. My boldness was born out of my consuming too much ale at dinner and little tea as he had, to balance it out.

He arched an eyebrow.

"Why, William. One would think you are using me for something more than my companionship."

"I would never, sir!"

I proclaimed it with such fervor it surprised even me. A solid round of giggles bubbled from my own lips for my cheek. His shoulders sagged the tiniest bit, and a smile as warm as the summer sun snaked across my lips. I knew I had won.

He walked the few steps to make his way into *our* room, and I slapped my hands on his shoulders and pushed him through and straight toward the bed.

"Now," I called to him after he toppled onto it in a small fit of laughter. I held up a singular finger to drive my point home. "Get thee undressed, sir, and climb into our bed—we have sheets that need warming."

He gifted me with a slightly humorous look as I fumbled about with my clothing. I nearly giggled from the sensation of his amusement channeling its way to me. I began to paw at my clothes even more because I could not gain purchase sufficient enough to remove them.

"William..." he intoned from directly behind me.

At the sound of his voice in my ear, I became stilled. Not a singular sway to my standing at all. Inwardly, I felt a strong pull from him, leeching away any inebriate feeling from my person.

He wandered through my being, flushing me with warmth to the point where I became overheated.

"Sleep."

At this, I found myself succumbing to his command. As I started to slip into the abyss of slumber, I felt his arms about me, guiding me back onto the bed.

"That is it, Will. Let go. Find peace in sleep."

My head came into contact with the pillow, his face just above mine.

I do not know what overcame me, but I reached for him and pulled him upon me and kissed him. The moment my lips touched upon his, my body electrified. With a swipe of his tongue, every pulse, every beat, every extremity caught fire and roiled along my vascular system, burning me from within.

He pulled away.

And I fell...

...into the blissfully laden black.

The morning came in a sliver of light from the bathroom door, slightly ajar, revealing the skylight open to the brilliant sky above.

Blindly, I stretched out my hand to where Joss had always lain beside me, only to find the sheets cold and barren. Indeed, the entire house itself was quiet.

Naked to the world, I maneuvered through the bedroom and staggered my way to the bathroom to relieve myself. Having completed that, I began the slow ascent from slumber to a fully waking self. Within five and twenty minutes, I found myself fully scrubbed and dressed for the day. Checking my watch, I found it to be not much more than half past the seventh hour of the morning. I walked out onto the second floor and made my way to the spare bedroom, thinking that after I...

I...

Did I truly kiss him?

I stumbled with the thought, reaching for the balustrade to steady myself.

I kissed him!

With terror pouring through me, I had to admit I knew I had. In my fall into slumber, I had pulled him to me and pressed my lips to his. And I...

Like ice water, dread flooded my veins. My breath hitched. Ashamed for my actions, I found I could not query Joss without sorting out how I was going to apologize profusely for my drunken actions.

Drink.

Yes, that was the way. I needed to just put forth that I was too out of sorts from the ale I had consumed.

Only, it had not been all that much. And had Joss not begun the process to leech it from me when it all happened? Nay, that tract would not suit my purposes in gaining his forgiveness. No, there was no way about it. I needed to profess my being out of sorts with whatever he had done to remove the drink from me. Surely, he would understand that. Would he not?

::Joss? Are you there?::

Silence was my only greeting.

Where could he be? Had I ruined the singular greatest thing that had ever happened to me? Surely, he would think it a drunken thing and put no greater thought or weight to it, would he?

I began to pace in front of the spare bedroom door, unsure of my next move.

Finally, I plucked up enough courage and simply opened the door to see if he was there or not.

He was.

Sleeping soundly, twisted up within the sheets so thoroughly. For a moment, I was left speechless at my folly. He had not answered me because he was still lost in slumber.

I found myself at the foot of the bed watching him sleep, lips slightly parted, and his waist-length hair strewn a tad wildly from the neat plait he usually wore. No doubt, he too had a restless night.

Before I would wake him, I slowly slipped from the room, gently closed the door, thinking it best that I descend upon the market and find us sustenance with which to properly break the morn.

I had thought to leave him a simple note. But then, realizing he would probably seek me out once he roused himself from sleep, I decided against it. I secretly hoped I could make my way to the market and back again and have breakfast put together before he got around to grooming himself, such as it was for him and our native ways, for the day.

So, with all haste, I made my way out of our home and hired a calash with which to make a most speedy return and welcome Joss with a morning meal equal to the one he had so generously provided me last night.

As I moved swiftly along, I could not help but take stock in the fact that Manhattan had changed so much in my few years upon this Earth. Gone were the aging wooden structures I had witnessed in my youth, in lieu of edifices of stone and wrought iron. They were proper modern buildings for a burgeoning world metropolis such as New York was becoming.

With traffic being so light at this hour, I closed the distance to the marketplace within a matter of minutes. I quickly made my purchases and returned to the house only to find a note tacked to the kitchen doorway. Joss had decided to gate to Akwesasne to assist Jacob and Thomas on their impending arrival later today, before their departure aboard the Red Sea ship. I should expect them all around one this afternoon.

I balled the infernal note in my hand and chucked it hard into the kitchen where it bounced haphazardly along the floor.

"Blast!"

I did nothing to hide my displeasure in his avoiding me this morning when I needed him most to sort out what had happened last night. I hoped he was listening in on me now and could feel my building disappointment. It served him right if he did.

I sent a cursory thread of inquiry to see if he was listening in, only to be met with a resounding wall of noncommunication. To be sure, our connection was strong as ever—he was just making it quite clear he wanted his space from me.

I walked into the kitchen and slammed the sack of this morning's purchases on the counter, breaking three of the eggs in the process, which only added to my growing ire with my companion as I hastily cleaned up the mess.

"Companion, indeed. Does he think me his innkeeper, then? Shall I bill the Grand Council for *services rendered*?" I warbled into the room with great affectation.

The whole thing was absurd.

"We are grown men, related by clan and by kin. So, it was a kiss. What harm was there to be had from it?"

At precisely one o'clock, the three of them arrived with various rolled packs and shoulder bags no doubt containing their clothing and sundries for the trip.

Joss did everything he could to avoid me. Taking up the job of sorting the luggage and their supplies and then excusing himself to hail a proper carriage to pick us up to see them to the harbor.

The wall was still there between us, though not so insurmountable—a wisp of a barrier compared to what it was before.

Thomas had already become adept at gating and levitating. He demonstrated, on a much smaller scale, that he could also defend himself by shielding from an attack—though my potatoes were scarcely the volleys of light and energy I knew would be his true adversaries.

But it was impressive how quickly he seemed to be taking to his new life as an apprentice Guardian.

"He is coming along quite nicely. Almost at an alarming rate. Supernaturally so."

"How do you figure?" I asked as I helped them move the final pieces of their luggage to the curb waiting for Joss to arrive.

"I cannot say, really. Just takes to it like a bass to a river, if you get my meaning."

"I do. Are you concerned?" We eyed Thomas as he sat on one of the trunks I had offered them to condense the number of items they were taking with them. Thomas busied himself reading a novel I gave him for the trip. I felt it also lent an air of respectability if their travels seemed to bode that they had enough to carry them to their destination.

Jacob merely shrugged, indicating he had not come to any real conclusion; he was simply letting me know the jury in this case had still not reached a conclusion.

As we repacked and sorted the last of their things, I was fairly bursting to ask Jacob if his former student had mentioned anything of my actions from the night before. I think Jacob saw my apprehension and bridged the gap to appease my conscience.

"Did you mean what you did, William?"

"Mean? What do *you* mean? What are you getting on about there, Jacob?"

He arched a brow.

"Oh, very well. I do not know why I did it. It...just seemed the thing to do. Something he wanted from me and I ran with it. I do not know what to make of it either, to be perfectly honest."

He nodded and looked down the road to spy Joss coming back on a broad carriage about a block and a half away. He turned to take advantage of the time we had before Joss arrived.

"He has always had those feelings for you, Will. I just did not know you would entertain them as well. With all the fillies you have had your fun, or bedded down with, I would not have guessed you would. He was rather resolved to leave it in that unrequited state. He would not do anything to make you uncomfortable, even if all it does is bring him great discomfort to do so on your behalf. He would endure that pain for you. That is how much he feels for you, my friend."

"But, Jacob, I would never want him to be in any pain!"

I released the utterance a tad more forcefully than I had intended, bringing a surprised look upon Jacob's face as well as Thomas who looked up from his book. In truth, I felt every word of my proclamation. I would protect him at all costs.

Tiyanoga's words were stealing across my mind. Had we begun the slow dance that would bind us in other ways than merely from mind to mind?

I softened my tone considerably and continued in all haste as the carriage closed the distance to where we stood.

"It was not altogether an unpleasant thing, if that is what you are asking me. Beyond that I am quite at the end of my tether. Uncharted waters and all of that."

I was flustered and tried like hell to get myself under control as the carriage pulled up alongside of us.

For the next several minutes, I helped Jacob and Joss load the luggage and carry bags. I paid the driver our agreed-upon fare and then took a collection of bills I had withdrawn from the bank and placed into a leather billfold along with a bag of coins for smaller purchases and slipped it into Jacob's carrying bag. Only I had forgotten how Jacob never misses a jot—even when you think he is not looking. He gripped my wrist as I withdrew from his bag.

"Will, what are you doing?"

"Nothing. Just merely making sure you have enough for your excursion, so no one questions the first-class passage I have booked for you and Thomas."

"So, you are seeding us with cash to make us look good? Is this truly necessary?"

"It is! If I am to have a single evening's restful night sleep while you are on the high seas then, I beg of you, let me do this. Will you be able to handle—"

"William," he sighed, wrapping a broad and strong arm around my shoulders, "you have always taken care of me in ways I could never bring myself to ask. It warms me that you are still inclined to do so."

"Family sees to family, do we not? Is that not the way of things?"

He nodded.

"Shall we to the harbor, then? We have only just over an hour before they have last call prior to departure."

"Thankfully, our journey there will not be all that long."

As Joss collected my things from the house and locked it behind him, Jacob concluded our prior discussion.

"Be gentle with him if you feel you cannot be for him what he most desires."

"You are not upset with what has transpired?"

"William, you forget that freedom is the hallmark of the people. Only the Europeans feel the need to judge, belittle, and persecute. That is not our way, as you well know."

"Well, for all of the avoiding he is doing with me, I doubt I shall have an answer to any of that for some time to come."

Jacob leaned forward as we took our seats in the carriage while Joss made his way from the door to join us.

"Nothing would make me happier than to see you both happy— whatever that may end up being. *That* is all I ask."

It was as near to a blessing from Jacob as I was likely to receive.

A tentative probing Joss's way as he handed me my walking stick, gloves, and hat found that while he was not as approachable as before, he no longer had a wall of silence between us.

The four of us seated, I tapped the stick against the roof of the carriage, and we moved off to our date with the *Báthory*.

We arrived dockside. The wharf's throng of people moved along, awash with maritime activities. People bustled about either stowing items on board ships or removing them. As we moved along the dock, I caught my first view of the ship.

Clippers, having recently made their appearance in the world, were impressive to behold. These vessels had but one word to describe them: awe-inspiring. They were built for speed. There was no doubt.

The *Contessa di Báthory,* however, had a dark weight to her that made my blood run cold. She was large for what I knew clipper ships to be, easily besting the other two I had viewed before. I stopped for a moment along the dock to take her in fully.

She was a darkly colored ship, predominantly black with gray and white her only accent colors. There was little joy or ornamentation in her design. She was powerfully sleek to the point of menacing. At her bowsprit was a carving I found most peculiar.

It was a woman in gilt battle armor with flowing hair that seemed to entangle onto the bow and hold her in place. Her powerful left arm curved up and held on to the bowsprit; her hand bore long sharp nails which could fillet a man with one rake of it. Her other arm stretched behind her, taking hold of the railing as if at any moment she would launch herself into battle. The fullness of her figure was a horrific blend of voluptuous beauty and maniacally driven evil. Her face, heart-shaped and sensual, might have been considered beautiful, but this was negated by the dark-red crystal eyes coupled with her mouth, displaying menacing sharp teeth and fully agape. Her expression seemed to be caught mid-hiss to a perceived point in the distance. The visage stood as a resolute challenge to anything Poseidon and his realm could unleash upon her.

::A most formidable presence, indeed.:: I pushed along to Joss who completed his activities of getting Jacob's and Thomas's things properly stowed into their first-class cabins.

I continued to take in the other travelers and realized an odd thing stood out: no one bothered to observe the ship at all. Everyone around her, either on the deck or along the wharf, took no notice of her pernicious existence, save for our quartet. Upon closer examination, I discovered that everyone seemed to be going out of their way *not* to take notice.

People moved along the dock at a normal pace, but as they approached the *Báthory* they averted their eyes and seemed to scurry past, as if being near her would consume their soul and banish it to a place from whence there would be no hope of return.

Once past her they would resume their normal pace and cast their gaze about as if the whole event had never happened.

"Is that not peculiar?" I inquired as I watched the comings and goings of the people along the wharf.

"That no one ever looks upon her?" Thomas added as he took in the surroundings, drinking it all in.

Smart lad. I could see why Jacob was both impressed and a bit reserved about how Thomas was progressing. It was almost too smooth a transition from quaking boy to the composed one who regarded everything with a deeply analytical eye. Jacob caught my watching Thomas and arched a brow at my observation.

"Now, you will be able to press the matter, should someone question your booking?"

"William, you forget you are talking to a Guardian. I think I can easily best anyone who should try to give us trouble."

"I thought your sort were not allowed to fight openly. Do you not have to keep things under wraps, as it were?"

"As you witnessed in the marketplace, we Guardians are very good at bending the rules, so it never becomes an issue. Plus, we have other ways to *influence* their decision-making process if needs be."

He smirked at this—*the cocky bastard.*

The final call for boarding had begun. It was time to say our goodbyes. At this point, I was sure my sister would have shown up to at least wish them well and a safe journey. Jacob sensed my immediate qualms and leaned toward me, out of earshot of his young apprentice.

"Becks and I said our goodbyes last night. I made it abundantly clear she was not to return dockside because I knew what she would try to do. She agreed. But we had the loveliest night two people in love could have. I mean that in every way a man can mean when he is with the woman he loves. And I thank you, William."

"Thank me? What on Earth for? What the blazes did I accomplish with such an amorous-sounding farewell?"

"She acknowledged that were it not for you, and Joss, she would not have ever plucked the courage to see a way back to us, our love for each other. She attributes it to the two of you. She is smitten thinking about you and Joss being together. She said if she were of a religious nature, she would have prayed for it to be so. That way the four of us would face the world together. Rather sweet, do you not think?"

I chuckled darkly. "And this from the mattress conquistador of our school years? Who would have imagined you would be tamed by such a filly as my sister?"

He leaned forward so his lips were nearly touching upon my ear. "Your sister is a great many things; a coquettish filly is simply not one of them."

"No, Joss says she is every bit the hellcat you deserve in life."

Jacob feigned a gasp and placed his hand upon his heart as if Joss's comment had mortally wounded him.

Joss returned to report their things were successfully stowed below decks and the items they would need were safely in their cabin. He also told Jacob not to become too soft lying in all of that luxury.

"And this from the man who has his own bed warmer" was all the cheek Joss and I needed. "Hellcats, then? I see you, Josiah Bartholomew Lightfoot. Just wait until I let Becks know of your name for her."

"Why should that change anything? She relished the idea when I told her."

At Joss's words, we glanced at each other and a smile broke between us. I was grateful for the small, if deeply loving words as Jacob took his leave of us.

We hugged them both warmly, and I made Thomas promise to follow every teaching his uncle Jacob gave him. Thomas was quite adamant that he had no desire to go astray, as he found his uncle's instruction to be most helpful. He actually looked forward to furthering his studies and wished they had more time to dedicate to them.

I turned to Jacob as we walked to the gangway.

"How are you going to manage the training if you are limited on where you can go to practice?"

"It is an easy enough thing to manage if we have land in sight. Gating to unknown places is limited to what we can see. Once there, we can return to the ship without actually seeing it. It is forever imprinted upon our minds, and we can make the gate to it with little effort."

"I see. Well, Godspeed and all that." I nudged him and he nudged me back.

We embraced briefly again, despite the stares I got for being so friendly with the natives.

"What shall you do while we are so far away?"

"Well, tonight I have the party engagement at Miss Covington's, which I am not looking forward to attending. She is…likened very much to a python, strangling the very life out of me."

"Are you taking Joss with you?" he asked while we watched Joss and Thomas discuss the trip.

"I want him to, but I do not know if I can bring him to it. Rebecca will be attending, so in that event, it should be a thoroughly raucous affair. But I would be so pleased if he came along too."

"Oh, well, if it is a matter of coercion, then I am sure something will cross your lips with which to convince him to keep close. I have a real feeling that were he to gain your attention, he would fight anyone to the death lest they try to wrestle you from him."

"It might well be worth bringing him to Sarah's soirée, then. If anything, just so I could watch the three of them do battle."

"You are a wicked one, Will. It is nice to know some things never do change."

I shook my head at his jest.

"All right, enough. On the boat with you. I have had enough."

A few minutes later, they were aboard the vessel, along its side, waving goodbye. There was a fair collection of people, though far fewer had booked passage than I thought a ship of this size would require to make the trip monetarily worthwhile.

Once they made their way well past the end of Manhattan, I turned to Joss.

"Come on, back to the house. We have to find something suitable for you to wear for the party tonight."

"Will…" he groaned in a most exasperated manner.

I took a step closer to him, my face mere inches from his.

"If you want me for yourself, Josiah, you will have to keep me close and defend what is yours. Only in that way will you ensure no harm will come to me. And as far as you are concerned, I am *off the market*. Is that not what the socialite youth say these days when one is taken?"

I knew it was quite bold of me to lay it bare like that, but in truth, I simply thought the most straightforward approach was the best course of action. Otherwise, we would devolve into a quagmire of *are we* or *are we not*s that would only cause a fair serving of grief all the way around.

"You know what Tiyanoga said, Joss. He implored that I do not fight it. So, I have chosen to heed his advice on the subject."

He stood there, somewhat surprised at my approach.

"You find no discomfort in saying his name now?"

"Not since you have identified him at Akwesasne. No. Since then, it has been fairly easy to say his name without any discomfort on my part. And *you* are *evading* my point, and you well know it."

We regarded each other for a moment.

Finally, he seemed to accede to my wish.

"Very well, Will. I shall accompany you to Miss Covington's affair. Pray that you do not regret bringing me there."

"You are not planning on blowing up the place, are you?"

"If she so much as lays a possessive hand on you, then I will not be held accountable for my actions. That is all I shall swear."

I smiled warmly, and he moved through me again, only this time with a possession to his presence that nearly stole my breath.

"I would have it no other way," I murmured to him with as much passion as I dared in the open.

We moved to the street to hail a calash to take us back to our home and the preparations for the party which was to start in less than four hours.

It might seem like quite a bit of time, but Joss did not know how much preparation a gentleman had to go through to properly prepare for such an event.

There was no more hiding between us.

And for some reason I could not fathom, it seemed like we had turned a major corner in our bonding, one that would strengthen it in ways neither of us could begin to understand.

As I boarded the calash, I could not shake the sensation that Rebecca had something to do with Jacob's prodding and Joss's pulling, with me the sole mouse amongst the *three* hellcats I found myself allied with. Joss snorted as if he read my small summation. I chose not to think upon it further or things could get quite awkward during the ride home.

Chapter Nine

Number Three, Beekman Place

Wherein William Hallett and Josiah Lightfoot attend one of the highlights of the social calendar, only to find how things are not always quite what they seem.

November 5, 1847
South Street Seaport, New York
1:57 p.m.

To be sure, the ride home was an unusual one. Had we proclaimed some sort of overture of love to each other? I was not altogether sure.

I could tell from a cursory reach between us that his confusion upon the matter raged as surely as my own.

Blast! This simply will not do.

He smirked but added nothing to which I could cling that would give me some much-needed direction. He was being rather coy about all of this. And a bit too cavalier with my emotions, if I were wholly honest.

Damn him!

::You think too much, Ohnehta'kowa...::

At this, he took his right hand and gently placed it over my heart. His dark-brown eyes, so intense I had no defense from them, nor did I want it to be so, held my gaze.

::You need only feel it here. Only there will you find the answer you seek from me.::

And at that, my breath hitched as a wave of warmth surged, a never-ending river of emotion poured forth from his hand upon my chest. It coursed over my body, leaving me undone.

"Heavens above, Joss...I never..." I whispered, my arms outstretched along the back of the calash seat to keep from falling forward and out of the vehicle altogether. It took all the strength I had to say those simple words.

He leaned forward until his lips were but inches from my ear.

"And I have not given you the full breadth of what I carry for you, William. 'Tis but a creek's worth to the raging ocean of what I bear for you. You would do well to remember that."

With that, he removed his hand, and the light and warmth that had burnished its way to the very tips of my fingers and toes faded and I nearly passed into oblivion with the despair of its absence. Never had I run the gamut of one extreme feeling to another, nor with the all-consuming voracity his simple act afforded me.

At this point in time, I knew the game had truly changed between us. I may have thought I carried the upper hand whilst traipsing through Venus's grove, but clearly with one touch Joss explained to me I knew nothing. All I knew to that point: the adventure I sought was not the Guardian and Flintling war. It was but a sidelong diversion. Parallel to my present course certainly. Only I had come to realize *Joss* is my adventure. The quiet nature of him, the purposeful, confident manner he moved through the world, the way he always seemed slightly amused by whatever I did—all of this and so much more held my attention. Say nothing of his striking good looks coupled with his supernatural abilities, which were extraordinary, to say the least.

A most bewitching man.

He smirked slightly but tried his best not to outwardly show it. Instead, he chose to busy himself with the sights streaming by as we made our way home.

Our home?

At this, he turned to me, his eyes wide and contemplative. I felt confident that he heard my thoughts on the matter. Would he accept?

My first thought was this had moved faster than I thought possible. Yet, the deeper I thought upon it, the enormity of the four years at Dartmouth, the ensuing two years since we parted ways, felt as if it had taken an incredible amount of time to get where we found ourselves now. A great deal of time indeed, if what he hinted at were true. Though for my tastes, when taken in that context, our unrequited love had not happened fast enough for my purposes. I meant to have him, and nothing would keep me from it.

Tiyanoga's words continued to haunt me on this. Some small part of me continued to be concerned that I might be playing into the hands of the enemy by pursuing the very thing he foretold would happen.

And it seemed even though the cat was out of the proverbial bag, as to Tiyanoga's identity, whenever I thought upon him and our conversation, they appeared to be my own thoughts, and Joss did not appear to have any sense I had them at all. That was comforting as it was troubling. It played out as if my mind were truly not my own, but a plaything between these two warring factions.

My heart, on the other hand, knew where it belonged.

A glance Joss's way fulfilled all I needed to know. That what I debated lay solely with myself. He appeared to have no knowledge of it. Another point of concern began to thread itself. I really did not know how I could express Tiyanoga's intent by providing me with this knowledge could be trusted, even if it came from the enemy. I just hoped Joss would see the truth in it and learn to trust that it came from a very honest place.

Though, while Tiyanoga's plea for my assistance seemed true enough, I needed to recall he could not, by any means available, be called an ally to the Guardianship.

He is but the enemy to you; you would do well to remember that, William, I reminded myself.

Was I really going to take the man who sat at the forefront of the enemy at his word on this? It gave me quite a bit to mentally chew upon as the calash wended its way home.

About twenty minutes later and we were pulling up in front of the house. I turned to Joss and placed a hand upon his knee. He looked at it, and his gaze trailed my arm up to my shoulder to take in my face. I offered him what I hoped was a winning smile. He smiled in return, almost embarrassed by my being a bit forward with him.

"I know you wish to keep your distance from me and my lot, but, Joss, I *need* you there. If anything, just to keep that bloody social piranha from consuming me whole."

He snorted darkly, far more possessive than I had ever witnessed before.

Sensing his mood, I added, "Yes, well, there is that. And it warms me so to know you feel that way, Josiah."

He wrinkled his nose slightly.

"What?"

"I have never cared for my proper name. Joss suits me better; do you not think?"

I tilted my head slightly to look at him fully.

"Not to me. You shall always be formidable to me. The ever-impressive Josiah."

He rolled his eyes. "Come then, *William*. Let us get inside and get you ready for this catastrophe."

"Us, Josiah, let us get *us* ready for this catastrophe."

We disembarked, I paid the driver, and we made our way into the house as if this were any other day. Yet, with each step we took leading to the front door, our emotional state simmered to the point of bubbling over. It was little wonder that we both did not take to dashing the final steps, tearing our clothing off as we climbed to the front door. As soon as the door shut behind us, I ceased holding back and pressed him against the door itself and my mouth devoured his. His arms came about me with a strength that nearly pulled the very breath from my body, bringing my hips crashing into his in the most delectable manner. His strength I found one of the most alluring aspects to our newfound romance.

A most passionate man, indeed.

After a few moments of colliding of teeth, tongues, and lips, we parted, panting, with Joss heavily breathing at the door, me a few feet back. Our eyes intense, holding each other's gaze, aflame with thoughts I never entertained before. In the span of those few instants, huffing at each other in the heat of the moment, every carnal thing I thought I could do with a man ran through my mind. It was as if he had reached in and extracted my heart's deepest desire. Indeed, my skin and body were ablaze with him. I had never wanted anything more in my life than I wanted Joss, with nary a stitch upon him.

I started to move to him, slowly this time, purposefully. He met me part way and instead of an intense mouth play between us, this was soft and delicate—though no less deliberate. His tongue swiped tortuously across my lips. Without question, they opened as if on his unspoken command. His hands gently framed my face as he continued to kiss me. Each pass of his tongue claiming more of me and bringing me closer into his tight embrace as he slipped his hands from my face and wrapped them around me. His thoughts came at me in a rush.

::You are mine, William Matthias Hallett. None shall know you as I do. Feel me, my love. Feel the breadth of me. Know me and know what

I have is yours. I give as freely as I take. I shall make you tremble at my touch, nay, my breath upon your skin will catch fire and inflame your lust and desire for me. I shall consume you, make you a part of me in ways you never dared dream. You are Kanien'kehá, my life's blood. You are blood to me, life to me, love to me. You shall know no other from this point forward. I am yours and you are mine.::

His impassioned words of love and his vow to me coursed throughout my body, as if every cell, every muscle, bone, and vein would carry this memory and make a home within me. The saliva from his mouth, the taste of him, the air he breathed upon my face—with our preternatural connection it took on a new meaning. Each breath moved through me, past my clothing through my skin to warm muscle and bone. As our kiss deepened, he mentally pursued me, and like a raging river or the ocean he had for me rampaged against it, I felt it rattle, shaking me to my knees and making me weak. I knew not how to explain it to someone who might ask why Joss and I would now be intimate lovers, but as he tore into me, pressing here and there, letting the well of emotion rage behind the part of him that said if he let go it would overwhelm me, I knew he had become the master in everything I knew about myself.

Somehow, I knew this was part of the adventure. My complete and utter subjugation to him. He would take nothing less than absolute surrender.

::Only then, when I know you have released yourself to me, trusting me with everything that is you, Ohnehta'kowa, can I give myself fully to you. Your trust must be absolute as is my love for you.::

I slid my hands down his broad back and came to rest upon his firm buttocks. His native clothing, I discovered, allowed me greater access to touch them more fully than my own. I began to understand why he wanted me to start wearing it now. We slowly parted from our prolonged kiss, forehead to forehead, our noses barely touching.

"William, I...I have dreamed of this." He closed his eyes, and the tears he had been holding back spilt forth. I leaned forward and gently lapped them from his cheeks, bringing a small laugh for my efforts. He opened them and stared directly into mine before continuing. I think in this moment, even if the world had met with some cataclysmic end, I would do what I could to stall it just long enough to know what Joss felt.

"For so long, this has plagued upon me. From the time we were in school and I first laid eyes upon you, I fell for you. Nay, it was before that, when you came to Akwesasne to see Jacob and inform him you would be attending with him and inquired whether it would be possible to share a boarding room together. I was there that night, and it probably began there. Or when your grandmother brought you to the town to meet my family over some family feast."

He sighed.

"The point I am desperately trying to make is it has existed far longer than I realized. Yet in all those times, I did not ever think you would return my affections. I thought you were lost to me—what with your barmaid stories between Jacob and you. I began to understand more and more that we were not so alike, as I had hoped. So, I relegated myself to love you from a safe distance. Friendship would be my home with you. It was all I dared ask for."

I could not allow him to wallow in that alone.

"In truth, I do not recall seeing you at university. And not because I would not have wished it to be so. For now, I cannot think of any other way to be."

He became sullen and remorseful. "That is because I visited you on the eve of your graduation while you slept and wiped me from your mind—to make it easier to forget me, to move on with your life when you left Dartmouth."

I was astounded by that admission, truly taken aback by his act. It bordered on a violation upon my person. But I knew of Joss now. I knew he thought it a sacrifice worth the effort on his part. It was something I would discuss with him later. Right now, he needed to hear of my love for him as he stood before me, not the misguided happenings of schoolboys suffering from harrowing, unrequited crushes.

"I cannot say I am comfortable with your altering my memories of you, but knowing you as I do now, I know you thought you were saving me from myself, if that makes any sense."

I sighed and placed a finger under his chin, forcing his gaze to meet mine before I replaced my hand to his hip.

"Be that as it may, from that evening in the warehousing district, I was smitten with you even before I could scarce put a name to it. I am glad we are bound already. It makes this pairing on firmer ground. I would not want it any other way, Josiah. Not for all the adventures to come. You shall be, forever and always, my greatest adventure."

He took my hands from his hips and kissed them gently, before turning his head slightly to rest his cheek upon them. My frustration chose this moment to make itself known.

"Blast this infernal party of hers! I want no part of it. Not now. I would much rather spend it wrapped up in you and in our bed."

"Nor I. But you *did* accept the invitation, Will, *and* you added your sister to the mix. It would not be wise in skipping it now. To be precise, it would be disastrous to abandon Rebecca when she expects us to be there. I do not fancy being on the end of that Mordant device she seems firmly adept at wielding."

"I know. Believe me, I am cursing myself a thousand times over for not having the fortitude to decline the invitation when it was offered."

He kissed the knuckles of my fingers again, gently rubbing the thumb of his hands along them. His gaze riveted to my hands.

"You have such lovely hands, William. I marvel at them all the time. Such manly beauty in them."

::Ohnehta'kowa.::

::All right, you must tell me if that means what I think it means...::

::And what do you think *it means?::*

I pulled free and pulled his mouth to mine and kissed him passionately.

::Little hands? Really, Josiah?::

He chuckled softly as we continued the kiss.

::Well, they are smaller than my own, lover.::

A shiver ran through my body at the sound of that word—*lover*—from him.

::So tell me, Ohnehta'kowa, what would you rather be doing if we did not have to go to this horrid party of yours?::

In reply, I did not think any words but instead conveyed my innermost desires of how I imagined our bodies would combine to the fullest of release.

He pulled back and slowly released me. He shook his head slowly as he kissed my fingers again. Though the wicked gleam in his eyes provided me with all I needed to know that my message was well received.

"The party first, William. We must maintain appearances at all costs, especially now, because as we have been watching the enemy, we cannot be so blind to think they are not watching us in return. And there is no way on the Creator's Earth I would let Rebecca deal with it alone. Your sister's embrace of us means everything. I shall not leave her to that same barracuda. If we told your sister we would attend, we shall attend. *End of story*, William."

"Blast bloody appearances. I have no need with which to maintain my social status. I have you now, and that is more than I shall ever require."

He sighed softly.

"Will, I am thinking of your standing in society even if you are not. *And* of our continued health with your sister, say nothing of Miss Covington. Upstairs and a thorough washing off of the day's activities and then a fine suit for the party."

"Well, we will have to find something for you to wear, then. We are of the same build and height. I should think I have something that would be more than suitable."

His mouth slanted into a quasi-smile that did not quite achieve smirking status, landing instead somewhere betwixt the two.

"I do not relish being trussed up into one of those confining concoctions you call a suit, William."

"Hmmm," I murmured. "I quite agree; I would much rather see you *out* of one, myself."

I made sure there was no mistaking my intent in the comment. The message had its intended effect.

"As I, you. But it will have to wait until the party is over and we have returned."

I sighed myself, resigned to no other recourse that would not set tongues a-wagging.

"Well, if we must. Let us to it, then."

Joss tugged at his collar yet again. I felt for him. It could not be a great feeling to have that noose-like sensation around your neck when you had never had any reason to wear one. He was stunning to behold. The double half-moons' brilliance only added to the romantic vision he cast.

"Stop tugging upon it, Joss. You look fine." I smiled broadly at him as the calash made its turn onto Beekman Place. Rebecca snorted the tiniest bit at our banter. She was encased in a rust-colored confection that set off her hair and eyes to sparkling effect. The very height of fashion we Halletts were known for.

Sarah's house was just a few buildings down and my anxiety swelled the further we moved along the road. I set it aside to concentrate on my companion for the evening, even if no one else could know.

"You look better than fine, in fact. Delectably edible."

He chortled a bit. Rebecca nodded her agreement with my assessment. "See, she thinks so too. So, that is done."

"You are entirely too silly being in love. You are aware of that, are you not?"

"As long as you find me amusing, then I shall go on being silly at being in love."

He gifted me with a disbelieving look but let me have the last say upon it. I snorted a bit at the suspicion he expressed in that look.

The calash came to a stop, we disembarked, and I paid the driver whilst my supremely handsome date slipped from the carriage and held out a hand for Rebecca to join us curbside.

The calash moved off, and another quickly started to take its place, prompting us to move toward the music emanating from the house.

Number Three Beekman Place was a solid stone edifice. Though a tad further south, it was built to the standards inherent in the sorts of people who were beginning to populate the northern half of the island. *My* upper-classed sort, as Joss rightly goaded me. To a fair degree, dressed as we were on our way to the Covington soirée, I could see his point.

::I feel like I want to take your arm. I am surely the one with the most handsome man at the ball.::

::William, whilst I appreciate your feelings upon it, we are entering a viper's den. Let us keep our heads clear so our observations will match, shall we?::

::Are you always this humorless when on assignment?::

"Will..." he whispered, exasperated.

"No need. I get your point. Clearer heads, clearer field of vision and all that rot."

"Precisely."

Joss offered his arm to my sister, and we took the first steps when his truer thoughts snaked across my mind.

::That aside, I shall be hard-pressed to not have my eyes riveted to you all night. You are the most fetching creature, even trussed up in this skintight male torture device you call a proper suit. That arse, William. Truly a wonder beyond all measure.::

I flushed, and he chuckled, knowing he had succeeded in besting me.

"Boys, concentrate. We are about to enter the snake pit of Manhattan society. Let us bring our combined talents to bear, agreed?" Rebecca reminded us of our true intent this evening. We schooled our faces and prepared for the onslaught to come.

Once we reached the top, we were greeted by a butler and footman who removed our outer garments and permitted our entry into the main section of the stately home. It was then Rebecca revealed the fullness of her spectacular dress. Deep rust hues, beaded with the finest amber crystals and metallic threadings, accented by a dramatic collar that stood upright along the back of her neck in the richest velvet brown, accompanied by the sweep of her hair into a curled confection replete with pearls and crystals. She no doubt had planned to completely undermine Sarah's outfit at her own party. My sister knew how to ruthlessly play society's game and succeed at every turn.

We arrived just as I planned. The party was in full swing, and we were making our entrance to find Sarah standing in the large main foyer chatting up Michael Astor, my chief rival at these events, who seemed to be reveling in Sarah's attentions—lapping them up like a thirsty dog on a hot summer day. He was ravenous for her. Why the bloody hell could she not be for him? As looks went, he was a very agreeable fellow, which is why we often competed at these sorts of events.

::He does not begin to hold a candle to that arse. I know. I have seen it.::

::Joss!::

Cheeky bastard.

As soon as Sarah's gaze flitted to the door to meet our entrance, she quickly cut off Mycroft, Michael's distant cousin, with a semi-polite rebuff and proceeded to snake her way in my direction with all haste.

"William, there you are!" She trilled loudly enough that several heads turned in our direction. Far more than I was comfortable with, but I could not see any other way to avoid it. Joss pushed his way through me with such force it felt, for one brief moment, that his arms came about me in public.

::Sorry, Will. I cannot help...::

I held a hand up in his direction, signaling that he need not worry about it. I was his to protect, whether Tiyanoga said it should be so or not. I just needed to make allowances for him to have at it as needs arose. This was new territory for us both.

"You naughty boy, but I should have known you would wait until the height of the party before you arrived."

I smiled politely but was sure it was perfunctory and did not contain any of my usual warmth.

"As ever, Miss Covington, you are the picture of health and beauty, as it should be at such an event."

I took her hand and kissed it briefly, and it was then she visibly bristled.

"I, uh, see you have brought along your divine sister and...a *guest*."

"Ah, yes. Allow me to introduce you to Josiah Lightfoot. We went to Dartmouth together. His *cousin* was my college mate."

Her eyes remained ice cold, but she was a crafty one and quickly painted on a smile.

"Mister Lightfoot. How delightful for you to come. You are no doubt Rebecca's escort?"

"Yes, well, more of a companion partygoer. I will make my own way as needs be, Sarah." Rebecca gave an icy stare Sarah's way that kept Sarah from commenting further.

Sarah's words were genial enough, though the delivery was left lacking. She managed to snake a hand into the crook of my elbow and to move us along.

"Mister Lightfoot, feel free to enjoy yourself and get to know people." Clearly giving Josiah the brush-off.

"Actually, Sarah, I thought I would use this party to introduce Josiah to several guests. He can be quite entertaining and should prove a delightful addition to the party. The hosts from our schooldays used to clamor for him to come along with me when invitations went around."

"Entertain? How so?" she asked with a point to her query.

"He is, uh, a fairly brilliant...*magician*. Far above the usual sleight of hand sort of thing."

::Will....:: he groused along our link.

::Indulge me, lover. I have a plan.::

All I got for that was a solid grumble so intense it nearly shook my ribs. I almost giggled from the feeling of it. Not quite what I would have thought would be my usual response. He was upset. I needed to placate and not set aside his feelings in the matter. Lesson one in my adventure with Joss: it seemed I could no longer claim to be my own master.

"Really? Well, I am sure any party can use a diversion now and again. But really, William, I was so looking forward to dominating your time at the affair. You did say you would be my escort."

"True enough. Though I see there have been plenty of suitors who would very readily take my place."

"None who would suit my needs, I can assure you of that, William."

"Oh, I am not so sure—Michael Astor seemed to be quite taken with you just as I arrived."

"A *Jew*? Are you mad? I'm English, not desperate, William. He's pleasant enough, but really, the way you jest about such things. I suppose that is why I keep you around. The shock value alone keeps me in high spirits."

"I have found the Astors to be most agreeable, and he is such a lovely dancer I cannot help but think this evening has been elevated with his presence alone—say nothing of your subscribing to what amounts to nasty idle gossip that has never been proven and should bear no cause for any disparagement if it were true," Rebecca replied, a raking of claw to her tone meant just for Sarah.

My sister was ever the hawk when it came to backhanded bigotry in any form. Being Mohawk, she was overly sensitive to seeing it in others and frequently called them out for it on the spot. Since this was Sarah's affair, no doubt my sister was taking a more tactful approach in her support of Michael Astor.

Choosing to ignore my sister's barb, Sarah turned a cold eye to Rebecca and Joss who walked a few paces behind us. "But I suspect you know that about William, do you not, Mister Lightfoot?"

"I know William quite well. *Quite* well, indeed."

At this, she gave a small acknowledging smile, but chose not to press Joss any further for the double entendre that may have been implied with his comment.

We navigated slowly to the room where a string quartet was playing to the delight of several couples who were busy sweeping across the floor to their superb musicality.

It was quite the party, indeed.

"Do tell me you will favor me with a dance, William?"

"But of course. Joss, I shall not be but a moment."

"Not to worry, William. Your dashing young friend there has already caught the eye of several of the ladies. He does cut quite the figure for a native..."

"Ah!" I held my finger up to stall her next word. "Do tell me you were not going to say what I think you were. Because I will not stand for that. Josiah is not only a friend, but if you recall, Sarah, he is also family by clan through the Confederacy, and thereby related to me. My mother and grandmother are both Haudenosaunee, as am I and my sister. So, if you are a tad bothered by Michael and his Judaic gossip, then let me relieve you of the necessity of feigning any further interest in me."

I smiled curtly and tipped my head slightly. At this, she turned with an icy glare, filled with barely controlled vehemence.

"Really, William. One would think I was rather bigoted, by your reaction." She forcibly retook my elbow, turning us back to the crowd and smiling the sickly-sweet smile the debutantes were so good at affecting at a moment's notice. "I was *going* to say 'native *warrior*,' for he is clearly that, the sort of man women like me often fantasize about meeting at such an occasion though rarely do. Josiah is a most attractive man. And I do say the suit you have supplied him only enhances that impression exponentially. Really, do you mean to catch me out at every turn? This is supposed to be my birthday, dearest."

::Let her run her course, Will. There is something going on in this house that is not right. Take her to the floor. It will allow me to mingle and see what I can sort out with this uneasiness I feel in being here.::

::Do you not think it is because of your aversion to Sarah, herself?::

::She is but the focus of it, for this house has many things wrong with it. Though, I cannot say why just now. Dance now, Will. I will find you later on.::

"How right you are. I do apologize. Shall we to that dance, then?"

She smiled warmly, though it did not quite reach her eyes, which remained cold and calculating. She did seem pleased to have won this round between the three of us, even if Joss had given up on it.

We took to the floor. I noted that Rebecca had scored Michael Astor as her dancing partner, so everything seemed to be in play as we had planned. But as I took my place with Sarah, Joss's eyes were riveted to me over her shoulder, his gaze pointed and extremely possessive. It was evident to me: *I was on loan.* On no uncertain terms did Sarah *win* me away by any means.

::And she never shall, so long as I breathe.::

And with that he turned and vanished on the spot. I glanced around warily to see if anyone noticed the Indian suddenly disappearing. No one did. Conversations continued, the dancing and merriment went on unabated by Joss's departure.

I wondered where he got to as the music started up for the next dance, which was a rather spirited reel.

For the next twenty or so minutes, Sarah and I cavorted on the dance floor, though cavorting with Sarah might be too suggestive. We were the best paired couple on the floor, save for perhaps my sister and Michael, though whether that was due to my prowess at dancing or that no one wanted to show up the hostess at her own party, I was not altogether sure. Rebecca mingled and conversed with all the other socialites as we normally did at such occasions.

The following forty or so minutes beyond that, Joss was nowhere to be seen, which left me to fend off the polite light conversations which did nothing to stimulate my mind much beyond keeping it hovering above rampant boredom.

The first hour down and no Joss, no real competent conversation to keep my mind properly in the game, I was beginning to understand the reason I took to seeking adventure in the Points as opposed to my own class. This lot would sooner drive a man to madness, than marriage.

No wonder I wanted out.

::Joss?::

::I am here, lover.::

::And where is here? I have not seen hide nor hair of you for lo these past couple of hours.::

::It has scarce been more than an hour, Will. Are you always this overdramatic, that the timetable is thusly doubled?::

::Has it only been an hour? Rescue me now. I feel like I have been in polite conversation hell for countless days. And I am not being overdramatic. But never mind that—where are you and what are you doing?::

::Investigating something in the top floor of this house. I was right about our Miss Covington. She is not who she claims to be.::

::Do tell, since I am surrounded and hounded by this wanton bitch in heat.::

::There is precious little in this house to mark that anyone actually lives here, or has in a great long while.::

::But the house is fully furnished and the guests seem to be having a marvelous time. Food constantly rotates and drinks are replenished. It has to be coming from somewhere.::

::Oh, of that, I have no doubt. I am speaking to the rest of the house. It seems to be corded off to the guests.::

::Then how did you...? Oh, never mind.::

"William, do try these canapés. They are simply excellent."

Sarah picked one off a tray being circulated, and before I could scarce beg off, she pushed it into my mouth. I had but little choice to finish it.

"They are quite scrumptious, are they not?" she inquired with a quizzical look. It led me to believe I had consumed something not altogether good for my wellbeing.

That alarm in me was all Joss needed—the house rumbled, the gas lanterns flickered, and the guests stopped their activities as soon as the music ceased. Everyone looked about. Someone mentioned an earthquake, which given the alignment of the moons this month was not all that improbable. It had happened before. Except I knew it for what it was.

The windows burst open, and a gust of strong air billowed through the curtains. By the time the guests had collected themselves, Joss was at my side. Rebecca soon followed.

"I think you should not have eaten that, William. You know what crab does to your constitution."

Following Joss's lead, I turned to Sarah. "Was there crab in that?"

"Why, I think there was." She looked truly astonished at that admission of her error in assuming I could consume it.

"I cannot easily consume shellfish of any kind. I do apologize, Sarah, but I must return home lest I become a greater imposition upon your hospitality. I do beg your forgiveness. Josiah, if you please."

He was at my side and took my arm and assisted me to the door while Sarah profusely apologized for not thinking about it. Rebecca made our farewells and did her best to stall Sarah from tailing us out the door, to no avail.

"It was not your fault, as I only recently discovered this about myself. Actually, it was Josiah who deduced it for me. Not to worry, Josiah has a remedy for it that will set me right as rain by the morning." My stomach gurgled a tiny bit but loud enough that she heard it. "I do apologize, but I really must be going," I offered, slipping into my coat and accepting my gloves, hat, and stick.

Josiah, already suited up for the brisk night, took my arm and nodded genially to Sarah.

"A most splendid party, Miss Covington. I thank you for your hospitality and allowing me to celebrate your birthday. But I shall see to William's recovery, waiting upon him hand and foot, if necessary."

"My, a most valued companion, are you not, Mister Lightfoot?"

"In ways, I can scarce thank him for," I added, then, "Josiah, if you please."

We reached the door and the butler opened it and we were out to the street. With no calash in sight at the moment, we turned right at the end of the property line. Once out of eyesight, I spared a glance back to the Beekman residence only to witness the entire house go dark as if no one were there at all before Joss gated the three of us to our home a second later.

"Joss, there really is something wrong."

"I know, William. She deliberately poisoned you. I am doing what I can to remove it."

"You can do that from there?"

"Kiss me," he bade me.

"Joss, my insides are starting to churn. I do not think romantic..."

I spared a glance at Rebecca. "Oh, do not stand on etiquette with me, Will. Kiss him as he asks."

His mouth was on mine, and at once I saw why he insisted on such an odd request. In that kiss he was leeching the poison from me and into himself. Once I knew his course, I immediately broke the contact. He began to paw at me forcibly to bring my lips to his once more.

"Joss, *no*! I cannot allow."

"It cannot kill me, William. But it may kill you. Let me deal with it in the only way I can at the moment."

His mouth connected once again with mine, and the pull from within me was intense, his tongue drinking profusely from my mouth. It was hardly the romantic gesture I had goaded him about despite the voracious nature born in that kiss. Indeed, it was as if he were siphoning my soul through a sieve. But within a minute or so I felt immensely better for his actions.

When he was sufficiently satisfied, he broke the kiss and sat upon the sofa and slowly slid to the side and onto his back.

"*Joss!*" I called out, deeply concerned.

Rebecca retreated to the kitchen to bring him a damp towel for comfort.

He feebly waved a hand at my protestations.

"It is all right, William. I am working through it. It was a toxin that would have rendered you unconscious within several minutes and left you quite incapacitated to respond to anyone trying to bring you around. I have nearly sorted it. I apologize if this alarms you. I just could not think of any other way to leech it from you other than through your saliva. The kiss was the most prudent manner. Other than a blood leeching, which would have been my second choice."

He rested a hand above his head and gently closed his eyes. Within a few seconds it appeared he had ceased to function at all.

"Joss!" I shook him and started to lean in to feel his breath upon my cheek only instead to hear him grumble.

"Lover, move away from me before I push you away. You cannot be near me right now. Please do as I say, I shall ex-plain la-ter. Whaat ev-ver hap-pens, do *not* come too close. I beg of yoou."

Those last few words were the hardest for him to say. When it seemed I had not moved fast enough, he forcibly pushed me as hard as he dared to get me away from him. I stared at Rebecca, feeling helpless that I could not do something.

And his resolve to shove me aside came none too late it would seem, as he convulsed and I had to struggle to do as he asked me and remain where I stood. Without much warning, a vapor of watery air burst from his clothing and hovered in the air above him. His eyes opened abruptly. Gone were the darkened eyes I had come to cherish when they looked upon me; instead they were a most brilliant green and amber—glowing ethereally in the most disconcerting way. When next he spoke, his voice seemed to come at us from every corner. It was everywhere and nowhere at the same time, both inside my head and without.

"Stay where you are, William. I am not quite finished yet."

And with that his skin seemed to glow slightly, building upon itself until it burst forth and evaporated the mist hanging above him.

A moment longer and the glow emanating about him dimmed and his eyes and body seemed to be returning to normal. He lay there with his eyes closed, slowing his breaths until they were almost imperceptible.

I started to move closer to him, thinking the worst of it was over, when he sat up, startling the life out of me.

"Jesus, Joss. You could have warned me," I exclaimed with a hand to my heart.

::My apologies, lover. But it has been some time since I have had to deal with poison as toxic as that.::

"You have dealt with the likes of it before?"

He nodded once solemnly. I did not like the warning inherent in his single acknowledgment. As ever, he seemed to know my line of thinking. He took the towel Rebecca offered him and gently wiped at his brow, nodding to her, thanking her for the thought.

"You would be wise in heeding that warning, William."

For the next hour, try as I might, Joss was in a sullen mood. I made him something to eat as we had precious little at the affair. He took the plate and placed it on the small table next to the sofa but had not bothered to touch it.

Rebecca retired to the spare room, seeing how the worst had passed. She bade us both a good night with promises that we would regroup in the morning.

Joss thanked me in the smallest of terms, bringing a weary sigh from my lips. As I turned to go, he grasped my wrist, stopping me from retreating to the kitchen to make myself a plate and join him.

He slowly turned my hand so the underside of my wrist was exposed, and he gently placed his lips upon it in the most tender of kisses. I opened my palm to him, and he leaned his face into it.

"I am sorry, William. I cannot bear the thought of losing you. Tonight was close. Far closer than you realize. I am not angry with you. I am angry with myself that I almost was the cause for your demise. Do not be cross with my frustration. I am trying to deal with it the only way I know how. When I do not know how to deal with something, I retreat. Far too many years of seclusion to understand where I went wrong. Being near you and knowing we are committed now is very new to me. I am at a loss on how to deal with it. Do forgive me for how badly I have handled it."

I slowly sat next to him on the sofa and took both of his hands into mine, turning him slightly so we could see the fullness of the other.

"Joss, there is nothing to forgive. Please do not mistake my frustration for anger. I have tried to talk to you along our link, but you have refused any contact from me. What was I to think?"

"I know. I know, Will." He pulled his hands from mine and ran them through his hair, pulling the braid out as he did so.

"I am ashamed for how I got caught up with all of the things wrong about that house and Miss Covington. I did not fully see what danger we were in until it was almost too late. When she put that crab cake in you, I realized just how far she was going to go to wrest you away from me."

"She could try."

"Nay, William. She very nearly succeeded. There is much you still have to learn about our world."

"Granted. I spied a few things myself that gave me great cause for alarm. Things were not adding up, as they say."

"That house is also not what it seems. Evil lurks there. Evil and pain. I could feel it coming off the walls. If a house can hold such things and remember them, that house is at the apex of such a structure."

I did not know what to say. A house having memories? I did not doubt the fullness of his words with what I had witnessed and been privy to these past few days.

A moment later he angrily wiped at his face.

"Joss, are you crying?"

He turned his head so I could see he was.

"I cannot lose you, William. I *will not* allow that to happen." He bit the words out as a curse to anyone who would try. "Woe be to anyone who attempts such a feat. I say to you now, William, do not think for one moment that now you are in my life, I will let any part of our endeavors come before what I feel for you. And it frightens me. I am consumed by how much the thought frightens me."

"But why, my dearest?"

"Because it goes against everything I stand for as a Guardian of the people. Until now, I was clear in my mission, in my life's work. You have supplanted all of that. You supersede my vows to the people, to our cause. That is why it frightens me. There is naught but you now in my world."

He leaned forward, slipping his hand behind my neck, and his lips were on mine, our kiss connected. He coursed through me with wave upon wave of love he had for me. In that moment, I saw the immensity of what he carried for me. As our tongues fought for dominance in the kiss, he pressed his advantage, and I reclined back against the sofa, his body stretching out on top of mine. I relished the feel of his hardened muscles flexing and relaxing under the fabric of his suit. The cascade of his hair enshrouded my vision, encasing me in black to where there was naught but him I could perceive. I felt the fullness of him against my own manhood. There we fought for sensual pleasures of the flesh bound in fabric.

My hands came up along his torso and under his arms, and I hooked them upon his shoulders. I snickered at the pleasures his tongue and mouth, say nothing of his formidable body, brought me. I was heady with how quickly he could make me soar, the heights he could take me in a matter of seconds. My skin was on fire with him, and I wanted nothing more than to burn.

A moment later, it was gone. I opened my eyes, and he was still sitting where I found him before any of it happened. I sat up, propping myself on bent arms to see him with his head in his right hand, his arm resting upon the arm of the sofa as if he had been there the whole time.

"Never doubt how deeply I am in love with you, William. That is but one tenth of a percent of how deep my love goes. You would go mad if I let it consume you as I wish."

I ran a hand along my face where I knew he had been suckling upon along my jaw, yet it was bone dry.

"I made you feel that. We never touched, William. I just let you feel and see but a glimpse of what I have in my heart. I would ravish you as you have never known before. Everything else would pale by comparison."

He quirked a brow, and my manhood engorged in the span of a second followed a moment later where I was racked with spasm after spasm of the most delicious orgasm into my breeches. He watched me writhe on the sofa, lost to my own euphoria. Out of my half-lidded gaze I saw he never lifted a finger the entire time.

"I am the master of your body, William. But fear not, for you own my heart. I relinquish it to you for good or ill. You have the power to destroy me with a single word of rejection. That is a far greater power than you realize. What I do is parlor tricks by comparison to what you wield in me."

To prove his point, he gifted me with another round of orgasmic pleasures the likes my body had never felt. I smelled my spent fluids from my groin; the musky scent filled the room. He breathed it in deeply as if it were life itself to him.

The next instant he was upon me, physically this time, his nose buried into my groin, his hands pressing hard upon my hips, holding me in place while he satiated himself on my scent. He shuddered as his nose moved amongst my privates, inhaling deeply as he did so. A moment later, with a wave of his hand the clothing was gone. I was naked to the room, and he hungrily lapped at what was there of me. In the next instant we gated to our bedroom and bed.

::This feeds me, lover. Food is secondary to what I find in you. Never underestimate that. I will always hunger for you. From the time I saw you I was lost to it, never once thinking you would find me to your liking.::

"Jesus, Joss. Never have I known..." His finger found my lips, landing firmly upon them to tell me spoken words were not necessary. He placed those same fingers to the side of my head. I knew what to do then.

::Come, Joss. Let us find sustenance in each other.::

A moment later we were both naked in our bed, bodies unfettered by clothing, slick with passion, seeking new pleasures we found in each other.

::Do not worry about your sister hearing us. I have silenced the room to anyone but us. We are quite free to discover each other.::

For redolent musk-infused hours did he school me in how two men could find solace in each other's arms.

When at last, hours later, he gave me leave to find my release, I nearly passed out from the state of bliss to which he took me. I wept from the experience. I could not help myself. The man had possessed every part of me, staking his claim, at times nearly violently so. Mind, body, and to the very depths of my soul did he plunder, only to pull me along, bringing me to new dizzying heights. I did not recede from his onslaught. I conceded nothing; I met him passion for passion and gave as good as I got. He laid his head in the crook of my neck, and within a few moments he quietly slumbered. It took me several minutes to come down from that carnal high.

I was his. I would never be anything but his, and he well knew it, now.

My skin tingled. Every fiber of my muscles felt rejuvenated from our lovemaking. I felt him course through me, his life experiences binding to my own. His memories of family, friends, and companions in his past all imprinted upon me. I knew him, I knew of him, I welcomed him to make a home within me.

His lips brushed against my neck. The soft kiss there I knew was the beginning of a lifetime of such moments. I was replete with the very essence of who he is. This afterglow was but icing upon the cake.

But it seemed he had other ideas.

::Do not find slumber just yet, lover. That was but a warm-up for what I am about to do. I needed but a moment to gather reserves. I am not done with you, yet. This is but the first of many if I have anything to say upon it.::

Sleep did not find us that night until ten minutes before dawn.

The midday came all too soon for us.

Us.

I found a new trust in that word to describe what we mean to each other now. I belonged to someone, and wonder of all wonders, he belonged to me.

Man to man.

I had heard of such things, but having played the field as much as Jacob and I had during our schooldays with the local collection of barmaids, farmers' daughters, and fillies who peppered the area at Dartmouth, never did I think what I shared with Joss last night would upend all of that.

I lay there, Joss lazily draped across my body, providing more warmth than any bedding I could deem to purchase for myself. Indeed, I was slightly overheated by the amount of warmth he brought and lay half-exposed outside of the bedding to find a comfortable balance.

My fingers toyed with a strand of his long hair, which draped about us like an ebony blanket.

In that moment I took stock of my own body, for Joss was no wilting flower when it came to making love. Indeed, he was nearly voracious about it, and nothing seemed to charge me up more for the challenge like Joss's appetite for me. My body felt slightly overworked, but on the whole not as damaged as I had imagined I might be from the rough and impassioned sex we had throughout the night.

Indeed, the part of me he took absolute glee in violating time and again seemed to be none the worse for wear. It was as he said; he took care of that for me so pleasure would be all I would know.

"It is the healing nature of me," he murmured against my neck. He started to kiss me there, his hands becoming purposeful again. The hardness of his cock pressed against my hip.

The morning soldier, at the ready for another entanglement, I suppose.

"You think too much in the morning, William. It is quite simple: when I am near you, I want to fuck. Never confuse that with anything else going on in that pretty head of yours. It is not much plainer than that."

With that, he moved so he could take from me again.

I sighed as he found purchase within me.

"A man could get used to waking like this."

He snorted as his lust for me built again. His hips cracking loudly as he claimed me once more.

We had not spoken a word between us from the time he took me again this day, nor did we *silently* say anything. I simply found my body knew what he wanted to do and followed through.

We discovered as we rose an hour later from the bedding that Rebecca had slipped a note under our door telling us she returned home, as she was sure what we needed most was quiet time together. Joss and I smiled warmly with my sister's continued approval of our relationship. He moved us to our bathroom, standing in the middle of the floor, still naked.

I did not know what he was aiming for, as my bathtub was to the left of us. Nor had either of us made the trek downstairs to start the fire to heat the water. I scarce heard the word in Mohawk he uttered that meant *warmth*, and the temperature in the room shifted slightly. The light from the skylight began to mist up; vapors, in small tendrils, snaked to the light above. The room became warm and inviting.

We kissed. In the background of his mind, I heard a whisper of a command.

::Rain...::

And a shower of warm water poured in a ring above us out of thin air. I glanced down, knowing it would collect at the floor of my bathroom, only to discover it vanished in a constant cloud of vapor which only added to the moisture of the room. Within moments, it was what so many books I had consumed had led me to believe it must be like in the tropics— humid and wet, yet not altogether too unpleasant.

He bathed the two of us, taking such loving care to ensure that every part of me was thoroughly cleaned to his satisfaction. I tried to return the favor, and he allowed me to do so for a while before taking over and finishing the job himself.

He never said a word about it, but I got the distinct feeling he relished caring for my body. It brought him joy to do this for me. I found I did not want to deny him anything.

We dressed in silence. He slowly buttoned up my breeches, my shirt, my waistcoat and jacket, all the while not wearing a stitch himself. I found this is how I wanted Joss most of the time. I loved seeing him bare; I reveled in his masculine nature. I loved his body. The sensations of having him claim me repeatedly. It seemed only natural that I enjoy seeing all of him whenever it was on offer.

A devilish smile was his gift to me for my thoughts.

He kissed me softly, his tongue barely brushing at my lips. I became hungry for the taste of him, and he let me take of him what I wanted.

God on the mountaintop, did I ever drink from him that time.

::Go down and hire a calash, William. We need to eat before what I have planned we do today.::

::And that is? Dammit, lover, you taste so good.::

He broke the kiss, bringing a whimper from my lips as he did.

"Focus, William. We have pressing matters at hand."

I reached for him and cupped his sizable cock and bollocks in my hand and tugged upon them with gentle purpose, bringing a small grunt from him for my efforts.

"I am nothing *but* focused. Now, you were saying?" I quirked a brow at him.

He gently extracted himself from my grip and moved over to the leggings and loincloth he had laid out for himself. He slipped into them and put on a simple ribbon shirt commonplace with our people now, and a warrior's jacket from the American militia. How he came upon the jacket was a mystery.

"No mystery, lover. I scouted for them for a short while. I earned this jacket. I am no thief."

"I never thought that. Not for one moment, Josiah."

He gave me a disbelieving smile and continued to put his moccasins on from the foot of the bed. Having accomplished that, we straightened the bedding and made our way down the stairs to the front door.

I held out a hand to a passing calash, and it thankfully pulled over to where we stood outside our home.

Our home, I repeated to myself, finding the tone of it most pleasing.

He smiled softly at my thoughts, and his love for me coursed through me, stroking my pride just a bit with it. Part of me relished the thought of our lives becoming entwined with each other. The other part was all too aware of the prejudice we would face if such an alliance were ever to make itself known to the populace.

And there was Jacob to consider.

::He would want us to be happy. Did he not make that plain enough to you before his departure?::

::Yes. But men say a great many things in theory that often do not bear much fruit when their presence becomes fact.::

"When have you ever known Jacob to be cast amongst their lot?" he queried with a fair amount of point to his question. I simply nodded, deferring to his opinion on the matter.

Several minutes' ride down to the edge of the common marketplace, there was a tavern with a sumptuous midday meal. It was a slightly upscale establishment, which could present us with a new problem if our conversation was overheard by those of my social circles.

"Two of the Cornish pasty specials, my good man, and two tankards of ale, if you please."

"Right away, Mister Hallett," the young lad responded as he made his way back to the kitchen area with our order. I had been served by the lad a few times on my previous visits and he knew me to be a most excellent tipper, so I was pleased our meal would not disappoint.

I noted for all of the splendor of my clothing, for Joss had pulled out my finest suit, that several patrons who chose to sup with us this afternoon did so from tables as far away as possible from Joss and me. A fair number of glances our way began to draw my ire for I realized they were keeping their distance because of my lover's presence at my table.

"This will not do," I muttered.

Joss placed a furtive hand onto my knee, out of sight of the others, catching my attention.

"Leave it. It is best they do not have so close an ear to our conversation, at any rate."

"We can manage our conversation by other means as you well know. I will not stand for idle prejudice to mire our burgeoning..."

::William!::

At once, my mind and my anger subsided at his calling of my name. His gaze softened considerably. The touch of his hand upon my knee became a small caress, stroking my anger to calm, keeping the bear inside me placated.

::You cannot draw attention to us for any reason. I have had to deal with such prejudice all my life. It is as it is. I thank you for wanting to defend me, but come now, do you really think anything you could say upon the matter would adjust their way of thinking? They have been taught to distrust us, despite their adoption of many of our ways to your form of government. Believe me, I have more than my own ire with their lot. But now is not the time or place. We must focus upon our more pressing matter, that of Miss Covington.::

I sighed.

"Yes, you are quite right."

Our server brought us our plates and tankards. He tried to smile at Joss, and when Joss returned it, I could not help but notice the color that flushed the lad's cheeks. He was *smitten* with my lover!

I felt Joss chuckle at the thought, relishing the jealousy inflaming my senses.

::Truly, lover. You astound me with how you jump from moment to moment, taking on battles here and there. I love you for the surprises you constantly bring me. But he is a smitten boy of our kind. Let him have his fun. You know the result of his flirtations already. No one can hold a candle to you, and you well know it. Or must I take you on this table in front of God and everyone to prove it to you again?::

I felt the need to slightly adjust my breeches as covertly as I could after his innuendo. And yet, his next thoughts left me in a state of bewilderment for the ease with which he expressed them.

::We could have the lad together, you know. I can tell he would be open to it. He is fairly itching to find another man to be with. No man should have to want that much and not find satisfaction.::

I gasped aloud and had to bring out a handkerchief and feign a small coughing spell to get over his wild suggestion.

Joss merely picked up his fork and knife and began to eat in earnest; a small curve to his lips left me wanting to rap him upside the head for playing with my lust-driven ways, instead of *focusing,* as he kept prodding me to do. Then I realized he was having a bit of fun with me.

::I tease you, but we do not have as many complications between what love and sex are. How do you think we achieved our heathen status amongst your father's kind?::

I began to eat, choosing not to let his erotic innuendos confound me. He seemed to be pleased I got over what he perceived were my feigned protestations. He knew the moment he suggested it I imagined taking the young lad and having my way with him as much as Joss had shown me what two men could do with each other.

*::Is that how you learned to be so voracious a lover?::*I inquired as I began to sup upon my meal.

::I stated I spent many years alone. It does not mean I did not have trysts along the way. A man must have what he must to satiate those desires. But make no mistake, lover, whatever I did in my past is nothing like what I have with you. You ignite me. They merely catch my attention and are forgettable almost from the moment anything would happen.::

I arched a brow at that, for I knew what he meant. Having been with him all night and this morning, I would never find sex with another to be anywhere near what Joss and I shared. We were simply too connected. He consumed me during our lovemaking to where I nearly ceased to exist—except within the confines of his lust. I knew he was lost to me in much the same manner.

::Can we move on? Have you sorted our sex lives now? We have Miss Covington and her party to discuss.::

"Yes, of course."

I drank from the tankard and wiped my mouth with the napkin.

"What do you wish to talk about there?"

Joss eyed the room and seemed to be sufficiently satisfied that we were well beyond earshot of the nearest dining guests before he continued.

"As I stated earlier, that house is not what it seems. I think we should go back there today. Pay a visit to Miss Covington, give her our apologies for departing so quickly from her party. Make up some sort of excuse to stay for a visit. I will sneak in and see if I can find out something further about the home."

"Will it not be dangerous?"

He shrugged.

"No more than usual."

I looked around and then leaned forward, drawing his attention close.

"But with the change in the Flintlings, has not the game become far more, er, complicated?"

"Nothing I cannot handle. I assure you, Will. I would never put you willingly in harm's way."

Half an hour and two minor flirtations with Lucas, our server, we found ourselves on the corner of Beekman Place and East 49th Street.

"Proceed to the house and make your inquiries. I shall not be too far off, I promise you."

I began to move down the street, and his hand at my elbow stopped me.

"Use our communication sparingly. I am not sure whether or not she can detect communication along our link. Her behavior at the party seemed to suggest she had some preternatural means to discover what we were all about. I have thought much about this. It is why I think you were poisoned. It is my belief that Miss Covington, or whatever she may be, wanted to subdue you to get to me."

"Not too full of yourself, are you?"

"William, it is no secret amongst our enemy of my peculiar talents. I am a known, and therefore, desired entity."

"Granted. And I know those talents intimately now." I wiggled my eyebrows to ensure he knew the measure of my jest.

"William..." he sighed.

I playfully groaned, mocking him.

"It is dangerous enough going into the lion's den; please do not take the wind out of my sails where my love for you is concerned."

"William"—his gaze became far more pointed—"you really must find your focus in all of this."

"Joss, I am sorry. Truly. You are correct; I need to focus and find my bearing in what I am about to do. I do apologize. I shall endeavor to do better."

"Precisely."

A visible relief came upon him. No doubt my doing, as what he asked of me would give him peace of mind. I did need to heed his warning. No one knew better how to do these things.

He took my hand in his; his eyes looked directly into my own.

"I know what we have is new. Believe me, I do not wish to risk it needlessly."

"You are quite right. Any last words before I go in?"

"No more than we have already discussed. Just go with every intent upon placating her about departing so abruptly. Woo her, if needs be. Do whatever it takes to keep her preoccupied whilst I complete my exploring of the other rooms."

As Joss bade me, I proceeded to call upon Miss Covington at her home on Beekman Place only to find the home cleared out. From the looks of it, it had been abandoned for far longer than I thought possible given my attendance at her party the night before. I stopped at the door and took note for the first time of the unique silvery metal framing the doorway. Interesting sigils and runes were engraved into it.

"Curious…" I muttered to myself, as I had not recalled that particular design element of the house. I ran my fingers along the metallic side panel, taking time to run a finger into the indentation of the nearest rune. It was not like any I had read about before. How could I have missed such a unique feature? Seeing the symbols and glyphs, I could not help but recall viewing something very like them upon the Mordant my sister possessed. This was most odd.

Indeed, another odd thing was that the building was unlocked. I gained entry without so much as a guard, doorman, butler, or policeman to stop me.

At first, I was hesitant about going inside, but after glancing around and detecting no one observing my entry, I proceeded with a fair amount of caution. Trusting Joss was somewhere nearby, should this venture prove too much for me to handle, allowed me to pluck up enough courage to continue my search of the premises.

The vestibule was laden with nearly an inch of dust and debris. This had clearly not been the case when I was here the night before. What few lighting fixtures had been present were in deplorable condition—again, not quite what I remembered. I was astounded. I stood in the drawing room where a fully furnished room was but a night ago. Paintings had hung upon the wall which now only bore the soiled outlines of those frames as if time had marked their absence.

I moved from the drawing room to the cavernous stairway of the main part of the house. Each step I took seemed more tenuous than the one before, despite my attempts to maintain control of my emotions. I proceeded up the staircase, which showed signs of serious neglect. How no one ever inquired as to the purchase of this structure was beyond me.

It was a fine building, if in need of some care. With the proper attention, it would make a lovely family home. How could such a building remain so...*empty*? It even had the benefit of prime location along the waterfront facing the East River and Blackwell's Island. Its neglect was a complete mystery to me.

I did not detect Sarah, her family, or her staff in attendance. I also could not sense Joss anywhere, which was most disconcerting. The home appeared completely devoid of any presence save my own. A ripple of distrust threaded its way through me. It was the closest I had to feeling Joss throughout the entire operation. I had to trust he would still find a way to save me, should something go horribly wrong.

Upon reaching the top landing, I observed the ceiling stood at least fifteen feet above me. Not unusual in and of itself, but without the fixtures and furniture from the night before, it loomed much larger than I thought it should—bending reality into something of a nightmarish state and adding to the apprehension I had about the place I thought I knew so well. I moved to the second room on the right from the staircase which was where Miss Covington's invalid mother was rumored to be kept. I never had the pleasure of meeting the woman on any of my previous visits; it was just a collective knowledge within high society that Sarah's mother was unwell and restricted to bed. A whispered piece of gossip that now took on new meaning. My nose wrinkled slightly as a foul odor permeated the area. I was not sure if whatever created that smell lay behind this door, but I was determined to absorb as much detail from this mystery as I could.

Joss was quite right. Miss Covington was not what she appeared. If, in fact, she was even *who* she claimed to be. Given the revelations of the Guardians and the Flintlings, I was beginning to have doubts upon what was real within my own world. This latest mystery did nothing to take away from that. Up until recent events, the universe had always been ordered to my mind. This whole experience ran contrary to those precepts. Another troubling point to ponder.

I paused momentarily at the door. Part of me remained unsure if I wanted to proceed further without some confirmation that Joss was nearby. I wanted to reach out to him along our link, but he had warned against it. We simply did not know enough about what we were dealing with to chance it.

I placed my forehead upon the door. The stench welled up behind it—no mistaking the simple fact. In that moment, when I needed him most, I felt him. Just at the outer reaches of my senses, as if something were preventing Joss from moving in closer. But he was there, if just out of reach. This did little to quell my apprehension. I would have to trust whatever lay beyond this door was enough to solve the mystery but not so overbearing as to cause me any great harm.

The silence was made all the plainer to me with the rattle of the doorknob. All I could think was this was the sort of setup where some horrendous creature Joss and Jacob had warned me of would wake from slumber, and attack.

Never, even when I considered my nights spent in the Points, had I felt more alone and more vulnerable than I did now.

Holding my breath, I pressed upon the door and found it unlocked. Yet something prevented it from opening to its fullest. I managed to just barely get the door to part from the frame. I braced myself and pressed in harder with my shoulder to force my way into the room.

The aroma gushing forth made my eyes water and nearly brought me to my knees. There, in the middle of the room, suspended from the ceiling by chains around the wrists and ankles, was the rotting corpse of what was most assuredly, at one time, a woman.

The remnants of her black dress, torn and shredded, clung to her form as did the last vestiges of muscle and sinew, to rotting bone. Her hair hung in wisps of shocking white against the darkness of the room. Her mouth gaped, as if she had died shrieking in utter torment. Only when I moved further into the room did I see the butcher's hook entrenched in the corpse's back. This was the means of her suspension, a grotesque chandelier. The shackles appeared to restrict further movement when the woman had met her horrific demise.

It was a most heinous sight. I thought I had a strong constitution and could endure just about anything. This tested my mettle. There was little in the way of ambient light. What I had allowed through the opened door, much to my dismay, was more than enough to illuminate the horror within.

"Invalid, my arse. Now there is a new definition for the word."

Bringing a handkerchief to my mouth and nose in an attempt to diffuse the fetid air, I made my way further into the room.

"What on heaven's earth could have possessed someone to treat this woman with such a violent end?"

"Oh, she wasn't as pleasant as you might assume. She was quite mad, I assure you."

Spinning around on the spot, I took in Sarah, standing at the door, leaning against the jamb, her arms crossed. I staggered in bewilderment. How long she had observed my wanderings, I cannot be sure, because I knew she was not there before I pressed for entry.

The windows were closed, and there was no other means into the room I could detect. She moved with ease about the space. Was it a trick of the light or did her form glide about and waffle in and out of existence? With the lack of ambient light, I could not be sure.

"But this is..." I struggled to define it, indicating with my free hand the corpse above. "Barbaric. What could *this* possibly have served?" While horrific in the extreme, my nights spent in the Points had sadly inured me to such things.

"Nothing but my own curiosity at human suffering, I assure you." She imparted this with such charm, laying bare the malevolence at its core. She moved around me slowly, as if we were still back at market and not strolling around a tortured corpse suspended between us. She was the one who was quite mad; I could sense it in the way her gaze beheld me. If I was sure of anything, it was that. I was a nuisance, a curiosity she was no more threatened by than a wayward ant—as expendable as the woman whose remains soared above.

Before I could comment further, she flew to me. I stumbled backward onto the floor with a resounding crash, her full weight upon me. She giggled and quickly pressed my hands above my head, holding me in place with one forceful hand by my wrists. Never had I encountered such strength. I could not move in her grasp. She leaned forward so the light of the hallway caught her face fully. In it, I could detect darkened eyes, completely obliterating any vestige of human quality. While my breathing became labored as I struggled to get free, she seemed to expend little energy. I gave up any pretense of my arrangement with Joss and tried to reach out to him.

::Joss!::

The building rattled most abruptly, shaking it to its foundations. No doubt Joss was pressing for entry into the room. Dust showered down upon us. Sarah gave it no notice, as if she were somehow preventing my Joss access to save me.

She leaned forward. Her face was but inches from mine. She cocked her head to the side slightly in a very unnatural way, as if she could not manage it easily.

"Shhhhh, Will. Quiet now. Be still."

She waved a hand in front of my face, and all at once I found my consciousness agreeing with her, yet on some other level I was struggling, as if trapped behind a thick pane of glass through which I could observe but not rouse myself to continue the fight to freedom. Her words seemed to be winning the battle.

Where is my protector?

She giggled maliciously again—her eyes wide with a childlike wonder infused with a clear sense that nothing was sacred to this creature, not even life itself. She sat up, releasing my wrists, though I found I could not move them from where she had them pressed into the floor above my head.

"Now listen very carefully, William. What I have to say is very important."

Her voice became like liquid, a calm and soothing stream of water that washed over me. My muscles relaxed to her voice. I found myself intent upon hearing her message; the little voice in my mind challenging her was growing fainter with each passing moment.

"You will forget all you have seen here. You will forget about me, about meeting me. You will excuse yourself from all social circles. Your friends and family acquaintances will move on without you. We have other plans for you."

I lay there, in a drowsy state, unable to do anything but concentrate on the sound of her voice. In some far-off corner of my mind I remained cognizant this was nothing but pure coercion. But none of that mattered now as her voice lilted about the room. The woman above us seemed to disappear from my view. I was already allowing the memory of this place to fade from my mind. I was willingly letting it go, like granules of sand slipping through my fingers.

She drifted above me, parallel to my reclined form. But somehow, I did not seem to be concerned with that either. She smiled wickedly, as if she enjoyed the snare of her charms and how it played heavily upon me.

"Now, William. One other thing."

When I turned my fullest attention to her, she seemed to float in the air slightly above me. Her dress billowed about her in a breeze I could neither feel nor hear. Again, she drifted in and out of existence, flickering between the two rapidly as if struggling to maintain her presence in this world, reminding me of the witch Tituba whom Christian had subdued. On some level, my mind seemed to work upon that, replaying what I could recall from Christian's successful counter to her attack.

"That delightful Indian you have following you."

A protest struggled to break free from my throat, but she shook her head. The building rattled again; this time much harder.

"Don't deny it. I know you sense his presence." She gestured to the assault she seemed to think emanated from him. "You would do well to let him move closer to you. *We* are very interested in him. Do everything in your power to bring him to you. Encourage him at every turn. Call to him. We desire to get to know him better, but thus far he has been most elusive. You will help to bring him out of hiding. Am I clear?"

I smiled, and it felt odd to express something so warm upon my face with none of the emotion behind it. I have often heard how some people wear their expressions like a mask. Until this moment I had not a clue what that meant.

::I am here, lover. She will not be ready for my assault. Hold but a moment further. Trust me, William. She will not touch what is mine.::

The building shook with a blast that cracked the walls and brought more dust to rain down upon us. The far wall buckled followed by a wave as if some mammoth earthworm had burrowed along it. My eyes drifted from watching Joss tear his way past whatever protections Sarah had put up to shield the house from intrusion.

"Most clear. Everything I can."

I heard my voice say it with little affectation as it echoed about the room, but I could not recall forming the words in my mind let alone within my mouth. For reasons I could not fathom, my arms were released and blood coursed through them, bringing them to life once more.

She moved closer and pressed her lips to mine. Her breath was intoxicating. I found my mouth opening to hers, and a coldness swept through me as her breath caught mine. She seemed to draw every ounce of warmth from me, yet I held on, almost desperately, as if her coldness held my salvation. I attempted to bring her to me by wrapping my arm around her waist, but it only slipped through her form. She could hold me but not the reverse. So, I hungrily clung to her lips, savoring the kiss in every rapturous detail. The scent of her breath reminded me of something, but I could not put a finger upon it. Slightly floral and sickly sweet, almost with decay.

How the thought pressed through the haze of her ministrations upon my brain, I would later reflect, was a complete mystery, but through that haze I heard Joss's voice pressing at the edges of my mind: "She is Death!"

The windows of the room rattled, the floor thundered, and the building shook so violently as the entire wall crashed inward. A brilliant blue-white light, brighter than if the sun itself had descended into the room, moved through the shattered opening.

I felt him move in. Joss's fury blazing hotter than ten thousand suns—catching the very air with fire. His rage pressed into the room, breaking the kiss. I had not realized that in our embrace she had drifted toward the ceiling, taking me with her. I fell three feet to the floor, my knees crashing upon its hard wooden surface. The pain brought tears to my eyes and me, somewhat to my senses.

Joss's radiance obscured him from my blurred vision. The light hanging above his head was simply too intense to discern his features, but the anger I felt raging between us clarified his position even if I could not witness it. I held my hand to my eyes, wiping the excess tears while attempting to block the exorbitant harshness of it all.

"Hell-Witch, look your last!" he bellowed. She soared into the air near the ceiling.

She maneuvered around the ragged corpse, hissing at Joss in defiance. *How did I forget about the corpse being suspended in the room?* I wondered amid the mayhem.

He bellowed words behind the power he wielded, so loud I could not make out clearly what he was saying to her. She wailed in response—a death siren so powerful I put my hands to my ears to shield me from the deafening cry.

I could tell he turned his head in my direction from the outline of his shadowed presence. He ascended and lunged after her. She cried out and produced a Mordant that crackled to life in the room. A bolt of energy lanced about, lightning discharged, scorching the walls and ceiling as they collided. As he lunged for her again, she chose to strike at him with the pointed end of the Mordant. It struck against the light above his head. The light somehow shielded him from her blow.

Rebuffed and enraged, she became maniacal in her subsequent attacks, lashing out only to be rebuffed by the light, which rumbled against her onslaught. The titanic fight thundered in the building, shaking it to its foundations. Large cracks appeared in the king beam, running the length of the room. The plaster of the ceiling, what little remained, rained down in pieces. At one point in the battle, the Mordant came too close to the suspended corpse, and it sliced through the thick metal links of the chains as if they were but cobwebs on a sill. The decrepit body came clamoring to the floor, which would have been of little concern to me had I not taken to hiding under it for protection, as it was the only thing in the room that could provide any cover. The fetid thing fell upon me with a decisive thud, its scent filling my nostrils; I struggled to free myself from the dead woman's embrace. Above, through the wisps of her hair, I could see Joss had maneuvered Sarah, or the maligned creature who I mistook to be Sarah, into the darkened corner of the room along the ceiling.

She screamed again and with an enormous force lanced out with the Mordant once more. This time she successfully scored past his shield. I thought he was going to be killed, but her success was clearly part of his plan. In the next instant, he seized upon it, shattering it entirely. The dust and debris from the expired device flung into the far reaches of the room. The radiant blast bounced against the walls in a shower of sparks and rubble. She screamed again, and he made his decisive move. He lunged for her and seized her around the neck. She clawed at him. He cried out as the blood flew from his wrist and arms as her razor-like nails slashed at him. She struggled to make another sound, and only when she was unsuccessful in getting the air to flow through her to produce it, did she take both hands and lance his ribcage using her fingernails which had elongated into sharpened talons. He cried out in agony but held firm upon her neck, crushing her air supply—a move similar to the one Christian had employed upon Tituba.

As I lifted the dead woman from my body and tossed it to the side, Joss reacted to Sarah with a move of his own. He seemed to draw the power of the floating light into himself and released it in a blast that consumed her before she could plot an escape. I saw her visage wither into a mass of embers and billow into the air. The blast threw me from my feet and dashed me to the other side of the room where my head collided with the wooden mantelpiece. Stars formed before my eyes, and I sank into oblivion.

I came around in a daze, and in the darkness of the room I caught Joss's eyes peering into mine. My head cradled in his lap.

"Rest, my love, I have you. I am sorry I could not reach you sooner. Her wards were stronger than I anticipated. Rest is what you need. You will recover."

As I succumbed into the abyss, the small signs of his gating us to our home enveloped me. I was with Joss. I was safe in his arms.

Darkness crept in as I felt him place me gently in our bed.

Chapter Ten

Beware Mohawks Bearing Gifts

Wherein William Hallett and Josiah Lightfoot recover from their entanglement with Sarah Covington, while the Guardianship finds itself in completely new and dangerous territory.

November 8, 1847
William Hallett's Home, New York
12:37 p.m.

The early afternoon sun shimmered into our bedroom. My body carried a dull ache to it. Joss lay next to me, his body curled up against me, his head resting upon my shoulder. For the moment I relished his warm breath against my neck. How long we remained in bed I did not know. I moved slightly, but not so much as to disturb Joss.

To my great joy, we were naked as I relished the feel of him. Then memories started to reveal themselves to me. Joss had been hurt! Sarah had punctured his rib cage. I scrambled, not caring whether or not I disturbed him. I had to reassure myself he was on the mend.

His arm draped across my chest held me firm.

"I am fine, lover. I have healed. You need not worry about it."

"But..."

::She did not cause me as much pain or damage as you might have thought. I am not easily broken.::

::How long have we...?::

::About a day and a half. It is the eighth.::

"Well, why did you not wake us earlier? We have missed an entire day."

He finally opened his eyes and lifted his head to meet my troubled gaze.

"Because you were far more damaged than I. I had to heal you, and that took more time than the few hours I required."

His words were true enough. My body still ached more than I was wont to admit. But not so much that I could not coax a kiss from him.

He snickered as my mouth met his in a chaste kiss.

::Our breath...the backside of a loose-stooled horse has a better scent.::

I laughed and playfully bit his bottom lip for his cheek.

"Can you move?" he inquired, deep concern mellowing across his face.

"I think so."

"She broke four ribs, and your head hit rather hard against the mantel. I feared I might have to call a few healers to help me get you back to where you are now. Luckily, our bond seems far stronger than I originally anticipated."

He rose, exposing the fine muscled body that warmed my heart and loins in so many ways. Even the remnants of the Sarah-like creature's attack upon his rib cage left no mark. Truly an astounding feat of healing on his part which left me to admire the wholeness of him once again, unfettered by my concern for his health.

He arched a playful but pointed brow with his next words. "William, you are in no state for that. I assure you once I am confident your wounds are fully healed, I shall ravish you as you should be. Until then, let us get downstairs and see what we can scrounge for a midday meal."

Luckily, Joss gated back to Akwesasne to his family to gather some food, as my resources were fairly thin, and we had more than missed the best choices at market. He returned an hour later. When he arrived, I could tell something plagued upon his mind, but he would neither speak of it nor allow me to *see* what it could be.

Instead, he went about preparing the meal, and we began to eat with little in the way of conversation. That was not to say we did not push between us how we felt being together.

"There is something we need to discuss."

I wiped my mouth. I reached out to him but found he had retreated. He shook his head briefly to let me know that now was not the time to pry.

"Okay, I am all yours."

He placed a soft hand on mine as it lay on the table. His gaze softened considerably.

"We have heard from Jacob," he started, holding a hand up to stall any query I might have. "Samuel conversed with him and Thomas to get an update on the *Báthory* and the Flintling operations as they make their way to San Francisco."

"Ah, yes..." I began, though having never seen San Francisco, I truly had no idea how to understand the measure of his words.

"It is a town along the Northern California coast. The Mexicans have a foothold there, but it is questionable how long that will last if the Flintlings are able to establish themselves. We think this is why you had the information that they have gone global and why the Russians are involved. Thomas was able to observe some Russian operatives talk about a fort just north of San Francisco where a Russian colony used to exist some time ago, but has since been abandoned. It appears the Flintlings are using it as the base of their operations within the area. That will be the focus of our attention for the time being. A council of Guardians is being called to Akwesasne tonight to disseminate assignments. I am, or rather, *we* are expected to be there."

I was astounded by these revelations.

"They want me?"

At that, Joss became thoroughly perplexed, setting his napkin down after wiping his mouth.

"Why does this confuse you? You and I are, for all intents and purposes, permanently linked, are we not? Samuel knows this. If I attend, then you must as well. There is no mystery to this, *Ohnehta'kowa*."

He leaned forward and placed a kiss on my forehead before collecting our dishes and moving off to clean things up. I joined him, relishing that we could share this simple chore together. The warmth I felt must have trickled across to him because he smiled warmly as he handed me the soapy dishes for me to rinse and dry.

With our special means of communication between us, we often moved about in a veil of silence. Indeed, nearly all of our communication was without words, more of emotions and loosely conceived thoughts that we were each learning how to interpret without the need for speech. Joss thought it a most excellent way to expand on how we communicated in case words were not an option. Even during my healing, I knew he was there, pushing warm thoughts of his slowly making love to me as he mended my broken body.

"You know, it was quite clever of you to keep me calm by pushing those ardent thoughts my way whilst you attended to my wounds."

He smiled before it faded a bit and a thread of worry coursed along his brow, bringing a new concern to me.

"There was the lowest point where you started to fail to respond. The only way for me to rouse you was to make you think we were..."

He stopped, clearly distressed over some troublesome part of my healing he had not made known to me before.

He shook it off before I could inquire further. His glance to me said I should not pursue it, at least for the time being.

"If this is as permanent as I want it to be, we shall have time for such conversations," he murmured.

I placed a hand to the crook of his arm, turning him from our chore to look at him fully.

"Never, for a solitary moment, think this is transitory by any measure. Do you get the fullness of my meaning? This is not some passing fancy. Do you think with what we share, with you consuming me and my passions as surely as if they were your own, nay, rattling my being to the core as you voraciously bring me to you, that I could ever entertain leaving you? Joss"—I took his hands in mine, kissing each finger softly, my lips speaking against them—"no one shall draw near to me in that way as you do, my dearest."

"Sarah Covington had you within her grasp, and you did not seem to want it to end."

"*She* had me bewitched."

An impish grin blossomed across his handsome face, clearly relishing that I rose to his baiting of me.

"You damnable man, you. You love to toil with me so."

It was his turn to take me harshly and bring me into a tight embrace.

"Nay, William Matthias Hallett. You are and always will be the most prized and precious element in my life. No adventure, no assignment, no man or woman will ever best what you bring to me. While I live and draw breath, you shall always be my first concern."

"But that's not your calling, Joss. The people, *our* people must come first, before you, before me. We know this. As lovely as our words and promises are to each other, we both know war seldom makes allowances for such things. But I love you for saying them."

He nodded and we kissed softly for a moment and I felt it, the elusive part of him that denied his calling, that indeed did say should it come to it, he would abandon his calling to the Guardianship if I stood in the balance. I did not comment on it or call him out for it because I knew in my heart of hearts it would be so with me.

A silent alliance. A lover's promise I prayed we would never have to face. I chose to let it go. He wiped his hands and handed me the towel so I could do the same.

"Come now. We must depart for Akwesasne before nightfall."

"Why would the loss of light make a difference to a Guardian and his companion?"

"Because security is heightened along the borderlands between the United States and Akwe:kon and in each of the villages. Incursions have been attempted, held off by us, but it makes the approach at nightfall a bit more difficult to deal with when crossing into our nation. Gating is monitored and followed after dark. The *Tewakenonhnè* get a bit twitchy at night, and for good reason too. You recall the news we read in your library? The Americans have been increasing their weaponry in ways we did not anticipate. While the treaties hold, secretly they have been testing our border protections. I fear Flintlings may be involved on their side."

"Surely, not."

"Think about it. Is it really so out of the realm of possibilities that Lord Flint would not pepper his kind within the higher ranks of the United States government? They were not happy when the British assisted us and backed us up in the establishment of our territories into a sovereign nation that has kept their westward expansion at bay. What better way to stymie our foothold than to assist the Americans in small ways to test our defenses and erode our perceived supremacy between our two nations?"

While the new Americans celebrated their victory over the British in the Revolutionary War, they watched in horror mingled with belligerence as they lost a good quantity of the land a decade later, pitched against our Confederacy with the British backing us in numbers and ammunition. Though it was the stealth of the *Tewakenonhnè* that truly made the difference in the balance of power in the region, a difference the Guardianship apparently kept hidden from the Americans.

"I recall those days at Dartmouth," I replied. "Where we discussed it in our history classes. Not so much as it was ancient history, but the topic came up and a vigorous debate ensued. It was clear that while Akwe:kon was acknowledged as a proper nation, the hostilities and animosity over its establishment was still quite raw for many of the American students in the class. Jacob and I treaded lightly."

Joss nodded before adding, "The whole endeavor left a bad taste on both sides as the United States felt betrayed by our people who had first assisted them in their war with the British. In the morass of creating our own sovereign nation, they forgot that our Confederacy, while taking a formal neutral stance during the Revolutionary War, knew the separate nations within the Confederacy took to helping the British or the Americans of their own accord."

"Rather than lose ground they so recently succeeded in gaining via their independence," I continued, "they acknowledged their borders as defined by the charter from the British Crown. Of course, it did not hurt in the negotiations when the Guardians revealed themselves at the time of the Treaty of Paris, demonstrating our abilities sufficient to hold their negotiators firm in establishing Akwe:kon."

Joss smiled. "It certainly helped our cause when the British realized we would stand in between Canada and the United States. Though it has not helped in the years since. Hostilities are mounting, thus the need for added security, especially at night."

We decided to let that go, though I found it troubling I had no idea tensions had increased to such an extent. I thought it best we should press on with our journey.

"Should I pack much?"

Joss could not help but allow a lust-filled smile to slither along those full lips of his.

"I think I prefer you out of your clothes."

I chuckled, allowing him to run away with his imaginings.

"You do, do you?"

He snorted. "Head higher than your breeches, love. I just meant while I appreciate what a romantic figure you cut in your posh European clothing, I fancy you in our traditional wear."

"Ah, I see. If we are in this together, then I need to claim my heritage to its fullest measure? Will that satisfy?"

"It would. But I am not speaking of myself, love of my life." He moved closer to me, his hands upon the collar of my shirt. "If you are to meet my family, it would be best if you looked like one of us."

With those words, my heart slipped past the soles of my feet and into the foundation of my home. He patted my chest softly, gifted me with a kiss, and moved off to the stairs and our bedroom to prepare for our departure.

To my great surprise, a collection of his traditional clothing was laid out for me to choose from.

"Will they not know they are yours?"

"I do not make my way home too often. Do you think I have not thought about this? All of these clothes are what I wear in the furthest reaches of our nation. *Istá* has not seen these. At least I do not think she has."

"Okay, I think despite how much I spend on choosing what I wear, that is for my social circles. In this case, I believe the best course would be to follow your lead. I want to make the best impression, especially if your *mother* is involved."

He leaned in and gave me a soft kiss for encouragement.

"With your inherent charm and stellar looks, not to mention your family lineage, you could handle that without wearing a stitch of these clothes."

I blushed rather intensely at his words.

"William! That was not my intent, as you well know. It is my mother we are talking about, and while your body is a work of art Michelangelo should have carved, we will spare my mother such an analogy, shall we?"

I brought him into a tight embrace, and we kissed softly.

"I just want to make the right impression, so you choose what you think looks best."

Our clothing was packed into a couple of deerskin travel bags, and we gated to Akwesasne. The first stop was along the border to check in with the roaming guards, then we proceeded to the council longhouse. After a short discussion with Samuel about the events of tonight, we had the rest of the afternoon to ourselves as the meeting was not set until six o'clock tonight.

"Time to meet my mother?" he suggested.

I could tell he was nearly as pensive as I was over this.

"Is she aware of your predilections when it comes to your amorous partners?"

"No. I have not spent much time home once I attended and graduated from Dartmouth. I took to my Guardian life and spent most of my time away. The last couple of times I came back here for supplies or to speak with Samuel, I did spend some time with my family catching up on what I had been up to. They are aware of my being in the Guardianship—though we do not talk openly about it. But they have never known me to have any romantic leanings. So, you will be a surprise to them should we choose to share that part about us."

"Do you think we should?"

He looked down at the ground for a moment.

I sensed his reticence in going down that path. I decided I needed to let him not concern himself with this sort of talk.

"Look, I shall follow your lead. Whichever way you want to go with this, I will not fight you on it, nor will I press to expose what we have. As with everything, we shall decide together when it is right for us. Will that do?"

He shook his head. "I do not want anyone to think I am ashamed of being with you. Least of all, you."

"I know you are not. Is that not what is important here?"

I wrapped my arms around him and quickly gifted his forehead with a small kiss to show my support, regardless of which way he wanted to go with it. I even pushed into him how fine I felt about how he wanted to approach it, just to give him leave to handle it as he saw fit so he would have no reason to doubt me.

It seemed to satisfy for the time being. That was until we walked toward his home, and then he became a bundle of nerves—despite outwardly keeping that native stoic face in place. From the time we arrived I could sense his apprehension, coming up with all sorts of reasons to stall meeting his family after our discussion with Sam.

Only when his youngest sister, Mary, spied us as she returned from watching their brother play a round of lacrosse with the other boys, did Joss run out of options with which to occupy our time.

"Have you been to see the family yet? Mama has been asking about you since she found out about"—she leaned in to whisper her next—"*the meeting* tonight."

"It is fine, Mary. This is William Hallett. He is one of us too."

"Oh!" She eyed me with a modicum of incredulity but decided after a few moments to accept her brother's assessment. "Well, it is probably high time you saw Mama at any rate. You can come along too, if you want."

I could not help but smirk at Mary's secondhand invite. It caused my poor Joss to turn so many varying shades of red I really could not think of a way to console him that would not tip our hand about our burgeoning relationship before he was ready.

She tugged him along by the hand while he groused a bit emotionally, not because he did not want to see his family but because it was not on his terms. His sister was calling the shots—quite the accomplishment for an apparent nine-year-old.

::She is ten...and a powder keg of a girl. Do not let her beguiling nature fool you. She is far more than she appears. Her words will never fail to make me pause, and take what she has to say deeply. I revere her in my life. I think she will be one of us when the time comes.::

I could not help chortle with his last comment. He turned his head, but instead of frustration or anger, all I observed was his imploring me to save him, stopping my laughter in my throat. I endeavored to sort out how I would greet his family once we arrived.

His familial home was built like a traditional longhouse but with large wooden beams instead of simple bent tree branches and raw-looking large shingles layered to resemble the more traditional bark fare. The home also boasted large panes of glass that gave a brightness to the interior. It was a most impressive home to behold.

Mary pulled us inside to find the various members of Joss's extended family. His mother, Anne, was at the stove, preparing a meal. Her soothing voice singing a song Joss had sung to me once during my healing. I had not recalled it until I heard her singing it now.

::You sang that to me while you were healing me.::

He nodded, but added nothing to what I said, though I did get a warm push of the love he had for me. He was subdued, though, unsure how to proceed now I was here amongst his family.

His mother turned and smiled as soon as she saw us. After placing a lid on the stew she was preparing, she came over and hugged her son. She dropped a soft kiss upon his cheek with words of love in Mohawk. She caressed his face, and her eyes were so bright to have her son home, no matter how brief our stay would be. Clearly, she lamented that Joss did not spend as much time with his family as she desired.

Then her gaze turned to me. She was a slight woman but with a steely countenance. She stood by my estimation at about five feet tall with her crown of white-and-black hair braided and pinned up to her scalp. She was dressed in traditional clothing with delicate floral beading and ribbons on a rich black fabric. Her children easily dwarfed her in stature. Joss's father had passed a couple of years ago, unexpectedly from what I had gleaned from knowing Joss's memories, and their height came from his father as he was a man of about my stature. Mary stood between us, her eyes moving back and forth among the three of us, unsure of what was going to happen, but she did not want to miss a beat of it.

Anne Lightfoot moved past Joss and Mary. She placed her hands on my biceps before pulling me into a warm and somewhat tight hug. She murmured words of love and welcome to me in Mohawk that for the life of me, whether due to the emotional height of the moment or because my Mohawk was failing me, I did not get the fullness of her meaning—just a smattering of how happy my presence made her and the importance that I remain with her son. To what end her spoken desires regarded Joss and me, I was unsure. Joss seemed to beam at hearing them, so I took it as a very good sign indeed. I returned her words in Mohawk as best I could. I think I did fine enough, though Mary sniggered so maybe I laid it on a bit thick. His mother did not seem to think so.

She hugged me again and left a kiss on both cheeks and my forehead before releasing me.

"*Istá*, er, Mama, William's Mohawk is not as fluent as he would like. He is improving, but it might do better if we spoke in English while we visit."

"I shall help you improve speaking our tongue. It comes more natural to you than you think. I was there at your birth, you know. You come from a great family. Elizabeth is a dear friend and cousin. Our home is yours. Never doubt that. Come, my son."

While she said *son*, it was me she spoke of and not Joss, much to Joss's and my amazement. She guided me over to their living space. I was introduced to Joss's siblings who ranged from his elder brother, Ross, at thirty years of age, to Mary who was the youngest. Twelve children in all, including Joss. Each of them were very welcoming, and I could not help but feel overwhelmed at the sheer amount of love and acceptance they had for me.

::You are family, Ohnehta'kowa. How else should they address you?::

::It is more than that. I think they know about us.::

Joss choked on the water he had poured for himself from the pitcher on the counter. Everyone turned at the sound of his little coughing fit.

::Yes, I thought that would gain your interest.::

Joss tried in vain to compose himself, but I think his family's response to my being here with him took him totally by surprise.

"You think you are the only one to know what is going on in the world?" His mother gave a knowing glance between us, a slight gleam to her eyes. "The *ahtahkwa'òn:we* telegraph works faster than you think, my son."

His family shared a small laugh with their mother's words. The *moccasin* telegraph was a salient feature to all native peoples. I had no doubt in what I had expressed to Joss. They knew. They all knew. We were fooling ourselves to think otherwise. What is more, they approved of the match.

Mary tugged upon Joss's sleeve. "I like him. He is good for you. We all can see it, especially now he is here. It is strong, my brother. *He* is strong. His love for you knows no bounds."

The air ceased to move; the sounds from outside ceased to chirp, play, or give us any clue that life still raged on around us. His family watched Joss closely. Clearly, this little revelation had upended his world as he knew it. I was just as surprised as he was. I knew traditionally the autonomy our people benefitted from extended to couplings like the one Joss and I shared. Only the Christianized village of *Kahnawà:ke* held beliefs that a relationship like the one Joss and I favored ran against the Creator's wishes. Their God was a wrathful god. One of the reasons why I could never subscribe to their concept of the world and how we moved through it. I did not think Joss or his family did either.

We spent the next hour talking with his family, or I should say I did the talking and Joss sat there in a bewildered stupor trying to absorb the turn our lives had taken with those closest to him. I realized I needed to be the stronger one here. I allowed him his space to work through the way his family took to us.

"Well, I am just glad my son will no longer be alone. He needs this more than I think he wants to admit." His mother patted my right hand between hers.

"You know, the day of your births, yours and your sister's, was a very auspicious day, what with your entry into this world and the terrible death of your grandfather all happening within the span of a few moments. One great life in exchange for yours. A terrible sacrifice to witness: an incredible high to a tragic, bewildering low."

She gently took her hand and wiped a tear that fell from her face.

The revelation left me bewildered. Joss turned to me, sensing my confusion over his mother's words.

"You say my grandfather died the same day my sister and I came into this world?"

A glance between us, layering more confusion over my response to her story, only made the moment more pressing. I had to know the truth of it. All Rebecca and I had ever been told is our grandfather had died of consumption at an early age. To hear it was not the case opened a list of questions on why our family held the lie against us from childhood. Joss's mother eyed me with a growing concern and eased me into a chair next to the dining table. She and Joss seated themselves near me. Her hands never left holding mine.

"Did you not know of this, my son?"

I slowly shook my head, cognizant of what I was admitting to her, to Joss, to anyone who bothered to take notice of my plight.

"Why would Grandmama tell me this fabrication surrounding a man she loved so much? It does not..."

"That day was a dark one, William." Her words were kind but firm, holding my attention to its fullest. "Audrey, the Eldest of the Clan Mothers present who guided you into this world, told me of things surrounding your birthing. They chill me to this very day."

"Pray tell me, for I am at my wit's end hearing this divergence from what I always assumed was true."

"What you need to know is Audrey was a seer. She often commented on things she saw that no one else did. So, whether you take her visions to heart or not, realize this was what she relayed to me after it all happened, and we were on our way back home. Several of the other Clan Mothers paid it no mind. I was young and therefore impressionable. Yet, I tell you this—" Her gaze became rather pointed, and we all leaned in, as if what she would impart next had a conspiratorial air to it. "I believed her. I do to this day. I cannot say why or point to some part of her tale that makes it truer than most would give credit for, but I just cannot set aside the wholeness of the tale as folly."

We eyed each other, unsure of where Joss's mother would take this. Her next words changed everything.

"Not all of us who gain the talents of a Guardian heed its calling. Some choose to remain as they are and cope with what gifts the Peacemaker or rather, *O'so:ra,* as we know he is the true father of the *Tewakenonhnè,* bestows upon them. Some of us remain in the shadows of what you Guardians do. But I believe Audrey was one such person. She carried the gift all right."

"How do you know this? Did she demonstrate some feat of Guardian ability that forever sealed it in your mind she was latent in pursuing them?"

"Silly child, you think I would bring this to you when I know you were told a lie to keep you from your birthright and what you should be to the people? Your grandmother did everything she could to keep you from it. I suppose if you were my child"—she spared a glance Joss's way that carried no less a point to her remark for me, as she obviously felt it about her own son—"I might feel the same way." She placed a gentle hand upon Joss's where it lay on the table. He gently squeezed it, realizing as his mother she too paid a price for his calling.

"But surely Grandmama would not intercede should I take up the calling."

"Your grandmother is a very formidable woman. I do not have to explain that to you. While her husband was carted away to be readied for the funeral, she made it quite clear how she would keep what happened from you and Rebecca so you never felt the taint of that wondrously horrific night."

I made to stand up. It went against the grain of everything I had ever known my grandmother to be. Sure, she could be unforgiving in her temperament whenever she felt the need to press her advantage. It was a trait all the females in our family possessed, my sister chief amongst them. Yet, I could not with any certainty think of why she would prolong this deception once Rebecca and I reached adulthood. Would it be because she thought our births signaled that we would indeed be influenced by such a calling and she could not bear the risk involved?

I had to wonder.

As I began to rise, Anne's hand came down firm upon mine, stalling me entirely and making us jump with her sudden movement.

"William Matthias Hallett, do not think for one moment that what I tell you is mere gossip amongst Clan Mothers. Because there is the truth of it. You see, while Audrey lay dying, drawing her last breaths upon this world, she called but for one person to come to her. Who do you suppose that person was?"

"I could not presume to guess."

"Then I shall show you. It is what she left me before she released her hold on this life and this world."

At that she leaned forward and placed both hands on either side of my head. I sensed them glowing upon my skin. Fear and apprehension clouded every thought. Joss made to get up and rush to my side and stop his mother.

"Josiah! Remain where you are. This is for William from Audrey. It was her dying wish that he see it as she did."

::Do not worry, Will. I am right here with you. I will stay as close to you as I can.::

Within the next moment the entire room dissolved. Instead of Joss's family home, I stood in a room I knew to be where Rebecca and I were born. The scene was awash with activity yet stalled for a moment so I could take in the enormity of our births.

Thunder rolled above my head, and I looked up not to the roof of Joss's home but to the ceiling of my familial home in Hallett's Cove. As my gaze moved from the ceiling, everything became active...for when I raised my hands, they were not my own, but a woman's hands. Audrey Brant. These are not my thoughts or words, but hers that are shared with me now, in the moment as they happened.

A current of Joss's love moved between us. I did not know if he saw what I did, but I prayed to whomever would listen that he did. I reached for him in the bewilderment of Audrey's offering and rejoiced when I felt him clasp hard upon me. We were in this together no matter how it played.

My eyes moved from the violence of the stormy night bellowing about us. A hurricane engulfed Manhattan and raged outside. The birthing of babies should present itself as a joyous occasion, a celebration. But this afternoon presented itself to be something altogether different.

As a Clan Mother of my people, the Mohawks of Akwesasne, I have often been present at birthings. It is the way of things and has been this way for far longer than the people can remember. Birthings are the most potent power women possess—the creation of life.

It was strange to feel this from within her, knowing that for the Haudenosaunee, women govern the culture and guide us through the forests of life. It is the Clan Mother's responsibility and birthright to ensure Haudenosaunee longevity. The chiefs and warriors may be out front, but only so the women can point over their shoulders to tell them where to go. A request for the Clan Mother to be present at a birthing in our territories was quite commonplace.

To do so elsewhere—not as much.

I could not help but smile at her sense of responsibility mingled with the humor we natives employed in every facet of our lives. Her thoughts and mine blended to such a degree I could not tell what she imparted to me and what was retold in my own voice so I could make some sense of it. A most bewildering sensation to say the least.

Yet I could sense through her that this birthing proved to be different.

Not to appear out of step with the times, it appeared Grandpapa had also sent for a doctor to ensure that should Audrey and the others fail in any way then the doctor would fix it.

Frustration roiled with me. I could not understand what he meant. As women, as well as Clan Mothers who not only birthed their own, but assisted in countless other births within the nation, we knew what needed to be done, and yet this young man who takes money for what comes naturally to us stood by to fix it should it go wrong.

As the English are fond of saying, poppycock.

Contented that two of our own had married into the prestige of being a Hallett of New York, they did the sensible thing to ensure the birth of their baby was going to be in the traditional way. It was a great comfort to me that even within the halls of New York high society we Mohawks were finally making headway in educating the Americans on civilized customs and behaviors.

The very breath inside me caught as my mother came into view. Without realizing it, my hand searched the table and found Joss clasping it in his. A thread of love pushed its way between us, and I found I needed him as close as I could. Somehow, I knew what would come to pass would rattle what I knew about my world, my life, say nothing of the way Rebecca and I were protected from this, the very truth of it all. Audrey's vision pressed forward, pulling Joss and me along in its wake, though I was beginning to feel more at ease being within Audrey as she saw things.

Rose, the daughter-in-law and my second grandniece, began to call out in pain. Her baby was close. Sweat beaded across her brow, and her breaths came out in a rasp. I instructed the burning of Seneca grass and sage to calm her. The bedroom grew thick with it.

Rose sipped the willow and white pine tea and winced, whether from the taste or the heat, I could not be sure. It helped for the most part, but her pains were strong. They raged as powerful as the storm outside. Indeed, the very walls of the great Hallett home seemed to rattle along with Rose's birthing pangs; the two of them wrangled with each other, caught in a horrifying rhythmic dance. When the storm relented, Rose cried out in agony; when she settled, the storm outside raged and rattled the house again. It did everything to shake our nerves.

The other midwives, who came along to help, tended to Rose as best they could—wiping her brow and gripping her hands to guide her through the waves of it. I was sure from Rose's perspective she was going through the worst pain imaginable, but having seen many of these, I thought it a relatively easy birth.

Thunder erupted across the skies above. All present cast their gaze momentarily to the ceiling of the room, eyeing the creaking and buckling noises warily. The Sky People, it appeared, had their own agenda tonight.

"She is calling for John, Elizabeth, and her own mother. I think she would even call for the Christian God himself if she bought into all of that and thought it would help," Kathryn murmured as she approached.

My eyes glanced over at Rose as she sat in the wooden birthing chair so it would be easy for her to produce the child when the time came. Many a child came into this world through that chair, though none of those before carried the weight of the birthing happening this night.

My gaze returned to Kathryn, and I gave her a look of resignation.

"Let her call them all she wants. The baby will be around for a long time; they can see it after it has arrived. She knows better, but that is the pain talking."

My pulse quickened when the door opened to the room and Grandmama entered. Though only twenty-six years younger, she possessed a more radiant glow than I ever imagined before.

Elizabeth swept into the room in a simple dark but smartly tailored no-nonsense dress. The rustle of her voluminous skirts turned heads in the room as she made her way to me.

Her confidence seemed to billow the aroma of Seneca sweet grass, giving way with little resistance to her formidable presence. Gracefully composed, as ever the proverbial eye in any storm, she returned to us carrying another small pot of tea.

"She complained about the tea being too bitter, so I"—in unison we stated the obvious—"added the maple sugar."

We shook our heads and allowed ourselves a small smile for we had been in Rose's position and knew we should have added the sugar in the first place. Willow-pine tea carried a brutally bitter bite upon the tongue.

Elizabeth grasped my arm warmly. It was her way of letting me know how much she appreciated my presence. Elizabeth smiled briefly before turning to take in the rest of the women busy with caring for Rose.

"Heavens, it is warm and thick with the grass in here."

"That is Anne's doing. She is always heavy-handed with the grass. She would burn the meadow bare if she had her way," I replied as I poured a small cup of the tea and handed it to Kathryn who spared no time in getting it to Rose.

Another cry rang out as a wave overtook Rose's resolve to remain calm. As it abated, the house groaned again as wind and water pounded heavily upon the rattled shutters. Not that any of us could spare the time to observe the storm as Elizabeth's husband had all of the home's windows shuttered up against it, say nothing of the birthing pulling focus. There was but one small sliver of light where the warp of two boards did not quite meet up. It was our only connection to the outside world. But we did not have time for taking in the storm, as a baby pushed to make its way into this world.

I moved in Rose's direction, to guide her through the final stages of birth, when the room swayed before me. The walls seemed to liquefy, rippling as if they were melting in place. Only one thing I could think of would cause this: the sight was coming on again.

Not now, the child needs me.

A shrill cry from Rose shocked the room. In that moment a chill ran through my heart for I thought I heard a small laugh nestled within that cry. It was a mirthless laugh, a malicious teasing laugh. I staggered for a moment. I felt the pull against my life, sapping energy from my limbs as it leeched across my body to my very core, and I had no way of stopping it. Like a seven-year-old girl being pursued in the forest, I found myself truly frightened—convinced I was on the precipice of my own demise.

Visions of Audrey racing through a forest as a young girl interspersed with current events, confusing me, but clearly the association was quite clear in her mind.

::Steady, Will. I am here.:: Joss softly intoned to me. The scene played forward.

"Audrey, she needs you." Elizabeth nodded in Rose's direction before turning to me where she saw my pained expression and asking, "Are you...all right?"

I braced myself against Elizabeth's offered hand and the small bedside table for support. I shook my head to try to clear it. When my eyes focused again, I was in shock at what I saw: there before me were two glowing points of light undulating within the belly of Rose, each bearing down toward their entrance into this world.

"Twins..." The word sputtered from my lips before I scarce realized I had said it.

I murmured the word aloud into the room, feeling Audrey take root in me so that every sense and thought available to her became my own. My bones and body seemed to curve with age. Joss did his best to grant me relief, but I knew I needed to go through this to the bitter end, no matter the cost to me.

"Twins? Did you say…twins?" Elizabeth asked in bewilderment as she helped me to a full stance. I nodded. The very air was sapped from my lungs; I struggled as if attempting to breathe under water. But through it all, my gaze never wavered from the sight of those two glowing lights as they made their way to the birthing.

"They are coming…" I barely managed a rasp out to the other women as I struggled to focus on getting back into the fray. The doctor came forward and placed a cone-shaped tube to her belly. With a sudden burst of energy I did not know I possessed, I knocked the boy-doctor aside.

"Out of my way, child. This here is women's work."

Rose's cry escalated into a piercing shrill, if that were at all possible, as she suddenly removed herself from the birthing chair and squatted as instructed. She bore down with a guttural cry as the crown of the first baby's head made its way into this world.

The door to the bedroom opened. John, the father, obviously concerned in the change of his wife's cry, had come to investigate. His father, James, was fast on his heels as they both stepped into the room.

My grandfather appeared far more handsome and beguiling in person than any painting that tried, failing miserably by comparison, to capture the reality of him.

"It's time, James." The doctor approached the men. "The Clan Mother thinks it's twins."

"Twins?" John murmured, as if the thought had never occurred to him that his family would be off to such a grand start. James clasped a firm hand upon his son's shoulder, and the men beamed at each other before embracing briefly.

"No time for celebrations just now. They have yet to be born," Elizabeth called to both of them. The men nodded and eased back to the edge of the room in an attempt to stay out of the way.

"Quiet now; here comes the first!" I called out as my hands cradled the head of the first child as it pressed its way into the room. Thunder roared overhead. The wind howled surrounding the arrival of the first child, announcing to the world that the birth of these babies carried an ominous tone.

To witness my own hands through Audrey receiving myself into this world astounded the senses. I reeled with the moment at hand.

::Easy, Will.:: Joss steadied me as I grappled with the sensation.

The great house shuddered and groaned. Thunder pounded upon the roofline. I looked at the boy I held in my hands as I received him into the world and began to wrap him up into a swaddling cloth. The other women moved in to tend to Rose as I guided the young boy to the birthing cradle. My eyes tried in vain to focus upon him, but he kept shifting and vibrating. I thought it must be something wrong with me, that I became overwhelmed with everything.

::It may be our viewing is causing her to not see you wholly. Time has wrapped in upon itself.:: Joss "whispered" to me.

To calm myself I ran my hands into a hot bath of water to wash away the birthing when my breath caught. A bone-chilling moment overcame me, leeching it out of my body and turning the water to an ice slurry in a matter of seconds. A puff of humid air billowed from my lips. The temperature of the room seemed to drop about twenty degrees within a matter of seconds.

Out of the corner of my eye, I saw the men in the room, seemingly unaware of the change in their surroundings, faces alight with delight of the birth of a healthy son. As I slowly turned, I became rattled by the way the room was beginning to lose its form. Walls rippled and undulated all about me, yet no one else seemed to take note of it.

A bright flash cut through the room as the shutters were forced open from their latches. In the brilliance of the lightning, the room became crowded with a collection of Haudenosaunee warriors. Unseen by everyone else, these spectral shapes dominated the available space in the room. I had never witnessed their likes. Proud warriors in full battle readiness, they were silent sentinels who had but one focus in the room: the birth of these babies.

I knew at that moment the Others were watching. This was no normal birthing. A new chapter in Haudenosaunee history was being born.

Though I had never witnessed them myself, I knew what they were: the Unnaturals, preternatural beings akin to the Sky People of old, spirits who seemed to look like us but with the pallid, violet blue-white skin of the beyond. Each warrior bore different images and small patterns and pictorials tattooed upon their skin that changed and undulated across their flesh. They were creatures of immense power. As the storm continued to rage, pulsating lights seemed to burst from within their expansive bare torsos, matching the intensity of the thunder outside as if somehow the bombastic nature of the weather were tied to them.

They did not simply come with the hurricane. They were the hurricane.

I could not bear seeing them any longer, and in haste I balled my fists to my clenched eyes to clear the vision. I did not know if I could make it through the birth of the second child. I feared losing my grip upon this world when I was needed most.

I kept my eyes closed to the horror of it, taking a moment to breathe deeply, begging for them to disperse...to leave us to our work. When I dared to open them, I was relieved that the warriors had all gone. But the oppressive feeling of their presence remained. They were still there, just on the other side, unseen. Their arrival served to underscore the significance of these births. These children were being watched and not necessarily by a benevolent presence, either. The Others were tricky; one never really knew the measure of their allegiance.

"Have to get back to her..." I stammered under my breath. My once sure and direct hands felt feeble and failing. The light flickered within Rose's groin. Too much time had passed between the birthings. She was going to lose the second child.

Rose snapped her head up, her eyes wild with fear. "Something is wrong. I can feel it."

She looked at me pleadingly. She began to panic. I plucked up every ounce of energy I could muster and leapt into action.

"Look at me, Rose." Placing my hands on either side of her frightened face, trying to pull the woman from the terrified girl, attempting to catch her frenzied gaze, I tried with everything I had to soothe her rattled heart. "You will not lose this one. She is much too important."

Now, why I said that to her, I was not sure. I had no reason at all to assume the second child would be female, much less the influence she would have in this world. But sometimes these things just come to you. I had learned not to argue with it when it happened.

Rose nodded—together, she realized, we could do this.

Joss joined in, pulled with us into the moment.

We began to chant a song her grandmother had sung to her whenever she needed calming. As soon as I cooed the first few syllables, the room shuddered. Some of the other midwives looked about the ceiling, wondering if the home would hold against the storm or if, in the next moment, we all would be swept into oblivion. Without much warning the flickering light of the second child grew in earnest and pressed forward.

Her time had come.

"Now, Rose...now!" I called out, and Rose did as I bade her. With every ounce of strength between us, we brought the second child into this world. She was radiant. Her skin literally glowed in my hands. The delicate flower of a girl already had the fine wisps of dark-auburn hair prevalent within the Hallett line. Did the brother have this trait as well? I honestly could not recall.

As I handed the girl to Kathryn and Elizabeth, I turned and saw the men as happy as they could be. I could only feel relief at making it through. The other women could tend to the cleanup thereafter.

Without warning, everything stopped. The sound of the storm abated. Silence descended. Even the babies had calmed themselves from their birthing cries. A soft shaft of sunlight poured into the room, giving the moment a subtle glow, bathing it in tranquility. Every person seemed rooted to their spot. No one moved a muscle.

Peace descended.

As soon as I moved, the action in the room seemed to pick up again, as no one else had been trapped between time, and for that single radiant moment the possibility of peace for the children was real.

I took up the birthing chair as the other midwives got Rose back into bed. I leaned my head back and closed my eyes, grateful the birthing was finished and somehow everyone had survived. For the next few moments I allowed myself to be wrapped up in finding a way to return to normal breathing. Just the flow of air to and from my lungs calmed me immensely, and I relished these few moments to gather myself from the entire event.

"The storm seems to have let up. Heaven itself is welcoming these two brilliant children into this world." James beamed brightly as he lit his pipe. How much I wished his sentiment were right, though inwardly I knew it could just as easily have been the reverse.

"Audrey, do you require anything? Something to eat or drink?" John asked as he knelt next to the chair, taking my right hand into his. I could tell by his touch how deeply he felt the blessing these children brought into his life. I gently squeezed his hand to let him know I appreciated his gratitude. A wave of nausea overcame me, and I became a bit light-headed.

My eyes fluttered open...and I saw her.

"*Tituba!*" My voice raged for I knew the woman from Christian's engagement with the vile witch! Anger roiled and seethed within me in the span of a few seconds for I knew where the truth of my grandfather's death lay.

::*Easy, lover, we know what happened to her with Christian. Let things play out so we may know the fullest of them.*::

I knew Joss was right, but still my blood boiled with the sight of this detestable visage.

The only creature that had ever truly frightened me. Gone, the days of forgetting her evil beauty. Gone, the intervening sixty-six years as if they had not happened at all. Within the span of but a few seconds, I was a frightened little girl again in the forest with Hell's Witch upon my back. Only now, instead of being upon my heel she faced me directly.

She stood there behind James Hallett, and to my great horror no one else seemed to notice or care. Time had not changed her radiant beauty. She was as luminescent as ever in the semi-darkened room. I lifted a hand and pointed at James. Every warning in my head began to sound, the horror of the witch's presence pressing upon me. I was rattled, in shock. I found, to my confused dismay, I just could not get the words out to warn them all.

John looked at me quizzically and turned to his father for advice. James shrugged at my bewildered state.

Why could they not see her standing there?

I stammered with some spittle flying from my lips, "There, look out! Get...away...from him."

I waved my hand about in the air as if swatting unseen flies. Everyone stopped what they were doing when they heard me. They looked quizzically to one another, not knowing how to respond to my frenzied antics.

The beautiful woman, completely shrouded in the same dark, ominous-looking tresses, her face and limbs the only thing protruding from the smoky visage, smiled wickedly as if this were the shared secret between us to which no one else would ever be privy. She flickered in and out of existence. My eyes widened. Wracked with frustration, I could not understand how no one else knew the danger the witch represented.

Though I had not laid eyes upon her in over sixty-six years, I knew that vile creature for what she was...she was death or something akin to it, and she had come to claim a soul.

Helplessly, I watched as the witch moved around to James's side and slipped one arm around his waist. The other she seductively ran up his chest and leaned her head against his shoulder. She pouted playfully at me, feigning an apology for what we both knew she was about to do, confident in the knowledge no one would believe me should I even speak about what I saw.

"No, not James...not today," I muttered mournfully, knowing the plea would fall upon deaf ears.

The seductress smiled again and plunged her hand into James's chest. I knew what she was doing; she was squeezing the life out of his heart. A man who had loved Elizabeth so deeply he had endured the scandal of marrying a Mohawk woman and bringing her into New York high society, of ensuring the family was firmly rooted in both worlds. A man who had a heart big enough to love all who knew him and to be generous with that love of life and spirit. And now it was being crushed, obliterated, swept aside as if his presence was no longer required. His smile faded from his face, the pipe fell from his hand, his eyes dimmed, and he was gone. He crumpled to the ground before his pipe hit the floor.

I openly wailed into the air—such frustration and anger I had never known consumed my senses that I became savage with it. Angry tears flowed freely from my eyes; my breath rattled; spittle drooled from my mouth. I cared not. Joss pushed his way through me, stilling me from doing any harm in their home, but I wanted to. I sorely wanted to shake the foundations of the Earth watching helplessly as my grandfather's life was snatched from his body.

Elizabeth screamed as she and John rushed to his limp body. When I looked up at the she-witch, Death's paramour, she had moved to a different part of the room. She hovered above the bed where the twins lay with their mother. Slowly, suspended from the dark billowing smoke that coursed about her, she lowered herself like a black widow moving in for the kill—a small hiss escaping from her lips. Her ravenous gaze moved slowly over each child, a cold hunger coursing through her. Then, without any indication why, she turned to look at me square in the eye with a deadly stare and a wicked smile before silently drifting up into the darkness of the ceiling and out of sight.

In the massive bed Rose sobbed as she cradled the crying babies in her arms. The room was consumed with grief from James's untimely death. The doctor had immediately rushed to James's side, but I knew it was no use. He was gone. There was no bringing him back.

I leaned forward and pressed my face into my hands and wept with the enormity of the moment. The children's birth would be forever marred with the ring of death. It was an inauspicious and yet a powerful revelatory moment, one that would prove to have far greater resonance in the time to come.

Several moments later I lay with my face upon my hands, weeping with such pain as I had never known. Knowing Christian had dispatched the evil creature did me little in the way of comforting the pangs of mourning at watching my own grandfather, a man I admired greatly, succumb to that witch's hand. It boiled my blood like no other.

Joss took my hands, wet with my tears, in his and pulled me forward into a tight embrace, saying gentle words of love and comfort to soothe my battered soul. I clutched to him as I never had while his family watched, silent and supportive with what his mother imparted to me through Audrey lo those many years ago.

"This is why it could only be you for my boy. Do you not see that what he is? What he represents could only be matched by the divine and ominous birth that brought you into this world. Jacob stopped here before he left with Thomas on their assignment."

She held a hand up to stall me or Joss saying anything further before she had a chance to explain.

"We know it was against the wishes of the *Tewakenonhnè* and how they keep their affairs hidden from the people—and as a people we know why this is so. So, when Jacob came to us to explain what he observed, before you both made it official, he touched upon my forehead an imprint that would allow me to know when you both became one. While I cannot see the fullness of your pairing, I do see how strong you both are together. There is an ease between you most couples aspire to, but they will never know the strength and true peace you both enjoy."

She turned to look at Joss for a moment. His brothers and sisters did the same. It was a reverential look, one that spoke of how they were all in agreement over our coupling. It was the first time I had ever observed Joss at such a loss on what to say or do. Even our link had become intensely quiet. Almost frighteningly so. I began to worry about him.

::Nay, do not fret so, lover. I am just beside myself with how this all came about. While I have never thought my family would react negatively, I also did not expect their response to it being you who I chose to bond with. It is that which I am trying to grapple with and bring close to my heart. I am overwhelmed; that is all.::

::As am I, love. As am I.::

::Konoronkhwa kowa::

It was the first time he said those words *I love you* plainly and in our language. I was deeply moved with the simple way he expressed it to me.

"But look at your clothes. Josiah, did you not think I would know these were yours?" Anne turned from Joss to me. "I will make you your own set of clothing. I have heard what a dandy you are in Manhattan. It is fitting for you to be so, there. But you are *Kanien'kehá*. This is how you should express yourself. It is in your blood."

She leaned in as if to share a secret. "And I want to make them to quietly express the bond you share with my son."

She giggled the tiniest bit, and I could not help but join in her little ploy.

"But come now. Food is ready, and you should both eat before the long meeting you have to attend."

While Joss's family, my new family, gathered at the table for dinner, I could not help but feel the love they extended me. It gave me a strength I sorely needed but had no way of putting a finger to until this moment presented itself. I walked as a different man now. With the truth revealed, I was in it for the win. I wanted nothing less than to crush Flint and his army. My own family bore the mark of Flint, and I wanted nothing more than to eradicate it. Resolve began to build and bolster itself within me. As much as Joss said his love was vast and never-ending for me, my resolve to see this through to a bloodied victorious outcome would become just as vast and all-encompassing.

As we said our Thanksgiving over the meal a thread of concern weaved its way to me from Joss, no doubt sensing the shift in my perspective of this war. I did my best to comfort him that nothing between us had changed, only that the game was on for me. Nothing would dissuade me from pursuing it to the calamitous end. No matter the outcome, I was going to be in the thick of it, doing my best to strike not at Flint's army but to the very heart of the man himself.

I meant to end Saweskira.

Yet, how does one go about killing a god?

Aware Joss eyeing me while we ate, I began to formulate how...

Despite the explanations Joss had given me regarding the Guardianship as we walked to the meeting, nothing prepared me for the secret gathering hall that had been forged by our Guardian ancestors some five hundred and fifty years earlier.

To start with, it is dramatically located at the base of a large white pine perched on a rocky outcropping overlooking Akwesasne, a large expansive room with seating for nearly all Guardians if called to meet, easily encompassing well over six hundred who entered the building now. Joss explained that in recent years these sorts of meetings had become all too common.

Indeed, whilst I took in the enormity of the Guardian hall with all its wonders like a child in a candy shop, I could not help but notice the sidelong glances I began receiving as we moved amongst my brothers and sisters. Clearly, the ahtahkwa'òn:we telegraph had worked even faster and more thoroughly than the rumination offerings Joss's family had received via Jacob. These Guardians were fully in the know, both in how they viewed me in relation to Joss as well as my just having a presence when I had neither been fully inducted nor properly introduced. I felt no more than an interloper, plain and simple.

For his part, Joss emanated a strong sense of protecting me and my presence within this meeting. It seemed to be working, as the most I received were eyes that held little in the way of judgment, but a thread of suspicion, nonetheless.

I feared it could not be helped, regardless. There was quite little I could do about it without Samuel making some sort of statement to them, so it was best I went along, keeping my thoughts and feelings to myself. Instead, I clung to Joss probably a tad more than warranted. He did not seem to mind as his gentle smile for me, as we made our way into the chamber, warmed my soul and granted me purchase to hold on throughout the ordeal.

As we entered with the other Guardians, the exposed roots of the large white pine glowed to provide illumination when we were all assembled, drawing its energy from the assembled Guardians. Joss explained mentally that during dormant times there are Guardians who provide the needed energy to sustain its care.

The most breathtaking element, culturally speaking, lay with the twisted roots of the white pine that suspended our symbolic weapons our people buried when we became a Confederacy, eschewing the internal warfare that had plagued our peoples since time immemorial. Seneca against Mohawk, Mohawk against Cayuga, and onward, the devastation prior to the Peacemaker coming into our midst nearly destroyed us all. It was he who determined the weapons of our internal strife needed to be buried if we were going to move forward as one confederacy of nations. The term *bury the hatchet* quite literally stems from how our people put down arms against one another and buried them here to embrace *The Great Law of Peace*. Sadly, we had no way of foreseeing we were trading one war for another. But it is the cycle of things, I suppose. At least that is how Joss explained it to me.

The walls of the great hall were carved out of the earth with the bulk of the room being made up of limestone, slate, and shale with enough quartz interspersed to glow and provide an increase in illumination. They appeared to be smoothed over as if gently worn away by a running creek over millennia. Its benches and seating were all gently carved out of the floor and raked at a slight angle to provide ample viewing by anyone no matter where they are seated within the structure.

As the Guardians took their seats, a prayer of Thanksgiving could be heard throughout the chamber. We quietly contemplated the words of thanks to the Creator for all that had been given to us—*such as it is*, to my way of thinking, though I did not openly express that. Joss seemed to pick up on it, however. As the prayer was read, I could not help but marvel at the room being so temperate, given the sheer number of Guardians within the chamber.

::The air and temperature are maintained by secluded vents and a device left to us by Spruce himself that regulates everything within the hall. How it works, where it derives its power we do not know, but it has sustained us over the centuries of our existence. It has never wavered in all that time.::

The most prominent feature, aside from the intricate illuminated root system encompassing our ceiling, was the long window occupying the left side of the hall toward the back of the arena. From the top level of seats in the speaker's theatre, it afforded us a grand view out into the valley below, but looking at it from the outside, it appeared as any other rock formation. You could see out, but from outside it appeared as part of the rock outcropping, indistinguishable from what surrounded it. A grand illusion, to be sure.

::Another wondrous work left to our keeping. It is an auspicious room to work from when you are just one man, holding down the fort, as it were. There are a great many things this room can do. You are seeing but one aspect of it. Oddly enough, it is to Tiyanoga's making as first Central that we owe this marvel. Each Central tends to its upkeep as part of their duties. Speaking of which, here comes Samuel now.::

The Thanksgiving prayer ended as Samuel took to the dais in the center of the cavernous room. The Guardians stood en masse as Samuel made his way to the speaking dais. His voice could easily be carried into the raked audience chamber. In truth, I kept having to close my mouth from the incredible sensations this hall offered. I was at a complete loss to the ingenuity and masterful engineering feat. It defied the mind.

::You grow inured to it over time. Though to be honest, I still find the technology Spruce left us overwhelming. I try to work through it and absorb how it all works when I have the time, but that has been woefully lacking as of late.::

Samuel took a moment to eye the room and its inhabitants. I was rather surprised at his lingering glance over Joss and me. Surely, he knew I would stand next to Joss now we were one.

"Thank you all for coming." Samuel's warm baritone voice echoed throughout the chamber. I could not say he strained to be heard; the acoustics were truly astounding. "There is much to cover; I would ask that questions be held until the end of what I need to impart to you."

He paused to see if there was any dissension in the hall. None came. His gaze changed to one of intense seriousness. The situation warranted it. I felt the shift in mood from the Guardians in attendance.

"The battle, as it has raged for so many hundreds of years upon our lands, is no longer in play. The *Flintlings*, those who are under Flint's control, have expanded their operations to the other end of the continent, and if one of our own is to be believed"—he glanced my way, and I was more than sure it was not missed by those in attendance—"they have now achieved a certain level of global expansion. To what end, we are not able to ascertain at this point. We are working on it. Indeed, one of our very best has taken it upon himself to investigate these movements personally. His words from a conversation I had with him last night should explain things further."

He rolled out the Central wampum belt. It illuminated, casting the dais in a silvery glow. Samuel ran a finger over whatever he saw on the belt, and Spruce's brilliance with their advanced technology expressed itself, leaving me with a bit of a cocked hat.

Before us the moving image of Jacob and Thomas. They were not fully formed but seemed to hover as if projected onto a transparent wall of glass. Then Jacob spoke, and I could not contain myself and gasped with his first word, bringing a soft smile and a touch of Joss's hand onto my own to calm me.

"We have been on the Báthory *for less than a week, but the distance we have traveled in such a short amount of time is beyond comprehension. By my estimates, we are now clearing the upper part of South America. At this rate, we will take the Horn by the middle of next week. This ship is truly astounding, and its feats could only be accomplished with either Spruce or Flint's influence."*

There was a strong stir amongst the Guardians. Several of them turned to face Thor and the Jemisons, as expected, but a fair number of them had turned Joss's and my way, given Jacob was now at the heart of our investigation. The faction lines could not be more evident between those who sought Joss's position on the matter and those who clung to the divinity of their cause by leaning upon the Jemisons' take.

But something else troubled me. Joss took quick note that in all the grandstanding formed with Jacob's words, there was but one point I focused on from the time the visage displayed at the front of the room.

"What is it, Will?"

::Look at Thomas. Even stilled as they are, his eyes betray him. He knows far more than he is letting Jacob think. We are only reaping the benefit of it because he stands just slightly behind Jacob. I am sure he schools his expression and mind whenever they train, but there is something there that may be Jacob's undoing.::

::Is this because of his prolonged exposure to Tiyanoga?::

::Undoubtedly so. He is in league with Tiyanoga. Think about it. When he came back to us after the escape to Salamanca and his family, he sought me out. When I asked him why me and not you or Jacob, he said in no uncertain terms that Tiyanoga instructed him to trust me above anyone else. Why would he say such a thing, other than the information I had tucked into my head by Tiyanoga could benefit him in some way? His alliances are clear, well, at least to me. The boy plays with us.::

Joss thought upon this briefly before nodding just once at my estimation.

"We should not have sent Thomas with Jacob. If I am clear about anything, it is that he has been played a fool and will surely come to some cataclysmic folly not of his doing."

From the events of last night's communication Jacob continued.

"The ship is laden with procured bodies: men, women, and even children lay subdued in ornate and technologically advanced boxes that keep them in deep slumber but also seem to be affecting them somehow. I have seen it with Thomas's help, but to what end these changes or this trip to San Francisco is quite beyond comprehension at this time. All we know is they are making excellent time to get them there and will waste no time in their return for another deployment in the ready there in New York."

At this, you could feel the ire consume the room. There may have been a slight factoring between those who saw fit to follow whom, but that changed with Jacob's last remark. Jacob opened his mouth to continue, but instead a low hum emanated throughout the chamber, cutting his voice off. Darkness enveloped the luminescence of the room without going so far as to obscure the visual of Thomas and Jacob, even though we could no longer hear what Jacob was saying. We moved quickly from our front-row position onto the dais to see what we could to do to help Samuel correct this latest incursion into the meeting before things spiraled out of control.

"Everyone, remain calm. We are trying to sort it. Yes, there we are..."

Only nothing Samuel contributed made its way into the room, as that too seemed to be silenced. Instead, a single silvery light intensified, and the visage of a man stood in its center, unharmed by the intensity of the witchery being used. I knew him for who he was: Tiyanoga now stood central to the chamber as he probably had over five hundred years ago.

"My brothers and sisters..." His voice snaked around the room, mingling with others seeming to hug the smooth walls of the chamber in a chorus that repeated and kept pace with Tiyanoga's words.

::He is using the Flintlings to augment his message, showing he has the greater numbers.::

"We should try to shut him down..." Samuel added as if hearing my thoughts or coming to the same conclusion on his own, realizing how quickly this whole event could devolve into a morass of mired opinions and misinformed suppositions that would only make things much more difficult.

"Do not fear me, for I was once one of you. The first Central, in fact. Yes, it is me: Tiyanoga. Though how and why I am still here, exacting Flint's revenge upon you all, is a long and sordid tale. One we simply do not have the time to cover at this juncture. Too much has changed."

He turned his gaze to Joss and me as if he were truly in the room and could address us as such. A most disconcerting moment to behold. But now was not the time to debate or weigh our options on opposing his intrusion. I felt within my bones that were we to engage, we needed to hear him out to its fullest.

"Bring your best to the battle at hand. Though I daresay it will lead you to places and situations that will truly test your mettle. The game is, you see, on. Time for skirmishes and playthings to be set aside. This time, the challenge is in earnest."

"What of our Thomas?" Thor bellowed into the room, as ever the bull in the china shop. Several of his family members and their followers gifted Tiyanoga with such vehement looks they left no doubt that, were Tiyanoga truly present, they would have done their level best to rend him limb from limb. Only Jacob, Joss, Samuel, and I knew what a lost cause that course of action would prove should they even try. Their form of manipulating the Guardianship and the *Dark* was over. I should have expected Tiyanoga's next point would become the lasting one.

"Thomas has always been in my care. He is here with me now." In that moment Thomas smiled brightly with such reverence for Tiyanoga as a prodigal son to his father that it brought gasps from Thor's family. *"Who do you think assisted me with getting Jacob into our midst? And make no mistake, he is captured and quite subdued now."*

With that, the silent vision of Jacob talking from the wampum's continued projection changed to showing Jacob trussed up, seemingly stripped naked, though the visual was partially obscured in darkness of whatever part of the boat they had chained him to.

"His powers are quite suppressed. A mere mortal now. Yes, we can change the game on all of you. It is not an easy feat. Rest assured; Jacob is a most capable foe. Even now, he weakens our subjugation of him. But I think we will get him to Fort Russe just in time to perform his more permanent change."

He walked over and caressed the side of Jacob's sweaty face, besmirched with soot and whatever vile excrement a seafaring ship such as the *Báthory* could boast. He gripped Jacob's hair harshly, horrifying some of the newer Guardians installed—sadly, I counted myself amongst them as I tried to reconcile the softly spoken and encouraging man with whom I spent time in the Battery less than a week ago.

"You should endeavor to bring your best, but there are only two who might stand a chance against us in our current state." He turned to make no mistake that those two were Joss and me.

"Yes, Joss and his companion, William Hallett, are more than welcome to engage, should the Central see fit to release them to the task." He took a step that removed him from the lighted aura he had been occupying, and the moment he did, he solidified into looking just like the rest of us.

The response from the Guardianship was what you would expect when faced with the enemy. They randomly attacked Tiyanoga who easily rebuffed their shards of energy, their flames and gases lobbied in his direction. Only my hand stayed their assault. I did it hearing Tiyanoga's voice in my ear instructing me on how to stop every one of the Guardians' feeble attempts to subdue him.

Within seconds, I had quashed all such attacks. The Guardianship itself was subdued no different than poor Jacob on the *Báthory*. How I managed this I had no way of knowing. It seemed to emanate from my being as if called up by Tiyanoga through me.

"Yes, you do understand just how much the game has changed, do you not?" He took to the center of the dais, forcing Samuel to relinquish his position. Tiyanoga leaned against it as if holding class to a bunch of miscreant and foolishly prideful students. Unworthy students.

"Oh, and to be fair, you need not hold William Hallett accountable for what just happened here. True enough, he bears some of my more salient talents in that incredible head of his. But make no mistake; Joss and William are your greatest assets and you would do well to follow their lead."

He turned to eye us once more as he took to the silvery glow Thomas remained in, though Thomas's eyes were pointed to his family in no uncertain terms as to where *his* allegiances lay.

Tiyanoga placed a fatherly arm across Thomas's shoulder, clearly indicating where the battle lines were drawn and that with Jacob's continued health hanging in the balance, it had all become very personal.

"Heed this, if nothing else: we are coming. For once the light will rise in the West and will blow East, laying waste to what is in favor of what is to come."

Screams could be heard in the village below the grand hall. All eyes turned to the window overlooking Akwesasne below; billows of smoke and small fires already dotted the landscape.

"It has begun; it is already here."

And with that, they faded and the room swiftly returned to normal. Without a single comment, several Guardians gated back to the village to see what damage had been done and what they could do to assist—save for Thor, the extended Jemison family, Joss, Samuel, and me. The image of Jacob lingered before the vision was wiped away, evaporating into wisps of nothing but leaving a deeply felt impression on all of us.

We gated with the others down into Akwesasne to a scene of devastation the likes of which I had never witnessed. It was akin to what I imagined the Revolutionary War had wreaked upon the land. Some dwellings were on fire—not of epic proportions, but the damage would have to be dealt with. Guardians were already putting them out and seeing to wounded and stunned people within the village. At issue, we could not determine where the source of this attack sprang.

"There it is..." Joss turned, and we spied the most unusual visage. Coming down the main road we stood on was a boy of no more than eighteen years of age, but the manner of his motion was both beguiling and horrifying. He leaped on all fours as if he were a bear. His skin had a silvery pallor, but the face was unmistakable: Christian Stuyvesant.

For a moment we watched his erratic behavior, not able to discern how he had arrived here and to what end he was quite literally clawing his way throughout the village.

He would stop momentarily, as if sniffing the breeze for a sign of something in the air. I did the same thing and at first I did not sense it. Just as I was about to inform Joss of my thoughts, he engaged Christian directly, shielding him from progressing further. I smelled something coursing along the air as well. A metallic scent that tickled my senses. Christian seemed to regard Joss for a moment, a recognition of some sort.

"Christian, it is me, Joss. Do you not recall our meeting at William's house in Manhattan?"

Christian stood up within the orb Joss had him trapped in and wiped a soiled sleeve across his upper lip, removing the sweat there.

"I am here for it" was all he said in return.

"For what?" I ventured.

"You know. You sense its arrival as well. I had hoped it was just for me, but I see I have company in that regard. *You* shall not acquire it."

He smiled, but it carried no mirth. No, he saw me as a competitor now. That gaze had nothing shy of a competitor's appraisal of his competition. To what end, though, still escaped me.

He slammed against Joss's shield with a few lighted arcs of power from his own hands. No doubt his rogue Guardian abilities were fully in play now. They rattled against Joss's shield but gave no ground to his advance. Again, he sniffed the air and his eyes narrowed. There was only one way to distract him I could think of.

"Where is Rebecca? Is she all right? What have you done with her?"

This stopped his advance for a moment. He turned his head slightly as if trying to understand the fullness of my question. Could it be he had subdued her or harmed her in some manner? My concern, nay, my ire was rapidly building with each moment he delayed his answer.

::He is not quite himself, Will. I do not think he harmed Rebecca. I think he broke free and his Flintling half is making him do this. He appears at war within himself.::

::Well, he would do well to answer me before I begin to forget myself.::

A large explosion erupted from the Guardian hall along the great window, and something hurled toward us with lightning speed.

Christian wasted no time once he caught sight of the impending object. Instead of trying to take Joss's shield down, he concentrated power within his hands, condensing it as I had observed Joss do back at the Flintling warehouse on the auspicious night that had changed everything in my life. I knew this would not end well. Joss was preoccupied, trying to discern what was heading our way. He did not notice Christian's move.

"Joss, he is doing what you—" I never got to finish. Christian released the immense power buildup into the ground at his feet, and the resulting explosion not only shattered Joss's shield but blew everyone within a twenty-foot radius, Joss and me included, off our feet and into the air. I collided with a wagon wheel some ten feet away and Joss crashed through the window of a small shop.

Christian was the first to regain himself from the self-made explosion and began running on all fours toward the silvery orb that could clearly be seen now it drew close to us. At his last few feet to the device he leaped in an attempt to grasp it, only when his arms swiped at it, the orb disappeared altogether before appearing behind him and continuing on its current trajectory.

Several of the Guardians on hand tried to subdue Christian, but he was able to defend himself quite handily, besting them all in a matter of seconds. Whatever this orb was, Christian was wasting no time in achieving his intended goal of possessing it at all costs. The only problem with that was the damned thing altered its course to pursue me!

I did not know what to make of it. In my confusion and without Joss to assist, I did what I thought best, and that was to run away from the cursed thing.

I ran into a nearby building, and the damnable thing blasted a hole through the wall to give chase. I emerged from the back door out into the open field beyond only to discover it *and* Christian barreling my way.

Joss suddenly gated to where I was and put up a shield against the orb's advance. Christian took this as his sign to finally acquire it and leaped once more into the air only to have a silvery whip lace itself around his neck. It quickly hauled him bodily into the ground.

The orb continued the short distance to where Joss and I stood, and as it contacted Joss's shield, it simply passed through it. Before I could react, the damned thing hovered above my head and stopped. We looked around and noticed that the person who had subdued Christian was Rebecca. The Mordant kept Christian down despite his best efforts to rise. She had a handle on it now.

Joss and I shared a disbelieving look at Rebecca's sudden arrival but realized we had precious little time to debate the how and why of it now. Our collective gaze moved to the orb.

The problem was it just hovered there. I moved slowly to Rebecca with Joss at my heels, our attentions never leaving the silvery object above us. By now, the Guardianship and several villagers had moved to where we all stood and watched how this was going to play out.

The orb made some high-pitched musical tones as if trying to communicate with us.

I looked to Joss, who simply had no idea what we were dealing with.

::Ohnehta'kowa, I do not know what this is. In all my years and teachings, we have never known such a device to exist, much less come from the chamber itself. It must be a construction of Spruce that would make itself known when the need arose. I suppose Tiyanoga's incursion into our meeting was all that was needed to release it from its restful state.::

::But what does it want? Why does it hover above me and my sister?::

For clearly, that is where it remained. It held no interest in Joss or Christian, despite Christian's desire to obtain it. The damned thing just kept chirping and making some other bird-like sounds as it wavered between my sister and me.

I took a tentative step forward. Joss seemed to think I was being hasty, but to what end should we let this carry on? It clearly was looking for a response.

"Look, er, I do not know what you want but—"

"*William Matthias Hallett,*" it called out loud for everyone within the area to hear. "*Rebecca Elizabeth Hallett,*" it continued. She glanced at me but shrugged. She had no idea how it knew who we were or why we would even be here now to show itself.

"Choose between you."

I worried for my sister's health because if this thing meant to do harm, then the brotherly thing to do was to protect her at all costs. Aside from all of that, I had Joss to assist me should some peril come from my voicing my assent.

"Me, then! I choose me."

"Will, are you mad? Look what it did to Christian. Do you think any good will come of it?" Rebecca implored.

"What choice do we have? It is either you or me. I have Joss to assist because of our bond. Well, I hope that will suffice should the worst come to pass..."

I turned to face the orb.

Some more chirps and then the blasted thing began to hum. I could tell Joss was prepared to protect me should something go awry, but given how easily it passed through his last form of protection, I did not think Spruce would allow any interference.

The orb expanded a bit. Christian began to growl and claw at the dirt, but Rebecca held him down with the Mordant. I glanced back at Joss, who gave me as encouraging a look as he could manage, given the circumstances.

"I am ready..."

The orb struck. It descended and surrounded me, lifting me bodily from the ground. Inside it I could see everyone below before everything went white, and I found myself in a large white room, not too unlike the Guardian hall. However, instead of the dais, it contained a single bench.

"William..." I knew without a doubt I heard the voice of Spruce talking to me. He slowly materialized and indicated that we should take a seat. He was a full foot taller than I, of a robust and muscled nature. Despite his youthful appearance, his long white hair braided down his back gave him a sage-like air. His clothing was traditional fare but also in all white. He bore huge antlers present in our chieftains save that these were his own and a full and impressive rack they were—also stark white and polished to a sheen that caught the light from every angle. The beading of his deerskin tunic completely adorned in white wampum of the finest and most delicate quality. Seeds fell from the fringe of his

clothing and hair, dotting the landscape with white flora and fauna. This man exuded life in all its great abundance. For the briefest moment, I could see why Saweskira had reason to be jealous. Spruce was nothing short of a god in the largest of terms. His warm baritone voice, comforting to me as a crisp warm autumn day, brought me from my wandering observations.

"Flint is raising an army. An army built upon the dead of the Guardianship. You know this to be true. Tiyanoga has demonstrated as much. There is much we must do to counter this threat. I am giving you the breadth of my knowledge. I am gifting you everything I know and what I have seen in my lifetime. It is my final gift to the people. I hoped and prayed it would never come to pass, that my brother would learn over time to let things be and allow your kind to find their way in the world we created for you. But he is Saweskira, Flint, ever the brother who knew not when to quit. He knows no other way."

At this, he seemed weary and tired, lost in his thoughts about his brother.

"Is there some way to defeat him once and for all?"

He had a small chuckle.

"I believe he is angry with me and takes it out on all of you because he cannot engage me."

"Why is that?"

"I am dead."

He let that one course through me, sapping every part of me I held on to in this conflict. He knew what effect those three words would have upon me.

"This is but a construct of everything I am. When I realized the lengths Flint would go to drive men mad in this world so he could dominate, I banished him back to our home world and set about constructing this device, should the need arise. Do not fret for me. I had a full life. What you need to know about my demise is important, because it holds a bearing on how it may all end. There is a passageway. Think of it like a hole drilled by an earthworm or, rather, a tunnel connecting your world and mine through the cosmos. I have been successful in keying it to deny him, based on who he is. He is trapped on our home world thinking of nothing but conquest to prove me wrong in this world, our birth world and, to his manner of thinking, his true home. So, when I closed it off to him, he became enraged and sought

vengeance upon me. I was in the tunnel between our worlds when it collapsed, taking me with it. I have several traps set for him on our world that keep him there. Believe me, he will be stymied as to how to return to this world. The only viable link he has through that meager remnant of a tunnel is to communicate with his horde here and find a way to open it from this end."

"His horde? The Flintlings, you mean?"

He snorted. "He might like that term. He's a complicated man, my brother. Simply complicated. But, make no mistake, he must be stopped. The Haudenosaunee, as well as the other peoples of your world, need to be able to move forward untouched by Flint or my involvement. Our argument is old and between us. Flint is just very unforgiving when he is on the losing end. And he has a singular mindset when he wants something—he pushes and pushes until he achieves it. It is my hope that with everything I have stored in this life sphere, which is now connected to you, you might find a way to seal him off forever. You alone can access it—though to what end Joss will be able to detect it remains to be seen. He is a resourceful one, which is why I sent him to you. The device will do a great many things that will no doubt surprise you and challenge you in your quest with Joss, Jacob, and your sister to put an end to Flint's campaign. Do you get the fullness of what I impart to you now?"

I nodded.

"He must be stopped at all costs," I reiterated.

"Yes." He got up, bringing me with him. "He will challenge you and take you to dark places that will shake what you believe in yourself. But you have Josiah. Your bond is strong. As strong as I intended it to be."

"You mean, you intended for Joss and me...?"

"I intended for you to share that bond. It is your interpretation of that which gave birth to your more amorous inclinations. It is what it is. Perhaps your love for each other will ultimately be Flint's undoing. It is a tactic I had not considered. Flint will not see it coming or know how to deal with it. Use it if you feel you can and must."

He looked off into the distance.

"It is time I released you back to your world and your time. Just know, I will always be here"—he touched my head—"and here." His hand moved to my heart. "I now live through you. You carry me forward in ways even I cannot see or know what the outcome will be.

But I knew it would be you. So, when my time came, I simply closed my eyes and prayed you would rise to the challenge and accept me into your life. Yours and Joss's life. You shall be the Peacemaker, the ever-powerful Spruce, the giver of life and all that goes with it."

He placed a warm hand upon my shoulder.

"It will not always be an easy road. The red road never is."

He moved back a little. A small warren of snow-colored rabbits slipped fully formed from his garments only to scurry off into the white grassy knoll that had formed during our short conversation. His eyes moved from the collection of newly born rabbits to meet mine. "But the rewards are wondrous to behold. I hope you get to experience it all. I love you, William Matthias Hallett, for you are now me."

I trembled at his words, feeling him consume every fiber of my being, taking root in my soul as surely as the trees and brush that sprung up around us.

"Call on me when needs arise. You have every ounce of my knowledge and expertise to draw upon now. No doubt it will confuse many, save Josiah. He is a most brilliant man. I admire him greatly. Lean into him and share with him what you experience now I have become a part of you. He has a truly gifted scientific mind. He will help you sort out things that may elude you."

I nodded, unsure of what to do.

He pulled me in for an embrace, and I smelled all the wondrous scents in life: flora, fauna, the wet soil after a good rain, the crisp scent of freshly fallen snow, the smell of a forest and river. He truly was the seed of life. He took his hands and placed them on either side of my face and gently put his forehead to mine, just as Joss had shown me before. We stood like that for a moment. I could not help but cherish this moment with him. I was deeply humbled by the experience. Then he smiled and began to move off into the whiteness of the room which seemed to grow brighter the further he stepped away from me.

"Nia:wen, Spruce."

He turned one last time and raised a hand.

"Nia:wen kowa" was all he offered, and then he was gone.

I slipped into a haze that left me with a feeling not of falling, but of rising up.

When I came to, everyone was standing around me, including my sister and Joss.

"Are you all right, Will?" Joss inquired as he sat next to me and lifted my head onto his lap. The worry in his face had me reaching up to stroke the side of his.

"I am unharmed. Just, um, overwhelmed. How long…?"

Joss looked to the others, then back to me.

"No more than a few minutes. The orb became translucent and descended all around you. You hovered within it for a moment or so before it gently put you down on the ground where you are now. Are you sure you are all right?"

I proceeded to sit up with his assistance. I glanced Rebecca's way. She had released Christian fully, who seemed to have lost his crazed look and instead seemed rather sheepish about the damage he had caused.

"I am fine. A little shaken, but otherwise I am unharmed."

"Good," Rebecca commented, leaning forward to take full attention of us. "Now, let us get on that damned boat and rescue my husband!"

Glossary

Mohawk Vowels

(variations may occur across Mohawk dialects)

Character—Mohawk pronunciation

A—as in *father*
e—as in *get* or the a in *gate*
i—as in *police*
o—as in *note*
en—like um in *umpire*
on—like oo in *noon* or as in *gone*

Mohawk Consonants

(variations may occur across Mohawk dialects)

Character—Also Used—Mohawk pronunciation

h—as in *hay*
k—g before vowels—as in *gate*
k—elsewhere—soft as in *skate*/or hard as in *Kate*
r—r or l—as in *right* in some dialects, or l as in *light* in others
n—as in *neigh*
s—sh, c—as in *sell*
s—before y or i, sounds more like the sh in *shell*
t—d before vowels—as in *die*
t—elsewhere—soft as in *sty*/or hard as in *tie*
ts—j, ch—as in *tsunami*
ts—before y or i—more like the j in *jar*, and
ts—before hy or hi—more like the ch in *char*
w—as in *wisk* or *way*
y—as in *yes*
'—a pause sound, as in the middle of "*uh-oh*"

NOTE: These are not hard rules as variations do occur across the many Mohawk community dialects.

Mohawk Terms Used In This Work

Word—Phonics—Translation

Ahtahkwa'òn:we—ah-tah-kwa-ON-way—Moccasin
Aiionwatha—ay-ohn-WAY-t'ha—Equivalent to Hiawatha
Akwe:kon—Ah-kweh-goh(n)*—All of us, together
Akwesasne—ah-kweh-SAHS-nee—Mohawk Settlement
Atená:ti—ah-t'e-NAH-ti—Elk
Ati'ron—Ah-t'i-ro(n)*—Raccoon
Atotarho—ah-toh-TAR-ho—Onondaga Chief Name
Dekanawida—de-gah-na-WEE-da—The Peacemaker
Haudenosaunee—who-de-no-SHAW-nee—Official name of
     Confederacy
Istá—IS-t'a—Mom (familiar)
Kahnawà:ke—gah-nah-WAH-kay—Mohawk Settlement
Kanien'kehá—gah-nee-YEN-gaha—Mohawk (people)
Kanien'kehá:ka—gah-nee-YEN-gaha-gah—Mohawk (language)
Konorónkhwa kowa—goh-no-ROHNk-h'wah-gohwa—I love you
     very much
Kyenawa's—key-nah-WAH's—Summon
Nia:wen kowa—nya-WEN-gohwa—Thank you very much
O'so:ra—oh-so-ra (no emphasis)—Spruce
Ohnehta'kowa—oh-NEH-T'ah-gohwa—Little Hands
Sátien tánon—sah-TEEYEN T'ah-no(n)*—Sit down
Saweskira—sah-wes-geer-ah (no emphasis)—Flint
Takwa'ahson—t'ag-wah-AH-so(n)*—Spider
Tek:orens—t'HE-oh-rens—He Who Splits Lengthwise
Tenìteron—t'eh-NIT-ehroh(n)*—Couple/lovers
Tewakenonhnè —t'e-wa-ke-NOOHN-h'ne—Guardians
Tiyanoga—t'hi-yan-OH-gah—Bear Clan Chief Name
Wá:s sentá:wha—wah's sen-t'ah'wha—Go to sleep

t'— soft clipped t sound (tip of tongue to the back of front teeth along the hard palate).

*—the n is only lightly pronounced (not a hard sound)

Acknowledgements

My humbling gratitude to James K. Moran, Wendy Stone, and Lou Sylvre for their invaluable feedback and guidance in the crafting of this work.

About the Author

SA "Baz" Collins hails from the San Francisco Bay Area where he lives with his husband and Zorro, a character of a cat. A classically trained singer/actor (under a different name), Baz knows a good yarn when he sees it.

Based on years of his work as an actor, Baz specializes in character study pieces. It is more important for him that the reader comes away with a greater understanding of the characters and the reasons they make the decisions they do, rather than the situations they are in. It is this deep dive into their manners, their experiences and how they process the world around them that make up the body of Mr. Collins' work.

You can find his works at sacollins.com, violetquillredux.com and as a co-host of the wrotepodcast.com series.

Email: sacollins@sacollins.com

Facebook: www.facebook.com/sacollinsauthor

Twitter: @sacollinsauthor

Website: www.sacollins.com

Other books by this author

The Angels of Mercy series
My Summer of Love
Before the Fall

www.ingramcontent.com/pod-product-compliance
Lightning Source LLC
Chambersburg PA
CBHW032208180726
48284CB00001B/247